FOREVER FABLED

FLYBOYS

GINNY STERLING

INTRODUCTION

Keep your eyes on the radar...

Austin 'Sparky' Calder wasn't dumb – he was a realist. If fairytales and fables were true? He was the ogre or troll in the story. Luck was not on his side and there was no magical potion, no charm, no magic wand that would change that fact. He was reckless to the point it was dangerous... and part of the reason he ended up in Ghazni in the first place!

...Just believe.

Giselle Beck was a daydreamer, an optimist, and was determined to always look for a silver lining or magical rainbow. It was just harder to see sometimes when your location was a desert, on the edge of a war-zone, dealing with the wounded, sick, or dying around you... until she got a mysterious invitation!

Now, she was falling for someone she couldn't have and this mysterious man was wooing her by words and with deeds, despite the obstacles between them... until it happened.

He kissed her.

What happens when suddenly you are questioning everything - including this fairytale? What is real? What is pretend? And what will happen when everything falls apart before their very eyes?

Wow! I was finally able to get into this series and wow! Wow! WOW! It's starts with tragedy and there's almost tragedy near the end and then this amazing band of brothers pull through for each other. There's also an amazing love story woven throughout. Each of these men, egotistical, loud, cocky and wonderful have hearts of gold and their own personal demons to overcome. I can't wait to binge on the rest. Flyboys here I come.

Marisa - Thank you for running through this one with me.
Abby - You are the best and I appreciate everything.

Ginny Sterling Newsletter

FLYBOYS
Family tree
Ginny Sterling

THUMPER (Jackson Sloan)
m. Harley Petersen
Samantha
m. Toby Saxon

ALPO (Hunter Petersen)
m. Glory Madison
Twins
Madison   Michael

ACE (Bryan MacKenzie)
m. Jessica Logan (Wolverine)

ROMEO (Lee Tarrant)
m. Dixie Lancaster
Lee's brother is Micah Tarrant in HH Remember Yours

ARMADILLO (Cody Fuller)
m. Delilah Chaplin
Luke   Plus Lots More
m. Nicolette Saxon

VALKYRIE (Aeron Saxon)
m. Marisol Jenkins
Toby   Caspar   Nicolette
m. Samantha   m. Luke   Fuller
Sloan

FIREFLY (Sutton Grainger)
m. Melody Green
Betsy
m. Johnny Marks
Betsy's father is d 'Mr. Clean'
Aunts are Karen & Emily Marks

REAPER (Ryan Merrick)
m. Sophie Lane
Ben   Ruby
m. Rose Griffin   m. Michael Griffin
Father is John Griffin in HH Remember Home

HOT CAKES (Jace Sorensen)
m. Karen Marks
Claire

VAPOR (Matthew Barlow)
m. Tara Sorensen
Julian
m. Charlotte Reed
Father is Daniel Reed in HH Remember Wishes

CABOOSE (Nick Evans)
m. Ivy Quinn (Maiden)
Quinn

X-RAY (John Masden)
m. Emily Marks
Lisette
Sister to Karen Marks & aunt to Johnny Marks

HANDSY (Mike Wheeling)
m. Meredith Bailey
d. Auren   Gwen

HOUDINI (Gage Walters)
m. Abby York
Penelope (Poppy)

GHOST (Jax Cunningham)
m. Mary West
Jolie

MAESTRO (Alex Wilcox)
m. Everly Briscoe
Caleb
Caleb's mother is Mallory Duncan

RICOCHET (Killian Briscoe)
m. Destiny Richards
Cate   Dillon

SPARKY (Austin Calder)
m. Giselle Beck

PARADOX (Joshua Parr)
m. Mallory Duncan
Caleb
Caleb's father is Alex Wilcox

RIPTIDE (Andrew Carter)
m. Megan Joaquin

Thank you, Abby!

PREFACE

Trigger Warning…

I always like to err on the side of caution – and the beginning of this tale starts with a very lonely person suffering from the onset of depression. This is not gone into heavy detail, but as it is a concept that many people deal with on a daily basis – so I wanted to mention it to you.

Beyond these pages, there is an action scene in one chapter that depicts a skirmish. I tried to tastefully create it without being too graphic. (*I do not like blood, guts, or scary stuff in the slightest.*) Again, this is me being overly cautious as sometimes something may not trigger me – but might be sensitive to other readers.

There will be an additional warning before that chapter.

Intense items tear me up mentally, so the Happily Ever After has to be just *that* much more significant in order to compensate… and I love a happy ending (like this one).

Enjoy!

CHAPTER 1

REAPER

One year ago...
Ghazni, Afghanistan

LOST in the memories that assaulted his mind, Reaper stood there stoically, thinking of how to correct an issue he never expected to face. This was not something he could bring to Reilly's attention because the man did not have a sensitive streak in his body when it came to requests from him.

Nope.

He was going to need to be… creative to fix this *'concern'*.

Sighing heavily, he searched his mind, lost in a time that seemed so much simpler despite the tragedy he'd witnessed in Ghazni. He missed some of those moments, before the painful memories, and treasured that innocence he once had when he first arrived here.

He found friends… and a family, brought together by a loss that left a mark on his soul forever.

"Fine boys, right here," Colonel Bradford began, shaking each of their hands as Lieutenant Colonel Reilly stood there stonily, refusing to look at any of their weary faces. "They saved lives today."

"Yes, they did," the Army base captain spoke, extending his hand towards Valkyrie, their new squadron leader.

Every second of this moment was searing itself into his mind as he watched it all unfold, committing it to memory. His buddies had always told him he had a weirdly analytical mind – and maybe they were right.

Army and Air Force didn't mix and rarely crossed 'lines'... yet, here their captain was, on their turf.

Thumper, his original flight leader, was gone.

In his place was a man Reaper truly respected and admired – his best friend. He was proud of Valkyrie stepping up and handling such a tough job, knowing he would have done the same if only given the chance by Reilly.

"Captain Logan – and grateful for your assistance today, son."

"Execute the mission, return home, do an honorable job," Valkyrie said candidly and Reaper almost smirked, standing there at attention as his buddy repeated Thumper's exact words verbatim. He'd heard the other squadron leader say that very thing several times in the past. "We never let our brothers down - and we are there for the team."

"Well, it's much appreciated," Captain Logan nodded. "If you ever need anything, please don't hesitate to ask. We are out here to work together and protect each other."

... Reaper shook his head at the memory from what felt like ages ago – staring at the men before him, watching one of them flounder silently, making his chest ache in awareness.

One of his team was sinking before his eyes.

Sparky.

The gangly man, that had once been all smiles when he arrived some time ago, was falling into the same pit the rest of them dragged themselves from.

Depression.

Loneliness.

Wondering if this was worth all the sacrifices they had made…

The bright smiles were gone, the chipper laughter and outrageous antics, the playful comments bantered back and forth between Sparky and Firefly…

All of it was fading away – including the kid's tan.

Reaper didn't think it was even possible out here, but staying inside, away from the heat and hiding from the world, would do it to anyone. The wiry man avoided the gym now, ate alone, and slept each chance that any of them had downtime… and was drowning.

That yawning hole of depression was something people didn't understand, how all-consuming it was… and Sophie had been a godsend to him. He'd mentally shut off every emotion to keep from losing himself, refusing to feel anything at all until she broke through his field of vision, blasting into his world like the hottest nuke, and laying siege to his heart.

God, he loved that woman… Reaper thought, smiling to himself. Making that reckless leap, marrying her after knowing her for two hours, seemed insane at the time – but he would do it all again in a heartbeat.

… And that is what Sparky needs, he mused.

A distraction.

Something, or someone, to get Sparky's mind from things, to pull him out of his funk, dragging him back into the world of the living… and it needed to be someone he could open up to – a friend that wouldn't interfere with work, keep him out on the weekends, or give him any bad habits… and he had just the answer.

… If the rumors were true?

Getting up from his seat, he ignored the curious looks of his squadron and walked out into the blazing heat of the hot Afghani sun.

"You!" Reaper barked, walking towards the fence, seeing a man running laps. "You there!"

"What, *Zoomie*? What d' ya want?" The man came to a stop, hanging his head down, stretching his back, and leaning his hands on his knees in fatigue.

Reaper bit his tongue to keep from dressing down the young man because he wanted his help with something. Crossing onto another base without express permission was not something he wanted to look into, nor crossing any distinct lines of protocol.

If they were in the States, this wouldn't be a problem – but here?

Here, things were very different. If there wasn't a line, he didn't want to be the one that forced them to draw it – or shine a spotlight on what he was doing.

Nope.

This was going to be something discussed… in secret.

"Tell Captain Logan that First Lieutenant Merrick wants to see him about a pen pal."

"Oh, geez. Seriously? You too?" the man groaned, straightening up and wiping sweat from his forehead, before rolling his eyes. "Will do, buddy - it's your life."

Reaper stood there at the fence, looking off in the distance, and ignoring the broiling sun above him… only to see a man walking towards him in the distance. As he neared, he recognized the captain from a few years ago in that brief discussion he'd witnessed and nodded politely.

"Can I help you, First Lieutenant Merrick?"

"I would like your assistance, sir," Reaper began, and hesitated. "May I speak frankly?"

"It's a hundred-and-two-degrees today... please do. Spit it out and make it quick," the other man replied, crossing his arms in a similar stance, but the curiosity in the man's eyes didn't stop him from being there.

He probably *was* curious – because this was insane.

Reaper knew it.

You don't rock the boat – and you sure don't borrow an anchor from an aircraft carrier... for a dinghy.

Just coming here, opening the doorway between both branches that kept things divided among their remote locations, was strange enough – but to broach something so insignificant?

It was unheard of.

Heck, most of the time the two branches took out separate trucks because they didn't even ride together into the city. Grunts stayed on their side of the fence... and his airmen remained on their own side.

The two did not mix – *ever*.

"I'd like to keep this between us – and I have a slight problem..."

"Okaaaay?" Captain Logan drawled, instantly wary. "What does this have to do with me?"

"I have an airman that is struggling and needs someone to talk to, someone he won't be meeting anytime soon, a person that would email or communicate with him – befriend him – and that's it. Neither of us needs a problem happening between our branches, but I thought if perhaps you had a person there that was looking for a pen pal, then...?"

"Then I could hook your buddy up with a pen pal on the sly?"

"Yes, sir."

"You know what you are asking, right?"

"I'm hoping it would be someone that could email from their personal email, keeping our secret, and just be a polite friend to listen. Look, I'll be blunt..."

"Don't let me stop you now," Captain Logan chuckled, his form not moving in the slightest. He was still standing there defensively with his arms crossed.

"Everyone has heard the rumors of your *'Romeo Squad'*," Reaper began bluntly. "I'm not looking to lose an expert pilot, nor can you afford to keep losing seasoned troops..."

"Watch it there, *Zoomie*..." Logan growled hotly.

"My point exactly," Reaper interrupted. "This guy is a good kid. He's lonely, lost, and needs a friend. I would rather Sparky have a buddy that he finds out is here 'next door' someday... than to have him spiral down or start sinking into a broken system that we both know needs work. He's struggling with the separation and just needs a friend."

"He needs a counselor or therapist."

"Can't a friend be both?"

"It could be *neither* and do more harm than good."

"That's where we both come in," Reaper countered. "I think if you have someone in mind, then I could drag him out here so we can have a chit-chat about nothing... and you can meet the kid. I don't want this to backfire for your service member - or mine."

"You want me to screen your guy? Seriously?"

"Don't you?"

"Would you let him email and talk to your sister?" the captain's eyebrow rose mockingly as he met his cool gaze.

"I don't have a sister," he retorted flatly.

"You know what I mean, Zoomie..."

"It's 'Reaper' or 'Merrick'... *Captain*," Reaper stressed and hesitated. "I would not be very comfortable with another man emailing my wife, but if I had a sister or cousin? I would approve of Sparky befriending them, if that is what you are getting at."

"Fair enough. That's all the screening I need," Logan said, smirking. "Give me a week and let me see what I can do. Any hints at his personality, likes, interests? I mean, if you are in for a penny, buddy? You are in for a pound now... or however the saying goes."

"Ah... he likes planes?" Reaper offered, suddenly feeling very unsure that he was the right person to be describing Sparky.

"You don't say...?" Logan drawled. "Is he easy-going? Friendly? Sci-fi nerd? Book lover? A foodie? Can you give me anything at all?"

"When the kid got here, he was always smiling, lively, playing around and vivacious. His call sign is Sparky for a reason, because he's a live wire and full of energy... and we need that back."

"I understand," Captain Logan said solemnly and hesitated. "Does Colonel Reilly know about this meeting?"

"Again, may I be frank?"

"Hasn't stopped you yet..."

"The man would rather see me bleed than know I was trying to help one of the guys – and if Reilly knew I was out here, talking to you? I would be running my butt off from here to China and back again. If I sneeze or look at him the wrong way? I have to run laps and can do nothing right according to him. So, does he know I'm out here? Heck no..."

"Yet you came anyhow?"

"My team is my family, sir. I think you can understand my motivation behind this request."

"You're okay, Reaper... you know that?" Captain Logan smiled – and finally relaxed his stance. "Let me see what I can do."

"Thank you, sir," Reaper acknowledged – and smirked.

"And I'm more than okay. I'm going to be Reilly's replacement one of these days and I'll take care of my family like they deserve."

"Ambitious, too… I see," Logan muttered, walking off and shaking his head before Reaper could say anything else.

CHAPTER 2

GISELLE
Ghazni, Afghanistan

"You, *Captain*, have got to be kidding me... right? A *Zoomie*? Are you serious? We are *Army*, Logan. We don't mix oil and water together – and we sure don't cross the streams, buddy."

"Gretchen, look... I know the guy and he's a decent person – or at least one that I'd want on my side in a fight," Captain Logan was speaking in hushed tones to her new boss at the remote Army clinic, Gretchen Perry.

Giselle hadn't had much time to get to know the other woman – and hoped she was super nice because there were very few of them stationed out here. In fact, all twelve women on base occupied one small barracks room that was once an office. They had bunks, lockers, and a small bathroom that had been renovated for them all to use.

She was an Army Medic Combat Specialist... and loved it. Helping people was what she always wanted to do, yet eight to ten years of college was not in the books because of finances – or lack of.

The youngest of eight brothers and sisters, it was always assumed everyone would make their way in life. She had two brothers who were tradesmen, one that went into the Navy, one paratrooper, and then her sisters held different customer service jobs back home near Wichita Falls, Texas.

Giselle was the 'baby Army brat'.

No matter the care and caution they took in the war zone, she would always be her Daddy's girl... and getting caught eavesdropping would put her directly from one war zone into another one, unarmed and alone.

Standing there, she listened to them whisper to each other.

"I never took you for sexist – does Juliet know that?"

"Who do you think taught me?"

"I doubt that..."

"Seriously, Gretch... I'm not taking anybody from your team. I promise," Captain Logan was saying in a hushed voice. "You just got here. We've got enough of a headcount. I'm not going to do it because I know what it feels like to have someone yanking people out from under you."

"Why then, is it one of my girls?"

"Because they are girls... duh?"

"Don't '*duh*' me, Logan – and it doesn't work out every time. I mean, Randy and I were at each other's throats at first."

"It worked out just fine – and yeah, Lily's track record is stellar."

"But she's not organizing this one... *you are!*"

"I can do it. How hard can it be?"

What are they talking about?

Is he taking one of the team?

They were already running around like crazy trying to

keep everything operating smoothly like it did when Houghton was here.

She already missed the grizzly man.

He treated her like a kid sister and could get awfully grumbly, but usually smoothed things over with sneaking them treats or getting the commissary to make something special for them. He had strings that he pulled all over the base and no one ever argued with him.

I want to be respected like that someday, Giselle mused, still listening.

"It's a pen pal, Gretchen. How hard can it be just to befriend someone?"

"You have a reputation, Logan – and my marriage is a direct result of it," Gretchen chuckled.

Giselle's eyes widened in shock.

Everyone on base heard about the '*Romeo Squad*' and how if you made it on the squad, you'd be married and outta there in under two years flat. There was only one straggler that made it to three years - and even he fell '*victim*' to his pen pal.

"You can be friends with someone... especially if you never plan on meeting them."

"Do you even hear yourself? How's this supposed to work? They are right next door, ya' big doofus... and what do you mean – '*never meet them*'?"

"Permission to speak freely granted, Mrs. Perry..." he laughed.

"Oh hush, it's just us, and we aren't talking about work. Seriously, though – how are you going to keep them from meeting?"

"Orders, Perry... it's called 'orders'."

"Wait, have you lost your marbles? The 'doofus' comment now remains and is no longer retracted. You _are_ a doofus, Logan!" Gretchen hissed, and Giselle could hear the woman slap her forehead, covering her mouth to keep from laughing aloud.

"You are going to *ORDER* someone to write one of the pilots next door, and tell them they can't say where they are at... and you think someone will agree to do that?"

Giselle had seen the handsome pilots in the distance, those dreamy jumpsuits, the funny motions that the ground crew made waving them forward... and the ones they made in return from the canopy of their planes. She loved watching the silent hand gestures and mimics they made, as if they were speaking another language.

It made her smile... and yeah...

They had caught her once or twice standing near the fence watching them takeoff and land while covering her ears painfully. It was fascinating to watch them signal to each other.

Just seeing some well-built guy in uniform strut towards the planes like he was in charge... and the way they would caress the aircraft during their pre-flight check?

Their hands touching the bombs, stroking the wing, checking the components of their sophisticated planes. The pilots had memorized every seam, every integral part, and knew every place to touch... and it was sensual – but in a very weird way.

Before Giselle could even think – her traitorous body rounded the corner and her equally deceptive mouth opened before her brain could control either of them.

"I'll do it," she volunteered – and slapped her own hand over her mouth, before stepping back into the shadows, praying that they didn't notice her.

"SEE?" Logan snapped. "Now, was that so hard? I've got my volunteer faster than I expected. This is excellent. Problem solved."

"Did you know she was there?" Gretchen hissed loudly.

"Duh…" he repeated once more, chuckling. "Blood, bandages, and boo-boos she can handle efficiently – but stealthy spying? Not so much. C'mon out, Beck."

Giselle stepped forward and expected to be reprimanded for eavesdropping on the duo that was obviously up to something.

"How much did you hear?" Captain Logan smiled and leaned back to sit on the desk behind him, crossing his ankles and looking at her. She had never seen the captain smile.

Oh, she'd seen him yell at people to keep them in line, but this was… weird.

Awkward.

"A lot," she breathed nervously and hated the way her voice shook.

"What do you think of taking the chance of a lifetime?" Captain Logan began softly, almost as if he was trying to 'sell' her on the idea.

Ha!

The joke was on him - Giselle was already 'sold'.

"What if I told you that you could have a chance to get to know someone, befriend them, and it wouldn't involve anything other than just writing an email? You never know who you might meet… it could even be your best friend or perhaps the love of your life?"

"But isn't the *'Romeo Squad'* stationed on <u>this</u> side of the fence?" Giselle said softly – and Gretchen barked out a laugh that got her a sharp glance from the captain.

"It is," he hedged. "And try not to refer to my guys as *that* – please? This would be a secret – on the opposite side of the fence. You couldn't tell anyone that you were writing to someone. It would have to be from your personal email, not your Army one, and absolutely no revealing your location."

"Why?"

"Security protocol, of course."

"Ahhh. Makes sense."

"See?" the captain said pointedly glancing at Gretchen, who rolled her eyes and looked at Giselle.

"He's setting you up," Gretchen warned openly, giving her a hard look. "It might work, it might not. You just never know what you are getting into, and I want you to be aware because not everything is sunshine and rainbows. There were a lot of bumps in the road at first with my own pen pal."

"I'm never going to meet anyone out here otherwise," Giselle said softly, feeling nervous and strange to be even having this discussion with them. What did it matter to anyone that she had a pen pal?

"I mean, there's a lot of guys, but I'm not interested. They are married, goofy as could be, or only have one thing on their mind..."

"Is someone bothering you?" the captain glowered and looked at Gretchen, before they both looked at her. "Say the word and I'll have it addressed."

"No. No. Nothing like that," Giselle began nervously. "I just would like... *more.*"

"More... *what?*"

Giselle wanted someone that would sweep her off her feet, carry her off, a protector, a friend, a lover, someone who thought of her with every breath. She wanted the fairytale that every girl, every mama, and any grandma wished for — someone just for her.

Her own prince of her dreams – and Giselle knew she would never find him here, in the middle of nowhere, slapping Band-Aids on boys that thrived on being disgusting like it was a competition. They were like her brothers, family members, and she wanted... well, *more.*

'*More*' seemed to describe it accurately in her mind, because she couldn't think of any other way to explain it. She wanted sparks, butterflies, a magic that could only be imagined. Legends, fairytales, princes and unicorns… she wanted the ultimate dream for any fanciful girl with a dreamer's heart.

"More than just this ordinary existence," she confessed. "I want more to my life and could use a friend – so yes. A pen pal sounds ideal and if it comes with strings attached? Then I suppose I shall dance for my puppet master."

"Oh, I like her," Logan snorted to Gretchen, looking over his shoulder briefly, before looking back at Giselle.

"Puppet master? Really?" he grinned, as he stood up, getting to his feet. "I found my volunteer, Perry. Thank you both for your time, ladies. Beck, I'll be in touch shortly."

"Yes, sir."

Two days later, Captain Logan walked in as Giselle was inserting an I.V. into a man's arm who had collapsed while doing physical training due to excessive dehydration.

"Just a second, Peña…" she muttered, slowly inserting the needle into the vein upwards, advancing it until the flashback of blood appeared, moving the cannula a little further into the vein. "You're doing beautifully. Just stay still and don't faint on me."

"Geeeezzz, Beck. I'm not gonna faint," Peña muttered weakly.

"Some do and it's okay, my friend," she whispered, focusing intently. Not moving her eyes from her work, she blindly reached up with one hand and popped the rubber tourniquet that she'd fastened a few moments ago, before applying pressure and removing the needle.

Diligently working, Giselle could feel eyes watching her as she loaded the bag, adjusted the drip, and then turned to yank off her gloves, disposing of the needles in the sharps container nearby, before patting the man gently on the shoulder… and moving to talk to the captain.

"Sorry about that," she began politely. "May I help you?"

"It's about our project," Captain Logan said candidly. "Do you have a moment?"

"Of course, captain."

She followed him into another room – and he wasted no time at all, shoving a folded piece of paper at her.

"This is his email. I would go ahead and send him a quick message, draw him out and get him to say 'hello' back. Then you can work on befriending him."

"Wait… me? I'm writing to him first?"

"Yes. Is that a problem?"

"I thought *he* was going to write *me*?"

"Plans change all the time. Besides, think of this as one of those little nursery rhymes or fairytales… coax *'Goldilocks'* out of the cave, hut, barracks, or whatever your new buddy wallows in."

"You mean *'the bears out of the woods'*?"

"Sure. Whatever."

"Is he blond? You said *'Goldilocks'*."

"I have no idea," he admitted, looking at her. "Does it matter if you are going to be friends… and that's it?"

"No. It doesn't matter," she murmured, staring at the piece of paper. "I'll email him this evening."

"From your personal email…"

"Will it matter?" she asked candidly, angling her head and feeling curious, throwing the captain's own words back at him boldly. It might have been a mistake because his expression darkened fractionally and she continued, hoping to ease the conversation.

"I mean, if we are not going to be discussing locations for

protocol – does it matter? If he asks, I can refer to security regulations or tell him I'm not at liberty to discuss this."

"Fine. Fine. Whatever… but no one put you up to this, okay?"

"Then how did I get this email address?"

They stared at each other for a few moments before Captain Logan sighed heavily and looked at her.

"Can you quit asking the hard questions and poking holes in all of this? *Please?* I mean, if push comes to shove? Tell him he's got some blasted fairy godmother watching out for his sour butt and he needs to pull himself out of whatever funk that he's wallowing in."

"I see."

"Good," Logan said glibly. "Anything else, Beck?"

"No, sir," she hesitated, holding back a slight smile. "No more hard questions – pull *'Goldilocks, The-Mysterious-Hidden-Flyboy'* out of his funk. I've got my orders, captain."

He gave her a hard look… but his eyes were glittering with humor.

"Thank you – and good luck, Beck."

17

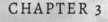

CHAPTER 3

SPARKY

"Jeez… will you get up and quit moping?"

Reaper was standing over his bunk, looking at Austin while several of the other men filed out of the room. They were heading for the mess hall for dinner, and he just didn't feel like eating.

Nothing appealed to him anymore.

Austin was out here, in the middle of nowhere, with barely any contact from his friends because they were too busy with their own lives. The buddies he'd made in high school playing baseball were now taking their own children to t-ball practice.

The friends he'd made at the Academy had been scattered around the world, in different locations, busy setting down roots or exploring the surrounding area… and he was here.

In the world's biggest litter box, surrounded by… well, poo.

A hot, steaming, smelly litter box… where the people in

the area recognized on sight that he didn't belong. Going into town was something the Army did on patrol – and they were armed or ready for anything.

Austin watched almost enviously as the trucks would roll out. He saw the troops climb on board, while he stood there in his flight suit that had zero-protection from a bullet. Oh, it would keep him from passing out, help him in an aerial dogfight if push came to shove… but he missed people.

He missed the adventure of stepping into a new bar or a club, seeing appreciative smiles, catching meaningful glances, dancing with girls, and playing a simple game of darts with the guys.

He never imagined that he would yearn for a bowling night at the Academy. The guys would get together on a free weekend – and play for hours at a time. Five or six of them would pile into a taxi at two in the morning, returning to the barracks.

He missed fun… and girls.

Flying was the best – but it was solitary.

Austin was alone in the Falcon. The ground far below him looked so empty, just seas of varying shades of green, brown, and tan sprinkled with blips here and there that were cities or towns.

The joy had just faded somehow and was replaced by a basic existence – and he felt like he was wilting away, losing a part of himself.

Reaper sat down on the nearest bunk.

"Look, I know this isn't someplace exciting like home, Germany, or Spain… but we are all here, thinking and needing the same things," Reaper said quietly, watching him.

Austin turned away to stare up at the ceiling.

"You are falling into a pit," Reaper began again, "And I know because you either drown or go numb just to keep from suffocating. Don't do this, Calder. Don't shut it off – funnel it, my friend."

"Go away," Austin uttered, hating that the man's words were reaching him, and his throat was getting tight.

"No."

"I'm tired – and nothing is wrong."

"If you are this tired, I'm going to recommend a medical evaluation to make sure you haven't picked up something."

"Can't I just want to be alone?"

"Occasionally – yes? All the time and bringing down the others? – No."

Austin turned his head and looked at him.

"Look, Sparky," Reaper began again. "You share a barracks with several other men who are watching you. Some miss their wives, their families, and some were alone before they ever got here. Don't be the anchor, taking others down with you… please."

At his silence, the squadron leader spoke again.

"Get up, plaster a smile on your face, try to find something that appeals to you, write some friends or family you have back home. Heck, reply to every email you get and have some fun with it. If they are trying to sell you a warranty for your car, tell them you're interested in full coverage on a blue Pontiac T-1000 from 1980…"

Austin cracked a smile for a second.

"That was oddly specific."

"The neighbor had one and always worked on it. It was a piece of junk, and I was terrified that my Mom would buy it when he finally put a sign in the window," Reaper smirked at him. "I'm serious. If it's spam or junk mail, harass them back. If you have a friend that writes – tell them to *keep* writing. If you have vacation time, go see my buddies in Texas and soak up the sun for a bit… just do anything but *this*."

Reaper stood up beside Austin's bunk, pointedly.

"Seriously. Get up and quit moping. Go get something to eat, hit the gym, go watch a movie, or get on one of the computers."

"Yes, mom…"

"That's First Lieutenant 'Mom', kiddo…" Reaper smirked.

Austin sat up, getting to his feet slowly, and looked at him.

"Try it my way for a month… and let yourself settle into a spot where you fit in. You don't have to be like anyone else, just be yourself. If you need more mental entertainment, friendship, excitement - if it's not coming to you or surrounding you? Create it – but do not sink," Reaper said quietly. "Never sink, because there's always another day and you are always welcome to talk if you need someone, brother."

"I'm fine," Austin said quietly. "I'll go get something to eat."

"Don't go sit in there if you are just going to mope…"

"Go. Don't go. What do you want?"

"I want you to take a minute, draw up your big-boy pants, and realize that in this part of the world? It's not just you alone. You are part of something bigger. Be a friend, part of the team, and get your head on straight… Now, c'mon."

"What?"

"I'm going to go check my email, write something that will make my wife either laugh or blush, and then literally drag your bum to the mess hall so I can sit across from you – and kick you in the shins every time you get *that* look on your face," Reaper said, putting his finger in Austin's face – before grabbing him by the shoulder and pushing him forward. "Let's go…"

Minutes later, Austin was staring at the computer screen while Reaper sat across from him, typing away.

Austin didn't have any family to write, making this all the more painful.

He grew up in and out of foster homes because his mother had a drug addiction that took her life when he was seventeen. She'd been a junkie for as long as he could remember – and it was really sad, honestly. He had no idea that having lighters and spoons in the bathroom, along with needles, wasn't normal... until he was twelve, when it hit him. The foster homes were nice and clean – and his own was a disaster.

Looking back now, it shocked him that he'd managed to come as far as he had. Opportunity seemed to find him, and he enjoyed every moment of it until recently... and wanted that carefree life he'd found in the Academy back again.

Logging in, he opened up his email and hesitated. There was a ton of junk and spam in there... but one email stood out to him.

It was a military email address... which was odd.

Army, too.

Weird.

He didn't know anyone in the Army – not even on the next base. Maybe it was spam too? Like the Prince of Sudan wanting a dollar for a plot of land... yeah, right.

Clicking on it, he hoped it wasn't some virus that he was opening that would end up shutting down all the computers or crashing the system... and stared in disbelief at the simple message.

> *I bet you are wondering what this is... and who I am, aren't you?*
> *Let's play a game, Sparky.*
> *Tag. You're it.*
> *Sincerely,*
> *A friend*

Austin looked up and stared at Reaper, who looked up a moment later.

"Something wrong?"

"Did you send me an email?"

"No. Why?"

"Do you know anyone in the Army?"

"The grunts next door? I know one guy, but that's it. Why? Did you get something from Logan?"

"No. This is from a person named G. Beck."

"Yeah, I have no idea who that is."

"Weird."

"Write them back and ask what's going on – let me know if we need to print it and turn it in to security…" Reaper said candidly and went back to writing his wife.

Austin clicked reply and sat there for a minute, his mind rolling with curiosity.

> Okay 'friend'… I'll bite.
> Who is this?
> You are right. I'm wondering how you got my email address and a little unsettled. The last time I heard 'let's play a game' it involved some puppet or marionette in a horror movie.
> I'd rather not experience that.
> If this is a friend – then refresh my memory of where our friendship began, because it's escaping me completely. I don't recognize the name in the email address.
> Tag… now you're it.
> Sparky

Austin clicked send – and jumped nervously at Reaper's voice.

"There!" Reaper began. "Whatever you just did… do that again tomorrow because I swear that I saw a glimmer of that fun kid who arrived here long ago and was throwing Skittles at people, telling them to *'Taste the Rainbow'.*"

"I should have eaten them," Austin admitted, feeling a smile touch his lips for the first time in forever. "That stunt nearly got me beat up."

"You know why it didn't?"

"Why?"

"Because it's candy – and you are so gangly we were afraid to break you in half," Reaper chuckled. "Let's go get some chow…"

"Yes, sir."

Austin logged out and hesitated, realizing that the other man was right. He felt better than he had in a few days and was curious to see how long it would take his mysterious person to write him back.

As HE STOPPED in to check his email again, he was stunned to see that there was a reply already.

> *… Ahhh – a movie buff, I see?*
> *What's your favorite movie?*
> *What genres do you like?*
> *Does it matter how I got your email address? I wanted a pen pal and unexpectedly had one fall into my lap.*
> *You.*
> *Let's pretend that real life isn't whatever this reality is…*
> *Let's play and instead, delve into another world. I think I will be a paladin with a bag of potions to heal people.*
> *What would you be – and why? Perhaps I should make up a name for my paladin, because I'm pretty sure Sparky isn't your real name, now is it?*
> *Tag – you're it again.*

Sincerely,
A friend

Austin nearly laughed aloud at this unexpected email and how intrigued he was. This person was neatly avoiding revealing themselves and wanting to continue their communications, garnering bits of information from him a piece at a time.

Alright G. Beck, I'll bite again...

(see what I did there, oh great and mysterious Paladin?)

My favorite movie is Robin Hood. I like the banter, the time period, the idea of knights and knaves, stealing from the rich and giving to the poor... and the fact that there is some swooning maid combined with epic battles. Yup. Nottingham was a jerk, but I get the appeal of Maid Marian. Let's be real - she would not have been happy with a pauper, no matter what she claims, and Nottingham could have won her over if he would have gone about things differently.

Swashbuckling (historical or sci-fi) adventures are my thing...

What about you? What is your favorite movie, why, and what genre?

I guess it doesn't matter how you got my email address... and sure, we'll write each other for a bit.

A paladin? Wow.

Hmm.

I'm trying to think what made you select that and wondering if you are in the medical field - or if you have a bag of potions. I guess you could also be working in some lab somewhere if the Army has stuff like that? I don't honestly know.

I think I would be a knight in this game. There is something appealing about going into battle with chain mail, a sword, and

25

knowing that people would look up to you as you rode through town.

So, a knight and a paladin. Where should our adventure take us?

No – Sparky is my call sign. My first name is Austin.

What's your name, oh great paladin?

Tag, you're it.

Your pen pal,

Austin

CHAPTER 4

GISELLE

GISELLE PUT her hair up in a bun just to get it off her neck and groaned. They were doing inventory *again*, trying to keep a close eye on their supplies because it took so long to get stuff out here sometimes.

She wasn't going to say a word in protest because she knew that Gretchen was just trying to get her footing, keeping a tight rein on the clinic, and making sure that the guys were taken care of if something happened.

It made her wonder if Houghton had given her the same story about that guy, Ethan Minter, that lost a leg a few years back... and she remembered when they pulled Reed's limp body from the truck only months ago.

Turns out that Gretchen was Reed's nurse at the hospital where he'd been flown out by chopper – and Giselle and Houghton had been the ones to get him ready to fly. She had never felt so scared or worried before – and could never forget his face as he struggled to stay awake, fading in and out, praying in a broken hushed voice as he lay there bleeding heavily.

Oh gosh, she had wept so hard that night when her shift was over.

Yes, out here, they always prepped and checked inventory because you just never knew. You could make do with a few things, but key items like medications, blood, supplies for I.V.'s or other things? Those items could make the difference between life or death - and whether you suffer in-between.

Making her way out of the barracks, she headed into the mess hall to get breakfast before hurrying down the cement walkway back towards the clinic. She was running behind, scarfing down a slice of toast with peanut butter just as fast as possible.

In the distance, she heard the jets powering up... and hesitated, unable to resist. Turning, she stopped to see if anyone was on the airstrip on the horizon and saw that it was still empty.

It was too early.

They were all probably getting ready and would be walking along the pavement in a bit. There was something so compelling seeing the line of pilots walking in the distance, holding their helmets, wearing their gear, and watching them look over their planes before climbing inside.

... And one of those mysterious pilots was her new pen pal.

"Beck!" someone called out. "Let's go! We are starting!"

"Oh, shoot..." Giselle muttered, realizing that not only she had gotten distracted, but she was also losing track of time - and now late. Racing off, she hurried into the building in the distance.

Hours later, her brain was gloriously numb, and she could hear numbers droning in the back of her mind as she kept counting... *two, four, six, eight...*

Yes, it had been a long morning and was finally lunch time. She was going to check to see if Sparky had written her back, before grabbing a quick bite. If she went now, there would be a line waiting for the food and this would work out best to wait.

Besides, she couldn't wait to see what he said.

Happily, as she opened her email – she saw that he had indeed written, and it was quite lengthy. Fascinated, she started to read and found herself smiling at his comments, replying almost immediately.

Hello, Sir Austin – oh noble knight of the realm! Very nice to meet you... finally.

Which Robin Hood movie are you referring to? There were a lot of them, and I prefer the Kevin Costner version. Have you seen Braveheart? Very bloody, very similar, and a wonderful movie along those same lines.

I like movies that draw you in or make you laugh. I don't do scary movies because I'm like a four-year-old that gets nightmares. My favorite movies are probably 'BIG' with Tom Hanks, 'City Slickers', or 'Clue'... Oh gosh, I simply love 'Clue' with Tim Curry.

I don't handle movies that make you cry either – 'Titanic', 'The Notebook', and a handful of other movies are my kryptonite. I'm just wrecked and cannot stand how they leave me mentally.

A detective, huh?

Yes, I'm a paladin – and a medic.

Excellent deduction, my dear Austin – eh, Watson!

So, you would be a knight? I could see that – walking up to your 'steed' before climbing in (on) I could definitely see that in my mind... but remember? There are two different types of knights.

A knight in shining armor?

29

... Or the black knight.

(A.K.A. - the evil dude)

People could be looking up to you in awe – or in horror.
Which would you prefer and why?

So, our story begins with its players:

A knight and a paladin.

Where do you think our adventures should take us? Some
far away kingdom? An icy, treacherous waste land? A concrete
jungle full of twists and turns, with danger at every corner?
Where would you venture... and for what would you search for,
oh skilled knight?

Tag, you're it now...

Your pen pal,

Giselle

Clicking send, she smiled.

THE NEXT MORNING, it was much of the same routine.

She got up, threw on her clothes, pulling her hair back in
a ponytail, before braiding it and pinning the bun loosely in
place. She had a massive jar of hair gel in order to put her
hair within regulation – but sometimes if it was windy out?
The sand would get stuck, making her hair and scalp so very
gritty that it was disgusting to wash out.

Walking out of the mess hall with a banana, a slice of
toast with fried Spam on top... she heard the jets in the
distance again, stopping to take a look at the horizon once
more.

Her favorite morning ritual.

You could already see waves of heat coming up from the
ground as the sun rose. It was going to be an extremely hot
one today and nearly choked as she took a bite of her food.

There was a single lone figure standing off in the distance, looking towards the Army base.

She could see the tiny outline against the glaring sun behind him, rippling in the orange and red hues, before he began to walk back towards the building. She couldn't see any of his features from this distance and knew he probably couldn't pick her out of the 'ant hill' that was milling around her as the base came to life around her here, during the early morning hours.

Surely, he didn't suspect that she was here… nearby… did he?

Feeling alarmed, she walked inside and checked her email to see if he had responded – and saw nothing there yet.

Sending him a quick one, hoping to throw him off the track, she quickly typed a brief questionnaire to draw him out just as requested (sort of) by Captain Logan.

He asked her to pull him out of his funk and she wasn't sure all the mind games were doing that. Yes, he responded, and the emails were getting longer and more frequent… but what was Logan really after? Information?

> *Oh, Sir Knight,*
> *Indulge me in my curiosity, if you please...*
> *Chocolate, Vanilla, or Strawberry?*
> *Basketball, baseball, football, or soccer?*
> *Car or truck?*
> *Northern guy... or good ol' southern boy? (or Texas, because it's in a realm of its own in my book! God bless the Lone Star State!)*
> *Hot dogs or hamburgers?*
> *Chips or fries?*
> *Coke, Pepsi, or Dr. Pepper?*
> *If you could go anywhere in the world – where would it be?*
> *Your friend,*

Giselle

Clicking send, she waited.

IT WAS ONLY a few hours later that she had a response.

Giselle was really grateful there was a computer in the clinic that she had access to. It would truly kill her to be one of the groups that only got to use it once a week. In fact, because of their 'accesses' to the internet, it did not put them on the rotation the rest of the troops were.

The troops, organized by groups, were given specific days and times to use the computers in the office – and they kept as many people 'off' the list as to give everyone a shot. If you worked in a room where there was a computer, they did not give you an allotted time slot. You had to work around everyone else, sharing... which meant she had company every time she sat down to check her email.

Sighing heavily, she clicked on 'Receive/Send' – and saw three responses from Austin.

Clicking on the first one, she swallowed heavily.

> *Giselle,*
> *Where are you stationed?*
> *Austin*

Whoooaaaaa boy, her brain seized while her heart screamed an '*Oh No!*' at each thump. This was not what anyone wanted or expected – and that profile against the sunrise this morning?

That *had* been him...

He was looking for her, and she now knew it.

Clicking reply, she remembered Logan's advice – and used it.

> *Austin,*
>
> *Military communications specifically state that you cannot give away your location. I'm assigned as a medic to a base – and even that will probably get scrubbed in the filters.*
>
> *Giselle*
>
> *P.S. – Why?*

Clicking send, she moved on to the next email… really happy that he was responding, and it gave her so much joy to just be able to communicate with someone – even if there were guidelines.

> *Giselle,*
>
> *What were your selections?*
>
> *You are asking me about my choices, yet you never tell me anything about yourself – and I am curious too. I still don't know how you got my email address, but I'm not questioning it anymore but enjoying the interactions – a lot.*
>
> *Please – tell me more.*
>
> *Austin*
>
> *P.S. Caramel… or chocolate is my favorite*
>
> *Baseball – I played all throughout high school and ran track*
>
> *Neither – I usually hitched a ride with friends or got a taxi. I suppose if I was to go buy one? I'd go for luxury because I want something a lot plusher than a bunk and a locker. Butt-warmers? Check! Steering wheel heater? Check! Cameras and dark windows? Check-check! How about SUV or extended cab truck? I wanna sit high… pilot, remember?*
>
> *Okay – I'm guessing you are from Texas?*
>
> *Ha ha ha!*

Apparently, I know several people from there and should probably go sometimes. I'm from Little Rock, Arkansas.

Hot dogs or hamburgers? – Meat, period. If someone is grilling, I'll eat.

Chips or fries? – Again, food.

I can put it away. Is a good macaroni salad an option on this one? I would pick macaroni salad with the crunch bits of celery over both choices above... but no peas. I don't like peas in it.

Dr. Pepper... All. The. Way.

If you could go anywhere in the world – where would it be? ... I would choose a coffee shop or café where we could say 'hello' for the first time – and it wouldn't matter where it was.

Austin

Giselle sucked in her breath at the last comment, suddenly feeling very strange within her. He was making this sweet... *friendly*... and wanted to say 'hello' in person. Her heart was back to hammering against her chest as she looked down at her frumpy uniform and sweaty persona.

This was *not* how she wanted to meet a guy – and meeting him would change so many things. What if she thought he was nice, but he turned out to be not her type or...

What if she really liked him – and he wasn't interested in her? She always heard that Air Force guys kept to themselves because they thought they were better than Army grunts... but Army was just as proud!

What was she supposed to say?

"Hey baby... your fence or mine?"

There were no cafes, no coffee shops, near here unless you went into town – and she really didn't relish that idea. Medics patched up what came back from patrols into town.

No, this needed to stay neutral, friendly, because she was definitely chicken.

Bock-bock-bock...

Giselle felt slightly cornered now too, because she had already answered one email. He would be expecting responses from the other two emails he had sent her. It wasn't like she could put it off or say there was no access to the computer. No, she was going to have to respond, or it would raise a red flag with her new pen pal.

Had she said something wrong or led him on?

She was now second guessing everything she was saying or doing. Was this what Gretchen meant when she warned Logan about giving her the pen pal... because things got weird fast when it was a guy and a girl chatting?

Clicking reply, she began typing... and it seemed to take forever to respond because she was reading and re-reading each response, looking for loopholes.

Austin,

My selections?

Oh, I'm a very simple person and pretty easy-going. I don't have a lot of favorites, probably very mundane, too. I mean, I find medical stuff fascinating, so I guess you could call me boring? I read medical updates for fun and to keep up with changes.

Let's see...

Chocolate – but gooey caramel is good. I had a sister that used to work at McDonalds in high school and she would give me both flavors on a sundae. Best-stuff-ever!

Marching band... I play euphonium. No sports here.

V-Dub-love all the way – it's a culture. My diesel Beetle is in storage at my parents' house. They start it every once in a

*while and drive her at least once a month for me. I should sell
her because I don't know when I'll get back... but she's my baby.*

*Okay – I'm guessing you are from Texas? --- Very much
so, ARRRRKansas fella! Wichita Falls, Texas – born and bred.*

Hot dogs... I don't do hamburgers. Blech.

*Mustard potato salad... I understand about the request for
macaroni salad. I'm not a 'chip' person and French fries can be
soggy or very overrated. I like a good tangy mustard potato
salad and can disgrace myself on it at picnics.*

Dr. Pepper... All. The. Way.

(Amen, buddy... there's nothing better!)

*If you could go anywhere in the world – where would it be?
Wow.*

*I'm really not sure what to say to your comments about
meeting at a café? It's terribly sweet, but isn't that a bit fast? I
mean, we are strangers just now chatting and this implies
meeting, building a deep friendship, or something else.*

Besides, why ruin a good thing? Right?

*I'm shy and this is easier for me – and we can't discuss
locations, so who knows where the other is? I don't plan on
traveling anytime soon... and well, yeah, a tremendously sweet
idea. I wish there was another time, or place, where it was
feasible.*

*How about we go back to the mental/email thing, my
knight? If I was a true paladin, I would look for some place
magical... maybe an oasis. Water, trees, a paradise like in the
books – and what if there are ruins of a castle nearby?
Dreaming of a time that knights and such roamed the earth.*

What if it was like in the renaissance paintings?

*What if there was a moat or some obstacle that had to be
traversed to get to where the damsel was? Perhaps in those
written dreams, we could canoe across a silent, still lake,
observe the fog touching the water, and wish for magical places
instead of lingering in this reality.*

Maybe there are fairies, sprites, unicorns, and magical mists that cover the land, giving it an ethereal look? See – so much easier to dream and imagine a world away from here. Let's not focus on reality but hover in our imaginations... It's so much more welcoming and easier on the soul.

Your friend and paladin on this journey,
Giselle

HER HEART HURTING and soul heavy, she didn't hit reply to the third email. Instead, she hesitated... and deleted the email, before logging off and leaving the clinic.

She went back to her bunk and got out a change of clothes, needing some solitude and peace of mind that she didn't just ruin the single bright flicker of joy that had touched her in months... and suddenly feeling lost.

Donning her shorts and yanking a t-shirt over her head, she slipped on her sneakers and went for a run. There was a straightforward path along the fence line, and the sun was finally starting to lower on the horizon.

She could hear the men in the distance talking as they walked towards the exchange, saw others also jogging along the trail through sand and rock... and tried to lose herself in the simplicity of the motion.

One foot in front of the other.

Step by step.

... Drawing to a halt by the fence line that separated the two branches.

Watching in the distance, she marveled at the planes landing. The scream of the engines, seeing them glide rear wheels down first before tipping the nose slightly and then coasting to their position in the line... quickly followed by the next plane, then the next. It was almost processional and there was a beauty to seeing them in motion.

Turning her head, she saw the Jeeps and trucks returning

to the base from their own excursions and held her breath. No mad rushes, no erratic movements, no skidding to a halt or screaming for medical help... just an uneventful day of patrol.

Looking at the sky, she watched the sun set standing there, knowing she was blocking the path and moving slightly for the other joggers — just intent on watching... and why?

She didn't know.

The blue on the horizon faded to an angry orange before settling into a deeper bluish purple as the sun moved out of sight. It would be pitch black out here before she knew it... and standing here for five minutes, twenty minutes, or three hours wouldn't change anything.

That was his world – and this was hers.

The two did not mix.

Looking one more time at the black shadows of the planes against the fading light, she sighed heavily and continued her run.

CHAPTER 5

SPARKY

Austin,

Military communications specifically state that you cannot give away your location. I'm assigned as a medic to a base – and even that will probably get scrubbed in the filters.

Giselle

P.S. – Why?

"SHE'S... *HERE*?" Austin whispered aloud, reading her email in shock.

Giselle hadn't said as much, but the abrupt withdrawal and terse response about protocol to push him away was telling. She could have said, *'I'm stationed in Alabama'* or *'I'm in Texas'...* or anything else – but she refused to answer him and then asked *'why'*?

Why do you think a guy wants to know where a girl is? he

thought wryly, realizing that if she was nearby, then perhaps he could meet her... and clicked on the other email from Giselle.

Yup, she was backpedaling and explaining that she was afraid. He also noticed that she never bothered to reply to his last email either. Yep, she was 'hiding' from him, as much as being the 'girl next door' could in this isolated, strange world. He understood her being afraid of what all of this was...

So was he!

Who wouldn't be afraid to put themselves out there and end up being smacked down... but the problem was if you didn't try, then you would never know.

Fear never stopped him from being bold, doing the unthinkable, or talking to a girl out of his league. Everyone put their pants on one leg at a time, just like him. If he let fear paralyze him, then he would have never made it as far as he had in his career.

Emailing her over the last three weeks had been the best time he'd had so far in forever... and didn't want it to end. Instead, he would need to find a way to draw her out of her shell, appealing to her curiosity.

He wanted to meet her, to see what she looked like, and say 'hello'.

> *Giselle,*
>
> *I understand, and you are right. I forget sometimes out here in the middle of nowhere about protocol... and appreciate the reminder.*
>
> *It's been a long week and I've really enjoyed taking a breather for myself, jogging around the base. People would say that's absurd, because of the heat – but if you do it early in the mornings or just before sunset, it's not so bad.*
>
> *So, let's chat about this mysterious haven we are dreaming*

*about. Would you want to imagine a place with ice and snow...
or maybe some place desert-like? You mentioned castles?
Wouldn't it be silly to imagine us touring a castle in Scotland
or England? What about Italy? It's not a long flight from my
secret location, but I don't know about you.*

*My squadron leader has been mentioning a place that I
should visit and it is located in Texas – but I've never been
there. Do you know where Yonder or Tyler is?*

*Just talking... thinking aloud and dreaming with a friend.
I think I'm going to get in a few laps before I turn in.
Off to go run...
Your friend,
Austin*

Yup. He was deliberately baiting the hook, hoping to reel
in something. It was hot out and he was exhausted, having no
intention of going running tonight since he'd already lifted
weights earlier in the day with the other guys... but this was
a chance he couldn't pass up.

Throwing on his PT clothes, he saw a few curious looks
and grabbed his water bottle from his footlocker.

"Where's he going?" Ricochet asked bluntly. "Didn't he
already exercise today? The bean pole is already rail-thin and
scrawny..."

"Maybe he's that way for a reason," Paradox muttered,
walking into the room with a towel about his hips. "I've seen
the guy at the gym, and he tries to bulk up, but it's just not in
him. You know that gangly kid eats like a horse and can
bench press his own weight?"

"With what?" Riptide laughed.

"He's scrawny," Copperhead muttered, smiling slightly.

"Don't mistake 'wiry' for 'wimpy'," Reaper interjected,
smirking at the other men. "I think he could probably hold

his own in a fight – and I'm glad he seems like his old self again."

"Me too."

Sparky looked over his shoulder and smiled – meeting Reaper's eyes. Nothing they were saying bothered him. He'd heard it his entire life. He was thin and never seemed to bulk up, no matter what he did.

"Yep. Someone told me to stop moping and pull my head out of my backside - so I did. I'm going for a breather. Don't wait up, *girls*...."

"Yup. Sparky's back," Paradox grinned, waving 'bye'. "*Arrivederci*..."

He grinned at Paradox and took off out the door to the barracks, nodding to a couple of guys in the hallway. As he stepped out into the night air, he grimaced.

It was still awfully warm out despite the sun setting in the distance. He walked past several buildings and looped his water bottle tether over his wrist, holding it in his hand, and began to jog.

He was on his third loop around the base when he spotted a figure in the distance... and kept going no matter how much he wanted to stop running and yell 'hello'.

Instead, he circled again and saw that figure standing beside a building, simply watching him. Running one more lap, he stopped, catching his breath very close to the fence line – waiting.

He took several sips of water with his back towards whoever it was, just listening, hoping, and praying.

... Then, out of nowhere, came a faint female voice.

"Drink another bottle of water before bed, too – it's hot out..." and he heard movement, turning quickly, trying to catch her and saw her running off into the shadows away from the fence.

"Giselle?" he hollered out painfully – and glanced upwards at the fence, feeling desperate.

It was exceedingly tall, with barbed wire angled at the top facing inward on both sides. Even if he managed to scale it? He would slice himself up before getting arrested for trespassing on government property they did not assign him to.

Pivoting, he ran inside to the communications room despite his state of dress and being covered in sweat… taking the first empty seat.

> *Giselle – was that you?*
> *I'll be running again tomorrow night, if that was you… and I'd like to say 'hello' – please. I know you are scared, but it's just a quick greeting. It won't change anything. Meet me – let's talk – please.*
> *I promise to drink my water and gulp down another one.*
> *Austin*

He clicked send and sat there for a minute, downing the rest of his water… and nearly choked as he saw her reply already. Clicking on it, he responded immediately before even reading it.

> *Don't move – I'm online too.*
> *I want to chat.*

Clicking send, he went to read her email… and smiled.

> *Austin,*
> *This is such a bad idea in so many ways. I mean, we are in different branches and there is a fence for a reason. I probably shouldn't have gone out there or even said anything, but my stupid mouth cannot keep from blurting out stuff.*
> *If you have a sports drink, it might be better to get some*

electrolytes – sorry, not trying to 'mom' you, but that's just the
medic in me talking.
  Giselle

Exiting out of the email, he saw she had replied.

I'm here – you know this is insane, right?

He replied immediately, trying to keep his shy girl from running away again. She'd already done it once tonight, and he wanted to draw her out.

Why is it insane?
Two friends meeting in the middle of nowhere? Perfectly
normal, I assure you.

Austin clicked send and saw she had replied again. His poor girl was panicking… and he might need to back off a bit.

Let's just keep writing, okay? Please?
Don't push me – I'm scared.

"Definitely time to back off…" he whispered aloud to himself, his mind racing as he tried to think of a way to reach through her panic, hating that this was the only way he could communicate with her.

Fair enough. Writing only.
Please don't back away or regret being my friend. I will be
going for a run tomorrow night – and if you are there, maybe
we can talk.
If not, that's okay, too.

Clicking send, he waited for several moments... and finally her name popped up on the screen.

Let me think – and maybe we can talk.

He replied immediately.

I'm not going anywhere... Ha ha ha.

I run in circles and keep coming back to this location – just like you. If you are there? Great. If you feel too nervous – that's okay. I completely understand, Giselle.

Get some rest and please don't worry – from one friend to another- okay? Now, I'm getting off the computer to get a shower because I stink.

Austin

Clicking send, he sat there for several minutes... just waiting. He was curious to see if she would respond again, especially if she thought he was 'gone' and his curiosity was killing him.

Of course it was insane!

His mind was wondering what she was like, imagining all sorts of things, and he kept finding himself drawn to her... and the odds of them being compatible at all were horrifically bad.

He could end up really liking her, and she could be completely uninterested – or worse yet? What if she was married and just looking for entertainment? He'd heard of guys that met up with women only to find out they were married to another service person that was deployed. Yeah, he was very cautious indeed – even if he wanted to meet her.

Just as he was getting ready to log out, her name popped up once more.

"Oh thank you, God..." he breathed softly, smiling and clicking on it.

> *Austin,*
> *About 8pm again tomorrow night?*
> *I'll bring two bottles of water along with some Gatorade powder...*
> *Two friends meeting and saying 'hello' – that's it – and we have to keep this to ourselves. Do not tell anyone at all we are meeting or talking.*
> *Giselle*

Clicking reply, he couldn't stop the stupid laugh that bubbled up from him as he wrote her back quickly.

> *Giselle,*
> *I'll smuggle a banana or two from the mess hall for 'dinner and drinks'. See you tomorrow... and now I'm really going.*
> *Phew!*
> *Austin*

Getting up from his seat, he couldn't stop grinning. He had a date!

THE NEXT MORNING, Sparky was trying to keep from gushing happily as he saw that he had another email from Giselle. The room was quite crowded, and other guys surrounded him, all using the computers during this brief break in the day.

"Sheesh... Ghost! Can you either stop radiating sunshine over there, or read it aloud so the rest of us can enjoy whatever has you grinning like the Joker..." Maestro said suddenly, causing him to look up and chuckle. The man looked completely sour and disgruntled, glaring at Ghost – who was blushing.

Well, somebody got a smutty email... Austin grinned, feeling slightly envious of the guy.

He couldn't even imagine what his own reaction would be, but he guessed it would be pretty similar – the dude was stammering and sputtering, looking completely beside himself.

"Oh, I can't read it aloud, guys," Ghost said, causing Austin's smile to widen even more.

Maestro groaned audibly and sighed, sliding down in his chair as he, Ricochet, and Inferno started laughing knowingly.

Yup. Ghost got something awfully juicy in his email box.

Austin hoped the guy didn't log off when he left the station… because he was gonna snoop out of sheer curiosity and glanced at Paradox, who raised an eyebrow at him knowingly. He would have company snooping and nearly laughed aloud once more.

The two men grinned at each other, conspiring silently.

His wingman.

"Ohhhh my gosh, I wish I had a girlfriend that would write me naughty things like that. You stupid, lucky cuss…" Maestro uttered despondently. "Noooo, I literally get a bill forwarded to me by my child's Baby-Momma-Drama that I get to deal with on a few rare occasions."

"So pay it, *big daddy*," Ricochet teased.

"How's that sister of yours?" Maestro taunted openly, harassing the other pilot, giving him a sly smile. Ghost looked so relieved in that moment that the focus was off of him and went back to reading his email.

"Single? Pretty? I bet she's some sensuous, seductive, young lady just waiting for a…"

Whoaaaa boy... Austin thought in a split second, knowing the two fought like cats and dogs sometimes – and saw Paradox's expression.

Yup.

Ricochet shot out of his chair, climbing onto the computer tables and halfway over the partition before they began to move into action. Maestro was laughing with delight, having gotten a rise out of the cool, arrogant man.

"Whoaaaa! Whoa! Whoa!" Austin snapped, grabbing at the belt of Ricochet's coveralls.

"Hang on, boys... not the computers!" Inferno snapped, going for Ricochet's collar and arms, tugging him backwards away from Maestro. "Off the desks, buddy!"

"I told you before, loudmouth, that she's way out of your league..." Ricochet snarled angrily.

"Time to batter up..." Maestro grinned, leaning back in his chair and putting his hands behind his head, taunting him again. "I'm gonna knock it outta the ballpark if I ever meet a sweet, young, hot *Miss* Briscoe..."

"Maestro, knock it off," Ghost whispered hotly, glancing around and looking distinctly worried. "I do not want to lose computer privileges. Ricochet? Inferno is right. It will take forever to get new computers if we destroy these. Remember the Army guys only have one computer that they have to share..."

"Man, that would suck..." Austin muttered openly and frowning. If he lost his computer privileges, he might just join in the fight because he would be livid at being cut off from Giselle.

"Right? I don't want that to happen to us," Ghost said firmly. "So, can you two please take it outside and leave the poor PCs alone?"

"My sister would take one look at you and laugh,

Maestro…" Ricochet goaded. "You aren't her type – unless she's slumming and desperate."

"Desperate girls need love, too," Maestro shrugged, giving Ricochet a sly look, baiting him.

"Is that how you got some girl knocked up?" Ricochet said innocently.

Austin and Inferno cursed at once, moving for him… as Ghost dove for Maestro almost immediately.

"You don't know anything about that!" Maestro roared angrily, surging to his feet and putting his finger in the other man's face. Ricochet simply slapped it away, smirking at him.

These two idiots were going to get busted for fighting if they didn't quit yelling at each other or making a mess of the area.

"Probably a classic '*touch-and-go*' move… or did you stick around for sloppy seconds?"

"Your sister didn't complain… and neither did your mother."

"You know nothing about my family!"

"If I ever meet any woman with the last name of Briscoe – I'm gonna say '*hello*' just for you, Ricochet…"

"You'd sleep with anything…" Ricochet taunted, and Maestro's face transformed. He was about to beat the stuffing out of the other man, and it was evident to everyone. The quiet man literally swelled up, both fists clenched, and his arms tensed up like he was fixing to throw a punch.

Bye, bye computers… Austin thought, getting to his feet because if they were going to throw down – he was going to get in a few swings for good measure because they would all end up cut off from the internet as punishment.

"Why, I ought to…"

"Knock it off – NOW!" Reaper said bluntly, appearing in the doorway with his arms crossed over his chest. "I don't want to know what happened, nor do I care, but I will tell

49

you this much – if *I* lose my computer privileges and cannot talk to my Sophie? I'll put you both in the clinic with blunt force trauma... am I clear?"

"Yes, sir."

"I can't hear you..." Reaper whispered, cupping his ear pointedly.

"SIR! YES, SIR!" All five men shouted in unison, snapping to attention as Austin felt his hands shaking with relief and the rush of adrenaline. *Thank goodness someone could get through to those two hot-tempered nitwits,* he thought silently, saluting.

"Good..." Reaper acknowledged. "Now, Maestro - not sure if you have heard, but Reilly is a genuine piece of work. That miserable man will cancel your leave at the drop of a hat if he gets mad. So, try not to act up before you fly out Friday? Ricochet, you too. Your vacation starts in two weeks, so try not to blow it before you get a break from the worst sandbox in the world... okay?"

As the men filed out of the computer room, Austin saw Ricochet stop Maestro, pulling on his shoulder and turning him around in the hallway, talking silently to him.

Paradox walked backwards right between the two of them and pretended to silently play a violin on his shoulder, smirking at the men. Austin wasn't going to pass up the opportunity to mess with them too, and needed an outlet for everything bubbling inside of him.

Honestly, he was a mess.

Adrenaline from the near-fight, happy to be emailing Giselle, and on cloud nine at the idea of them having a secret date(ish) tonight at the fence.

Austin followed behind Paradox, playfully playing 'drums' loudly on the wall with his palms and fists, causing a few heads to pop out to see what the commotion was.

"*Concerto-time... Signore Maestro y Ricochet!*" Austin sang out loudly, wanting to get everyone's attention and have a little fun. He heard Paradox laughing ahead of him, knowing where he was going with this, and looked backwards, meeting Reaper's gaze down the hallway.

The cool, stoic squadron leader was actually grinning and shaking his head at him.

"*Arrivederci! Ciao! Molte belloooo.... Ayeeee-ya-ya-yaaa! Cielito lindo, que a mi me toca*! Sing it with me, boys!" Austin hollered wildly, putting his arms over his head and pretending to conduct music, being deliberately annoying as could be...

He was singing and laughing as several voices began to sing with him from the other rooms, making up words with him. Some were enthusiastically singing, and Austin laid a hand over his heart - and the other flung into the air, serenading anyone who would listen.

As he moved down the hallway, Cajun leaned out of the barracks doors... and handed him a hairbrush to use as a microphone.

"Oh! I'm a professional now," Austin grinned – and began belting out the lyrics once more, not dissuaded in the slightest as someone else nearby hollered '*shut up*' in the distance.

Throwing open the doors as the end of the hallway, Austin exploded into the sunlight, still singing and humming happily, tucking the brush into his pocket so he could return it later – making his way towards the mess hall for lunch... and feeling like a million bucks with plans to smuggle two bananas or two cookies out of there for his hot date tonight.

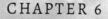

CHAPTER 6

GISELLE

THIS IS CRAAAAZY...

Giselle was silent as she harshly brushed out her long brown hair and began to plait it tightly into a braid.

She had always been accused of being an optimist, a dreamer, or focused on the positive and never seeing the negative... yet, knowing she was breaking a rule that Captain Logan had set down for her, Austin guessing her location, and the fact that they were going to try to talk in person for the first time?

Every negative thing was crashing down on her shoulders, making her feel so insecure and self-aware of how badly this could end up being.

Austin wasn't helping things either.

He was pointing out facts, coercing her to meet him, wanting to say 'hello' in person... and meeting someone out here, in the middle of nowhere, was so far from any of her dreams or fantasies? It almost felt like someone was taking the possibility of a fairytale away from her – from the person she was truly coming to like a lot.

It was a bitter pill to swallow.

She would never meet her Prince Charming if she settled for starting a friendship or budding relationship with the first guy who was sort of sweet to her.

Was it settling? she mused silently.

Austin was very nice, but everything within her was screaming that this was never going to end like she hoped it would, because reality wouldn't let it.

No, reality was a harsh taskmaster, and the daily grind would forever remind both of them that they were in different worlds despite being in the same location.

"Come and meet me, Giselle," she mocked bitterly, making a face and staring at the mirror as she finished tying her braid with a rubber band. "Let's say hello and meet. I'll bring you a banana. Be still my aching heart."

She dropped the braid, looked at herself in the mirror, and sighed heavily. Dropping her shoulders, she put her face in her hands and took several deep breaths to call her nerves.

"This is nothing," she whispered into her palms. "This is nothing and you've got to quit making it more than it is, because that is how you'll get your feelings hurt."

Looking up, she took a deep breath, held it, and let it out, before shaking out her fingertips.

"Just go for the run, enjoy the evening air, and keep your head on straight. It's no different from talking to anyone else... so don't make it that way."

Except she desperately wanted it to be different.

Yesterday evening, Perry showed up at the clinic at the end of Gretchen's shift with a piece of paper in his hand. Giselle watched the two of them for a few moments as they silently whispered to each other, smiling, before Perry unfolded the paper to reveal a crayon drawing… of badly sketched flowers.

It looked like a two-year-old drew them… but his smile, the love in his eyes for his wife, and the look on Gretchen's face were mesmerizing.

"I brought you some flowers, babe…" Perry had said, giving his wife a goofy grin – who immediately drew the curtain, blocking them off from everyone else.

Giselle knew the two were kissing – and exchanged a pointed look with her coworkers, who were also fawning over the sweet attempt at romance. There were no flowers out here – but the fact that he'd drawn them, was thinking of his wife, obviously worked in his favor.

It was stupidly romantic and if some guy had done that for her? Yeah, Giselle would have had much of the same reaction. In fact, she *wanted* some guy to do that corny stuff for her.

She wanted Austin to be 'that guy' and was scared to be disappointed.

Picking up the two water bottles, she taped the packets of drink mix pouches she'd ordered online for herself to them. Getting to her feet, she stretched for a minute, before putting a bottle in each hand to start her run.

Leaving the building silently, she nodded to one of the other girls that was headed into the barracks, rubbing her eyes wearily in fatigue. Man, she understood that exhaustion. Sometimes the heat just zapped you and other days it wasn't as bad.

As she entered the evening air, she took a deep breath. It wasn't too bad out, not like the other night. The sun was setting, glowing on the horizon. She saw a few others taking advantage of the evening, jogging as well.

Yeah, this was going to be a mess, a mistake. It was going to get back that '*one of the Army girls was talking to an Air Force guy at the fence'* and then she would have people breathing down her neck.

… People like Captain Logan.

Trying not to be obvious, she glanced over towards the fence and saw a few people doing the same thing — jogging. It was getting late and usually the base went 'lights out' around nine in the evening. As she made one lap, she began the second one and started looking for her pilot.

Her pilot?

Her shoe slid slightly on the gravel and sand as she straightened up, following the path once more. Her eyes were searching the landscape as she got closer to the fence in the distance… only to spot someone had stopped and was kneeling, tying his shoes.

A dark-haired man… just like the other day.

That had to be Austin.

Goldilocks, ha!

Her heart hammered in her chest and her brain started chanting out a mantra obnoxiously…

Don't be excited, keep it real. Don't be excited, keep it real… Don't be excited, keep it real. Don't be excited, keep it… reallllly cute?

Nuts!

The man was handsome.

As she jogged forward, she slowed and caught her breath… only to see a smile appear on his shadowed face.

"Giselle?" There was such a hopeful, wistful note in his voice that the tiny girl inside of her perched on a prim cushion in the dark recesses of her mind literally squealed in delight, making herself known.

"Austin?" she began hesitantly, looking around and saw most of the others had left the path, heading up to the buildings in the distance. "Hello. It's nice to meet you."

"You too," he said simply, and then they both stood there for a few minutes awkwardly.

"Water?" she asked, holding out a bottle towards him. He nodded, and that seemed to spur him into motion as he revealed a napkin, holding two large cookies that had seen better days.

"There were no bananas," he admitted, smiling sheepishly as he looked at her in the dim light. She couldn't tell what color his eyes were and almost wished there was a spotlight nearby. "I certainly wasn't coming empty-handed either."

"It's no problem," she began politely and extended the water bottle through the fence towards him. "There's an electrolyte drink pouch on the side, if you want it."

He took the bottle, and she hesitated, extending her hand through the fence… and he shook it politely, before she drew it back to her side.

"Again, nice to meet you."

"I'm glad you decided to come."

"Curiosity killed the cat," she offered nervously and looked away.

"Cookie?"

"Oh yes, thank you."

He tried to slide his hand through the fence and hesitated, carefully trying again… and laughed nervously. Instead, she stuck her hand through the fence and saw his sheepish smile.

"Well, that's a bummer," he began. "I guess any handshakes will have to be made by you reaching through. My palms are too wide and it's getting hung up where my thumb is attached."

"It's fine," she offered nervously, taking a bite of the cookie gingerly and opening her water bottle. "Did you have a nice day at work?"

"Yeah. You?"

"No busted noses or bodies," Giselle volunteered absentmindedly and winced. "Sorry, that's kind of a thing that I smart off to my boss. Gretchen usually asks how things are going and I always respond with *'No busted noses or bodies'* – just like if you ask her? Gretchen will respond with, *'Well, I didn't kill anyone... yet'*," she finished, feeling like a dolt explaining things – and heard him chuckle softly.

"It sounds like you have a good rapport with your boss."

"She's amazing."

"I'm glad."

"What about you? Do you have any 'things' that you do on a daily basis?"

"Oh, um, before a flight we always huddle up and talk about what we have going on with ourselves personally, keeping our group close and tightly knit... and then each of us has a 'theme song' that we use to get us in the right frame of mind," Austin volunteered – and winced.

"Two things," Giselle said quickly, marveling at what he said and liking it immensely. "First request? Don't share about this meeting – please. I could get in trouble. Second request? What is your song?"

"Oh gosh," he chuckled, reaching up and rubbing the back of his neck... and it enchanted her at this bashful side of him. "I wish it was something edgy or glamorous. Let's just leave it at 'peppy'... okay?"

"Uh noooo?" she laughed in disbelief. "I really want to know now."

"No judging?" he said warily, smiling at her. "And meet me here again tomorrow night?"

"Fine," she agreed, surprising herself with the ease that she did so – and saw his smile widen. "Now fess up... what song do you use to get your head in the right place for a flight?"

"Well, ah, uh..." he was stammering, and she was really enjoying this.

"I bet you dance to it – don't you?"

"Oh, geez…" he chuckled, looking away and taking a sip of his water. "You are going to make me sweat this, aren't you?"

"You pushed me," she smiled. "I'm just pushing back, *friend.*"

He barked out a laugh loud enough to make her look around quickly as she marveled at the sound of it. She took another bite of her cookie just to keep from sighing or saying something stupid, really adoring his laughter.

"Fine, fine…" he began, grinning at her. "Have you ever seen the movie *'Trolls'*? Some guys play Led Zeppelin, some guys play *'Sabotage'* by the Beastie Boys. I know one guy who plays classical music, and another that is partial to The Black-Eyed Peas… but yeah, my song I use is *'Can't Stop the Feeling'* by Justin Timberlake – and yes. I do dance in my cockpit – a lot."

She felt her smile widen and felt something shift inside of her, realizing that this guy was just so stinkin' nice yet down to earth. He liked peppy upbeat music, stole cookies, negotiated meeting her again, and she really liked the attention… plus, he was adorably cute.

"I like it," she admitted softly, meeting his eyes.

"You don't think it's stupid?"

"I have the same song on my iPhone," she replied openly. "I like music that makes me happy, feel good, or bouncy… and I think it's an excellent song to get your 'head' right, if you need to keep from feeling stressed."

She heard announcements on the speaker system in the distance and met his eyes.

"Light's out," he volunteered simply, and looked almost regretful that they were out of time already. "Tomorrow? Same time?"

"Sure. I'll bring the water again."

"I'll bring a treat."

They stood there nervously for a moment, and she smiled politely, raising her hand silently to say 'goodbye'. Her eyes roved over his face in the shadows and wished there was a little more moonlight or something, so she could see him better.

He was a little taller than her – and she came to his chin. There was a slight goatee on his face, outlining that smile… and noticed that he was looking over her just as intently, making her instantly nervous.

"I guess I'll be seeing you tomorrow evening, then."

"Until tomorrow, Giselle," he said gently, raising a hand to wave 'bye' as well, before stepping back from the fence. She nodded, and they both began to jog off towards their respective buildings.

AN HOUR LATER, she was still smiling as she lay there in her bunk, thinking.

CHAPTER 7

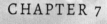

SPARKY

Austin lay there in his bunk, his mind racing. It was four in the morning, and he was already wide awake and ready to start his day – just so it would hurry through the hours so he could see Giselle again.

She was pretty, from what he could tell in the shadows, and really liked her voice. There was this soft southern drawl he recognized and gave him a slight pang of homesickness that he never thought would hit him since he bounced from house to house in foster care.

Yet, when she talked?

The way she rolled her 'Rs' and drew out certain words – it was there – and he could have listened to her talk for hours about nothing. He wanted her to look at their get-togethers like he did... to him it was a date(ish).

Gosh, yesterday he'd been so angry that the bruised bananas looked so bad in the mess hall that he'd skipped them and grabbed two of the tiny chocolate chip cookies instead.

Today would be a little different, though.

The exchange was supposed to be getting a shipment in, which meant that there would be new stuff… and it would pack the small shop with airmen looking for prizes to set aside. Last month he got two cylinders of Pringles that were near crumbles and a package of Sour Patch Kids. While he wasn't exactly a fan of sour candies…?

Candy was candy – let's be honest.

Getting up, he padded silently down to the communications room in his socks, t-shirt, and running shorts… just to send an email to Giselle. It was empty, and he was grateful that he would have a little time to himself without having to make sure no one was looking over his shoulder.

> Giselle,
>
> Thank you for yesterday. I know you were nervous, and I would never breathe a word. Trust your honorable 'knight' to do the right thing. I can't wait to see you later.
>
> Have a great day, my fair paladin…
>
> Austin

Getting up from his seat, he suddenly had an idea and sat back down. He opened up a tab on the computer and started searching, looking for a surprise to have shipped here for Giselle – just to see her smile.

It had to be small enough to get through the holes in the fence – or unbreakable if he had to chuck it over the tall chain-link fencing. It wouldn't really be special, friendly, or even romantic if he had to 'pitch' it over, but he wanted something to slip in her hand… just so she could store it or look at it, and think of him.

"And I think I want her to think of me," he breathed, his eyes scrolling across the screen rapidly.

Clicking on a few things, he put them in his basket online and moved to check out. They were silly little trinkets. Things that would probably mean nothing to anyone else – and he hoped that they meant something to her.

"You're up early."

Austin jumped in his seat to see Reaper standing there in the doorway, looking at him curiously. The other man was in the same state of dress he was practically in, and looked like he'd just rolled out of his bunk.

"Morning, sir…"

"It's before seven in the morning. Call me Reaper and knock off the 'sir' stuff until required," Reaper said easily. "Did you start the coffee in here?"

"Not yet."

"Ughhh…" he groaned, rolling his eyes – and thumped the switch to the 'on' position. "What are you up to, Sparky?"

"Couldn't sleep."

"So, you thought you'd shop or email someone?"

"Yeah."

"Anything special going on?"

"Just a friend and getting a few things for myself."

"Ah… I see," Reaper said quietly, smiling. "I thought I'd come email Sophie to start my day – and finish hers. I'm hoping she sent a photo of my son. She tries to send one every week, and he's grown so much."

"You miss them," Austin said simply, not asking because it was easy to see as Reaper nodded.

"More than anything. Sometimes I wish things were different, but then again I wonder if that old adage, *'Distance makes the heart grow fonder'* works well for us. I mean, I can be quite annoying and make her mad sometimes… but she seems to put up with me."

"Sometimes we enjoy annoying or pressing buttons on the ones we care about," Austin admitted, thinking of how he'd pressed Giselle into meeting him at the fence last night... and hesitated.

He cared – but as a *friend*.

It was going to be tough to even dabble with the idea of anything else, because she was right.

They were on different bases, different fields, and different teams. They could be the best of friends... but that blasted fence would certainly put a damper on anything else. I mean, it was hard to be interested in a girl when you couldn't hold her hand or kiss her.

... And the tiniest voice whispered an intriguing idea in his mind.

What if there was no fence?

"Are you okay, Sparky?" Reaper asked bluntly, looking at him strangely.

"Huh? Yeah. Why?"

"Well, I was asking if you wanted to see the picture Sophie sent of my son and you never answered, combined with this weird look plastered over your face. I wasn't sure if you were having a stroke or holding back a severe case of the runs..."

"Ughhhh... really?" Austin blurted out, making a face and drawing back physically.

"Whatever you were just thinking had you completely out of it and looking like you were quite bothered."

"I've got a lot on my mind."

"Your friend?"

"Yeah... wait... how'd you know?" Austin hesitated, feeling stunned – only to see Reaper laugh softly.

"You just told me a second ago that you were buying stuff and emailing a friend. Are you sure you're okay?" the man asked, smiling and watching him closely.

"Yeah. No. Yeah, I think so," Austin admitted and then looked at him. "When things are new and you don't know what's going to happen, it's a little unsettling. I'm sure you had the same issue with your wife."

"I'm happy for you," Reaper said quietly, nodding.

"I mean, it's not like that," Austin blurted out nervously. "We are friends and just talking right now, but she's so pretty. I can't stop thinking about her, and I know it's crazy, but…"

"Whoa… whoa," Reaper interrupted, smirking. "Being friends is a fantastic basis for a relationship – and that's kind of how we started. I wanted to be friends, and she wanted to wring my neck."

"Oh."

"I irritated her – a lot and probably at a horrific time in her life. Someone very close to her had just died and in swoops a man with zero tact. I really don't know how she puts up with me, but I can't live without her… which is why I'm here," Reaper said openly. "She starts and finishes my day – every day."

"I see," Austin said quietly, thinking about his own friendship with Giselle. He looked forward to the emails each day and this newest twist where they were going to meet. He wanted to see her every day, even if it was only for five to ten minutes under the cover of darkness so they could keep this a secret.

"I think I'm going to have my coffee and write Sophie now," Reaper chuckled, shaking his head… and Austin nodded, feeling chagrined. He wasn't very good company, if the man was talking to himself.

Opening his email again, he wanted to draw her out a bit more…

> *Giselle,*
> *Let's do something fun and different… let's create our own*

story. Each of us writes a line and the other builds on it. We
can keep this going between us and have some fun with it.
What do you think? I'll start – because I'm lame and taking the
simple route.

    "Once upon a time..."
    Now you create the next line in our story.
    Yours truly,
    Austin

Getting up from his seat, Austin nodded to Reaper.

"I think I'm gonna go hit the showers and mess hall,"
Austin began and hesitated. "I really appreciate you listening
and talking to me. It's nice to know that I've got someone to
talk to if I need it – and I'm really glad you set me straight."

"Everyone needs someone they can talk to, Sparky,"
Reaper said quietly. "Valkyrie was my person, and he never
said much, but when he did – I listened. He really pulled me
through when my mom died and was there again for a few of
us when one of our own crashed."

Austin nodded silently. It was strange to think of having
someone to support you when he could only depend on
himself for the longest time.

"Anything you need – just say the word, brother."

"Thank you… and I mean it."

"You're welcome," Reaper acknowledged – and smirked.
"And I mean it."

Grinning, he gave him a loose salute and walked off,
ready to start his day.

SEVERAL HOURS LATER, after lunch, he popped in quickly to
check his email and couldn't help the laughter that escaped
him as he read Giselle's email.

You slippery fiend!
What a great idea... and a lame start – really?! REALLY?
Fine. Two can play that game and now the ball is back in your
court, Sir Knight.
      "Once upon a time...
      Long, long ago..."

Giselle

Austin grinned – imagining her reaction. He quickly hit reply and knew she would be boiling (or laughing) when she got this email back. She had taken the easy way out also, in retaliation to him – and knew exactly how she would reply once more.

That was perfectly okay, too.

He was giving her this 'out' so they could play along and relax… and he was enjoying this so much.

Fiend? Fiend?
Pshaw... never! Me? It's called creative writing (and I'm
dying laughing over here)
      "Once upon a time...
      Long, long ago...
      There was a HANDSOME knight..."

Austin

P.S. – See what I did there? Oh! And to make sure you show
up tonight for our 'fence rendezvous'. I've got a treat for you!

AUSTIN LOOKED up in surprise as someone cursed loudly from the hallway and there was a commotion. Ricochet was getting to his feet, and he saw Copperhead running just as someone started screaming for security.

"What the…" Riptide said openly, following him as two security guards went racing into Reilly's office… and heard more screaming as the door opened.

"I HATE YOUR SMUG ATTITUDE AND HOW YOU THINK YOU ARE BETTER THAN EVERYONE! YOU ARE NOBODY! DO YOU HEAR ME? I WILL HAVE YOUR WINGS FOR THIS STUNT AND YOU WILL NEVER…"

"Sir, Lieutenant Colonel Reilly, you need to remove your hands from First Lieutenant Merrick – now, sir," one of the security detail began as the door started to close behind him…

Ricochet threw out both of his arms to stop them, catching Austin in the throat painfully… and Riptide caught him bodily to keep him from hitting the ground. He gagged and coughed several times, before glaring at the blond man before him.

That really smarted!

"Are you okay?" Ricochet asked quietly, before holding up his finger to his lips at the men surrounding him.

"What is the world is going on?" Riptide hissed. "Oh man, Colonel Bradford, too? Ohhhh boy, someone's gonna hang!"

"Maestro's in there," Ricochet said grimly.

"Oh no… no, no, no."

"Sup, fellas," Paradox said from behind them as Austin turned and burst out laughing. His buddy was standing there holding a bag of popcorn – and threw a popped kernel in his mouth, chewing and grinning broadly. "Has the show begun?"

"How did you know?" Austin asked, grinning – and reached for a handful of popcorn.

Paradox shrugged evasively, but there was a glimmer of

satisfaction in his face that told him the man knew exactly why security was in there.

"Shhhh!" Ricochet hissed.

"… Escort Lieutenant Colonel Reilly to his quarters, and I need a report from each of you on what has just transpired."

All of them stepped to the side, immediately saluting – and not making eye-contact as the security team walked Colonel Reilly down the hallway.

"Merrick, you know you cannot jump two ranks, but dang, son…" Bradford was saying just before the door shut.

"… And we need to go," Paradox chimed in quickly, grabbing Austin's arm and dragging him into the nearest room – and the others followed immediately. "We don't want to be caught eavesdropping on Bradford – especially if Reilly is in trouble. I'm going on vacation, and I'll be darned if I lose my trip out of sheer curiosity."

"What do you think just happened?" Austin asked openly, grateful Paradox was watching out for him because the temptation to go peek at the debacle that was unfolding was awfully strong.

"I think we are getting a new leader."

"Reaper?"

"Depends if Bradford actually bumps him two ranks," Ricochet said openly, looking at Paradox. "You just made rank – and Reaper got bumped two years ago, but he's still BPZ."

"You think he'll do that with Reaper being 'below promotion zone'?"

"Let's just say that I would prefer if Reilly didn't return."

"I think we are all in agreement on that one…"

"Reaper would be fantastic, truthfully," Austin admitted. He had literally just thanked the man that very morning and thought he was excellent leadership material. He cared – and that was rare.

"... But he's not staying. I think he's got a year or two left."

"We can get the dirt from Maestro when he gets out of there..."

"No," Ricochet said quietly. "He's very closed-mouth when he wants to keep his secrets. None of us knew about his son until recently."

"True," Austin agreed.

That had been quite a shocker to everyone. Maestro rarely said much and talked mostly with Caboose before he'd left. It had to be hard getting transferred here, making a friend, that friend leaving... and then your wingman was gone?

Ghost had been Maestro's wingman, but got out a month ago to return home to his wife.

"I'm shocked."

"I'm not. Reilly's been horrible to everyone. Remember Handsy? What kind of jerk has someone stand there for hours on end in a salute just to be petty?"

"Reilly," Paradox muttered, shaking his head and held out the bag. "Popcorn?"

Austin listened to the conversation around him as his mind raced. If there was a chance in command, then it would ripple the 'pond' – which meant that there would be a new squadron leader. It wouldn't be him. He was too low in rank, too new, but that person could also make or break his time here.

Suddenly, he really wanted to get away for a bit.

Let the destruction happen, let the chips fall where they may, and then he would find his 'place' once more among the remains. The last time there had been a shakeup, he was given new orders here... so that was enough for him to feel unsettled at this moment, especially when he was finding a nugget of happiness in his world.

All of them grew quiet as they heard voices once more.

"… Man, that felt a little too good, and remember – say nothing," Reaper was speaking to someone, and the four men looked at each other, unmoving.

No one wanted to get caught snooping, especially while tensions were high. They could hear nervous laughter and Austin recognized who it was. The man who'd kept his personal life a secret from everyone – and had just revealed that he had a son back home.

Maestro.

Maestro was in that office with Reaper, Bradford, and Reilly. Something was going down, and it was just a matter of what and when. He could practically hear the whine from the bomb that was about to fall in his lap – and would be completely unaware because the man with the zipped lips would never blab a word.

"I guess we wait?" Austin whispered in disappointment.

"I guess so," Ricochet agreed.

"And I guess I'm not in trouble after all," Paradox volunteered – walking boldly out the doorway with his bag of popcorn, tossing another kernel into his mouth.

Austin watched his friend leave, wishing he could put on a front like Paradox… and knew the other man was thinking the exact same thing as him. The 'poo' was about to hit the fan - and they would all be ducking to avoid that nasty crosswind that was about to hit the entire team.

He let out a soft curse, and heard Copperhead laugh softly at him, standing nearby, looking at the other man knowingly.

"Exactly, my friend… exactly."

CHAPTER 8

GISELLE

SHE SNORTED, looking at Austin's email, and rolled her eyes. What a silly guy, and what exactly was he trying to say? Was he trying to push her into thinking he was handsome?

Uh... too late?

Would she ever admit that? Absolutely not!

He was pitching underhanded, taunting her with the idea of creating a fairytale... yet using tried & true phrases already there. Where was the original stuff? The *good* stuff? Stuff he was thinking of, dreaming about, or creating?

She wanted to know that – and this was practically cheating...

The stinker!

Austin,
Seriously? Again?

Two can play that game... I thought you wanted to create our own story? When are we going to get past the quotes and clips that make up every single fable?

"Once upon a time...

Long, long ago...

There was a HANDSOME knight...

And a frustrated but BREATHTAKING paladin with infinite patience..."

Gauntlet thrown.

Giselle

P.S. See you soon for the 'fence rendezvous'... LOL.

GISELLE GOT in a chow line to eat with Donna, Carla, and Madeline, so she wasn't sitting alone. The line was out the door, which meant it was something good to eat... or the rumors were true. She'd heard that there was a restock at the exchange if there was a large delivery – that meant treats.

As she got her tray and slid it down the railing, she watched as they doled everyone up the same thing unless you spoke up quickly. Chicken tenders, whipped potatoes, cream gravy, buttered corn, and...

Giselle hesitated, smiling.

There – at the end of the line, was Captain Logan.

The man was seriously awesome on so many levels, and everyone respected him. He was taking his time, talking to each person, which explained the long lines, and literally plopping scoops of ice cream on top of cherry cobbler.

Her esteem for the man only grew, because this was a brilliant strategy to meet, speak, and talk to each person on base. No one expected this. This was not required or assumed. This was something he'd taken on himself to bond with his people.

"Hey Beck," Captain Logan smirked. "How's *'Project Sparky'* going?"

"Fine," she squawked nervously, clearing her throat. "Just fine. Why?"

"What's 'project Sparky'?" Donna whispered under her breath.

"Just some paperwork…" she replied quickly, and saw Logan's wink as he handed her a dish. "Thank you, sir."

"Let me know if you need anything, Beck."

"Will do, sir."

"Oh my gosh, the captain was so nice…"

"I know! Can you believe that? He was just smiling and…"

"He's so hot and dreamy…"

"He's insane about his wife and very happily married."

"Y'all… Ewww? Just no," Giselle shuddered, setting down her tray. "He's intimidating sometimes, and I've seen him seriously yell at some people before. I would rather stay on the good side than get on the bad one."

"Sometimes I wish I hadn't divorced my ex, but then he will contact me, and I remember exactly why I did."

"Not me. I'm not ready for the hassle of it all."

"My man is waiting on orders to come open to see if he can get assigned out here – or I can get assigned there. What about you, Giselle? Do you have a guy? You never say anything…"

"Sure, I have a guy," she sputtered nervously, wanting to fit in. "He's nice."

"Is he back home in Wichita Falls?"

"He's active duty…"

"Oh? Where's he stationed?"

Giselle winced. She knew that was coming and blurted out the first thing that came to mind. "Langley."

"Langley… Air Force Base? Your guy is in the Air Force?"

"Yes."

"Wow…" Donna said, raising her eyebrows. "You go for the ones with the egos, the attitudes, and the checkbooks, huh?"

"Wow… that was pretty derogatory," Giselle muttered, surprised. "I mean, can't a guy be *'nice'* if he's in the Air Force? You can't believe the hype and stereotypes… or people would think we are a bunch of angry people that fight all day long. Let's be honest, unless trouble shows up on our doorstep? We do a lot of paperwork and prep-work for when that day comes."

"She's got you there, Donna…"

"True that, girl…"

"I, for one, hope it never comes," Giselle admitted, raising a spoonful of cherry cobbler and ice-cream up. "Let's stick with Band-Aids, dehydration, sprains, and broken noses."

"Amen, sister!" they said easily, each lifting their spoon in a mock toast.

A FEW HOURS LATER, Giselle was running down the path, looking for Austin in the distance and fully aware they were both waiting for it to get a little darker out. Fewer people, less visibility, and a whole lot fewer questions…

Glancing up, she saw him standing towards the back half of the fence, waiting. Jogging forward, she gulped in air and let out an out-of-breath 'Hey' in greeting.

"Evenin' paladin…" he smiled easily, tilting his head to the side. "How was your day?"

"Fine," she began and handed a bottle of water through the fence, speaking distractedly. "Just busy work today and a few visits for headaches, dehydration, and one accident with a box knife."

"Ouch."

"Yup. What about you? How was your day?"

"Meetings," he admitted. "Going over maps, discussing flight plans, and lots of boring stuff."

"Stuff we aren't supposed to discuss," she smiled, guessing.

"Stuff we shouldn't discuss," he agreed, matching her smile. "H.I.P.P.A."

"Exactly, but I didn't tell you a name or describe the person."

"Clever, paladin…" he whispered playfully.

"Speaking of clever…" she began, looking at him. "You think you are sooo smart with that fairytale-stuff, don't you?"

He laughed softly, grinning at her.

"Would you forgive me for any annoyance, frustration, or silliness if I reminded you that I had a treat tonight?"

"There's not much to forgive," she replied and chuckled, "but I love a treat. Did you get a hold of something good? I heard we got a delivery and assumed you guys did, too."

Austin held up a bag and wiggled it.

"Are gummy worms good enough to qualify as a treat?"

"Shut the front door…" she gasped – and he laughed loudly. "Shhh! Did you seriously land some gummy worms?! Austin! That is like the lottery out here. I'm shocked."

"Fresh, soft, unmelted gummy worms to share with my girl…" he teased and ripped open the package. "Want one?"

"Hold it up to the fence and let me breathe in the sugar," she ordered softly. "It's been well over two years since I've had gummy worms or gummy bears… when I was little my parents got me a gummy snake one time and I puked red for an hour straight."

"Ahhh the memories," he laughed again. "I had gummy tarantulas."

"Ewww… no," she breathed deeply, smelling the sweet

fruit scent – and hesitated, realizing he was watching her. "I'm weird, aren't I?"

"I like your weirdness," he replied easily. "Can you reach through and get a couple?"

"You go first."

"Nuh-uh," he countered. "Ladies, paladins, and princesses are first. Every knight worth his salt knows that. Now, please. We'll run out of time – get yourself a handful to snack on."

"Are you sure?" she asked quietly and saw him step forward closer to the fence, realizing that she could see him a little better… and really liked his smile.

"Positive," he murmured, holding the bag for her.

Reaching through the fence, she let out a small laugh, realizing she was like a kid reaching into a candy jar behind a cage. She picked up a few worms and tried to pull her fist back through the fence, only to realize it didn't fit. Her fist was too big for holding the worms.

"Uh oh," she giggled nervously and heard him laughing softly as he tried to catch some worms to keep them from falling in the sand. He cupped his hands under her single fist, chuckling.

"Open slightly and make a triangle with your hand…"

"I'm gonna drop them…"

"You'll drop them if you don't…"

"Austin, oh my gosh… this is too funny…"

"Don't drop the gummy-gold…" he whispered conspiratorially, making her laugh even harder as she looked up at him and met his smile.

"Thank you," she said sincerely, not fighting this budding attraction. "I'm really glad to have finally met you. This is better than I ever imagined."

"It's the worms, isn't it?" he asked softly, smiling at her.

"Things you never thought you'd ever say aloud..." she uttered softly, teasing him, and they both laughed again.

"Okay, trying this again," she announced quietly in a hushed voice, cracking her hand as a few worms dropped and adjusting her grip to slowly squeeze it through the fence.

He took one of the precious gummy worms that he'd caught and bit it in half... sighing happily.

"Tastes like childhood memories," he murmured as she bit into one of hers.

"Oh, yeah... that's the stuff," she acknowledged softly – and then laughed as they shared a look. "I sound like a druggie getting a hit from her dealer."

"You sound like it too," he chuckled, grinning. "Does that mean I can tempt you out here for another 'fence rendezvous' tomorrow night?"

"I would come anyway," she replied, feeling suddenly shy as she met his eyes and saw his smile widen.

"I'm glad," he breathed. "I'm really glad."

"Tell me about yourself before the speakers announce lights out," she whispered. "Let's talk."

"Not a lot to talk about on my end," he admitted, wincing. "I had a pretty messed up childhood and bounced around in foster care until I got in at the Academy. They saved my butt."

"Ahhh," she acknowledged, not judging in the slightest. She was really proud he got himself out of a messy situation and seemed to be doing well. "I'm the youngest of eight..." and saw his mouth drop open in shock.

"Eight?"

"Yes," she smiled. "I grew up in a very loving home, very family oriented, and dirt poor. Pass-me-downs were a legitimate thing in our home, so going into the military to learn a trade was a simple choice."

"Do you miss home?"

"Sometimes," she admitted. "I miss Sunday dinners at my parents' house, but I do not miss tornado season. Wichita Falls seems to be a magnet for storms – or so it feels like. If I hear the sirens, it's like instant PTSD for me."

"Have you ever been in a tornado?"

"Yep. We all crowded into a concrete storm shelter that was half sunken into the ground to keep it secure. You stepped down into it and bolted the door from the inside. The creepiest moments of my life because it really sounds like a freight train. I was twelve."

"I can honestly say that I have not had the pleasure," Austin chuckled. "And I'm okay with that."

"Right? I could go without that experience again."

"I can imagine. You said you were from Little Rock?"

"Yes."

"Did you like it? Like the area?"

"It was just a city like any other," he said openly. "It wasn't a matter of 'like' or 'dislike'… it was where I grew up."

"Home is different now, isn't it?"

"Very."

"Same for me – despite my upbringing," she admitted. "I feel like 'home' is on pause right now and I'm existing out of my footlocker."

"Exactly."

"Someday, though," she smiled. "Someday I will look back at this and think *'man, that footlocker was so much easier to keep tidy'*…"

She met his smile in silent understanding as the announcements sounded in the distance.

"That's our cue, flyboy…"

"I know," he began, and hesitated. "This is so nice. I enjoy this more than I ever thought possible."

"Me too."

"How about tomorrow night I bring an iPod or something? We should be able to listen to one or two songs, maybe dance slightly through the fence or…"

"Let's just talk," she smiled ruefully. "I'm not sure there is a way to dance here and that might be a distant future thing someday. Besides, I bet you like your toes, don't you?"

"Are you a terrible dancer?"

"The worst," she hissed playfully and treasured his laugh as he shook his head. "I'm only warning you."

Stunned, he rolled up the package of gummy worms and held it through the fence towards her.

"Here, Giselle…"

"Oh Austin, that's sweet – but no. Those are yours."

"Give a poor guy a break," he teased. "I'm trying, you know. '*Sweets for the sweet*' and all that? Take them and think of me."

"Worms?"

"Exactly," he grinned. "Take them and enjoy… I'll see you tomorrow."

"Same time?"

"It's a date."

"Now, I think I'll go check my email and see if I can taunt my favorite pen pal before I turn in…"

"Oh mercy," Giselle laughed and accepted the bag of gummy worms, meeting his eyes in the dim light. "Thank you."

"We'll have that dance someday," he breathed. "I promise."

"Knights, paladins, castles, and fairytales, right?"

"Exactly."

"You are too sweet."

"Better than those worms," he smiled. "Goodnight, my sweet Giselle."

"Sweet dreams, Austin," she acknowledged, unable to hide the flush of pleasure that hearing him call her '*his sweet Giselle*' made her feel. Walking back towards the barracks, she heard a faint tune whistling in the darkness… and realized he was whistling 'A Whole New World' from Aladdin.

What a mysterious and charming man, she thought, smiling to herself.

Disappearing inside the building, she saw that the computer in the clinic was available and slipped inside to check her email. Sure enough, that sneak had managed to write her back.

Smiling and chomping on a gummy worm, she clicked on it.

> My sweet Giselle,
> Let me give this a try again… and we'll see what you think as I try to impress my harshest critic.
> Once upon a time…
> Long, long ago…
> There was a HANDSOME knight…
> And a frustrated but BREATHTAKING paladin with infinite patience…
> Who put up with the devilish rascal, because it made them both incredibly happy to take five minutes a day to see each other, share brief messages, and snack on unexpected delights in the moonlight…
> (Does it count if it's a run-on sentence?)
> Austin

Giselle's heart fluttered wildly in her chest as her nose suddenly burned and throat ached with emotion. This was so wonderfully sweet – and romantic. Could this actually be happening? Could something so crazy unfold into something so beautiful?

Hitting reply, her fingers trembled as she typed.

> Austin,

That was an incredibly beautiful run-on sentence, and your harshest critic approves heartily. Now, it's my turn.

Once upon a time...

Long, long ago...

There was a HANDSOME knight...

And a frustrated but BREATHTAKING paladin with infinite patience...

Who put up with the devilish rascal, because it made them both incredibly happy to take five minutes a day to see each other, share brief messages, and snack on unexpected delights in the moonlight...

But what that knight didn't know was the paladin yearned for what she could not have, searching the world over for a treasure few would discover...

I adore this idea you had – Sweet dreams, my friend.

Giselle

CHAPTER 9

SPARKY

"Ten minutes, men... then line up at the outside near the airstrip," Reaper ordered and glanced over them. "In uniform, too. We'll have company."

He shut the door and Austin turned to look at the other men, who were already moving into action. They'd been given the morning off due to meetings that didn't involve them – and had been sitting around, playing cards, listening to music, and some of them were still in their underwear or running shorts, just like they woke up this morning.

Austin was one that was in running shorts... he moved swiftly, dressing quickly, and bolting out the door to see that he wasn't the last to line up. *Thank goodness,* he thought wildly, moving into a parade rest position just like the others. Colonel Bradford was there and waved Reaper aside, causing the airmen to look at each other warily.

Were they about to meet their new commander... instead of Reaper?

He looked in the distance, beyond the Falcons lined up along the runway to see a few people milling around on the Army base next door... and wondered if Giselle had written him.

She had him hooked... and he knew it.

His eyes scanned over each form, looking for his girl... and then skipping to the next as he hoped he would get a glimpse of her. Just a hand raised in the air, a pause in her step, anything at all to let him know that she was looking for him – as much as he was looking for her.

... And there it was!

He swallowed, staring at the figure in the distance that stopped along the sidewalk between buildings... and saw a hand near her waist wave briefly, just before adjusting her camouflage cap, and continuing on her way.

Austin almost kicked up his heels in happiness and felt a smile touch his lips... only to realize someone was talking. He snapped up tautly as he realized Colonel Bradford was addressing Reaper – and pinning a new rank on the man.

"With pleasure, sir," Reaper said... and Austin heard Paradox curse under his breath. Yeah, it would be really hard to get away with some of the stuff he did behind the scenes. The man pulled pranks and some of them weren't exactly funny – especially if you were on the receiving end.

Reaper had always followed rules closely – and would expect them to, which wasn't a bad thing in his book.

"Men, I hope that you know I stand before you, excited to take on the task and relieved that we can have one of our own representing us. I take pride in what we do, who we are, and have always believed that our squadron is our family... and none of that will change – although your wingman will, as of today."

"What?"

There was a ripple among the team – and Austin swallowed. He was just getting used to his wingman, Paradox... and now they were changing things up?

"People come and go," Reaper continued quietly, his voice commanding respect. "And we've been through so many changes over the years that I believe it's been healthy to shake things up a bit. With change – comes growth... and my job is not only to make sure you come home after each flight, but to prepare the next leaders of tomorrow – you."

Reaper paused and glanced at Colonel Bradford – who nodded. Yup, this move had already been cleared and decided. There was no changing it. Austin was getting a new wingman.

"We've recently lost two of our own, demoted to civilians," Reaper joked, smiling faintly. "Ghost and Maestro will always be in our hearts, but in their departure? We have a few fresh faces among our team."

No one moved – not even to glance at the newbies that arrived this very morning. Austin assumed this was an introduction, a kind of *'meet the team'* get together... and that wasn't the case.

"Ricochet, step forward please," Reaper said loudly, pausing. "First Lieutenant Briscoe... Ricochet," he repeated in greeting as the blond-haired pilot stepped forward and saluted their new leader. "It is my distinct honor to move you to squadron leader... Captain Briscoe."

Reaper yanked the insignia off Ricochet's uniform, replacing it – and nobody breathed. Austin wanted to chance a glance at Paradox, his own wingman, to see if he was okay. He knew his friend had to be boiling mad right now, because it was always assumed that he would take Reaper's place as squadron leader next.

"The pleasure is mine, sir!" Ricochet said loudly, saluting both officers before returning to his position in line with the rest of them. He didn't dare chance a look down the row… especially not as Reaper spoke again.

"Ricochet, your new wingman will be Cajun – who was just reassigned to our squadron. Welcome aboard, Cajun."

"Thank you, sir!"

"Outfield, welcome to our team," Reaper continued stoically, "And you'll be flying at my side as my wingman."

Austin snorted.

Man, that had to chap the other guy's hide. He couldn't imagine being assigned to the boss the first day, as if you needed to be babysat or something. There was a lot more freedom and fun if you weren't under the microscope… and saw Reaper's gaze focus on him sharply.

"My apologies, sir. Allergies," Austin said openly, standing completely still, almost ramrod straight in his body's alignment.

"Sparky and Copperhead – you are now paired up," Reaper announced, and he felt a rush of gratitude at the choice.

If he couldn't be assigned to Paradox anymore, then Copperhead would have been his next request. He was a little more hotheaded than most, but he genuinely liked the guy.

"Thank you, sir!" both men said in unison, saluting.

They paired the rest of the team up, just before they were dismissed with orders to be prepared to fly at thirteen-hundred hours. As everyone relaxed their stance, Ricochet was called away almost immediately… leaving them standing there with Paradox.

"What the heck, man…" Riptide uttered bluntly as several sets of eyes swung around to look at the tall man that was staring daggers at the doorway that Ricochet and Reaper had just disappeared.

Austin knew he had to be seething and if nothing else? Paradox was a proud man… weird, but proud.

"Paradox…" Austin began – and froze.

Paradox looked at him with so much hostility and pain in his eyes, that he didn't say anything else. His friend needed time and space to come to terms with the obvious rejection and being passed over for promotion.

"If you need to talk…"

Paradox walked off abruptly, spitting on the ground.

Yep. Things were going to be tense and for the first time in forever, he truly wanted to get away… fast. He was going to put in for vacation, a break, a breather – and an idea hit him.

He was going to ask Giselle to go with him tonight.

CHAPTER 10

GISELLE

GISELLE HAD BEEN HEADING BACK towards the clinic when she saw the airmen lined up on the airstrip, all standing there formally at parade rest with their hands behind their backs. Something was going on and she was curious… and spotted Austin standing there at the end of the line.

She wondered if he ever looked for her like she searched for him – and decided to take a chance to give a small, nervous wave… only to feel like an idiot two seconds later because he could not obviously wave back.

Stepping inside, she checked her email again and saw it was empty. Sending a quick email to her parents, she smiled. It was strange to tell anyone about her friend… because it made it real.

Getting up from the desk, she only hoped that the rest of the afternoon flew by because she couldn't wait to see him this evening – and show him the surprise that she had picked up for the two of them for their 'fence rendezvous'.

Around seven o'clock, she checked her email again – and saw there were two responses waiting there for her. One was from her mother and the other was from Austin.

Giselle,

You'll have to tell me all about your friend, honey. I hope you are doing well and everything is going well here. We miss you and love you very much – but it does my heart good to hear you are happy.

What's this boy's name?

Do you have a picture?

What does he look like?

Do we get to meet him?

Oh! Your sister is going to have another baby – Georgia just told me yesterday that she was pregnant again.

Isn't that wonderful?

Love,

Mom

Smiling, she didn't reply yet because she had no idea how to answer half the questions… and felt a little unsure at some of them. No, she had no photos, and they weren't really at *'that'* phase yet.

They were friends, and she didn't want to make it weird if he wasn't interested in her like that, too. She thought he might be, but he was playing it very cool sometimes… like he was interested, but only mildly.

She was the one going at the speed of light and had to keep reminding herself that they were *'just friends'*.

Clicking on Austin's email… her breath caught in her throat.

Once upon a time...

Long, long ago...

There was a HANDSOME knight...

And a frustrated but BREATHTAKING paladin with infinite patience...

Who put up with the devilish rascal, because it made them both incredibly happy to take five minutes a day to see each other, share brief messages, and snack on unexpected delights in the moonlight...

But what that knight didn't know was the paladin yearned for what she could not have, searching the world over for a treasure few would discover...

What a journey it would be - especially if they traveled together, pairing their skills and attributes that made each of them special...

See you soon,

Austin

This 'story' they were creating was definitely leading her down a mental path that made her wonder if maybe he actually was interested in her. After all, he'd asked her to dance at the fence... and she'd brushed him off, feeling frightened and shy.

Mentally, she was feeling a little unsure of herself and having gotten that email from her mom... she was definitely a little homesick. Everyone seemed to be moving along in their lives and she was really happy for her sister – but all of it seemed so far away for herself.

She couldn't even fathom calling her mother to tell her she was going to have a baby because there was no room for that right now in her world – much less any of the other stuff that came with it.

It was sad that her single best relationship involved a ten-minute discussion with a man she barely knew, parted by a fence, in the cover of darkness, so they had a little privacy without being questioned.

Hitting reply, she wondered if Austin would see it before or after seeing him… and almost didn't send it. What did any of this mean? There were so many ins and outs, so many innuendos, that she was afraid to let her heart hope too much – and wished there was some sort of sign or clarification of what exactly was budding between them.

If it was just friendship, then she needed to quit feeling like each moment at the fence was two people, meeting under the stars, against all odds – because that just made it romantic in her mind.

> *Once upon a time...*
> *Long, long ago...*
> *There was a HANDSOME knight...*
> *And a frustrated but BREATHTAKING paladin with infinite patience...*
> *Who put up with the devilish rascal, because it made them both incredibly happy to take five minutes a day to see each other, share brief messages, and snack on unexpected delights in the moonlight...*
> *But what that knight didn't know was the paladin yearned for what she could not have, searching the world over for a treasure few would discover... What a journey it would be - especially if they traveled together, pairing their skills and attributes that made each of them special...*
> *Though she was scared, the paladin was intrigued – wanting to know more...*
> *See you soon,*
> *Giselle*

GETTING UP FROM THE DESK, she went to busy herself and change – eager to see how he reacted to her little surprise.

Two hours later, Giselle was jogging and on the third loop around the base, standing there waiting and feeling slightly nervous. They were going to run out of time today if he didn't hurry when she finally spotted him headed in her direction.

"I'm so sorry I'm late," Austin began quickly. "I got stuck talking when I was checking the calendar for dates."

"It's no problem," she smiled easily, watching him dig into his pockets for something. "Just glad you are here now. Do you want some water?" she asked, holding out a bottle she'd brought for him.

"Oh… ah, actually?" he began and hesitated. "I kinda wanted to talk for a few minutes about something – and I brought a cream soda. It's a little shaken, but I think it will be okay."

"Cream soda?" she chuckled, surprised. "You must have made out like a bandit at the exchange the other day. Gummy worms and now a cream soda? Talk about a jackpot! What did you want to discuss?"

He was still glancing around, looking awfully distracted as he twisted off the top of the soda and jumped back slightly as it fizzed up, going over the top of the bottle.

"I had a cup…" he said distractedly. "Dang it…"

"No cooties here," she teased and hesitated. Would he think she was weird even saying that? I mean, sometimes you did what you had to, and it wouldn't bother her… but maybe it would bother him.

He looked at her and appeared to visibly relax, handing her the cream soda through the fence.

"If you are good – I'm good."

She nodded and took a sip, handing it back through to him… and watched him do the same, digging out her own surprise for him – a tiny Bama pecan pie that was slightly crumbled and broken in the shipping.

Donna had ordered a box of them on Amazon… and she bought one from her as a treat for Austin. He'd been so sweet with the gummy worms and wanted to return the favor.

"I have a surprise for you too…" she began as he rubbed the back of his neck nervously. "Are you okay?"

"Yeah. I had this idea and I'm afraid you will think I'm weird, but I think I really want to do this," Austin began and hesitated, looking at her, pausing. "What's that?"

She had her hand through the fence, holding the tiny pecan pie for him.

"I think we are loading up on sugar during our fence rendezvous… dessert and drinks," she smiled up at him, meeting his eyes as he stared at her.

"Go away with me," he whispered, not moving. "Let's go away somewhere and get to know each other better. I jotted down some dates so we could put in for leave if possible."

He took the tiny pie out of her hand – and put his hand there instead, holding hers.

"I… ah…" he stammered, looking like he wanted to say more – and she stopped him, feeling her heart slam against her chest at the feeling of something so simple as holding hands.

"Yes," she breathed, not looking away from his eyes.

"Yeah?" he smiled softly. "I've got some time and…"

"I do too," she confessed. "I was just thinking today that I wanted to get away and was thinking of home."

"Let me take you there then," he urged softly. "Let's go on an adventure together. There is a place in East Texas that has a bunch of airmen – and we'd have access to a private plane. I could fly us to Wichita Falls or wherever you want to go…"

"Really?"

"Say the word and consider it done," he breathed and withdrew slightly, smiling nervously. "As friends."

"Of course," she nodded, pulling back slightly. "Do you

want the cream soda?" she asked, taking a quick sip again and passing it through as he took a bite of the pecan pie.

"Mmmm," he groaned. "I have such a sweet tooth and love pecan pie. Have you ever had possum pie?"

"Ugh, that sounds disgusting," she laughed. "Tell me it's not made with possum."

"Nope, but it's got a pecan shortbread crust, and this tastes kinda like this. Possum pie has chocolate and cream cheese in it, too."

"But no possum?"

"No possum," he smiled and handed her the tiny pie, letting go of her hand for a moment so they could switch treats… before reaching for her hand, clasping it again quickly. They traded twice more, finishing both tiny treats, and continued talking between bites.

"So, you have some dates you could take leave?" she began, feeling her heart beating nervously. She was actually going on a vacation with a guy – someone that she was only getting to know?

… And she couldn't be more thrilled!

"Yes," he scrambled, digging in his shoe to pull out a slip of paper. "Sorry, no pockets."

"I get it," she laughed softly and saw his shy smile as he handed it to her.

"Just circle whatever you get approved for-and I'll put in for the same timeframe. I'll book our flights, too."

She nodded. "I'll get the hotel rooms."

"Not necessary," Austin smiled. "My friends? They have a place for us to stay so we don't have any additional cost."

"Really? That's fantastic… and I'm pretty sure my parents would let us stay with them. They turned our bedrooms into guest rooms, so whenever any of us come, we have a place to sleep."

"Sounds like I'm meeting your parents," he murmured

and smiled at her. "Does this mean that I can perhaps take you to dinner... for a proper date?"

Giselle looked at him, her eyes searching his, and stepped forward towards the fence – at the same time he did. They stood there, holding each other's hand awkwardly through the chain link, and time seemed to stand still as they both ignored the sound of the PA speakers in the distance announcing 'lights out' in ten minutes.

"You want us to go on an actual date?"

"Very much so," he breathed softly, his dark eyes holding hers. "Do you mind? Does that make it weird since I just asked you to fly away with me?"

"No," she chuckled, hating that she was feeling so relieved and emotional in that moment. "Not at all. I would love to go out with you, Austin."

"Let's pretend for a week we are a normal couple, no fences, no clearing things with the boss... it would be just you and me, going halfway across the world on an adventure together."

"Knight and paladin in a far-off land?" she teased thickly.

"A quest," he smiled tenderly. "Remember our story? This will only enhance it – and we should probably go, so neither of us gets in trouble."

She laughed softly, touched at the ideas he was putting in her head, and nodded.

"I'll let you know as quickly as possible what I get approved. It would probably be faster to email you the dates."

"Sounds good. I'll check my email several times tomorrow."

"There's not many of us, so it shouldn't be a problem for me."

"Perfect."

They stood there together, waiting, and finally she smiled tenderly at him.

"I'm going to need my hand to come back through the fence, so I can go inside... which means you'll need to let go, Austin," she murmured softly, feeling incredible in this moment and how she felt.

He released her hand slightly, holding onto her fingers. As he turned her hand just a bit, her heart skipped a beat as he bowed and unbelievably kissed the back of her hand, like she was some medieval princess... before releasing her hand completely.

"Goodnight, my sweet Giselle."

"Sweet dreams, my knight," she whispered, withdrawing her hand and laying it against her chest, above her heart. Her other hand clenched the noisy wrapper of the little pecan pie, crinkling audibly as he picked up the empty glass bottle that somehow got propped against the fence in the sand at their feet.

"I'll see you tomorrow... same time."

"I'll be here."

AS SHE WALKED INSIDE, her entire being was humming with joy and she felt like she could dance upon the clouds at this moment. Austin had held her hand, asked her to go away with him so they could pretend to be a normal couple, and asked her out on a date.

Could life get any better than that?

Just for giggles, she checked her email one more time – and let out a tearful chuckle, touched beyond belief that he'd snuck in another line to their story.

> *My lovely Giselle,*
> *Once upon a time...*
> *Long, long ago...*

There was a HANDSOME knight...

And a frustrated but BREATHTAKING paladin with infinite patience...

Who put up with the devilish rascal, because it made them both incredibly happy to take five minutes a day to see each other, share brief messages, and snack on unexpected delights in the moonlight...

But what that knight didn't know was the paladin yearned for what she could not have, searching the world over for a treasure few would discover...

What a journey it would be - especially if they traveled together, pairing their skills and attributes that made each of them special...

Though she was scared, the paladin was intrigued – wanting to know more...

And the valiant knight vowed to sweep her away to a foreign land – far, far away...

I hope you'll go and won't think I'm crazy – I'm just a guy who's found a girl he really admires. See you soon... and ignore me if you see me crossing my fingers and toes. I'm nervous you're going to discover what a dud I am one of these days.

Austin

She quickly replied back – adding her line to the bottom and smiling tenderly, realizing that she really needed to thank Captain Logan one of these days if this continued along the path as she hoped it would.

CHAPTER 11

SPARKY

Austin got up the next morning to see if Giselle had replied... and literally fist pumped the air.

> *My dear knight,*
> *Once upon a time...*
> *Long, long ago...*
> *There was a HANDSOME knight...*
> *And a frustrated but BREATHTAKING paladin with infinite patience...*
>
> *Who put up with the devilish rascal, because it made them both incredibly happy to take five minutes a day to see each other, share brief messages, and snack on unexpected delights in the moonlight...*
>
> *But what that knight didn't know was the paladin yearned for what she could not have, searching the world over for a treasure few would discover...*
>
> *What a journey it would be - especially if they traveled*

together, pairing their skills and attributes that made each of them special...

Though she was scared, the paladin was intrigued – wanting to know more...

And the valiant knight vowed to sweep her away to a foreign land – far, far away...

So, she took his hand, feeling more alive and happier than ever before...

And I am – I'm so excited about our conversation and making plans. I do not think you are a dud at all... just the greatest of friends. I'll let you know ASAP when I get my request approved.

See you tomorrow evening.
Giselle

GLANCING AT THE COMPUTER, it hit him hard that it was Christmas and the items he'd ordered for Giselle hadn't come in yet – and he wanted to gift her a little something special.

Riptide passed by the doorway at that moment and leaned against the frame, crossing his arms and looking at him.

"What's up with you, Sparky?" he asked openly. "You've been humming, smiling, cutting up... and don't think that I don't see you talking with that girl on the other side of the fence every evening. Are you slumming, brother?"

"What?" he whispered, stunned.

"She's cute, if you like them in camo and skinny? There's nothing to hang onto with that one," Riptide chuckled, uncrossing his hands. "Girls are supposed to have a waist and hips…" he said, holding out his hands. "Something nice to hang onto, you know?"

"It's not like that," Austin protested faintly, feeling his face and neck heat up. He never even thought about Giselle like that – but listening to the man that probably could date any woman he wanted, unbidden flashes were going through his mind like a strobe light.

Would she even be interested in him like that?

Yeah, Austin wanted to kiss Giselle, but because he felt drawn to her. He never even considered intimacy or what a deeper relationship would bring between them. He always wanted her to look at him with respect, treat her with honor, and believed deep within him that the right person should be treasured… not manhandled, not like the obnoxious pilot was mocking.

"Y'all meet every evening?" Riptide asked, grinning. "How do you even manage with that fence? Do you wriggle underneath it to land some personal one-on-one time or are you two just chit-chatting and smooching between the links?"

"That's none of your business."

"Oh my gosh… that *is* what you are doing?" Riptide asked in disbelief. "How long has this been going on?"

"Drop it, Riptide," Austin growled protectively, getting to his feet.

"What's going on in here?" Ricochet asked openly.

"You want to tell him about your sweet little thing?" Riptide asked, laughing. "Our boy is in *'La La Land'* doing the *'Walk to Remember'* and talking with *'The Princess Camo-Bride'*… and wishing he was doing some *'Dirty Dancing'*…"

"That's enough, Riptide," Austin snapped angrily, yelling hotly and seeing red.

"West Side…Boring?" Riptide grinned – and Austin lost it.

He darted for the man at the same time Ricochet went for him, neatly sliding under the squadron leader's arm, using his wiry frame to his advantage – before tackling the smugly grinning, surfer-looking pilot against the wall noisily.

"Hit a nerve?" Riptide grunted as Ricochet pulled Austin off of him.

"What is going on, Lieutenant Calder?" Ricochet snapped angrily. "And what is he talking about? What *'sweet little thing'*?"

Austin ground his teeth and looked at Ricochet, painfully silent. Ricochet met his eyes and without turning away, he spoke.

"Riptide, can you return to the barracks and wait for me?"

"Yes, sir," Riptide grumbled… and thirty seconds later, Ricochet asked him again, his voice infinitely quiet.

"What is going on – and you might as well tell me because everyone will know shortly if I have to get Reaper to pull security footage?"

Austin swallowed.

"I haven't done anything wrong," he whispered, looking at Ricochet. "I have a friend that is stationed at the Army base next door – and when I go running, we meet up and talk at the fence for a little while."

"Have you trespassed on Army grounds? That is a smaller installation and they do not allow unauthorized people to just come and go like they are back home. In the States, all you must do is flash your I.D. and answer a few questions at the security gate. Here, they'll ask questions later because of our location and constant threat. Have you requested permission?"

"No, sir," Austin admitted. "I haven't crossed the fence line – and no one knows that I'm talking to her."

"Her, huh…?"

"Yes, sir."

"And you haven't broken protocol?"

"No, sir."

"Ignore Riptide," Ricochet said simply. "The man is jealous and bored. Don't engage him or you could get in trouble for rough-housing... and then there would be no more freedom to go talk to your girl."

"Yes, sir."

FOLLOWING RICOCHET back to the barracks, he was surprised to see that the man had gifts for all of them that his wife had shipped in. He was grateful for the razors, soap, socks, and other goodies... putting his cookie aside to split with Giselle this evening. Saying 'thank you' to Ricochet – and touching base with Riptide to make sure there were no hard feelings... he headed for the exchange.

The idea that losing his temper with Riptide could end his conversations with Giselle was the only reason that he went and 'ate crow' – apologizing to the man. She was putting in for leave and hopefully would hear something soon because the first date available was two weeks away.

Browsing the sparse inventory, he searched and searched for something, anything remotely nice to get Giselle... and spotted the perfect gift.

There, in the case, against a blue velvet box, was a pair of earrings that were perfect. It was nice, simple, not too fancy, and would show that she was special to him without making things weird. Earrings were an easy gift, and the tiny box would be easy to slip through the fencing.

... That stupid, blasted fence.

Purchasing them, he slipped the box in his pocket and threw away the receipt quickly, afraid one of the guys would find it. Last thing he needed was the entire team taunting him about having not even gotten to kiss the girl he was falling for.

Austin hesitated – and smiled.

Yeah, he was falling for Giselle and wanted to take his time about it. He wanted it to be right for both of them, not rush into anything, and make sure that it lasted because things could be hard enough as it was – especially with the forced separation between them.

He couldn't wait to surprise her tonight for Christmas.

Two hours later, he received his present... via email.

> *My dearest knight-of-the-realm,*
> *I just got my leave approved!*
> *January 15th-22nd (including the weekend) Do you think*
> *you can get yours approved that fast? I'm so excited!*
> *See you later – and Merry Christmas!*
> *Giselle*

Logging out, he ran to Reaper's office and winced, remembering he was in Texas for the holiday with his wife. Bravely, he went and tracked down Ricochet.

"Something you need, Sparky?"

"Honestly? Yes. How long will Reaper be gone?"

"He took two weeks for this visit to spend it with his family. They are trying to have another baby and he wants to spend time with Ben and Sophie," Ricochet smiled. "What's wrong?"

"I'm trying to put in for leave – and I need to start planning things, buying tickets, etc. but, well, Giselle got approved for mid-January and I'm not sure I can wait. Can you approve leave requests?"

"Fill out your form and let me have it," Ricochet offered. "I'll walk it down to Colonel Bradford and get it approved tomorrow morning."

"Oh man..." he whispered, grabbing the other man's hand

and shaking it. "Thank you, Ricochet. I mean it, thank you so much."

"I know what it's like to want to take a break with someone you care about," Ricochet admitted. "I can't wait for May to see my wife again. Make your plans, have an enjoyable time, and good luck, my friend."

Austin returned to the communication room to hurry and email Giselle.

> *My lovely paladin...*
>
> *I put in my request and should know an answer tomorrow. As soon as I get approved, I will buy our tickets and forward yours to you. I want to put us on the same flight, sitting beside each other out of Kabul.*
>
> *Gosh, I am so looking forward to this!*
>
> *Here's my addition:*
>
> *Once upon a time...*
>
> *Long, long ago...*
>
> *There was a HANDSOME knight...*
>
> *And a frustrated but BREATHTAKING paladin with infinite patience...*
>
> *Who put up with the devilish rascal, because it made them both incredibly happy to take five minutes a day to see each other, share brief messages, and snack on unexpected delights in the moonlight...*
>
> *But what that knight didn't know was the paladin yearned for what she could not have, searching the world over for a treasure few would discover...*
>
> *What a journey it would be - especially if they traveled together, pairing their skills and attributes that made each of them special...*
>
> *Though she was scared, the paladin was intrigued – wanting to know more...*

And the valiant knight vowed to sweep her away to a foreign land — far, far away...

So, she took his hand, feeling more alive and happier than ever before...

He grabbed her hand, smiled at her, and whispered, 'Baby, let's run away together and never look back...'

See you soon – and Merry Christmas!
Austin

CHAPTER 12

GISELLE

GISELLE WAS SO EXCITED, and couldn't wait to see Austin this evening.

His last email, his addition to their story, just absolutely melted her heart. Oh gosh, this was all so new to her and seemed so incredulous. She had accepted him as a pen pal by sheer chance... and to learn how wonderful he was? Yes, this was more than she ever imagined.

"Boo!" Austin jumped out, causing her to leap and let out a yelp, as she slapped her hand to her chest to calm her wildly beating heart.

"Oh mercy, you scared me to death!" she hissed at him in the still of the evening air – only to see his infectious smile and hear his laugh.

"Don't be dead... because dead people don't get Grandma's Oatmeal Cookies," he smiled, holding up the package. "I thought I would save this for our little fence-rendezvous. Do you like oatmeal cookies?"

"Only if they have really plump raisins," she laughed. "A cookie should not have meager raisins."

"I heartily agree," he laughed, winking at her as he tore open the packet and broke the cookie in half – handing it to her. "My sweet tooth says, *'good evening'* to your sweet tooth."

"Right back at 'cha…" she chuckled, accepting it and breathing in the rich brown sugar smell and scent of oats mixed with cinnamon. "Mmm, it smells like home."

"Right? Well, not my home growing up – but one of the foster ones. That woman used to bake a lot, and I was there for six months. I barely remember her name anymore because I was young and, unfortunately? There were a lot of places I bounced in-between. I think her name was Dee-Dee? Or Deidre? Donna?"

"I'm sorry you went through that," she whispered, taking a bite.

"Me too," he admitted. "But I think it makes you stronger because you know what your life will never be like… you know? I would never touch drugs or let my kid get lost in the system. I would fight it with everything in me to make sure he had a stable place to grow up happy."

"That's beautiful," she smiled tenderly. "I really like that – and I guess you are right. I know how I would want my home, my family life to be like because I loved how I grew up. We were so broke, but never knew it because there was always laughter and love… but I understand because I think a kid should have new clothes on the first day of school. It's a matter of pride."

"Oh hear! Hear!" he acknowledged. "I heartily agree with that. I was a garage sale nerd, meaning I was picked on because I wore stuff that was 'new to me' as my new clothes."

"Same," she agreed. "Do you have any Christmas traditions you would want to pass on? Since it's Christmas, I thought I'd ask."

"Now that you mention it," he smiled, giving her a mock-innocent look of dismay. "It is Christmas, isn't it?"

"Yes, you goofy man..." she chuckled. "When I was growing up, we had knitted booties that held empty coffee cans for our stockings. Everyone knew which stocking was theirs because of the crocheted patterns. Mine was squares with a pink 'chained' tie on my boot."

"Nice..." he grinned. "Hmm. Christmas traditions? I can't really think of any – oh wait! I know. Eggnog with cinnamon sprinkled on top. No matter where I was, someone was giving out eggnog, and that was one of my favorite things."

"The sweet tooth?"

"You know it."

They both stood there smiling and chewing on the cookie, hesitating for a moment just as Giselle broke the silence between them.

"Can I tell you something without it being weird?"

"Of course. You can tell me anything."

"I doubt that," she said wryly and heard his laugh. "But I really truly enjoy these moments and look forward to them every single day. I had no idea how happy exchanging emails would make me, nor how much I would come to treasure our friendship... and I think this is the best present I could have ever gotten this year."

He stood there quietly, just looking at her, and she felt nervous.

"This is the part where you make a corny joke to break the silence or tell me I'm being weird," she ordered nervously, feeling like maybe she said too much, or he was taking it the wrong way.

"I think that was a beautiful way to phrase the jumble that is in my head, because I feel the exact same way," he mumbled. "I think another tradition should be oatmeal cookies under the moonlight before Santa arrives."

Giselle looked up at the stars and smiled. It was beautiful here and the night sky was so clear, so unpolluted by light from the cities, that you could see the nebulas making it look like dust around the brightest stars.

"When I was a girl, I believed in Santa for so long…" she whispered softly. "I used to put oats with glitter in the front lawn, pretending to feed the reindeers because I was determined they would come to my home first," she laughed silently. "I think I was nine or ten when I found out my parents were our Santa and cried all night long on Christmas Eve."

She drew in a deep breath and let it out.

"That seems so long ago – and it's funny the things you remember when you feel safe and want to share them with someone who understands."

"That's the sweetest thing I've ever heard," Austin murmured, and she turned to look at him – and hesitated as he met her eyes, giving her a shy smile. "Perhaps Santa looks a little different when you get older, but the sentiment is still the same, no matter what."

He was holding a small black box in his hands.

"You didn't…" she smiled shyly.

"Of course, I did," he replied tenderly. "Merry Christmas, my sweet Giselle."

She reached in her back pocket and held up the small case proudly – only to hear his laugh.

"Giselle…" he growled playfully.

"Merry Christmas, my sweet Austin," she teased, matching his wide smile as she stuck the case through the fence for him. Laughing, he handed her the box and hesitated.

"Hang on," he urged and looked around. "Come closer."

She stepped forward obediently, and he waved her closer still, putting his shoulder against the fence and his hip.

"Match my stance," he smiled, "Because if we were having a real Christmas and this stupid fence wasn't in the way? I would be sitting next to you on the floor by the Christmas tree or on the couch, watching you open your gift."

Giselle immediately obeyed and looked at him, his face so close to the chain-link that she could see his dark eyes. She nearly sighed aloud as she saw his smile, and loved the fact that he had a nicely trimmed goatee on his chin. It made him look so incredibly gorgeous.

"Hi…" he whispered.

"Hi…" she replied, feeling that smile on her lips again. He made her feel so alive, so thrilled to be here, despite all the challenges and nastiness of the world circling them. Here, she was at peace.

"Open it," she urged.

"You open yours," he ordered, chuckling.

"Same time?"

"Deal."

They both counted aloud and when they got to 'three' – she opened the case and hesitated.

Inside lay some tiny gold earrings that looked like suns with tiny diamonds in the center. She heard him whisper her name and didn't dare look at him because her vision was blurring from the tears that suddenly flooded her eyes unexpectedly.

She loved *Tangled* – and recognized this emblem. This sun was from the princess' kingdom where she returned, falling in love with Eugene.

"Do you like them?" he said softly. "I thought the little suns were appropriate because we are out here in the desert…"

"It's from the Disney movie called *Tangled*," she whispered and looked at him in that moment, despite the tears. His eyes widened in alarm for a moment before she spoke. "It's my favorite movie and I love them. This is the best Christmas I've ever had, Austin. Thank you."

"Put them on for me."

She nodded and removed her plain silver studs, putting the tiny gold suns on her earlobes, fastening them.

"How do they look?"

"It's the most beautiful thing I've ever seen," he breathed, still staring at her. "I can't tell what shines brighter – the stars in the sky, the stars in your eyes, or those earrings…"

"You flirt," she laughed easily – and then spotted his unopened gift. "You didn't even open your gift from me."

"I wanted to savor these last few moments."

"Open it," she ordered playfully. "Now nothing is as nice as this, but I saw them and thought it was perfect."

He opened the case and hesitated – glancing at her.

"Oh Giselle," he breathed, smiling widely. "I love them…"

"I thought the yellow polarized lenses were perfect because you are my ray of sunshine each day," she smiled impishly. "And you gave me little suns – so I guess I'm your stinkin' ray of sunshine too."

He laughed easily and slipped them on.

"How do I look?" he said in a mockingly deep voice.

"Oh-so debonaire," she whispered breathlessly, laying the back of her hand to her forehead to pretend to faint… causing him to laugh once more as he put them back in the protective case. "You really like them?"

"I love them. They are perfect and I can wear them all the time."

She stood there, her shoulder to his, in this little haven that they'd occupied for a brief moment each day… and heard his voice, faint and nervous.

"I wish there was mistletoe," he breathed softly – and she looked at his profile in wonder. "Is that so wrong? I'm just so happy and I feel the need to express it, but there's this darn fence, cutting me off from everything I treasure. I wish I could hug you, hold your hand, or cuddle like a couple of teenagers…"

"Austin?"

"Yeah?"

"Why don't we try it – despite the fence?" she whispered bravely, staring up at him. "Because I wish you could kiss me, too."

He turned slightly – and she did the same as both leaned towards the fence. This felt so weird, so strange, because she couldn't embrace him fully and he couldn't hold her at all. His lips brushed against hers softly and felt him sigh heavily.

"This feels so wrong," he began sadly – and Giselle swore her heart stopped at his words, only to see the burning desire and regret in his eyes. "I want to sink my fingers in your hair and hold you close when I finally taste your lips… and it feels so clinical when I cannot touch you. Like I'm close, but still so far out of reach. It's almost cruel," he grimaced painfully, his eyes darting along the perimeter of the fence looking for an 'out'.

"I understand," she breathed, not moving away as they remained so close to each other, trying to kiss the other person. "I want to touch your face or pull you to me, or wrap my arms around your shoulders…"

"I'm gonna need a cold shower…" he laughed softly, trying to kiss her again, except she was laughing too. His finger reached through the fence and touched her cheek barely as the announcements began alerting everyone about 'lights out'.

"I'm gonna yank those speakers down one of these days," he confessed wryly, smiling at her. "I hate them - and the interruption every single night."

"I know."

"Okay, quick stuff we need to talk about," he breathed,

still not moving away. "I'll find out tomorrow about my leave and email you. Then I'm booking the tickets for us, so be prepared to cuddle for fourteen hours on a plane with your friend."

"I think I can handle it," she smiled.

"Prep yo' self…" he taunted devilishly in a soft voice. "Do you care if it's a window or aisle seat?"

"No."

"I might need some information from you… like a date of birth and other stuff, but I'll need to check. I usually book American Airlines or Delta, so if we can both look – send me the info as soon as possible, because we are getting out of here together for a real rendezvous - *without a dang fence.*"

"Whatever shall we do?" she said innocently with wide eyes, causing him to laugh again.

"I can think of lots of things… but the first is holding hands, then hugging, and finally? I'm kissing you."

"That sounds perfect."

"Go head inside, my sweet," he breathed, leaning forward to barely brush his lips against hers again. "I want to make sure you are safe."

"No one is going to touch me on base. We're safe here."

"I know. It's a guy thing… please."

"We need to both go," she said, leaning forward to kiss him once more. "I really hate this fence."

"Loathe…" he drawled, smiling.

"Abhor…"

"Despise…"

"I can't wait for our vacation."

"Me neither."

"Goodnight and Merry Christmas, Giselle."

"Sweet dreams – and Merry Christmas, Austin," she uttered one last time before stepping back, seeing his eyes on her. "Thank you again for the beautiful earrings."

"You are welcome – and thank you again for my awesome sunglasses. I love them and will get a lot of use out of them."

"You're welcome," she said pertly, lifting her hand to wave. "See you tomorrow. Same time?"

"You got it, babe."

She felt herself blush as she walked away, preening at the fact that he called her 'babe'. Entering the building and ducking into the first room she saw with a computer unoccupied - she sat down.

She was still emotionally high from the evening's atmosphere and dreamy soft kisses, and quickly replied to his email from earlier in the day.

To my favorite elf this Christmas...

Once upon a time...

Long, long ago...

There was a HANDSOME knight...

And a frustrated but BREATHTAKING paladin with infinite patience...

Who put up with the devilish rascal, because it made them both incredibly happy to take five minutes a day to see each other, share brief messages, and snack on unexpected delights in the moonlight...

But what that knight didn't know was the paladin yearned for what she could not have, searching the world over for a treasure few would discover...

What a journey it would be - especially if they traveled together, pairing their skills and attributes that made each of them special...

Though she was scared, the paladin was intrigued – wanting to know more... And the valiant knight vowed to sweep her away to a foreign land – far, far away...

So, she took his hand, feeling more alive and happier than ever before...

He grabbed her hand, smiled at her, and whispered, 'Baby, let's run away together and never look back...'

She laced their fingers together, holding fast to this miracle before her, and whispered, 'I'm ready when you are...'

Thank you for being the most amazing person I've met, Giselle

CHAPTER 13

SPARKY

AUSTIN WAS SO thrilled and could barely contain himself. They had approved his leave, the plane tickets were purchased, and time flew past so quickly since Christmas.

They were departing in the morning from Kabul.

As he waited by the fence for Giselle for their evening tryst, he mentally went down the checklist of things he would need. His cell phone was on a charger in Reaper's office, his passport was on top of his clothing to wear in his footlocker. His bag was packed... and all he needed was to sleep – and catch a ride to the airport.

Reaper refused any of the other pilots volunteering to drop him off, claiming that they would make a security guard available. So, there was one change with the new regime already.

"Not being difficult, but if something happened? You can pick up a gun and defend yourself... but they cannot fly your plane. I need everyone I can," Reaper had explained, almost apologetically – and he knew why.

Reaper had done shuttle duty for a couple of the guys willingly in the past, just to keep the rest of them safe. It was dangerous to be on the roads by yourself and alone – and the ride back could be a short or treacherous one.

Finally, he saw Giselle.

"Hey…" he smiled and easily stepped forward, his fingers holding the fence as she pressed herself to it, brushing her lips against his easily.

"Hi there…" she breathed softly, smiling happily. "Are you ready for tomorrow?"

"Very."

"My ride is heading out of here at noon, so I'll be there in plenty of time for the flight."

"Mine isn't leaving until one – so I will be there, but you might be alone for a bit."

"No problem."

"I don't see why they wouldn't let us drive together."

"I'm going to suggest it again," Austin admitted, because it made sense and fewer resources were used. If they were stateside, there would be a shuttle available to any military personnel on base… one vehicle would be so much better.

"I emailed my parents and told them it would still be a few days, that we were going to fly into town together," she said softly, and he couldn't help that melting feeling inside of him as he marveled at the warmth of her eyes. Gosh, what would it be like to see her in the light of day, away from the shadows… to see that lovely smile, bask in that warmth, and be close to her?

"I emailed a couple of the guys at Flyboys to let them know I was flying in for a visit," he began softly, feeling her fingers touch his where he had them on the fence. "I told Caboose,

Firefly, Ghost, and Maestro, that I was coming into town with a friend – and they said we were welcome to use the facilities to stay there onsite for free. Reaper also told me we were welcome to a few rooms at his wife's bed-and-breakfast."

"What do you want to do?"

"I thought we could stay at Flyboys," he admitted. "There's two beds according to Firefly, a kitchenette, and it's not too far from town… plus we can borrow a car to do a little sightseeing."

"Flyboys, it is…"

They heard the speakers already – and sighed.

"I'm sorry I was late," Giselle apologized. "I was doing a few last-minute things and getting my bag ready."

"It's fine."

"Can you imagine a week not hearing that?" she smiled.

"I'm looking forward to it," he laughed easily. "I'll see you tomorrow. Try to get some rest, okay?"

"You, too."

They whispered their goodnights to each other as he kissed her softly, treasuring the gentleness of her presence and the way it made him feel.

No, leaving together was probably the best idea he'd ever had in his entire life… and he couldn't wait to hold her close to him finally. His eyes drank her in as he watched her leave once again.

Soon, he kept telling himself… only to hear a tiny voice making themselves known at the back of his mind.

… And then what?

THE NEXT AFTERNOON, around noon… Austin couldn't wipe the grin off his face as he slid his sunglasses on his face, hefting his bag onto his shoulder. The truck was waiting for him just outside the gate, and it was time.

Walking up, he was a little surprised to see it was a covered vehicle, but then again? It made sense. Make this look like a normal run, a truck full of soldiers and military personnel, so they weren't stopped or bothered.

Moving to the passenger side door, he saw a man in camouflage sitting there and hesitated. The man looked at him, raised an eyebrow.

"Where do you think you are going, *Zoomie?*"

Austin hesitated.

"In the back," the soldier said bluntly, smirking.

Heading around to the back of the truck, he raised the flap... and stared.

Giselle was sitting inside, with her back against the back of the truck opposite of the driver – and smiling. Without questioning a thing, he threw his bag in the back of the truck, climbed in, and saw her stand... moving forward to take her in his arms, hugging her tightly.

Closing his eyes, he inhaled, breathing in the scent of her hair and marveling at the way she just fit in his arms.

"Heading out..." the soldier called in warning, just as the truck lurched forward, nearly dislodging the both of them. Giselle quickly sat down – and dug out two helmets and vests from the side compartment, handing him one.

"What's that for?"

"Your head," she smiled, slipping the vest over her head as she strapped the helmet to her chin, and heard the driver laugh knowingly.

"Hey Zoomie... down here on earth, among the plebes? When we go into town, we protect our bonedomes from stray bullets," the driver called out over his shoulder, easily. "Put the gear on and humor everybody. Nobody wants to explain why someone ends up dead on a run."

Austin actually forgot about this part when he first arrived in Kabul. That had been quite a shocker as he'd sat on the truck with a few other guys, all donning protective gear. It was protocol now for everyone because when they had first started setting up the bases, one truck had been fired on from the street.

Austin slid the vest over his head, donned the helmet, and yanked off the precious sunglasses, putting them in the case and in his bag. He then reached for Giselle's hand automatically... immediately lacing his fingers with hers. The sight of their hands together was more poignant than he ever expected, making him swallow back the knot in his throat.

He needed this.

The closed flaps of the truck reminded him of their rendezvous along the fence line in the dark. It was dim inside, with so many shadows and only the occasional bump would cause the flaps to move, allowing in a brief glimpse of light.

They sat silently together, hands clenched, and bracing themselves on the rough roads before arriving to the airport finally.

"I'm not putting it in park," the driver said bluntly. "Get your things and tell me when you are good – then I'm out. Leave the gear for the next person and have a nice flight. Be safe, you two."

"Will do," Austin began, quickly standing as they both shrugged off the gear, stowing it, and he hopped down. Helping Giselle down, he grabbed both canvas totes and slung them onto his shoulder, before glancing at her... and swallowing again.

Now was not the time to be fawning over her – he had to get her inside to safety. Seizing her hand, he pulled her with him towards the door.

"We're out," he said simply – and heard Giselle.

119

"Thank you so much, Keyes," she began. "Be safe!"

"You, too, Beck."

Surprised, everything in him wanted to ask how she knew the soldier, but didn't want to come off as a possessive lout.

Of course, Giselle knew the men on base. Heck - she probably had seen half of their backsides giving *'peanut butter shots'* or medication straight into the cheek. She was a medic and had dug out bullets, stitched up people, gave fluids, and helped save lives... and he needed to acknowledge that – not be jealous.

The truck drove off and people were moving all around them. They stood out. Giselle pulled her bag off his shoulder, hiking it on her own. He nodded tightly as they both moved forward silently, hurrying into the building to go check in and get through the security checkpoint.

As they finally got to the gate for their flight, he set down his bag and looked at her... seeing her watching him. Neither said a word, but moved easily into the other person's arms, seeking contact.

Now he was free to memorize her features, here in the sunlight. She had a warm peach tint to her cheeks and pale golden-brown eyes that reminded him of amber. Her hair surprised him. He assumed it was a dark brown because of the shadows, but it was actually a rich, heavy auburn.

He stood there, drinking in her features, loving the way the light danced across her skin... as his fingers brushed against her cheek. It was so soft and she was more incredible than anything he could have imagined.

She reached up to touch his face, her fingertips brushing against his chin near his goatee... before touching his lip – and he was lost. He could feel her trembling in his arms, knowing how overcome he was himself, and it was too much.

He reached up and sank his hands into her hair, cupping her head as he tugged slightly before capturing her lips. The feeling, the emotions within him, was insanely strong. This attraction between them was made even more intense by knowing how the other person's mind worked.

As he kissed her, he felt her hands on his back, cradling him and craving the sense of belonging.

He belonged *here* – in her arms.

Someone nearby hollered at them, and he felt Giselle jerk against him.

A man was sitting there, waiting for the flight… and had poked her with a cane, still mouthing something and pointing at her. His hands were gesturing, pointing at his own head, frowning angrily – and Giselle pulled away.

"I need to cover my hair," she whispered painfully. "He's offended, I think."

"If he pokes you with that cane again, *I'm* gonna be offended," Austin snapped hotly, looking at the man. "No," he said simply, putting Giselle behind him protectively.

"Let's walk over to that shop and I'll get a scarf."

"You don't have to do that."

"Austin," she began. "I'm here, in their country, and a foreigner. It's a sign of respect and this isn't going to be a one-off event. We've got another thirty minutes before they even load us onto the plane. Watch my bag and I'll be right back."

"I'm coming with you."

"Alright."

It seemed like such a shame to cover her hair or any of her face now that he was finally getting to see her in the daylight – but he understood. She glanced at the hangars, finding a sedate large scarf that looked almost like a shawl, and held it up.

"Is gray my color?" she teased softly, pulling it off the hangar and moving to purchase it.

"Everything is your color," he replied without thinking – and saw the look of pleasure and surprise in her eyes, just as they crinkled slightly at the corners when she smiled.

"Oh, you are good…" she teased openly. He picked up two candy bars he couldn't identify or read the labels, two bottles of water, and pushed her hand away when she moved to pay.

"I've got it," he said simply, purchasing everything.

"You don't have to do this," she protested faintly. "You bought the tickets."

"And you are my girl," he countered quickly, paying the clerk and nodding politely, before handing the scarf back to Giselle. Picking up the bag, he turned to look at her… and saw her watching him, the scarf clenched in her hands, as she stared.

He felt his heart quicken as he met her eyes, taking the scarf slowly from her and unfurling it, before draping it loosely to cover her hair.

"There might be something to this…" he breathed softly.

"What's that?"

"All that beauty is only mine to look at," he murmured and saw her shy smile, just before he leaned forward to kiss her forehead. "C'mon. Let's go back to the gate before anyone else decides to reprimand us again."

CHAPTER 14

GISELLE

Forget 'cute'...

Giselle couldn't stop staring at Austin.

It was like seeing a new person now that all the shadows and darkened smiles were gone. He was standing there before her, vibrant and incredible. Rich, dark, warm eyes held hers... and his hair that she suspected was black, was actually a warm dark brown shade, nearly the same color as his eyes. The scruff on his chin was a little darker, but it only served to accentuate the tan skin of his face.

He was simply beautiful... and kept looking at her like he was thinking the same thing as her own revelation. The shadows and dim lights of their meetings at the fence had hid so much, never realizing it.

Every time he held her hand, smiled at her, or gave her a look - she felt it straight in her core.

Her fingers were itching to trace his features, to see that soft look in his eyes, and reveled at the feeling between them when he finally, truly, kissed her. Oh goodness, the moment she felt his fingers in her hair, her knees gave…

Had anything ever felt so good?!

And the way he put himself between her and the man who'd poked at her knee, causing it to give… well, she practically purred aloud. He was watching out for her, calling her *'his girl'*, and saying so many things that were creating a fervor in her mind.

Even now, as they loaded onto the plane… he was caring for her. Giselle went first onto the plane and checked her carryon at the gate, just like Austin.

As she moved down the aisle of the aircraft, he was there at her back protectively. She hesitated for a moment and glanced at him, only to see his smile.

"Take the window seat," he urged softly. "You'll enjoy the view."

Nodding, she slid into her seat, and he followed, taking the aisle location. She noted that he put a bottle of water in front of each of them – and tucked the candy bars into the pocket, smiling at her… and winked.

"Sweet tooth…"

"I see," she chuckled easily, pulling her scarf further down until everyone was on the plane. She was getting pointed looks and frowns from several of the older men as they were getting on the flight.

"Are you okay?" he murmured, looking at her. "You look nervous."

"I'm fine, just ready to get to Texas," she admitted – and it was true. There was nothing like being home.

The wide-open skies, the plains, seeing the cattle, horses, and expanses of land along the highways in the country. Smiling faces, soft drawls, and gentle people. Bluebonnets, primroses, cactus, and mesquite trees… yes, there was nothing like it.

"I'm craving a Whataburger," she breathed softly, closing her eyes. "With extra cheese and spicy ketchup."

"We'll have to go there then," he smiled at her. "There was one in Little Rock, but I grew up on the other side of the city – and zero in Colorado where the Academy was located. I promise we'll get you one of your burgers before we fly out."

"You think I'm silly…"

"No," he disagreed, taking her hand in his. "I think you are ready to go home."

"I am."

"And I am happy to be along for the ride," he said softly, his voice teasing, as he leaned forward to kiss her tenderly… and pulled her scarf slowly forward, causing her to open her eyes – meeting his.

He was there, smiling at her, and they were both hiding under the scarf, laughing softly like children.

"Boo…" he whispered, just before he leaned forward to kiss her again.

The kiss was much too brief as the announcements came on overhead, causing them to part. Giselle adjusted her scarf back and saw his bold wink, making them both chuckle again knowingly. He was a feisty, playful thing, and she loved it.

Austin sat up straight, held her hand in his… and brought it up to kiss her knuckles before resting it on the armrest as the plane started to roll backwards. They were leaving Kabul, and it almost felt like a couple leaving for a honeymoon.

Startled at the thought, she glanced at him… and saw his amiable smile, wondering if he thought the same thing or felt the same way. This week would be very telling between them, and she hoped it was everything she prayed for.

"What are you most anxious to see when we get there?" she asked as they taxied forward, accelerating at a breakneck speed pressing them into the seat. She felt heart jump in her chest nervously and looked at Austin, seeing his relaxed, knowing smile as he watched her.

"We're fine," he breathed. "I promise. If you see me bolt for the cabin, *then* you can panic. I'm never going to let anything happen to you."

She nodded nervously.

"I'm a knight, remember? Protector of the realm? Well, this," he said, circling his finger between the two of them, "Is our realm and I'll guard it with my life. Just like if I was injured? You'd fix my boo-boo."

She laughed nervously, rolling her eyes at him referring to an injury as a 'boo-boo'.

"What?" he scoffed. "You mean to tell me that you wouldn't? Have I been misled this entire time?"

"No."

"Then why would you laugh? Boo-boos are serious business. Gangrene is deadly, you know - and it starts with a simple infected cut."

"Austin, really? A boo-boo?"

"*Owie?*" he grinned playfully at her – and she burst out laughing at the impish smile combined with the way his eyes danced merrily. "Maybe an *'ouchie'* or a *'yowwch'*? Tetanus too, now that I think about it."

"Oh my gosh, where do you come up with this stuff?" she chuckled.

"I'm inspired – and we're off the ground, sweet Giselle."

Looking out the window, she saw the landscape below them. A myriad of browns, beige, greens, and dark gray mountains made the barren land so incredibly beautiful from this vantage point.

"You are so lucky to see it from this view every day," she breathed.

"I can honestly say I am a very blessed man in all my daily views…"

She turned – and saw him leaning to peek over her shoulder out the window, but smiling at her.

"Everything I have laid my eyes on in the last two-to-three months is just so incredibly beautiful and I couldn't be happier," he breathed – and she reached up to touch his cheek, needing the connection.

Her thumb brushed across his skin, reveling at the differences between them. His skin was rough where he'd shaved and the barely there stubble was catching her thumb. Her finger moved slightly to caress his hairline at his temple.

"… Giselle," he breathed.

This time, she leaned forward, moving to kiss him… just to prevent her from whispering aloud the feelings stirring within her.

THE FLIGHT WAS UNEVENTFUL, and they landed in Heathrow for their layover before the long portion of their flight across the Atlantic. Traveling with him was incredible. He indulged her, encouraged her to look at the gift shops and explore what she could while they were there briefly… and she purchased two Cadbury Crunchie's for them to enjoy.

Giselle knew Austin loved sweets, and every time they'd been together, he had something to snack on. This was a British candy sold here that was distinctly different from anything back home. It was a honeycomb coated in chocolate that smelled divine.

As they boarded the next plane, Austin stopped her almost right away.

"We're on seventeen…" she said, pulling out her ticket.

"Not anymore," he countered, winking at her. "I upgraded our tickets while you were in the gift shop. We are right here."

"First class? Are you kidding me?"

"Nope. Do you want the window seat again, babe?"

Giselle coughed to keep from bleating out the squeal of happiness at the way he called her that, combined with the fact that he was going out of his way to impress her... and it wasn't necessary.

She was a fish on a hook and not going anywhere.

Oh gosh, if this wasn't falling in love? She couldn't imagine what that would be like, she mused silently. *I cannot stop thinking about his smile all the time.*

As she sat down, he joined her – and promptly lifted the center arm between them, pushing it back between the seatbacks.

"Well, hello…" he said flirtatiously in a playful voice. "Come here often, miss?"

"I am traveling with someone," she replied, fighting back a laugh.

"A coworker?"

"Not really," she smiled. "He works nearby, though."

"Oooh it's a 'he'? Is it serious?"

"Well, he just upgraded my flight on the sly, and I think he's trying to impress me. Do you think it's serious – or am I making too much of things?"

"It sounds like he is definitely serious," Austin murmured. "Upgrades are a big deal – and if he's meeting your parents? Hmm. Could be very interesting indeed."

Giselle searched his eyes silently and stared at him. Was he still playing with her? Was this trying to hint at how he felt?

Neither spoke.

It was like the conversation had just died on both ends. She didn't know what to say, and he'd grown quiet - as if he was afraid to continue on this pathway.

"Sir?" The flight attendant walked through, pausing at

their row. "We need you both to buckle. The captain has the 'fasten seatbelt light on' and we are preparing to take off."

"Certainly," Austin said distractedly, still looking at Giselle.

"A-Austin...?" her voice trembled, feeling very exposed and insecure.

"Sir – if you and your wife could please buckle up? Once we are in the air, we'll be bringing around warm nuts and champagne," the flight attendant pressed again.

... Wife?

They were still sitting there – and neither of them argued over the term, and how it fell between them. It seemed to echo in her head, bouncing against something within her, almost like it belonged... and she wanted it.

"Sir? Ma'am? The plane is waiting to depart. Do you need assistance?"

"No," he said finally, moving to buckle... and the moment was gone.

Giselle grabbed her buckle, latching it, and slid open the shade on the airplane window – just so she couldn't look at his face, nor could he see hers. As they took off and got above the clouds, she finally heard Austin's voice quietly beside her.

"Man... she used the 'W' word, just kind of tossed it out there like it was nothing," he breathed and before she could comment on it, telling him to relax, the flight attendant was handing out champagne flutes to the first-class passengers.

Austin handed her one and took one for himself.

"I'm sure it was just an assumption," Giselle began nervously.

She was trying not to let it show that her hand was trembling at the way he was acting at the term 'wife' being bandied about by the flight attendant so easily... nor the fact that he didn't say anything. Usually a guy would interrupt with a firm *'that's not my wife'* statement.

Austin didn't.

"An assumption that I'd want *warm* nuts?" he began. "That's a little bold. Of course, I'd want warm nuts. What other 'W' word would you be referring to?"

The people in front of them started laughing.

"A window seat?" Austin said innocently, taking a sip of his champagne. "I don't think anyone brought up walruses, watermelons, or whiskers."

"You know what I'm talking about."

"Walnuts? Water buffalo? Wyoming?"

"Austin…"

"Wainscoting? You think?"

"No."

"Hmmm. I have to say that any other 'W' words have quite slipped my mind."

"Good. Forget it."

"You could refresh my memory," he teased softly, smiling at her.

"Warthog," she muttered, raising an eyebrow. "A warthog, okay?"

He laughed easily, taking another sip, and then smiled knowingly at her, reaching for her hand, lacing their fingers together, and setting it on his knee.

"Warthogs are my favorite."

"They would be," she muttered – and chanced a glance at him as she took a sip of her glass, only to still see him smiling at her. She felt the corners of her lips turn upwards, smirking… and heard him call for the flight attendant again.

"Miss?" Austin began easily. "Could we have another glass of champagne?"

"Certainly, sir."

"Austin…" Giselle began, feeling her pulse become

thready, wondering what was going through his mind as he just continued speaking, like all of this was nothing.

"We are celebrating," he told the flight attendant easily, not even looking at Giselle as he held her hand in his. "This is going to be an incredible trip."

"Congratulations, sir."

"Thank you."

"What are you celebrating? An anniversary?"

"Warthogs," he said casually – and Giselle choked on her champagne as everyone around them started laughing again. "My girl adores her warthog right down to her pretty fingertips, and that's definitely worth celebrating."

"I see," the flight attendant laughed easily, shaking her head, as Giselle tried to catch her breath, staring at Austin like he was insane. He was sitting there, grinning, and released her hand, moving to rub her back, patting it gently.

"Are you okay, babe? Getting all choked up?"

"You are something…" she gasped, still laughing painfully as she looked at him sitting there beside her.

"Don't get so freaked out about the word," he whispered, smiling at her. "Someday you'll want that 'W' word used around you…"

Her eyes met his as he continued.

"… And that warthog might be excited to be a part of this crazy world. You just never know about those strange animals. They do all sorts of weird things, and they are completely unpredictable creatures."

"I guess so," she managed to strangle out as the flight attendant brought them both another glass of champagne. He handed her one and continued to rub her back between her shoulder blades gently.

"Are you okay?"

"Yes."

"A toast," he said softly, smiling at her. "To warthogs,

wonderful women, waffles, wizards, wives, and all those other beautiful 'W' words in our vocabulary."

There was something in his voice that touched her as she realized he wasn't teasing her, taunting, or playing around. He was simply testing the waters, and she was fully aware of it.

Holding the glass, she ignored the pale alcohol that was sloshing against the glass as he wrapped his arm around hers in the sweetest way, like a groom making a toast at a wedding.

... Another 'W', her brain said, seizing on it as she met his eyes.

"To the future - and words that begin with 'W'... like wondrous," he murmured, taking a sip and she nodded, almost afraid to speak as it might break the spell.

"To wondrous things, Austin," she breathed, basking in his smile, and took a sip as well.

A COUPLE OF HOURS LATER, they were watching Tangled together with the headphones on and she was leaning against Austin's shoulder, feeling awfully languid after the champagne – only to nod off during her favorite movie.

"C 'mere," she heard him order softly, gathering her in his arms as he spread a blanket over her shoulders. "Benefits of First Class – you get a blanket... and I get to hold you."

She snuggled against him, the temple of her head resting against his shoulder as she sighed, completely exhausted. His arm wrapped around her, and she felt his hand stroke her upper back as he kissed her forehead, then the tip of her nose, before whispering to her.

"Rest, sweetheart... I've got you."

GISELLE SLEPT hard against Austin's shoulder. She opened her eyes blearily, blinking several times – only to feel pressure on her head. A heavy sigh disturbed her hair, and she realized that he'd fallen asleep, resting his head against hers.

Glancing out the side window of the plane, she saw that the sun was starting to come up. There was a pinkish-orange glow behind the clouds and the white peaks looked like whipped egg whites or cotton candy.

This was heaven.

Instead of moving and disturbing Austin, she wrapped an arm around his waist and leaned into the embrace, holding him as he slept. He was such a sweet man, and everything he did seemed to touch her soul in just the right way.

He was breathing deeply, one arm around her shoulders and the other limply in her lap, where he'd been holding her hand at some point. She loved that he wanted to touch her. He was always reaching for her hand, touching her cheek, or hugging her.

She smiled at the stewardess, who came by to check on them silently, reveling in the knowing look the woman gave her. This was wonderful, wondrous, wow, and welcome in so many ways.

All 'W' words, she smiled, staring at the sunrise.

"Good morning passengers, this is your captain speaking from the flight deck. We are currently descending towards our destination and should be arriving in twenty minutes. In the Tyler area, it's currently fifty-one degrees, which means it's going to be a balmy day for east Texas for January. The time there is six-twenty-two..."

She listened as he continued to speak, giving instructions to the flight crew and saying that they would need to fill out customs declaration forms for any goods brought into the country. As she sat there, holding Austin, she realized he was touching her hair, stroking his hand down her back.

"You woke up…"

"In the best way possible," he said gruffly. "Sorry, I'm hoarse. I hope I wasn't snoring in your ear all night."

"Never heard a thing."

"Giselle?" he breathed, kissing the top of her head. "I really like this and adore holding you close. I hope you don't mind."

"Not at all," she admitted faintly, feeling surprised at how open he was being with her, marveling at his words. "This has been so nice."

"And we have a week of it," he reminded her and sat up slightly, stretching like a cat, smiling at her. "I'll be right back," he said pertly, leaning forward to kiss her as she was sitting up in her seat.

She watched him go as he shut the door to the restroom – emerging moments later, drying his hands. His hair was disheveled and utterly adorable. It was sticking up in a few places, looking like he'd run his hand back and forth on his head.

He rubbed his face, trying to wake himself up, and smiled at her lazily.

"You look like a big house cat…" she smiled.

"Wanna pet my belly?" he said huskily – and she shoved at his shoulder, making him laugh easily. "When we land, I'm supposed to text Caboose. He's going to swing by and pick us up on his way to work. We'll grab something for breakfast at one of the shops, if that's okay?"

"That's perfect."

"Once we get to Flyboys, we can meet everyone and

introduce you. I know some, but a few were before my time in Ghazni."

"This won't be weird?"

"They *are* weird," he laughed easily. "Our squadron is a bunch of characters, and we are all very close. They've become my family, and it's like they thrive in being wild or different. Just roll with whatever they say or do – and don't worry. If they didn't want us here, they wouldn't have offered the room."

"We certainly don't need much, just two bunks – or a recliner and a couch. Just something remotely comfortable to sleep on for a few days before we get to my parents' house in Wichita Falls."

"Exactly," he smiled. "And your parents are not going to be bothered about their baby girl bringing her *boyfriennnd* home…?"

She hesitated, feeling almost radiant as he drawled out the word 'boyfriend' playfully, smiling at her.

"I guess they'll just need to be happy for me having a *boyfriennnd*, now won't they?" she teased back – and then grew serious. "They might have a lot of questions for you that you might not be ready to answer."

"Oh?"

"About us."

"Giselle," he smiled softly, reaching out to touch her cheek. "I would be happy to answer anything and have a very nice open conversation with your parents. I want our friendship to grow, for *this* to grow, and I don't have any secrets from you. If you want to know something, then ask it."

She nodded as the captain started talking again.

They were landing.

CHAPTER 15

SPARKY

Tyler, Texas

As THEY GOT off the plane, Austin couldn't help but laugh as Giselle dragged him towards one of the vendors that was opening shop there in the airport talking about *'tchotchkes'*...?

"What in the world is a *'tchotchkes'*?" he chuckled and allowed her to lead. His precious girl had her canvas bag across her shoulder and her body was at an angle, dragging him forward, trying to get him to hurry. They had plenty of time because he needed to text Caboose – and then who knows how long it would be before his buddy got here.

"Not *'tchotchkes'*... kolaches! Kooo-laaa-cheese," she drawled pointedly. "They are the best thing on God's green earth and a delicacy of Texas that all of us know about. It's yummy pockets of dough stuffed with sausage and cheese, or fruit, or... *holy cannoli's!*" she practically hollered and slapped a hand over her mouth.

"Whoops sorry about that," she told him – and

pointed, putting her chin up in the air and making a face, before dancing in place. He laughed in disbelief at how adorable she was away from military life, and relaxing in the civilian world. She was home – and knew this place.

"Austinnn…" she whined. "They've got biscuit-and-gravy kolaches!"

"So get one?"

"One? *One?!* This is about to be *obscene*…" she sputtered distractedly, moving to the counter and immediately ordering. "I need four biscuit-and-gravy kolaches, a cherry kolache, and one Texas mild."

"They are really mild…" he heard the clerk say.

"Oh – thanks for the warning. I'll take the hot then," Giselle smiled and turned to him. "That's my order. What do you want?"

He stared at her in disbelief – and shook his head. His girl was gangly like him, but he had no idea where she was going to put that much food… unless it was 'that' good?

"Double it," he simply said, having no idea what he was getting into and didn't want to regret not getting enough.

"Alright!" Giselle fist-pumped the air happily and quickly kissed him pertly on the lips. "You'll love it."

"I already do," he replied simply and hesitated the second she turned back to the counter, talking with the man. She was chattering along as he wanted her profile, marveling at the woman before him… and how the truth had just slipped from him so easily.

He loved her.

"Wait till you try spicy ketchup," she was talking to him again as the clerk was handing them several warm bags. "Man, I'm going to gain big-time being back home. Fresh taquitos, Whataburgers, Taco Casa chips, Taco Bueno Muchacos with the hot sauce, warm kolaches… I will be going through cholesterol-withdrawal when we go back to Ghazni."

Laughing, Austin pulled her into his arms, hugging her, and felt her kiss his chin before nuzzling it.

"Let's find a place to sit down and feed my sweet girl before she starts nibbling on me," he teased – only to feel her pretend to do so on his chin, causing a sharp sensation to surge up his spine as he giggled.

He actually giggled like a girl.

That was not sexy or hot in the slightest – and she was laughing at him, clasping his hand, and beaming with so much emotion in her eyes that he felt his heart skip a beat.

"Let me show you what heaven is..." she ordered, pulling him towards a table in the distance. "Biscuit-and-gravy kolaches are the best ever and when you bite into them, the flavors just..."

Her voice carried as he only half-listened, marveling at how beautiful and strange life was. He was here, having met the woman he loved by sheer chance. She wanted to show him 'heaven'...?

He already knew what heaven was.

It was the way she looked at him – and how he felt when he was with her. Hell would be any life where he couldn't see her... and that voice inside his head spoke up once again, only this time a little louder.

... You only have a week.

A week with the woman of his dreams, in a place where she was obviously happiest, and would be completely surrounded by friends or family members the whole time. Having time alone would be rare - and when they got back to Ghazni? It would be even rarer.

He would lose those sweet kisses, those touches, those hugs – all because of a stupid chain-link fence and rules.

What was he going to do?

Suddenly, Giselle was frowning at him.

"Hello? Austin? Aren't you hungry? I mean, I hate to start without you, but once I get a bite? It's going to be a throw-down, and someone could lose a finger."

He laughed easily and gazed at her frowning face, realizing he would need to make the best of this week and every moment he had with her.

"Let me text Caboose – and go ahead. Pick what I should try first."

Moments later, he was biting into what had to be a lava pocket.

Giselle's eyes were watering as she chewed happily, but he was pretty sure he was going to have a blister on the roof of his mouth from scalding hot gravy shooting straight onto it. The kolaches were insanely delicious and just cooked, so he was very careful with his next bite.

Pretty soon, Austin received a text message from Caboose that he was there – just as they were finishing the last of the doughy orbs of deliciousness.

> Flyboys taxi service...
>
> Tips are appreciated!
>
> And a big tip will get you to your destination...

> On my way – LOL
>
> Missed you, bro!

"He's here. Are you ready?" Austin smiled and saw her grimacing yet smiling at the same time.

"My belly is soooo full. I'm a happy camper."

"C'mon, sweetheart," he chuckled, hefting her bag up and his. "Let's go."

"You called me *'sweetheart',*" she asked softly, smiling in wonder up at him as he stood next to her seat. "I like that."

"You are my sweetheart, and I'm your *boyfriennnd,*" he teased, winking at her. "C'mon. Caboose is not the most patient person."

She stood up and groaned slightly, rubbing her stomach, and put her hand in his – and he understood. His stomach was unbearably full, and he felt like he could take a nap.

Walking out of the airport towards the parking lot – he saw Caboose standing there with his dark aviator sunglasses on his face, grinning… and then he saw Firefly.

"Well, lookie what lil' Sparky brought home with him?… See, Caboose? I told you my favorite little mutt would go into heat one of these days when he got old enough to come running home. How's my favorite puppy-wuppy?" Firefly teased, throwing an arm around Austin's neck, causing him to laugh nervously.

Austin glanced at Giselle. Her eyes were round with surprise, as she had her hand over her mouth, obviously laughing.

"Are you house-trained yet, runt?" Firefly asked, running his knuckles on the top of Austin's head playfully, like he'd done several times in Ghazni in the barracks.

"Hi Firefly," Austin began, "This is my girlfriend, Giselle."

"Awww, Caboose – did you hear that?"

"I heard," the other man smiled. "Either of you need a conversation about the birds and the bees, because I've got the perfect person to…"

"NO!" Austin barked out, feeling mortified. "Things are not like that."

"My pup ain't got no bite?"

"Your 'pup' is not in heat, Firefly," Caboose grinned.

"Oh my gosh, kill me now…" Austin muttered, mortified.

His face was so hot from embarrassment that he didn't dare look at Giselle right now.

"So you *are* in heat? You know what comes next, right? Little puppers with big brown eyes running around yapping happily at everyone."

"Guys… please?!" Austin begged, nearly hysterical at the sheer embarrassment he was feeling, even though this was how his buddies showed 'love' for a brother.

Firefly had taken him right under his wing when he arrived at Ghazni, keeping some of the bigger guys away from him until he knew his ground, finding his footing.

Everyone assumed he couldn't take care of himself because he was a tall, wiry man. He wore a size 28 x 33 pants – with a belt. He was trying to free himself from Firefly's grip, but the guy easily had a hundred pounds on him.

"Have they at least descended, young 'un?"

"Firefly?! Seriously?"

Giselle was roaring with laughter and wiping her eyes, watching from a safe distance nearby, holding the straps of the bags that he'd accidentally dropped.

Caboose was shaking his head and smirking.

"I think he missed you, kiddo."

"I'm a year younger than the both of you…" Austin grunted, trying to shake Firefly.

"AWW," Firefly began, chuckling. "Isn't he precious? Like a scrappy puppy trying to get free. Gosh, I love this kid… I sure missed you, Sparky!"

Austin got his footing and pressed up bodily on the other man, lifting him off the ground and shoving him off – only to hear a slow clap from Caboose… and a slow whistle from Firefly.

"Very nice," Firefly said proudly. "You've been benching like I showed you. Now, introduce us to your lady."

"I did."

"Well, do it again, *cadet*, until you get it right," Caboose taunted, and gave Giselle a thumbs up.

"Sergeant Giselle Beck," she said, extending a hand towards the men – and both men turned towards Austin instead of shaking her hand.

"Oh my gosh, you didn't cross the line, did you?"

"What? No. Now you sound like Ricochet…"

"Pup – are you frolicking in the 'neighbor's yard'?" Firefly asked in disbelief, and Austin knew he was referring to the base next door. "She's Army?"

"She's standing right here, fellas…" Giselle said pointedly. "And yes – she's Army."

"Oh, Alpo is going to luuuvv this," Firefly drawled.

"Have you got a fascination with dogs?" Giselle asked – and all three men turned to answer at once.

"Yes."

"Firefly loves dogs and always has – I think he thinks like them and was flea-bitten in Ghazni," Austin teased.

"Who isn't?" Firefly grinned and stuck out his hand to Giselle. "Welcome to the Darkside – you'll love it here."

"Welcome to the family, Sarge," Caboose grinned, shaking her hand. "You realize that nothing in your noggin will be the same after this, right? You are here, with our gang, and you'll be indoctrinated – so I hope you two are serious because nobody gets out alive."

"What?" Giselle said, paling and looking at Austin.

"We'll be alive," he blurted. "He's just being funny."

"Sure, kiddo. Let's go and you can meet everyone, Sarge."

"You can call me Giselle…" she said quickly, frowning.

"Oh no, *Sarge* is definitely a much better name and you'll fit right in with the gang," Caboose grinned – and bumped knuckles with Firefly. "I freakin' love this part of my job."

"Why do you think I came with you? The best part of

wakin' up is picking up my Sparky-pup..." Firefly sang happily.

Austin opened the car door for Giselle, and she sat down in a feminine manner that made him nearly sigh aloud. He loved the delicate movements she made, tucking her feet under her.

"No neckin' in the back seat either, you two," Firefly grinned.

CHAPTER 16

GISELLE

Austin was holding her hand as they pulled onto a side road in the middle of nowhere. She could see the fence line, and fields as far as the eye could see, with a massive looming hangar in the distance - doors wide open.

"It's early and we are just getting started…" Caboose said easily, as if reading her mind. "We run on rotations because we have so many team members. It gives us a chance to stay active, brush up on our skills, and spend a lot of time at home with our families, too. I think Alpo, Harley, Thumper, and Houdini are the ones here the most."

She didn't say anything because she didn't recognize any of those names. The car pulled in, turning past the fence, onto a gravel road and then coming to a stop beside a few other vehicles.

"We're home, honey…" Firefly joked, already getting out of the car. "C'mon and meet everyone."

Giselle glanced at Austin, who was smiling and already

opening his car door. She needed to not quite be so nervous and relax, because he was obviously at home with these people.

On base, everyone was dedicated and driven. They talked about work, orders, medications, procedures, and occasionally family life – or at least that was how it was in the clinic setting.

This seemed... foreign to her.

These guys were so... happy?

As she got out of the car, people began emerging from the building and the hangar. She heard several shouts as Austin was almost immediately tackled by two men.

"Houdini! X-Ray!" Austin was grinning and laughing, "Oh my gosh, fellas! How are you all doing?"

They were hugging him, patting him on the back, and welcoming him like a long-lost brother – and she was just *there*.

... But that feeling only lasted seconds.

"Glory? Harley?" Firefly began in a booming voice. "Meet Sarge."

"Oh my gosh," Giselle muttered under her breath as every eye suddenly focused on her and some woman with pigtails did a double take before squealing aloud, sprinting across the runway, and launching herself at Giselle.

"Oh.My.Gosh.You.Are.So.Dang.Cute!" – each word punctuated with a shake as the woman grabbed her by the shoulders, punctuated by a flurry of high-pitched words, rattling her teeth.

"Glory! Babe!" a man was walking over, and Austin was rushing to her side. "Honey, *hugs*... okay?"

"Hunter..." the woman whined. "She's sooo stinkin' cute and her call sign is Sarge? I mean, how precious is that?! I didn't even know you could pick something like that..."

"It's not a call sign," Firefly chimed in with a sing-song

voice.

"Hi. I'm Glory and welcome to our world. You are gonna love it here and such a cutie-patootie! When did you and Sparky get married? Should we get Dixie to make a cake? Do we need to get FlyGIRL shirts made up? See Harley? I told you we should get some. I mean, just look at her. She's precious and already one of us. Can you imagine the business cards with Sarge on the front? Sheer perfection…"

"Glory!" several people said at once – smiling – as Giselle stood there unsure if she was being attacked, greeted, or when the verbal bombardment would start again.

"Umm…" Austin began, coming to Giselle's side and prying the fingers from her shoulder. "Let go - *please…?*"

"Oh? Oh, yes. I see. Yeah, Hunter is picky about guys touching me, but you are completely safe. We are both girls and my door isn't revolving – it only swings one way… and that's in my sexy-pookiebear's direction," she said, throwing a thumb over her shoulder towards the man that was standing there, grinning. "He's my magnetic north."

"God, I love that wild woman…"

"Her mouth just does not stop, does it?"

"Never."

"I'm so glad she's family."

"Sarge is family now, too."

"Hang on, team…" Austin began.

"Oh no, let everyone get it out," Firefly interrupted, grinning and clapped a hand over Austin's mouth. "This is amazing, and it should absolutely keep going."

"I think it's sweet. Remember how we knew Abbykins and Houdini would be perfect – same here? I mean, just look at them together."

"She's like a tidal wave of energy."

"Just as destructive."

"Nahhh… her heart is in the right place."

"Your kids will never have a chance at growing up normal."

"I'm their dad – and we thrive in weirdness."

"True that."

"We're twins – you aren't weird because that makes me weird."

"You *are* weird… weirdly genius."

"Okay, fine. I'll accept that."

"Back to our newbie, Sarge — welcome! Are you and Sparky staying for the week? I know Sparky mentioned you were staying here, but we've got bunk beds, and if you two are going to be 'bouncing bedsprings' then maybe we should call Sophie…"

"Somebody save me…" Austin muttered in disbelief from behind Firefly's hand, who was now laughing aloud.

"What did he just say?" Giselle whispered in wide-eyed shock as all the guys started talking among themselves quickly.

"You know, copulating and populating?"

"Bonkin' and zonkin'? That's when you know it's really good."

"Wedded and bedded?"

"Et fais dodo... with my favorite bro?"

"You forgot 'Hide the soap'…"

"Stuffin' the turkey?"

"Eww? Really? How does Karen put up with your lame brain, Hot Cakes?"

"Pounding the pup? Or should it be 'tup the pup'…"

"**STOP!**" Austin blurted out in a booming voice, looking almost as stunned and horrified as Giselle. "Y'all, we aren't married… and nobody's doing *that* and even if that happened? I would never tell you for this very reason."

"He's shy… how sweet."

"Sarge looks like she's about to have an aneurism... I wonder why?"

"Hot Cakes' turkey comment."

"Hey man, everyone got that joke and understood it."

"True."

"Stuffin' the muffin..."

"Bakin' the burrito..."

"Stop!" Giselle croaked out nervously, almost afraid to glance at anyone – including Austin. "We aren't sleeping together, and we aren't married. We are just friends."

"Friends?" three guys uttered – and the two women sighed dreamily.

"They're in *that* phase..."

"Oh goodness, I loved those moments."

"So romantic, right?"

"Jackson was so sweet."

"I'm still sweet, honey."

"Yeah, you are, but it's different when the guy is trying to win over the girl. There's an excitement of the unknown, a spark... oooh? Sparky? Is that how you got your call sign? Making all the girls fall in love you with, you charmer..."

"No – and this is all mildly uncomfortable. Is there coffee made? Can we put our bags in the room... with the bunk beds?" Austin began pointedly. "You can have round two of *'humiliate the newbies'* in five minutes."

"Oh," a woman said and stuck out her hand politely. "I'm Harley, Sarge. If you want to follow me?"

"My name is Giselle – and thank you."

"Why did he call you Sarge then? Is that your call sign?"

"I'm not a pilot."

"Firefly... why...?"

"She's a sergeant in the Army," Firefly called out, grinning – only to see every eye turn to Giselle again.

"What?" she uttered, starting to feel slightly defensive. "What's wrong with being in the Army?"

"Nothing."

"At least she's not a puddle-pirate," someone whispered loudly, causing her to laugh at the derogatory term for a Coast Guard member.

Each branch had their slang. Grunts, jar heads, zoomies, squids... they were all full of pride when it came to their own branch – and teased the others mercilessly.

"Sparky, you playin' on the other side of the fence?"

"Does Reaper know about that?"

"Nobody crossed a fence," she and Austin said at the same time – and then smiled at each other.

"We're friends," she finished, putting her hand in his as they walked up the steps to the building.

"Hunter, you never hold my hand anymore," the woman said behind her, causing Giselle to glance over her shoulder as they entered.

"Because I'd rather hold you against me."

"Guess we all better start going back to the basics."

"I think I'll go call Dixie."

"Good idea. I'm gonna call Delilah."

"I'll be back, fellas," one man said. "I'm taking Marisol some flowers."

"Ohhhh smart..."

The storm door shut behind her, silencing the commotion behind them.

"I'm so sorry about the confusion," Harley said openly. "Most of the time, we get to meet the significant other when they are becoming a spouse or not long afterwards. I apologize if we made either of you uncomfortable."

"You didn't know," Giselle said softly. "It's fine. We just appreciate you putting us up here."

"Are bunk beds going to be okay? I mean, we really don't mind. I can call my friend Sophie and ask her if there are any rooms available – and I'm sure there are because the town is tiny."

"Can you give us a few minutes to talk, Harley?" Austin interrupted politely. "We'll be right out."

"Of course. I'll go make a fresh pot of coffee – that isn't Hot Cakes brewed sludge."

As the woman left the room, they both put down their bags.

Giselle's eyes darted, taking in everything. The room was very simple. There was a very sturdy, dated-looking set of bunk beds in the corner... and a recliner. A small end table near the bed had a lamp on it and a tiny shelf that had mini deodorants, mini shampoos, and tiny soaps. They were ready for whoever came or needed something.

"Are you going to be okay with bunk beds – or would you like a genuine room with privacy?"

"This is fine – as long as you are fine. I mean, we'll have privacy and it's quiet."

"Are you sure?"

"Austin, we'll be here for two days before going to my parents. If I trust you to sleep in the next bedroom over, inside my parents' home? I think I can handle you sleeping in the bunk above me."

"So, I guess I'm on the top bunk?" he teased softly, his eyes dancing.

She smiled – and stepped forward to hug him, savoring the way his arms came around her easily. They just fit well together, and she loved breathing in the scent of him.

"I would prefer the bottom bunk, if you don't mind," she whispered against his shoulder. "And your friends are a lot to handle sometimes."

"They mean well, I swear," he breathed against her hair.

"You are amazing and they love me like a kid brother – so when they see someone so incredible as the woman in my arms is? I'm not surprised they are pushing us or making comments. They are all happily married and want that same thing for everyone."

She looked up at him in surprise.

"Don't you want that for yourself someday?"

"Still trying to figure out how any of it would work, you know? I mean, Ghazni isn't exactly a quaint town to raise a family or buy a house in."

"I see," she said simply, moving to step away – only to have him tug her back into his arms, hugging her once more.

"…But I never said that I didn't want it for myself," he began softly. "I'm trying to wrap my head around some really big details, and I think as my best girl, my confidant, and my favorite fence-rendezvous friend… you'll be the first to know when I am ready to make a change."

"You're assuming I would want to know," she said loftily, trying to hide her feelings. "I would be happy for you though, my friend."

She felt him pull back slightly and turned her chin upwards, making her look at him… and saw the emotion in those beautiful brown eyes that made her knees weak.

"Be happy for *us* someday," he whispered tenderly, "because we both know I'm crazy about you – and a little nervous to share so much of myself, but it's there."

Giselle stared up at him, feeling her emotions bubbling within her. She gazed at his beloved face, treasuring his soft smile, and the way it made her feel… understanding completely what he meant about 'sharing himself' because it was scary to open up to someone, giving them the power to hurt you.

"So, I should quit wondering where we are at in this?"

"I was hoping you would pick up on that when I called myself your *boyfriennnd*," he breathed, touching her cheek.

"Let's pretend I'm completely dense and hard of hearing. Dumb it down for me and spell it out."

His smile widened, and he leaned forward to kiss her lips softly.

"You just want to hear me say it, don't you?"

"Yeah."

"I'm completely infatuated with you," he began hoarsely, looking so intense yet afraid at the same time, and she understood. "I can't imagine us not talking or being close to each other."

Austin paused for a moment, searching her eyes.

"I think about you every morning and dream of you each night... so yeah, I'm very interested – and proudly at your side. You can label it whatever you want. Boyfriend, friend, significant other... just so long as you call me 'yours'," he murmured, brushing his lips against hers once more before deepening the kiss between them.

She melted in his arms, wrapping hers around him and savoring the feel of him being so close. His lips held hers as his mouth opened, tasting hers... only to hear a knock at the door.

"Do you want some coffee?" Harley said, interrupting their kiss. "I can show you both around and you can explore the area."

"Yeah, we'd love a cup and will be right out," Austin hollered easily, and dropped his voice as he stared at Giselle. "Tell me we are okay, sweetheart?"

"We're... serious?" she whispered, searching his eyes and feeling tears sting hers at the revelation that this was big between them both, and he was indeed in the same mindset as her. That was such a relief because she found herself wanting to tell him so many times how much she cared.

"We are *very* serious, sweetheart," he breathed, "and if you ever worry or need reassurance? Talk to me, Giselle. We're a team and I'm never letting go now that I've found you."

She threw herself into his arms again, hearing his soft chuckle of happiness, and kissed him.

CHAPTER 17

SPARKY

It surprised Austin at what a gig the team had going here.

There were three classes scheduled today – and Houdini taught all three. Caboose, Valkyrie, Thumper, Firefly, Hot Cakes, and Romeo were on rotation – doing flights with the students. Glory and Alpo worked/played around in the hangar all day long... and Harley, Thumper's wife, did all the bookkeeping.

The guys took turns on the coms, making sure the way was clear or that there weren't any problems... and while it was chaotic with planes taking off and landing all day long?

It worked - really well, in fact.

Giselle was talking with Harley and he was half listening, watching the planes soar off the ground... smiling. They sure weren't his Falcon, but it was nice to see the serene atmosphere around the place. The breeze was cool on his face and the sunshine was bright, making this feel so welcoming.

The flying lessons were actually making money, too – which surprised him. He figured when they told him they were on rotations, everyone was 'part time' and making a little paycheck here or there.

Except that wasn't the case.

They got paid by flight hour. Some guys did longer training flights if requested. They had people driving in from an hour or two away for a chance to fly the planes, look around, buy t-shirts, or even take photos with the pilots. Each man had a coverall with their call sign over the pocket, just like a name badge in the Air Force.

Hot Cakes was looking into what charter flights would involve for the company because of a recent issue that cropped up. Doing charters or emergency runs would really expand their field, and they could compete with private businesses... or even the smaller planes at the airport.

Their children would be there later today – and they had that handled too. None of the little ones were enrolled in daycare. Instead, it was a team system too: Marisol, Harley, Glory, Delilah, and Melody, each took one, two, or three children for the day that was needed, putting them into a rotation and giving them the chance to stay home, raising their own.

Melody still worked full-time opposite of Firefly, but only because they were heavily remodeling their older home one room at a time. Harley only worked once a week as daycare, because the rest of her time was spent at the office — maintaining the financials, the marketing, and the scheduling to keep them all busy.

Yeah, Flyboys (and their families) were thriving.

"Are y'all hungry?" Romeo asked suddenly, popping his head into the office where Giselle and Harley were sitting nearby. "I heard there was a special request for Whataburger and something about 'spicy ketchup'?"

Harley chuckled knowingly – and Giselle looked up at Austin, her eyes full of affection.

"Did Austin tell you that?"

"A little birdie might have said something…" Romeo grinned. "I like the dude and wish he was there when I was. Man, that would have been fun."

"I'm going to gather up the orders and take Sparky down to the hangar," Romeo began… and Giselle spoke up, not looking away from Austin.

"Could we all go?"

"Of course," Harley agreed, putting the phone 'away' so the voicemail would pick up immediately on the first ring. "Let's go."

Austin felt Giselle take his hand and couldn't resist smiling at her excited face. He loved that his girl reached for him – and that the simple things made her happy.

They strolled along the side of the runway, watching the planes take off and land, reveling in her bright, expressive face. She looked so happy to see this up close – and he couldn't wait to see what she thought of their flight to Wichita Falls in a few days.

As they got closer to the hangar, Austin froze as he heard a shriek… a clamor of metallic noise followed by several curse words.

A pink roll-around tool cart came flying out onto the runway… followed by a very irate looking Glory. As she banged on something, she started screaming bloody murder and jumping around frantically.

Alpo was climbing down off a ladder, and they began to run towards the woman - when Glory brandished a spray can in one hand, held up her other hand, and a stream of fire exploded forward towards the tool cart.

"WHAT THE…" Harley shouted, looking behind her.

Austin did the same to make sure a plane wasn't coming down.

"GLORY!" Alpo hollered, racing towards his wife, knocking the can out of her arm and shoving her behind him as Austin ran up.

"Where's the fire extinguisher?" Austin asked quickly.

"Was that brake clean, Glory?" Alpo asked bluntly. "Or was it gasoline? Throttle body cleaner? What was that in the can?"

"BURNNNN, YOU NASTY THING!" Glory yelped angrily, glaring at the pink tool cart that was engulfed in flames on top and smelled like burning rubber combined with something else. Harley pulled her aside and Giselle stepped back without having to be asked, because Austin was afraid something would pop or explode from the heat.

Alpo obviously thought the same thing, because he was removing bottles from the bottom of the cart and tossing them in Austin's direction.

"What were you thinking, honey?" Alpo yelped, moving quickly.

"Where's the fire extinguisher?" Giselle prompted again as Harley pointed to the wall in the distance.

Glory was trembling and crying now, slapping at her arms in disgust and Harley was brushing her off, both of them exceedingly upset.

"What is wrong?!" Alpo asked, moving to her side as Austin took over, trying to put out the flames with a towel he found on the ground... only to back away. There was a massive spider sac underneath it.

He looked at the woman who was beside herself, sobbing now as Alpo held her.

"Did she get bitten?" Austin yelled over the sound of Giselle spraying the cart with the extinguisher. "Giselle, back up, love. Something's wrong!"

He got up and pushed her away, taking over and looking at Alpo again.

"Something hatched and I think it got on her…"

"What?" Giselle and Harley shouted in unison – and Alpo picked up his wife, jerking her inside the hangar and began stripping her clothes off of her.

Austin whipped his head around, putting his back towards the frantic couple and focused on the roll around cart.

"I'm going to get her a coverall, so she isn't naked," Harley announced, running for the other building.

"I'm going to get the first-aid kit," Giselle followed – running after the other woman.

"Alpo!" Austin yelled, without turning. He could still hear her sobbing in the distance, completely freaked out but calming down slightly. "Is she bit? Did she say what it was?"

"A wolf spider got on her hand," Alpo began. "She knocked it off, and the babies started crawling onto her – and the cart. That's why she lit it on fire. I think she's okay…"

"No, I'm not…" Glory said angrily, sobbing. "I'm never going to be okay again! There were a bazillion spiders crawling on me and… and…"

Glory started crying again.

"Baby, I'm gonna get pest control out here right away, but you gotta remember – we are in the country. There's going to be spiders, snakes, and scorpions. You know the routine. Check your shoes, don't pick up sticks, and shake out things before picking them up."

"I *was* shaking out the rag, Hunter," Glory snapped. "That's when the eight-legged-Trojan-horse decided to scurry up my sleeve!"

Austin heard Alpo laughing behind him – and his wife's righteous fury.

"Quit laughing! It's not funny!"

"You are so sexy when you are mad, sweet cheeks."

"Because I'm standing here in my skivvies, surrounded by... Sparky! Thank you for not looking and putting out my tool cart. I actually love that thing even though it's contaminated now."

"It's not contaminated," Alpo chuckled.

Austin was smiling as Giselle walked back up with Harley, moving quickly to Glory's side. He stood there, listening, and looking over the things in the tool cart. The rubber or plastic was marred, blistered, and melted on several tools, but would still be functional once they cooled and cleaned off.

"Hey... a plane's landing," Austin called out, grasping the cart and pushing it to the side.

"Is everything off me?" Glory yelped nervously. "I've got to get dressed."

"Yes," Giselle said. "I don't see any marks or bites on you."

"Gimme a few minutes... and there might be," Alpo uttered playfully, and Austin chuckled with his back to the scene at the man's innuendo

"Annnnd - she's fine," Harley announced. "C'mon and let's leave them here."

"Yep, go away, sis... and quickly."

Glory's throaty laugh was heard as they walked away from the hangar.

Harley glanced over her shoulder at the couple, quickly walking and shaking her head.

"They are always like that... and I'm so happy for them."

"It's sweet," Giselle said, glancing over her shoulder – and Austin stopped walking in awareness. She obviously wanted him to play with her and be a little more openly affectionate, like the duo behind them in the distance.

He could certainly do that!

It was easy when it came to Giselle and wanting to reach

her. He craved that sweet sideways look or faint blush on her cheeks like a dying man begging for water.

Romeo interrupted his thoughts just as Austin was getting ready to reach for his girl's hand…

"Are we ready?"

"Oh yeah, I forgot to ask what Hunter and Glory wanted…" Harley began and shook her head again. "Nope. I'm not going in there and neither should anyone else for a bit."

"Geez… really?" Romeo muttered, frowning. "Are they seriously at it again? Never mind. They'll have to be happy with whatever they get. C'mon, Sparky."

Austin nodded – and leaned to kiss Giselle quickly.

"I'll be right back," he promised, winking at her. "Spicy ketchup time."

"You remembered?"

"Always."

AN HOUR LATER, they were all taking their seats in the empty classroom, taking advantage of the side of the room combined with the empty seats. There were twelve of them there today, and it made things a little snug in the kitchenette.

Thumper walked in with a twelve-pack of Diet Dr. Pepper and handed everyone a cold can where the box had been stored in the fridge all morning long. As he took a seat next to Harley, he looked around the room.

Austin saw a few knowing glances and smirks coming from the guys as Romeo spoke up.

"You know what the rest of us would say…"

"Go ahead, Thumper."

"You know I, for one, would be in full favor – that's my

puppy-wuppy-baby-bro…" Firefly grinned – and Caboose rolled his eyes, but gave a silent thumbs up.

Alpo was handing out burgers and containers of onion rings, with a stupid smile plastered all over his face that matched Glory's, who was humming happily. Giselle leaned towards Austin, her face a myriad of expressions from disbelief and laughter, changing to shock and delight.

"I think they…" she began, whispering softly.

"Hon, don't think it – KNOW," Harley muttered – causing the couple to laugh and smile at each other… as Firefly shot to his feet.

"Maaaan! Don't touch the food, you nasty thing! Gimme the bag of burgers and go wash your filthy mitts, Alpo. I swear…"

Everyone burst out laughing.

"If he hadn't been neutered already…" Caboose muttered, swapping his wrapped burger with one Firefly just sat down on a desk nearby.

"No kidding," Houdini glared, swapping his burger with Thumper's, who rolled his eyes.

Austin couldn't help but look around the room at these people, loving the relaxed and playful atmosphere, realizing that the best part of being in the Air Force in Ghazni was alive and well here, in Texas.

… And as if they could read his mind, he heard words that he never imagined spoken aloud.

"You know, Sparky, if you ever make a change? You'd have a job the moment you set foot down in Texas. We'd love to have you," Thumper said openly as Austin looked at him in surprise.

His eyes scanned the room and saw the approval on everyone's faces, several smiles, nods of welcome, and swallowed the lump of emotion in his throat… until he saw Giselle's expression.

She looked... sad?

"I truly appreciate that guys – and it gives me something to consider," he began openly, unsure of what to say or if they were expecting an answer from him right now.

"I'm happy but if I decide to ever leave, there will be a lot of discussions had between us..." he said, reaching over and pulling Giselle's desk a little closer to him pointedly, claiming her and wanting to show that they were a package deal.

"Oh, of course," Harley smiled. "It's just something to put on your radar if the need should ever arise."

"I appreciate that."

"When is your reenlistment coming up, Sparky?"

"July," he whispered, staring at his burger in sudden awareness. By the end of the summer, he needed to have more of a concrete idea of what he wanted his future to look like – and contract dates hadn't been something either of them discussed yet.

He had no idea how long she was going to be stationed in Ghazni or what her plans were for the future. They had been so focused on each other, communicating, and falling in love, wrapped in their own private bubble... that real life hadn't intruded – yet.

...But it was here now.

"Giselle?" Harley said gently. "When is your reenlistment date for the Army?"

"July," she said quietly – and Austin's head whipped to the side to look at her in shock.

They were both up... *this year?!*

"Hmmm... interesting how things work, isn't it?" Caboose said openly. That single brief statement spoken aloud was obviously what was echoing in everyone's mind.

"Medic, right?" Glory said quietly, watching her.

"I think that's the shortest sentence you have ever

spoken!?" Firefly retorted openly as Alpo walked back into the classroom. "Apparently us men need a few lessons from the love-guru, because if it got Glory quiet…"

"Speak for yourself," Caboose uttered, and Romeo laughed.

"Right?"

"Firefly – stuff something in that mouth of yours, would you?" Glory glared at him as Alpo took a seat beside her, putting his hand on her back. "I'm just thinking about a few things and…"

"About me, babe?" Alpo interrupted, grinning.

"Always, pookiebear."

"Oh shoot," Austin muttered, getting to his feet. "I'll be right back."

He got up and walked towards the kitchenette where they had originally started to put the food for lunch – and grabbed the bag he'd picked up for Giselle.

As he walked back, getting close to the doorway, he froze.

They were talking to Giselle in hushed whispers.

"So you two – is it serious? I mean, should we be looking at planes, houses, apartments, business cards, or some jobs for you? What can a medic do? Are you a doctor? A nurse?"

"What? Uh… no, I'd have to get licensing I'm sure, and I don't know how it works because I never imagined leaving the Army. I mean, I never expected any of this. A plane? A house? What do you mean?"

"We'd help you two find a place to live…"

"Sparky would eventually want an aircraft, I'm sure."

"That's actually a thing?" Giselle said, sounding almost as shocked as Austin felt. He hadn't considered anything past this week, and it was all slamming home in his head. He needed to decide what he wanted, make plans, and talk to her about where they were going…

"Are y'all serious? Has he said he loves you or talked about marriage yet?"

"Glory!"

"It's a legit question and he can't hear me."

"She can though – and you don't want to pressure either of them."

"It's not. This is girl-talk and..."

"Y'all," Giselle spoke again, sounding so painfully quiet that it made his heart hurt. "I don't think we are there yet or anywhere close. This is new between us. I mean, we were literally talking and just friends a few days ago. This is all so sudden and fast. I don't ever want to pressure him into doing something he would regret or that might hurt him – so please don't bring this up in front of Austin. We're... friends."

Friends.

"Gotcha. I see," Firefly said – and his voice was different. It wasn't the playful guy he knew, but more like a disappointed parent.

Austin stood there, waiting, his mind whirling.

Maybe Giselle wasn't there yet, but he certainly was. He was insanely in love with her and couldn't see a world without her at his side – the problem was, he never focused on what creating that life would look like... and it was time to start.

He needed to think, plan, and talk with someone he trusted, who had been there before... and there was a room full of those men not ten feet away.

Plastering a smile on his face, even though his heart was hammering with nerves, ideas, worries, and a flurry of other emotions... he walked back into the classroom with the bag.

He didn't say a word – and saw her eyes widen in surprise as she stared up at him in amazement, a smile touching her lips.

The entire to-go bag was filled with little buckets of spicy ketchup for her, so she had plenty… and could possibly take back a few of the packets if we smuggled them just right.

He wasn't normally a rule breaker – but he would do anything for Giselle.

In talking to Romeo, they figured out that if they put the ketchup containers in Ziploc bags, wrapped them in bubble wrap, put them in a box, and hid it in her clothing… it might make it. Either that – or chance mailing a box of them to Giselle on base right before they left Texas, and it should be in Ghazni in a week or two…

"You didn't…" she breathed, smiling at him with so much joy.

"It's just ketchup," he countered, meeting her smile.

"You are the best person ever."

"I'm your person."

Please say it, he thought wildly. *Please say you are my person or that you love me... please?*

"Thank you so much, Austin," Giselle said quietly, hesitating, and looking around the room nervously. Was it because of what they were just talking about? Their future?

He felt something plummet inside of him and sighed. She obviously wasn't *there* yet.

… And he didn't know how to reach her.

Silently, he sat down and ate.

CHAPTER 18

GISELLE

'OVERWHELMED'... barely scratched on the surface of what she was feeling by the sudden hushed conversation directed at her. She had ten people all looking at her expectantly, smiling, and so eager... but everything she seemed to say, every question answered, those smiles began to disappear.

No, she wasn't sure what was going to happen.

They were talking about massive purchases like houses or airplanes, not to mention major changes to her life and Austin's. She couldn't answer because she had no idea that 'buying an airplane' was a thing for normal people – and they all seemed pretty normal, so far.

They had barely just defined that Austin was incredibly interested in her. Nobody said anything about love yet... and she was terrified to put herself out there. If he didn't feel the same way, she would be crushed. She already felt vulnerable in a way she had never felt before, because she loved him.

She'd fallen hard.

If it wasn't the smiles and how he looked at her? It was the way he put himself out there, talked with her, and did silly things like the bag of ketchup packages sitting before her.

He listened and acted... and it touched her deeply, but couldn't acknowledge it except with a thank you. How did you just blurt out *'I love you'* over Whataburger spicy ketchup?

You didn't.

There needed to be a moment and every good fairytale, fable, myth, and legend had a penultimate point where something changed. A crossing where there was no going back, no turning, but a burst of change that would forever mark that person.

Snow White bit the apple.

Aurora poked her finger on the spinning wheel.

Elsa, let it go – literally.

Cinderella lost her shoe.

... And Giselle had spicy ketchup.

Lame.

"Excuse me a moment," she said quickly, moving out of the classroom. The moment she was in the hallway, she bolted for the bathroom because she was going to freakin' cry. What was wrong with her that things would be so good one moment and then so far off the next?

A sob escaped her brokenly, causing her to yank some paper towels from the dispenser, quickly wetting them. She pressed the cold, wet towels to her cheeks to keep them from getting splotchy.

Austin was so sweet, so kind, so wonderful... and so thoughtful, but it just felt so pathetic that it was ketchup that made her so stupidly happy. Okay, maybe it wasn't the ketchup, but that he listened, cared, acted, and it was all for her happiness.

Ketchup.

Was this actually her pivotal moment?

Did her fairytale involve ketchup?

"Giselle?"

"I'll be out in a moment," she said simply and took several deep breaths, trying to pull herself back together. No, this was something she would need to be patient about – and if spicy ketchup was her moment, the moment that everything changed?

She would never use any other condiment — ever.

Relax, she thought to herself. Focus on the sweet moments and quit holding your breath for more. Maybe he was just slow to make a move because he wanted things to be right between them.

What if Austin was backpedaling because he felt pressured, too? She was taking him to meet her parents. His friends were asking baldly about his future – and hers? It was all just a lot and combined with the jetlag? She was a mess... and imagined he was too.

Letting out a shaky breath, she wiped her face once more... and opened the bathroom door only to see Austin standing there, leaning back against the wall. His arms were crossed over his chest, and he looked positively miserable...

His dark eyes met hers, and she teared up again.

Austin pushed off the wall, put a hand on her shoulder, and pressed her back into the bathroom, locking them inside. He gathered her into his arms, holding and hugging her closely... whispering to her.

"Talk to me..." he urged softly.

"I guess I'm just tired."

"Is that what's wrong?"

"No," she whimpered, burying her face against his shirt and neck. "I don't want to talk about it," she uttered, muffled against him. "I think there's been enough talking."

"It's a lot, isn't it?" he said softly, kissing her forehead. "It's okay to feel overwhelmed because I'm not the best planner. I mean, I've been so focused on us getting here, seeing each other, and going to your parents, that I never looked past that… and that's my fault."

She pulled back and looked at him.

"They mean well," she whispered in a hushed voice, looking at him. "And they are so incredibly nice… but they are pushy. I don't even know what a medic does in the real world. I mean, I guess I'm an EMT or a nurse? There's testing and licenses – and the military handled everything for me. I didn't have to depend on *me* figuring it out."

She took a deep breath, swallowing back her anxieties, before continuing now that the floodgates were opening wide.

"I had no idea that people like us buy airplanes. We follow orders, get transferred to places. I can't even fathom actually having a permanent residence and…" her voice trailed off as she tried to slide back into his arms for another hug, burying her face once more – but he held her away.

"And *'what'*?" he encouraged softly, his voice full of emotion. "Talk to me."

"I can't yet," she whispered openly, looking at him. "I'm so scared because you are so close to me, so special, that I don't want to ever push or force you into anything you would regret."

"So, you would withdraw and hide, shutting me out?" he breathed – and sounded relieved. "It's not that you don't want this to go further between us – you do. You really want this, don't you? You are scared… and it's not just me worrying or wondering."

"Oh gosh, no," she hissed, hiccupping. "I want this… and yes, I'm very scared. This is so fast, so wonderful, and so intense, that I feel like I'm on a rollercoaster. I'm enjoying the thrills and savoring every twist and turn – but waiting to be told to 'get off the ride' or 'your turn is over'."

"What if the coaster never pulled to a stop – and no one told you to get off the ride…"

She stared at him, his eyes searching hers, and hesitated as he clasped her hands in his, bringing each hand to his lips and brushing a kiss on her knuckles.

"What if the ride never ended?" he repeated softly. "Would you be happy with me, if I made sure no one ever made you get off of our beautiful rollercoaster?"

"What do you mean?"

"If we started looking at what a future would look like maybe six months from now, so we could make decisions together on our re-enlistment. If you wanted to stay in Ghazni? I would stay there with you and there would be 'fence-rendezvous' every night. If you wanted to transfer to another base – I would transfer to the nearest air base just to be close to you."

"Oh Austin…" she whispered, moved by the intensity of his eyes and the promises he was making.

"And if you wanted to put down roots and find a way to enjoy the civilian world? We have an avenue to talk about together here, but our thrill ride never has to end, sweetheart," he said hoarsely, looking at her.

"Are you sure? Like I said, I might be just jetlagged and…"

"I told you to talk to me if you were scared," he reminded her gently, smiling tenderly as he released her hand, cupping her face. "This includes our future, and whatever it may look like."

"See? You are getting to know the real me behind that tough girl attitude," she teased tearfully, smiling at him. "Now, can I have a hug, or are you going to hold me at arm's length again?"

"Never," he whispered, pulling her into his arms and

kissing her tenderly. She savored the feeling of closeness, the way he made her feel so alive, and knew deep down that she was just antsy and scared. If this was how his friends had reacted, she was expecting much of the same from her parents.

She'd never brought a guy home to meet them – not even when she was going to school dances or when she entered the military. There was an unspoken rule at home that you didn't just bring 'anyone' home. You brought *the* one... and she was doing just that.

He was the one for her – and always would be.

"C'mon," he murmured against her lips. "Firefly asked me to run a few errands with him this afternoon – and Glory is getting our plane ready. I thought maybe you'd like to go to Wichita Falls tomorrow instead of waiting another day."

She smiled gratefully and nodded.

"I'm crazy about you and would do anything to see that smile again," he chuckled breathlessly, nuzzling her nose. "I love it when you are happy with me."

"I am," she whispered, kissing him again. "I couldn't be happier."

"Then these were happy tears?" he asked softly, teasing her.

"Sure," she chuckled, hugging him again as he laughed aloud.

"Hey Sparky!" Firefly called out, banging on the door. "You two aren't pulling a *'Petersen Maneuver'* in there, are you? There are more romantic places, buddy... and the bathroom at Flyboys just ain't it. Open up! I gotta go."

Giselle looked at Austin – and they both smiled.

"That's my girl," he whispered, dropping a quick kiss on her lips. "We'll talk more later when we are alone. I promise."

"Okay."

THE AFTERNOON WORE ON and before she realized it, Giselle was being herded into a car with a few women, being plied with babies, and completely lost track of Austin.

"Where are we going?"

"Dinner, of course," Glory answered simply, as if that was everything that needed to be said.

"Y'all didn't tell her we were going out to eat?"

"Of course, we did… I think."

"I'm pretty sure we did… didn't we?"

"Is Abbykins meeting us at the restaurant?"

"Yep. Houdini went to pick her up – and Cessna. They are bringing my sweet '*pupparoni*' with them."

"I don't think they are going to like that at the restaurant."

"Luke, Betsy, and the kids will…"

"True."

"The motormouth has a point…"

"How come Glory isn't a jumble of words tonight? She's actually… sedate. Did you drug her? Hello, I'm Melody and this is Betsy."

"I'm Sophie," another woman announced, waving. "Ben is in the car seat beside me and I'm not sure how he sleeps through this."

"Cause my wretched brother banged her in the hanger – I swear he is a walking sexual harassment case," Harley muttered angrily before glaring at Glory, who was sitting there with a very happy smile on her face. "I love you both dearly, but seriously?! Put a leash on Hunter and quit encouraging him."

Several heads whipped around to look at Glory in the minivan – and Giselle almost felt sorry for the woman… except for the obviously proud grin of happiness all over her face that made her laugh instead.

She didn't look remorseful in the slightest.

"Harley – did you just say *'banged'*?"

"Seriously?"

The two women, Harley and Glory, looked at each other and shared a smile… just as the woman with pigtails sighed happily.

"Your brother is simply the best," Glory smiled again, looking out the van window and letting a little giggle slip, causing everyone to gawk at her in shock.

"Dang, maybe I should have him talk to…"

"If *anyone* finishes that sentence? – I'm telling your husband. There is no way… *NO WAY*… that she is that happy, because *I'm* exceedingly happy with my spouse, and I do not sit there looking like I'm in some drugged stupor."

"You try having some man save you from hundreds of evil creatures, undress you in broad daylight, whispering promises to you, and then he makes love to you just to stop your tears…" Glory sighed happily, closing her eyes and smiling once more.

Giselle grinned as Harley rolled her eyes, and another woman spoke up. That wasn't quite how the spider incident went down, but obviously in this woman's mind - her husband had done just that.

"I seriously love and dislike you so much right now."

"Delilah, you have the same issues as Glory, and we all know it. Just because your boobs and ankles are swollen from baby number three doesn't mean that you are not happy at home with your husband. That belly tells a much different story, girlfriend."

The woman shrugged – and winked at Giselle.

"Cody's got the van with the kids, but I wanted to hitch a ride to meet our newbie…"

"You mean you wanted a break from teething?"

"That too."

"Y'all are too funny…"

"It's pronounced *'Down to earth'* and *'tired mama syndrome'*…"

"Not all of us," a woman mumbled. "Hello - I'm Dixie."

"Hi – Giselle."

"Dixie, why don't you talk to Romeo and tell him you are ready to have children?"

"Because I don't know if I am or not," she answered honestly. "It's a big move and we've had enough enormous changes in our lives. It's kinda nice that it's just us and things are in a routine, settling down. We certainly don't need any more drama or tragedy in our lives."

Giselle wasn't sure what they were talking about – but something in the woman's frightened eyes told her that she'd been scarred badly by something in her past.

"Babies are wonderful… a joy," Marisol said easily from the back seat beside Sophie. "I'm Marisol, and my husband has my kids in his vehicle."

"So says the woman who pops out nine-pound quarterbacks at birth… but if you asked Meredith or anyone that's lost a baby or someone they love? They would understand that fear that lingers in both of our minds. No, we aren't in any hurry, but the urge comes up."

"That would be your biological clock ticking…"

"I know."

"Would you pass on…"

"Can we change the subject?" Dixie said firmly, wiping her eyes on her shirt collar. "I really don't want to go down this path right now, and it's just a hormonal phase. Tomorrow I will be glad that it's just Lee and I…"

"We are here," Harley announced, interrupting her. "Any teary eyes? Wipe your faces… and someone pass Dixie a baby wipe please? Romeo will freak if he thought she was crying –

and for Pete's sake? Glory, will you stop smiling? Seriously? You are going to give us all a complex."

Giselle couldn't help but admire the bonding between the women who all opted to ride together while the men took their cars – and the children – giving them a much-needed break to talk.

It was actually really sweet.

They were all there for each other, helping each other, not holding back, and were a genuine family… and she loved it. It reminded her of her own sisters' back home, who had married and moved away over time.

This was simply wonderful, she thought warmly and smiled at Harley.

"Everything okay?"

"This is nice, you know?"

"We're just all the best of friends – and try to keep things open between us all. Sometimes it's hard because we all get upset, envious, jealous, or frustrated… but we care and love each other too. These friends I would call my sisters – and I am blessed to have each of them in my life," Harley said gently, reaching for Giselle's hand. "I can't think of another place that seems like heaven, then here."

"I have my husband and daughter, a job I never imagined, a home that works for us, and a family that we've built over time. Do I want a nicer car, a bigger house, more money, or nicer things? Sure… but I would never sacrifice the other aspects that I have. The indescribable gift that it is to help a friend get on their feet here, to see their lives take shape, and see how our Flyboys family expands."

Giselle swallowed, knowing Harley's words were designed for her.

"It's a beautiful thing," Sophie volunteered in the silence. "I love our group so much and knowing someone, anyone, has your back at any moment with just a single text message between us."

"We're family and sisters…"

"I promise it's not a cult," a woman said, opening the door, startling Giselle. She hadn't even thought about this being a cult and the moment that word was out – it all started to click for a moment. Was this a cult? Was she in trouble?

… And then she saw the newcomer shake her head 'No' in silent understanding as Houdini waved in the distance, walking off.

"Hi, I'm Abbykins according to Glory – and the biggest skeptic. Y'all should really roll up the windows if you are having a moment. It's called privacy, ladies. Dixie, honey, you have a little mascara under your eyes, sweetie - and Romeo is headed this way. Can someone give her a mirror? What's your name, newbie?"

"Giselle," she smiled nervously. "And I'm not really new – I'm just visiting."

"Sure you are," Abby grinned, winking at Harley. "C'mon, hon. Gage is getting our table already, and I think he wants Sparky at our end when he gets here. Melody? Firefly told Romeo he's at our end and said he was 'taking his favorite puppy for a quick walk first - and that he would be late'? When did you get a dog?"

"We didn't – it's a long story. Yup – Sutton just texted me. They are on the way now," Melody said simply, climbing out of the van and then groaning aloud. "Whoa boy…"

"What's wrong?"

"Sutton got Betsy's ears pierced…"

An audible groan rose from all the women, startling Giselle.

"What's wrong with that?"

"Nothing at all," Melody smiled tenderly with this

faraway look on her face. "Except that my sweet man probably is going to be mush."

"I bet he bawled like he did at your wedding."

"I'll take that bet."

"You all need to stop it. I love my sweet, emotional man."

"Sutton is Firefly..." someone whispered to her -and Giselle balked.

"Firefly? The same guy who's been teasing Austin... *cries?*"

"Hey! Hey," Melody snapped her fingers, frowning protectively. "Let's focus and go inside. Margaritas were promised and I'm hungry – and *everyone* cries."

"Who can enjoy a margarita this month?" Glory asked.

Harley, Dixie, Giselle, and most of the women raised their hands – except for four of them. Delilah, Marisol, Abby, and Sophie did not raise their hands, and it did not go unnoticed.

"Sophie?! OH MY GOSH, ARE YOU..."

"I don't know, but I can't take a chance at this point. I'll let you know in a few weeks and if I'm not? Then I want my margarita and Midol immediately."

"Done!"

Abby smiled at her and hooked her arm around Giselle's, leaning in so she could whisper an explanation.

"They've been trying for over a year now to have another baby. Her husband is still stationed overseas and only comes home once every few months for a week, so it makes things tough. I know she's been tracking her cycles, bought an ovulation counter, and trying everything she can because she wants Ben to have a sibling... but nothing's happened yet."

"Oh, I can't imagine how hard that must be for them."

"Yup. Last time he was home and got her period again? Sophie cried and cried. Dixie made her favorite cupcakes, and we had a period party at the house."

"What's a *'period party'*?"

"Midol, maxi pads, Kleenex, heating pads, pajamas, and

ice cream… we all sat around, watching Hallmark Channel, and sobbing like fools while talking about babies, our husbands, and the kids. It's just nice to be around people that understand, you know?"

Giselle nodded… but she did not know any of that. Not anymore. Being on base, away from her family and friends, had taken that bonding from her and she really wanted to be a part of a group once again.

Abby pulled her forward as everyone poured inside, taking their seats, and she was laughing at how they were saving seats like children. Melody, Abby, and Giselle all had their purses in chairs to hold spots for their men… and she marveled at the smiling faces as everyone walked around the table, saying hello, greeting each other, and reinforcing those bonds.

She remembered that Harley had them on shifts, so it made sense that they were saying 'hello' because it might have been a little while since the friends saw each other… and there were so many of them! It was staggering to see people still walking in the room, saying hello, and greeting everyone.

… And then moments later, as the servers were bringing several baskets of chips, in walked Austin and Firefly. Sure enough, the man was smiling and his eyes were shiny as he cradled a little girl against his shoulders, who was sucking her thumb.

"What made you decide to…" Melody began, and Betsy stuck out her arms, immediately diving for the safety of mommy's arms. "Oh, you look so pretty! Doesn't Betsy look lovely?"

Everyone at that end of the table immediately began praising the child as she gingerly touched her ears, happily, the soreness forgotten completely.

"How are you doing, Sutton?" Melody said gently as Austin took a seat beside Giselle, moving to hold her hand.

"Me? I'm fine," he said gruffly, rubbing the back of his neck. "I'm always fine and…"

"I love you, sweet man," Melody smiled tenderly as the couple shared a knowing look with each other – just before Firefly leaned forward to kiss his wife.

"You went with Firefly?" Giselle asked quietly, looking at Austin, who was looking at her. "You didn't miss much. We haven't ordered yet and…"

"I like this," he interrupted softly, giving her hand a slight squeeze. "I like us holding hands and being a couple."

"I do too," she replied, blushing slightly as she looked up to see several people watching them — all smiling knowingly.

"Let's talk later," she hedged, wanting privacy. While this was nice, it was also like having an entire mess hall watching or holding a conversation with you.

Austin nodded silently, still holding her hand.

CHAPTER 19

AUSTIN

AUSTIN SAT THERE at the table, holding Giselle's hand and treasuring how wonderful it was just to be there... all while lost in his own thoughts, replaying the last hour in his mind.

Firefly and X-Ray pulled him aside, dragging him away so they could talk to him away from everyone else. Within seconds, he was in a car staring at a little girl about two years old with shockingly white hair, watching him with fascination.

"So? How serious are things between you two?"

"Wow. You sure don't sugarcoat it much, Firefly."

"Never have, never will..."

"He wants to know if you are happy," X-Ray smiled easily. "And we've all been in your shoes, knowing how wonderfully scary falling for someone can be. It affects your life, your thoughts, and your dreams of the future – so we wanted to check on you."

"I'm good."

"Are you sure?" X-Ray said gently – and Austin looked at the man that had occupied the bunk directly across from him the moment he'd arrived in Ghazni.

"You're not engaged," Firefly interrupted bluntly, putting the car in park finally and getting out. "You're not foolin' around. You're going to her parents' home, so does that mean you are asking her daddy for permission? Is she pushing you for marriage?"

"What? No? Wait - do you think she's expecting that? I mean, we are kinda serious but…"

"Did you buy her a ring?"

"Noooo?!" Austin balked, feeling nervous now as he saw the jewelry store before them, wondering if they had dragged him here to buy Giselle an engagement ring.

"Dude! She flew halfway across the world with you – alone – and taking you to see her parents. The girl is gonna be expecting you to pop the question or marry her."

Austin looked at X-Ray, who smiled and shrugged.

"Really?"

"You probably should be ready if the discussion comes up," X-Ray began carefully. "I know that Firefly had the whole thing set up for Melody… and well, I ran away with my girlfriend, and we ended up married, waking up beside each other in quite a mess. It was hard because both of us were terrified at that moment because of our own issues. Then I had to leave again. It was tough on me because I couldn't see her… but for you? You'll see her, but be separated, too."

"How well do you know her?" Firefly asked. "I feel like you are my kid brother and kinda always have – so I just wanted to check on you."

"I'm… I'm confused. Why are we *here*, of all places?" Austin admitted hesitantly in a hushed voice. "I really like Giselle so much and feel drawn to her, but sometimes I feel like we are so different, too. I mean, I've never felt like this and she's so quiet sometimes."

"You are pretty outgoing, pup."

"What do you mean?"

"You love life, you do everything you can to bring joy to a room – whether it's singing Madonna at the top of your lungs in the middle of the gym on base, throwing peas at the next table in the mess hall, or pretending to suntan on the runway and asking Reilly for sunscreen…"

"Oh gosh, Reilly was really fuming about that…"

"Yeah, you have no regard for your own safety," X-Ray admitted, grinning.

"It was funny."

"Only because there were five of us out there with towels and in our running shorts pretending to be… where was it again?"

"Bermuda."

"Oh yeah," X-Ray cracked up laughing at the memory. "Inferno, Paradox, Firefly, and Armadillo were out there…"

"Remember 'Dilla was wearing his stupid boots because he was leaving the next week, claiming he needed to 'break them in again'?"

All three men burst out laughing – shaking their heads at the memories, before Firefly smiled easily, scooping up Betsy and holding her close as they walked into the jewelry store together.

"C'mon," Firefly invited. "Miss Betsy is getting her little ears pierced immediately before I lose my nerve. Melody hasn't done it yet because she'll cry, so I told her I would take our girl."

"Melody?"

"Shut up," Firefly admonished as the two men laughed. "I'm not telling you to rush into things or even suggesting you take the next step. I'm saying that I don't want you to change and I'm really happy to see you."

"Just be ready if the moment comes – and if it doesn't? That's okay too, because you will always have a home and family with us."

"Thanks guys," Austin said gruffly, deeply moved because he knew their pasts – just like they knew his. X-Ray was kicked out when he was in high school, and Firefly grew up in a children's home. All three men were close and like brothers because they had no one else – and it meant a lot that they were trying to look out for him.

"It could be the best thing that ever happened to you too," X-Ray said quietly, nodding at Firefly. "Just remember that. Issues and fears only compound if you don't address them – so if there is anything going on? Talk to her about it."

"Absolutely. Melody and I talk about everything… and then we do whatever it is that she wants," Firefly grinned.

"Same with my Emily," X-Ray smiled knowingly.

"I guess I just need to talk to her and figure out what makes both of us happy, because I guess I always assumed it was just 'boom' and that's the person you are supposed to be with."

"Sometimes it's not a boom."

"Sometimes it's a slow progression…"

"Or a splash of cold water."

"Y'all are not helping," Austin chuckled, smiling. "Everything you are saying is only confusing me more from what I thought I felt, understood, and knew…"

"Just doing our jobs."

"And we do it well," Firefly bragged, grinning and elbowing X-Ray. "We just both want to make sure you know what you are doing before things get too far or you get hurt. All three of us have been through enough stuff in our pasts,

and when the good stuff is standing there in front of you –
it's hard to accept."

"I get that."

… And Austin really did.

Sitting there at the table beside Giselle, listening to all of
them speak nearby, he realized that he was curious about
what she thought of all of this – because it meant a lot
to him.

These were his people, his family, and he couldn't share
this part of himself with her in Ghazni. It was like they were
from two different worlds, almost like Alice looking through
the looking glass and seeing an entire universe she couldn't
touch.

That fence between them in Ghazni was the surface of
that mirror. Her life differed from his – and she would never
experience a part of his environment… unless it was here,
among his friends.

Just thinking that made him feel weird.

In less than a week, these moments would be gone…

Again.

HOURS LATER, those same thoughts were rolling through his
mind.

CHAPTER 20

GISELLE

Giselle was a little surprised at how quiet Austin was and how strangely odd everything felt right now. He'd unlocked the door at Flyboys and they had gone inside, amid the shadows, feeling for a light switch.

As the lights came on, she expected him to talk or say something... but he was quiet. He just held her hand, before releasing it to gather up a t-shirt and shorts to change into in order to sleep. She did the same, tagging off with him down the hallway where the bathroom was located.

She was so exhausted from the trip, from being around so many people, that she knew her body was ready to crash into dreamland... yet her mind was churning like an ocean before the storm.

Entering the bunkroom, she saw Austin had already climbed up onto the top bunk, turned towards the wall, away from her... and she hesitated.

This was not how she wanted her evening to end.

Setting down her things, she murmured a brief goodnight

to him… and left the room. Padding in her slipper socks down the hallway towards the front door, she exited the building and found herself standing in the middle of the airstrip, staring up at the stars above.

"What are you doing?" his voice said quietly from behind her, and she didn't turn around to look at him, but waited there in the chilled air. "You'll catch a cold standing out here in… almost n-nothing."

She smiled to herself, noting the tremor of his voice.

"I'm trying to center myself," she admitted. "Whenever I feel overwhelmed, I used to exit the barracks and stare up at the night sky. It made me feel like I must be special to see a glimpse of Heaven that I never noticed before back home in Wichita Falls."

She laughed softly, not turning towards him.

"I know it's the light pollution that ruins the view of the stars from the city, but I was hoping I could see a few tonight to relax my mind… and draw some comfort."

"Comfort?" he asked, quietly. "Are you okay?"

"I don't know."

"What's wrong?"

"Besides feeling overwhelmed and alone in a roomful of people? I'm nervous about seeing my parents, scared about this, anxious that I'm making a mistake, plus dreading going back to a life full of nothing but emails and being separated again by a fence…" she whispered openly, not holding back.

"Why are you nervous about seeing your parents?"

"It's been a while," she shrugged. "I can't explain it – I just am."

"You felt alone tonight?"

"Austin," she began, feeling her throat tighten painfully. "I feel alone *now*… something's off and I don't know what it is or what has happened. You know? I went from happier than

I've ever been - to feeling pressured, overwhelmed, alarmed, and very alone…"

"Me too," he admitted, sliding his arms around her waist and she couldn't help but jump at the unexpected hug. "Is this alright?"

"Yeah. I just…" she began and then sighed. "Nothing."

"Talk to me."

"I just didn't expect you to hug me or touch me, because I figured that I had done or said something wrong at some point. I thought you were mad at me."

"No," he said, holding her close. "I don't know that I could ever be mad at you – and if I was? I don't think it would stick."

He laughed softly, pressing a small kiss to her temple.

"There is something about you that just calls to me… and it would be like being mad at myself. I kinda like who I am," he chuckled, teasing her.

"I really like us being friends and having each other," she whispered tearfully. "And if I have done something wrong, pressured you, or made you feel badly…"

"Giselle," he interrupted softly. "I just don't ever want to let you down – and I'm scared because what I feel for you, for us, is very intense. One guy mentioned that you might be taking me to see your parents for a reason and…"

"You volunteered to take me," she reminded him.

"Oh yeah," he chuckled. "I guess I forgot that part. I've been so focused on making sure I do or say the right things to win you over that…"

His words struck a nerve in her, ringing like a bell on a clear night within her soul. She pulled his hands off of her, freeing herself, and turning to look at him, stunned by the admission… and how it made her feel.

Austin was standing there, looking at her worriedly, and

those shadows of darkness reminded her of Afghanistan, their repeated fence-rendezvous…

"I wish it was like this back home," she whispered, reaching up and touching his face. "I've wished for this so many times…"

His hand rested on her back, holding her close once more, as they stood there both wearing socks on the asphalt that was quickly cooling and looked at each other.

"I wanted to touch you, hold you close, so often back home… and I'm already wishing we never had to leave this particular quest we are on."

"A 'quest' indicates we are searching for something, my handsome knight," she smiled, tracing his eyebrow and moving to trail her fingers over the shell of his ear as he tucked a strand of her hair behind hers.

"I don't want you to feel alone, Giselle," he said tenderly in a hushed voice. "If you feel alone, then I am failing in my quest or knight's journey."

"There you go again with that word…" she teased tearfully.

"I am searching for something," he began, causing her to pause her hand that was tracing the back of his neck now, memorizing these moments and trying to commit them to memory.

"What?"

"I'm searching for… my long-lost dance partner," he smiled lovingly – and she laughed because it was so silly, so unexpected, and just so him.

Whenever anything got serious or too much, he would throw her for a loop… and usually those 'loops' made her feel wonderful. The gummy worms, the champagne on the plane, her stupid ketchup…

"See, I wanted to dance with my fabled paladin that I found on distant, sandy shore, but a chain-linked monster separated us," he smiled, winking at her. "A terrible, fierce monster that keeps her away from my loving arms."

"Oh nooo," she whispered dramatically, playing along with him.

"But now, Sir Austin of the Yonder has conquered that foe…"

"Conquered? Really?" she said flatly, arching an eyebrow at him.

"It's my story and I can conquer if I want to… now where was I?" he retorted glibly, grinning wildly, and looking even more impetuous than ever before as he pulled her close, taking one of her hands in his and holding it upwards like they were going to waltz.

"Don't we need music to dance?" she smiled up at him.

"Let me let you in on a little known 'knightly' secret," he whispered, leaning forward to kiss her on the cheek. "If you listen closely enough, the song is there… in your heart."

Giselle caught her breath as he slowly began to glide with her, taking a few steps to the left, then the right, and spun her slowly like they were in some magical castle's grand ballroom… instead of in socks, and getting cold feet, in Texas.

Nothing was going to stop this magical moment they were sharing, she thought silently as her heart beat wildly, falling under the spell he was weaving around her, turning her about in the rapidly cooling moonlit wonderland they were in.

"Perhaps," he said softly, his eyes holding hers. "Instead of listening to all the mysterious soothsayers, fortune tellers, and elemental guardians who give out a lot of contradicting advice… maybe we should listen to what our hearts are saying and just talk to each other."

"Yes," she whispered tearfully, nodding and smiling up at him. "That sounds like the best suggestion yet, Sir Austin — knight of the realm."

"You can drop the *'sir'*," he flirted playfully. "We don't stand on airs here."

Giselle laughed aloud, her voice echoing in the night air as she threw her arms around him, hugging him close.

"I just needed this…" he whispered against her hair, holding her close. "Don't be upset with me, feel alone, or think that you can't talk to me. If you want or expect something from me – *tell me* – because guys can be a little dense when they are in the arms of a beautiful woman that they care for and admire."

"I need this too…" she admitted. "I don't want either of us to feel pressured."

"Me neither."

"I want us to just take our time, be together, and…"

He lifted his head from where he was holding her close, looking at her there in the moonlight. His thumb caressed her cheek as he gazed at her so openly with so much emotion, standing there within her arms.

"I want no one's advice or suggestions on how our relationship should go, what we should do next, or how we should act… because I just want *us*, Giselle."

"Me too," she whispered softly.

"I want our own kind of perfect as we fall in love…"

Her breath caught in her chest because that was the first time that he truly said anything about love. He said he cared, told her he felt strongly, but hearing this now in the moonlight reminiscent of their fence-dates just felt so special somehow.

"Our story is so beautiful," he whispered against her lips, kissing her softly, his lips brushing against hers so gently as he spoke. "And growing every time we touch. It's just our hearts and our souls involved - and we are fools to let others tell us what we need… when it's this sheer perfection between us, that we found by some miracle."

"It is…" she breathed, clinging to him.

"Let me treasure you," he continued softly. "Let us learn to love each other and discover what we need from each other. I will take you soaring through the clouds tomorrow, we'll visit another castle, and share so many moments that will build memories that will last a lifetime… if you'll let me flounder around at your side as I learn how to love you, my paladin."

She couldn't stand it anymore - a noise escaped her, sounding between a sob, a squeak, and a laugh as she pulled his head to her, kissing him soundly.

They stood there in the dark, holding one another in no rush as they kissed in the moonlight. He didn't press for more or push for things to get more intense, rather it was like he was savoring just being close to her… and that was what she needed.

… Only to hear the most incredible thing.

Austin had begun humming faintly, taking her hand from his neck and holding it in his, as he started to step slowly with her.

"Dance with me in the moonlight," he beckoned. "Continue weaving your spell, my beloved paladin, and never, *ever*, let me go."

They danced, held each other, until they were shivering and yawning from exhaustion. It had been an endless day, full of people, travel, misunderstandings, and… clarity.

As they walked inside, he kissed her once more before climbing up onto his bunk as she lay down on hers… only to see a hand drop down beside the bed, wiggling his fingers at her.

"My hand misses yours already," he chuckled playfully, punctuated by a yawn, as she moved to hold his hand with hers for a brief moment.

"… And as for dreading going back to just our emails or a

fence, maybe that is something we should figure out together — *alone* — and away from any helpers?"

"I would like that… because I am not ready for any of this to end."

"Me neither – and I don't plan on letting go… even if I need to let go to get to sleep. It's a different 'letting go' I assure you," he teased again, and she could practically see his smile in her mind.

"You are a goofball," she laughed softly, kissing his fingertips before releasing his hand. "Goodnight, my precious knight."

"Sweet dreams, my beloved paladin."

Giselle closed her eyes – only to hear his voice again in the stillness of the dark.

"I'm so thankful for that first email."

"I am too," she admitted.

CHAPTER 21

GISELLE

"Upgrade time!" Austin called out excitedly, bursting into the room, just as she finished dressing.

"Uh hello? Knock, knock?" she gaped, shocked... and saw his astonished look right before it melted into a smile.

"You're decent."

"Barely?!"

"I'm sorry," he apologized immediately. "I just wanted to get our bags and throw them on the plane. I've already done the preflight and we are ready to go as soon as you are... and you look beautiful."

Giselle rolled her eyes and smiled at him, seeing his warm expression. Something told her he wasn't actually *that* apologetic and wouldn't have minded walking in as she was zipping her pants.

"I'm wearing jeans and an Army t-shirt..."

"Somebody give Sarge a Flyboys shirt..." someone

hollered in the background, but Austin just smiled at her, giving her a thumbs up in silent support. Just that understanding that he didn't want to change her meant a lot. Her father was retired Army, and she was proud of what she did for the military… despite being surrounded by former and current Air Force pilots.

"You look beautiful," he repeated and bent to pick up his bag. "Is yours ready to go?"

"Yes, give me just a moment to throw on my shoes and get a cup of coffee."

"I've got our coffee made in two insulated tumblers that Harley gave me – and Glory picked up donuts."

"Oh really?" she smiled, realizing it was nice having everyone help and take care of them – and maybe she had been a little quick to judge. It had been a while since anyone stepped up to support her and she had been on her own for so long, it was hard to fathom that there wasn't some ulterior motive behind it.

"What did you mean by *'upgrade'*?"

"Let's go – and you'll find out," he grinned – and left the room.

Giselle laughed, recognizing that the playful man was up to something and yanked on her boots, lacing them quickly.

As she walked out of the room, she put the sheets in the basket as directed by Harley and saw Houdini was in the middle of teaching a class. It was so strange to see that a working business was thriving around them, while they were just living in the space like it was nothing.

Harley waved happily from her desk, holding a phone to her ear… and pointed back to the next room, angling her free arm around the door frame. Walking in, she saw two insulated Flyboys mugs waiting with lids beside them and a small bag of donuts.

"Now, don't be getting jelly filling on the controls," Firefly grinned, winking at Valkyrie, whom she had met at dinner briefly – plus it helped they were wearing name tags.

"We got you something," he smiled and held out a name tag... that said 'Sarge'. She smiled up at him, unable to resist. "You take care of my little brother, okay? He's a good guy and wears his heart on his sleeve."

"I promise."

"Good."

"...And thank you for this," she smiled at the two men, realizing they were accepting her as one of their own. It was sweet, very unexpected, and touching.

"Relax and enjoy this – because this is our world and you are welcome because you're Sparky's girl. I don't think we've ever had a *Sarge* come through before, have we?"

"Nope."

"*Birdbrain, Wile-E-Coyote, Grandma, Sugarbuns...* yes – but *Sarge*? I don't think so. Maybe we should start a logbook, so we don't double up on call signs."

"I heard that, Firefly," Harley called out loudly. "Don't think you are going to make more work for me. Start your own logbook, buster."

"Yes, *mom*," he said dutifully, as all three laughed.

"Have a great time, Sarge," Valkyrie said openly, reaching out to shake her hand. "And seriously – grab some t-shirts for your family. How many do you need?"

"There's eight children and my parents... plus my nieces and nephews, so I would need," she drawled knowingly, seeing the two men look at each other, realizing they'd opened their mouth without thinking. "Just one or two for my parents — if that is okay?"

Both men exhaled with relief.

She withdrew from the rack three rolled up shirts that

were tied with ribbon – one for each of her parents... and one for her.

"Giselle? Are you ready, hon?"

"I am," she smiled easily over her shoulder at Austin, who had appeared in the doorway. "I was just getting a shirt for my parents – and our things."

"Gotcha," Austin acknowledged and shook hands with both men happily. "Thank you, guys, for letting me borrow the plane."

"Just don't wreck it," Valkyrie shrugged – causing the three pilots to laugh easily as she swallowed hard. That was not funny and not something to joke about in the slightest, yet they acted like it was nothing.

"Do we need to worry about that?"

"Not in the slightest. No loops, no aerial stalls, and no diving... I promise. Let's go. I'm hogging the runway and Thumper is going to be landing soon with a student."

"Okay," she nodded in comprehension – and turned to the guys, hugging them both quickly. "Thank you again – for everything."

"You betcha, kiddo."

"Have a nice flight, Sarge."

"Thanks guys," Giselle smiled and looked at Austin, who was looking a little warily at his friends, before pulling her to his side. She looked up at Austin, surprised and a little touched that he was so possessive, disliking the quick hug between her and Firefly immensely.

"Relax, pup. Melody would maim me or cry... and I don't honestly know what would be worse. Your girl is all *yours* – I swear it."

"I was just saying *'thank you',*" she chided and saw his nod.

"Let's go."

As they walked out the door together towards the plane, she looked at him in surprise.

"You know that was nothing, right?"

"I know."

"Then why do you look so… grumpy?"

He stopped and hesitated for a moment before looking at her.

"I'm not grumpy – I'm a realist," he said simply, yanking open the door to the plane for her as she stood there silently watching him, trying to figure out what made him tick. He looked very insecure, quite grumpy no matter what he said, very frustrated… yet incredibly handsome.

Austin was wearing a white button-up dress shirt to meet her parents and the gold reflective sunglasses she'd given him from Christmas were perched on his nose. His hair was slightly spiked somewhat from his shower earlier… and his goatee was trimmed nicely, framing a very sullen looking mouth.

The man was upset.

As he slid into the seat of the Cessna, he looked at her.

"Did you want to go – or would you rather stay here with Firefly?"

"Oh my gosh… you're jealous?!"

"You told me not to be."

"Exactly."

"So I'm not."

"Then what's wrong?"

"Do we have to do this now?" he asked simply, looking at her across the seat. "Yes, I'm jealous – very much so – and exceedingly insecure, okay? Do you want to hear me say it? The man is built like a bodybuilder and I'm a toothpick next to him. He's a great guy and if that's your thing, then…"

"Austin?" she interrupted softly, looking at him.

"Yeah?"

"He's not the man that I want to dance with in the moonlight until I'm a hundred years old… so relax," she said tenderly and held out her hand to him. "I want our story, so let's open up our next chapter by getting this plane off the ground so I can show you off to my parents."

"You're sure you want me, because if you say 'yes'? I'm never letting you go… I want to make sure you know what you are in for. I don't mean to sound like a jerk, and I love the guy to pieces - but if Firefly is in *our* story? He's the Donkey in Shrek… and I'm forever going to be your knight, prince, king, whatever you want to call me – but he's the dang sidekick donkey and that's it. Got it?"

Giselle laughed at him as he took her hand, stepping up on the footpad and climbing into the plane beside him. Her eyes gazed at his beloved face, seeing that insecure smile on his lips, as she leaned forward to kiss them.

"I'm sure that I want you, my beloved knight."

He leaned forward and kissed her again softly, before whispering to her.

"Definitely time for an upgrade…"

"What do you mean?"

"Here," he invited, handing her a set of headphones. "You just leveled up from *'paladin'* to a *'passenger princess'*. Put these on and pull the speaker close to your lips so we can talk."

He helped her buckle, before reaching over her lap and latching the door closed, running through a few things on the strange 'dash' before her… and giving her a smile.

Leaning back in his seat, he tapped the mouthpiece, and she heard his voice… looking at him in disbelief.

"Mic check one… and two! Yo, is this thing on? Party people in the house say 'Heyyyy'…" he sang playfully.

"*Heyyyy!*"… Came the immediate response in the speakers, making her burst out laughing and seeing his immediate grin of awareness that she heard him playing around.

He held up two fingers, his index and middle, making a 'gang sign' and holding it up playfully in the window towards

Flyboys – only to see several of the guys standing at the window, making hand gestures back at him.

"Spark-dog is on the mic, G! My princess is ready to go. If I take it low-n-slow, with a clear tempo… am I clear ta' go?"

She heard several people laughing now in the background of the radio as Harley got on the coms.

"You are clear to take off, Sparky… Thumper is south-bound and lining up for the runway. He can already see you, so get to moving – and avoid the 'low and slow' pace, my friend," Harley ordered. "Have a great time - *and hustle* - or you'll need to wait for my husband to land and taxi forward."

"I'm out! … Clear the skies," Sparky replied – and Giselle was shocked at the speed at which the small plane suddenly rushed forward, accelerating quickly and pressing her into the seat.

He meant business and before she could caution him, question anything, they were off the ground and soaring into the skies turning slightly to the right before swinging back slightly to the west.

"Can you hear me?" he asked easily, his eyes checking the gauges and the surrounding air.

"Yes. No more rapping, Spark-dog?"

"Flyboys – this is Cessna 631, going to channel nine on the radio. I'll text when we land… and thank you again."

Harley's voice came through, crackling slightly as the distance between them grew.

"Have… great… t-time… care…"

Austin reached for the radio, changing the dial, and then spoke to her in the mic.

"Can you still hear me?"

"Yes."

"Perfect," he smiled at her. "I meant to ask, have you ever been in a Cessna? Do you want to fly her for a bit?"

"Me?!"

"Yeah, you. I'll show you a few things if you want to try it..."

"Oh no, no, no. I don't think so."

"Put your hands on the yoke," he instructed... and she numbly complied, feeling almost strange at this whole idea. Who would have thought that she would ever have her hands on something that looked like a steering wheel of an airplane – when there was really nothing to steer?

... *The 'yokes' on me? I guess?* she mused.

"In the Falcon that I fly, we have what looks like a joystick or a yoke... but these little things are a dream. It's like riding a bike with training wheels because it's so different. I mean, I'm not trying to minimize it but it's just so incredibly dainty compared to that monster I get to shoot into the sky all the time."

"Do you like flying a Falcon?"

"Love it," he admitted openly. "It's like driving a Bugatti or Lamborghini compared to a Ford Focus. Both will get you there, but one has all the bells and whistles with enough power to put you back in the seat while the other putters along nicely."

"So, you're a speed demon?"

"No, but I certainly appreciate quick responses from my machinery. If my brain thinks 'bank right' – I need it to move immediately, because there might be an issue."

"I guess it would be like me using a scalpel versus kindergarten blunt-nose scissors. It would cut, but my goodness - it would be terrible."

"Right tool for the right job," he laughed softly. "Feel the motion as I move the plane a little bit."

She watched as he glided it slowly and she felt it dip slightly, angling the side he was on downwards just a bit before straightening up.

"Course correction," he smiled at her. "I think it might be

easier to fly north of DFW before turning west towards Wichita Falls."

"I'm just along for the ride," she joked and shrugged. "Whatever you think is best."

"Do you want to do anything while we are in town?" he began. "I wasn't sure if you wanted to go on a date or just spend time with your family. I want to spend time with you and thought a date might be nice, but I'll be cutting into your time then. We can do whatever you want, so long as we are together. Do they like to play board games, cards, watch movies?"

"They just like to hang out and talk."

"Oh man," he chuckled nervously. "I'm not exactly a good talker sometimes and…"

"Austin, relax," she smiled, taking her hand off the wheel since he was holding onto it too – and smoothed his hair, needing to touch him. "They are going to adore you as much as I do."

He nodded nervously and glanced at her.

"They are going to fall for this sweet guy beside me because of how wonderfully happy their daughter is when she is with him," she whispered, moving to trace her finger just inside of his collar.

"I'm really glad to hear that," he said quietly, his voice echoing in the headphones on her head. "I know I get nervous sometimes and I didn't mean to make a fool of myself, but I just think you are so incredibly wonderful that sometimes I wonder what you see in me."

"I see a part of my soul that I didn't know was missing," she whispered, staring at his beautiful profile as he swallowed, before glancing at her. He reached for her hand, clasping it in his, before kissing it firmly and held it against his chest… before nodding silently.

Her words moved him, and it was easy to see.

"Thank you," he whispered moments later. "Thank you for just being you – and being here with me."

"I can't think of anywhere else I would want to be than right here beside you," she admitted openly.

CHAPTER 22

GISELLE
Wichita Falls, Texas

TIME PASSED as they flew for a few hours, talking here and there, but mostly she was grateful for the bench seat as she could snuggle a little closer to Austin, marveling at some sights in the area. It wasn't long before he turned to her, kissing her swiftly, and held up a finger to his lips.

"Wichita Falls Reginal, this is Cessna 631 out of Tyler… We are coming in southbound and requesting permission to land."

Cessna 631 hold your pattern…

Giselle listened fascinated as Austin and the person on the other end of the speaker began rattling off gibberish to her, talking about runway numbers, letters, a specific altitude, and advising to taxi to a certain building.

Yes, this was complete Greek to her... but Austin looked at her, nodding and smiling, as he immediately moved the plane to make preparations to land.

To her, if she was giving out readings, rattling off stats such as pulse, oxygen levels, told to bolus so many cc's, or start a drip at a certain millimeter per thousand... that was nothing.

That was her 'language' – and this was obviously his.

"We'll be on the ground in ten minutes if you want to go ahead and text Harley or your parents. I'll request an Uber once we land and..."

"My parents don't live far and will probably be excited to meet you. I'm betting they are going to want to run right over to pick us up. Is that okay?"

"This is your visit, darling. It's whatever you want to do," he said easily, staring at the displays and checking around the plane again distractedly as they got closer and closer to the ground. She realized he probably wasn't even aware he'd called her 'darling'... and smiled.

She liked diverting him, if that was what happened. He let down his guard when he was distracted elsewhere? Oh, she would need to keep that little tidbit in mind.

Marveling at his skills, she watched as he glided the Cessna down effortlessly and taxied it forward, heading directly for a building in the distance. It was so strange to think that they could just 'borrow a plane', go anywhere, and 'park' it here at the airport... yet as Austin hopped out of the plane, telling her to wait just a moment for him?

She realized that this was exactly the case.

He climbed back inside, smiling at her.

"We're going to roll it into that hangar in the distance and tie it down," he explained like it was nothing... yet her mind was still a little flabbergasted that this was actually happening.

…Just like that – he was 'going to valet' the plane.

Seriously.

She smiled at the craziness that life was turning out to be. If someone had come to her and said *'Hey, you are going to email this guy and fall madly in love with him – but he's on the other team – and oh yeah, he flies for a living'*…

She would have told that person they were insane… yet here he was.

They'd met by chance.

He swept into her world, winning her over one step at a time. He had become her best friend, her rock, the best part of every conversation, and treasured being in the same space as him. Just something as simple as holding his hand, or touching his temple, made her feel connected in a way she never imagined… and she loved their bond.

"Do you want to text your father?"

"I'll text my parents."

"Perfect. I'll let the team know we are safely here with the plane and tell them thank you again."

"… From both of us, because this meant a lot," she asked quickly, only to see his smile as he looked at her from his seat.

"Of course," he said softly. "Always."

She nodded nervously and turned back to her phone, texting her parents.

> We just landed. I wasn't sure if you were available to pick us up at the municipal airport…?

> We are already on our way and will be there in a few!

> Oh wow! Thank you! XOXO

> We can't wait to meet your young man...
> your mama made a roast tonight and her
> homemade potato rolls are rising right now.

> Mama made potato rolls???

> Of course! Her girl is home, and she wants
> your man to be well fed!

"Oh wow..." she muttered in disbelief.

"What's wrong?"

"Nothing," she admitted, and glanced at him. "I hope you are hungry?"

"Why?"

"My mother makes potato rolls from scratch once a year and won't share her recipe with anyone... but she made them today. I guess she wants to impress you."

He chuckled and rubbed his flat stomach, grinning playfully at her.

"I'm not about to let your sweet mama down," he teased. "I will make sure she knows how much I appreciate her cooking – and how much I care for her beautiful daughter."

"Oh yeah?" she teased playfully. "And just how much is that?"

"Meh, enough to carry her bag," he shrugged – and ducked, pretending to avoid her playfully swatting at his shoulder.

"Austin..."

"C'mon, my princess..." he teased, getting out of the plane and smiling at her from behind those sunglasses. "Let's get moving."

"Yup. They are already on the way."

"So no chance of running away screaming from anxiety and nerves, huh?"

"Nope. You are too late," she called out as he shut the door and circled around to her side, opening it for her and silently offering her a hand like she was some delicate queen from a gilded age.

"I guess I'll gather up my courage and fight the fierce dragons," he whispered playfully. "I'm hoping they are as easygoing as you said. I have a tendency to make a poor impression sometimes – or I did at least growing up in foster homes. Sometimes I can really open my mouth and shove my foot in it."

"They are going to love you," she promised, smiling up at him.

"… Because their daughter does?" he asked gently, with a note of hope in his voice as he gazed at her… and she hesitated, unsure what to say at his softly spoken question.

They stood there together for a moment, neither saying a word as she stared up at him – before pulling off his sunglasses so she could see his eyes.

"Or at least, I hope she does?" he amended nervously, his voice infinitely tender as she felt something in her shift.

"Legends say that the princess falls for a rogue knight."

"I hope it's not the same legend where she's married to King Arthur already and poor Lancelot is left out to dry..."

"Nahhhh," she said thickly, her eyes stinging as she saw the emotion in his gaze and watched him swallow. "This princess is very single and cares for her knight deeply, but she's scared to say the words aloud…"

At that moment, before either could say anything else, her phone started ringing noisily. She winced, looking at him and saw him nod as he stepped back slightly, and she answered the phone.

"Hello?"

"Heyyy! There's my baby girl – we are here, Giselle," her father boomed happily in the phone. "We are parked right up front in the 'No-Parking Zone' for you."

"Daddy – you aren't supposed to park there."

"Then you had better hurry, young lady, because we are right in front of the doors," he chuckled. "I'll see you in a moment."

Hanging up the phone, she looked at Austin and hated that their moment got interrupted as he hefted up both bags onto his shoulders, nodding to her.

"They are illegally parked right in front."

"I heard. We probably should hurry."

"I know."

"It's alright – we can talk later."

Giselle looked at him, feeling such a sense of loss and yearning that the precious bubble was broken... and she wanted to see him smile, have him 'wear his heart on his sleeve' like Firefly said, but that beautiful soul was there and retreating slightly.

She knocked one bag off his shoulder, grabbed him by the waist, and kissed him passionately with everything in her. She heard him drop the other bag to the ground just as he pulled her close to him, his hands gripping her as he kissed her deeply, making her heart flutter in her chest as her knees buckled slightly... only to pull away.

"I love you," she whispered – and saw his precious wide smile. "Now, let's hurry."

"We are still talking later," he said hoarsely.

"You've got my pink lip tint on you," and he immediately licked his lips, beaming happily as he gazed at her like she'd just set his world on fire. Just seeing him do that did things to her, and she felt herself blush at the intimacy of the simple act.

"Is that coconut?" he asked huskily.

"Pina colada," she replied... as he hefted up the two bags and held out a hand to her as they began to walk towards the exit.

"IF YOU LIKE PINA COLADAS…" he began singing at the top of his lungs – and she joined him, laughing wildly at the sheer joy on his beloved face. That walking soon became dancing, as they made their way forward and he playfully spun her around.

When it came to the 'have half a brain' lyrics, he crossed his eyes and stuck out his tongue, making her laugh wildly as she hugged him close – and he hugged her back, still walking forward awkwardly together, before kissing her pertly to sing the next lines… only to stop suddenly.

Her father was standing there, watching them.

"Hi Daddy," she called out happily, grabbing Austin's hand and pulling him forward. "This is Austin Calder," she beamed and saw his nervous expression.

"Sir," he croaked out nervously, sticking out his left hand… and then realizing it was the wrong one – pulling his hand from her, mouthing a quick 'sorry' – and stuck out his right hand to her father.

"It's nice to meet you, Mr. Beck."

Only to have her father jerk him forward into a bear hug – and Giselle covered her mouth with her hands as tears stung her eyes at the immediate acceptance as her father smiled at her over Austin's shoulder.

"I'm not much into health food – but I do like champagne," her father sang off key to Austin, winking at Giselle.

She heard Austin's precious laughter as he relaxed into the hug, patting her father on the back. She couldn't imagine a more perfect welcome to the man she loved than this.

"Is mama in the car?"

"Yes – and she'll be just heartbroken that she missed you two serenading each other," her father teased, ruffling Austin's hair. "I'm Maxwell – call me Max, young man."

"Will do, sir," Austin grinned happily, reaching for Giselle's hand immediately. "And I promise you, I'd be happy to belt out another song or two to your daughter just for your lovely bride, sir..."

"Oh, she's going to absolutely love you," her father chuckled. "My bride, huh? After eight beautiful children... it's more like she's my own sweet saint."

As they walked out to the car, Giselle saw her mother looking at the three of them with such happiness and pride, she gave her a thumbs up – seeing that her father and Austin were talking on the way to the vehicle, but Austin wouldn't let go of her hand.

He was clinging to her, telling her silently that he was still nervous... but she knew the moment he felt 'safe' or felt like he 'fit in' – there would be no holding him back.

... And she couldn't wait.

A SHORT TIME LATER, they were at her childhood home. She saw Austin's entranced expression and the longing in his eyes as he noticed the simple things that she had taken for granted every day.

The hallway was lined with photos of all eight of them in various photographs, different outfits, different locations, some costumes from Halloween and others a variety of terrible school portraits. Her favorite pictures had to be the ones that were candid and raw – showing the genuine joy of family... and she wished he'd experienced that.

She saw him stop, gazing at one of her favorite pictures.

When she was eleven, they had all gone on a camping trip to Lake Arrowhead for vacation because it was so expensive for that many people to travel. They pitched tents along the banks of a small stream near the state park and it had rained, causing everything to get soaked and muddy... the photograph was of the eight children – ages eleven to twenty –

there together, covered in mud from wrestling around in the creek bed in the rain.

She was in a t-shirt and blue jean shorts, while some of her siblings were in swimsuits, underwear, or cut-offs... all of them were laughing, smiling, and hugging on each other in a mass of limbs, smiles, and filth. It was always like this when they got together. There was no single one person, it was a family... and it was beautiful.

"This is incredible," he whispered reverently, his voice hoarse with emotion as he stared at it.

"We should all go camping again sometime, because our family has grown. You forget how fast time passes and how people change. I think this was right before Gideon joined the Army – he's a paratrooper and ornery as ever. I'm sure he would probably tell me I started my fire wrong or tied my fishing line wrong... because that's what brothers do."

"I wouldn't know," he said sadly – and she hugged him, spotting her mother in the distance passing the hallway.

"Yes, you would – because you have a whole slew of brothers in your team and I just met them," she whispered, kissing the shell of his ear from where she stood behind him.

"Just because they aren't blood doesn't mean that they don't care for you. Quit focusing on what is missing and be grateful you have something so beautiful with your friends. Firefly would do anything for you and we both know it, *puppy*..." she teased and heard him laugh softly as he nodded.

"You're right – and I guess I never looked at it like that," he began, turning to smile at her. "Sorry I got distracted."

"It's fine. I think Mom is making a pot of coffee and my dad is turning on the television. Let's put our bags down and..."

"I love you," he interrupted softly, brushing her hair back as he gazed at her. "I just wanted to say it again when we weren't rushed and marvel at this for just a moment, if that's okay?"

"That's perfectly fine," she smiled at him, touching his brow before tracing his hairline at his temple. "I love this spot and I don't know why..."

"We should hang out more, because I bet there are a lot more spots on me to love," he invited softly, causing the two of them to share a knowing smile.

"Oh yeah?"

"Very much so..." he whispered, leaning to kiss her but picked her up, wrapping his arms around her waist and hefting her upwards just enough to keep her feet off the ground.

"Which room is ours?"

"*Yours* is over here..."

"And yours is...?"

She pointed, smirking at him as his eyes danced in laughter.

"Then that's where mine is."

"Not under this roof buster... no bunk beds."

"My daughter is right, son," her father answered, interrupting them. She expected Austin to freeze or clam up, but he winked at her. "Nobody sleeps together in this house unless they are married."

"Does that mean you don't mind?" Austin said easily, not letting her down and turning to face her father as her mouth dropped open in shock.

"What?" she whispered in amazement at his boldness and the unexpected question from him.

"You're a cheeky boy, aren't you?"

"Your daughter loves me that way..." he smiled happily, putting her down as her father shook his head.

"The coffee is ready, and your mother said there will be

about another hour on the roast, you two," her father said, walking off and shaking his head as he laughed.

"Is that a *'Yes, you don't mind if I pop the question one of these days'* or a *'Yes, I'm cheeky?'* – I just wanted to clarify, sir…" Austin asked loudly, not looking at her, but that telltale dimple was there peeking out, telling her he was trying not to smile. That sweet little mark only appeared when he was smirking or holding back.

… And he was asking her father's permission for her hand – in marriage?!

"Yes – to both questions," her father replied loudly. "Gigi, do you want to call the kids and see if they want to come and meet Giselle's young man?"

"Gigi, Georgia, Giselle, Gideon… do you all have G names?"

"Except Daddy… yes – and I can't believe you asked him that."

"Come here," Austin said simply, picking up their bags and throwing them haphazardly onto the bed in one of the rooms, before shutting the door behind her.

"What are you doing?" she whispered nervously, pacing and nearly having a panic attack as her mind was bombarded with all these new issues that would come with the word 'marriage' tossed about randomly.

"Don't tease my parents like this because then they'll only be asking me a ton of questions. Now, my brothers and sisters are coming over for dinner, which means a ton more attention… Oh gosh, they are going to start asking to see a ring and all sorts of stuff we are not prepared for in the slightest. Austin – they are going to really be pushing. You don't know how they are going to be. I mean, my brothers and sisters just don't let up when they've got new stuff to pick on the other about. This is a big one! We just told each

213

other we loved the other person and nobody's ready to field a bunch of questions about rings, wedding dresses, or…"

"What makes you think I'm not ready?"

"Austin, it's… *it's my family,*" she whispered passionately, realizing he didn't understand what can of worms he had opened.

She stopped pacing to look at him standing there with his head slightly angled to the side. He looked confused – and she was feeling devastated, nervous, bordering on hysterical, because there was no way this was actually real – no matter how much she wanted it to be deep in her heart.

"What if," he began softly, his eyes watching her. "What if… I wanted to be a part of your family?"

… And before she could answer or ask him what he meant, she saw him kneel before her.

"What are y-y-you d-doing?" she stammered, feeling her nose begin to burn as tears stung her eyes as she stared at him. "Get up. This isn't funny at all…"

"I love you," he whispered, staring up at her as he took her hand in his. "I'm an insecure idiot who never imagined finding someone that he would chance building a life with, because I don't know what a normal life looks like. I had a horrible childhood. I'm scared that I won't be good enough for you, but I also know that I don't want anyone else to join our story," he smiled. "Firefly is definitely the donkey from Shrek. He means well, but he's just there and keeps butting in when I'm trying to impress you. Sidekick material, for sure."

Giselle laughed tearfully at his words as he smiled.

"I want us to have our happily ever after – even if neither of us knows what the future brings," he admitted. "I want to figure it out together. Whether it's here, in Yonder, some-where else at another base, or even still in Ghazni together with our evening fence-rendezvous… I really want to be a part of your world, Giselle."

"Really?" she whispered, softly as he brushed his lips against her knuckles, reminding her of paintings where a knight is bestowing a kiss on the maiden's hand... except there was no armor, no chain-mail, no horses, or sweeping gowns.

"Just two people that found their way through extraordinary means... to this moment together."

A knock on the door interrupted their brief interlude.

"Just a second...?!" both of them called out in unison, causing them to laugh softly while neither moved.

"Your sister Gemma is here, and the coffee is ready, honey," her mother called out.

"Give us five minutes, Mom..."

They remained still, listening as she heard her mother's footsteps walking off down the hallway and voices in the distance. She looked back at Austin, who was digging in the pocket of his jeans and not looking away from her... and pulled out a ring.

She drew in a ragged breath, waiting.

"I want us to be partners, to unite our kingdoms and make little infidels someday that know what being part of a family is," he smiled tenderly at her, his eyes growing shiny with emotion.

"I'm not sure what anything would look like down the road – I only know that I want you by my side, we can make our choices together, tackle our dreams, and build on this love that I never believed I would be lucky enough to find."

He drew in a shaky breath and looked at her hand as he slid a diamond engagement ring onto her finger slowly, before looking back up at her with so much adoration in his gaze that it was breathtaking to behold. The ring, a symbol of his love and a silent glistening promise to her, was sparkling on her finger as he still held her hand.

"I know this is fast or seems that way, but I've been crazy

about you for months now. Giselle Beck, my beloved paladin, princess of my heart, would you do me the greatest honor any knight could have bestowed upon him," he uttered emotionally. "Will you marry me?"

"Yes," she breathed... and saw his smile touch his lips as he rose to his feet before her.

"Yeah?" he smiled, his voice trembling and there was such relief in his expression that she couldn't help the small laugh that escaped her as they hugged each other tightly.

"I love you," he whispered against her hair, burying his face like a scared animal, taking refuge as she cradled him in her arms. She couldn't imagine how insecure he felt, putting himself out there to be accepted once more than he had probably done so many times in the past when settling into a foster home, hoping someone would accept him.

"I love you so much," she breathed, stroking his back and holding him tightly. "We'll figure this out together, through thick and thin..."

He nodded, not letting go as he pulled himself together and she waited, knowing how much he needed these precious moments. They simply stood there in the silence holding each other as she heard him take several shaky breaths, whispering to him softly words of encouragement... only to hear another knock on her door.

"Giselle? Gary and Greg are here... so are Grace, Gemma, and Georgia. Are you two coming out? Dinner is almost ready, and everyone is ready to meet your friend," her mother called out again.

"We're coming, Mama..." she said simply and smiled at him as he apologized softly, wiping his eyes and clearing his throat. He was emotional, and it touched her that he was so moved at this moment. He wasn't one of those gruff, tough guys, but so sensitive behind his playful exterior.

She cradled his beloved face in her hands, a palm laying against each cheek as she looked at him.

"Austin," she whispered gently, "Smile and be yourself – my family will love you."

He laid his hands over hers where they rested and pressed his forehead to hers.

"I just need *you* to love me – and never give up if things get tough," he said softly, putting himself out there and opening up, realizing just how deeply wounded he was and what a leap of faith this was for him.

"That's not what family does – and if we are doing this, then you are part of my family, so you are stuck with us through thick and thin."

He drew in a nervous breath and smiled at her, before clearing his throat, nodding.

"I think I still owe your mother a song," he smiled softly, lifting his head away from hers and dragging in one more deep breath.

"It's going to be just fine – I assure you," she began again, reassuring him and opening the door as the voices flooded the room. Instantly, she felt a burst of warmth in her chest at his intimidated expression, realizing that he had probably never been around such a chaotic, loving family.

"Look dork, just because you are the banker on Monopoly doesn't mean you get to help yourself to the money. That's not how real-life works…"

"Good thing this is a game, Gemma."

"Greg! You aren't the banker."

"Why not?"

"Georgia is going to be the banker."

"I could do it…"

"NO GARY!" everyone snapped hotly in loud voices before laughing.

"Daddy, why won't Aunt Georgia let you be the banker?"

"Because your Daddy cheats…"

"Because your Daddy doesn't play fair."

"Hey now, let's not tell my children I cheat – even if I did that one time…"

"It's pronounced *'every time'*, dear brother…"

"Don't be a sore loser, Gemma…"

Austin let out a little laugh beside her as they listened to the siblings bickering in the distance. She could smell the warm potato rolls cooking and the scene of food lingering in the air.

As they came around the corner, there was a clattering of chairs sliding back across the linoleum flooring as her father sat in his recliner, looking pointedly at her hand. He kicked the footrest back, getting up to his feet as her mother entered from the kitchen, drying her hands… and also looked at her hand, before smiling warmly.

"Looks like I've got another person to love," her mother said tenderly, walking over and hugging Giselle – and then hugging Austin like he'd been a part of their world for years on end.

She saw the shocked expression on his face and felt him squeeze her hand tightly, knowing he was trying not to break down. This was probably the most perfect welcome to her family that someone could have given him… first from her father and now her mother.

Someday Austin would understand what 'family' truly meant and she couldn't wait to be at his side during this entire process.

"Congratulations, you two. I'm so happy you are here, sweet boy."

"Mommm… I'm your sweet boy, remember?"

"You're all my sweet children," her mother said placatingly. "Are you hungry, honey? Let's get you some coffee and some food…" and shockingly enough, her mother pulled

Austin away from where Giselle stood – immediately taking him under her wing.

"I guess we are chopped liver," her father chuckled knowingly, watching her mother walk off. "I knew your mother would take to him – he's got this puppy dog look in his eyes. She calls it 'soulful' and loves the shy ones."

"He's *not* shy," Giselle smiled knowingly as her mother introduced Austin to her brothers and sisters, watching them shake his hand, hugging him, and then handing out wooden spoons to everyone.

"… And here we go," her father whispered, grinning at Giselle.

The strains of 'Dancing Queen' by ABBA began to fill the house, and one thing she never brought up was how much her mother encouraged singing and dancing. Giselle grew up in a home full of music and when she heard Austin singing? That was her moment of clarity, where all other doubts and fears just melted away.

Spicy ketchup… and wooden spoons. Who knew?

Oh, she knew she loved him, but the moment he started belting out in song? That's when she knew she was meant to meet this man in so many ways. Chance, fate, a miracle… whatever you wanted to label it?

Austin was meant to be here, now.

Giselle went to grab her spoon, holding it up to her lips as they all started singing together, like it was nothing.

From the Everly Brothers to Smashing Pumpkins, there were always songs playing in the house, and each bedroom had a radio in it. As a girl, there had been so many 'talent shows' in their pajamas, Christmas' caroling, and hymns sung off-key at a time but full of love… and by some miracle?

She had found *him*.

Her perfect match.

Austin was smiling in amazement as her brother hooked

an arm around his neck playfully, reminding her of their arrival and Firefly's greeting… as her sister swatted her brother Gary on the arm, immediately releasing Austin, who was right there in the thick of it.

Her mother had welcomed in her 'lost stray'… her family was enveloping and indoctrinating him into their group – and her very own fairytale was unfolding so magically before her very eyes.

She was home… and Austin was too.

CHAPTER 23

AUSTIN

Hours later, they were all sitting around the table with aching stomachs from the massive feast her mother had made to welcome them home, cutting up laughing and talking with such ease. Her sister had left to take her husband a Tupperware bowl of food for dinner at the hospital where he worked, her brother left to meet his wife and the kids for ice skating practice for his twin daughters, and slowly – one by one – they started to leave the house for the evening, leaving them there.

Austin sat back in his chair, his arm around her chair back, listening and talking as if he had been born into this world, she was blessed to be a part of...

"So did you surprise my daughter?" her father said, pointing at the ring.

"She surprises me all the time, sir."

"I told you to call me Max..." her father ordered, reaching

over and ruffling Austin's tousled hair once more. He always had done that to the boys and tugged the girls' braids or pigtails when they were younger. It was a show of affection that touched her heart.

"It might take me a moment to get used to that... Max," Austin smiled at her father, before her father turned to look at her.

"Were you expecting him to pop the question?"

"Oh no," she chuckled openly, glancing at Austin shyly. "It's been so wonderful being friends and talking to each other, that it completely blindsided me."

"We'll need to start looking at venues, dresses, and..." her mother began, and Giselle stiffened slightly, looking at her mom nervously.

"Actually, Mom?" she began and glanced at Austin, "This is all so new and unexpected, we really haven't had a chance to talk about plans or details. I mean, this *just* happened."

"What do you want?" Austin asked her softly, touching the back of her neck tenderly. "For me, it's easy. Whatever we do – I just show up, wear my dress uniform, and enjoy the moment."

"I want something like that," she admitted. "I just assumed that I would wear my dress uniform because it's a part of who I am... and I like easy, you know? I want to enjoy the moment too, without all the stresses or worries."

"Then it sounds like we both know what we want," he began, smiling at her as she glanced at him, before looking at her parents.

"I'm not trying to be difficult, it's just we are all spread out so far," she began. "My coworkers and acquaintances are in Ghazni – just like you. You've got friends in Yonder. My oldest brother is stationed goodness-knows-where this year... Mom, where *is* Gideon stationed now?"

"Fort Bragg, honey."

"How long of an engagement are you wanting to have?" her father asked the two of them, causing Giselle and Austin to share a glance.

"Again, this just happened, and we need to figure out some things…"

"Giselle," Austin began quietly, and she looked at him over her shoulder. "We're here," he paused, glancing at her parents, "I don't want to rush you or press you, but I'm pretty sure your parents would want to be a part of your moment…"

"What are you saying?"

"What if we got married here, had a reception back in Yonder, and then we could see if there was some way to celebrate with our teams back home in Ghazni," Austin suggested gently.

"I knew I liked you… son," her father said, mussing Austin's hair again, while her mother looked at her, smiling tearfully.

This was more than she could have ever hoped for or anticipated – to have every imaginable chance, including almost everyone they cared about, and at the end of it all? She would still be at Austin's side – no matter what.

"We can do whatever you want, and if you'd prefer a long engagement, then maybe we can travel back here later this year or…"

"No," she interrupted firmly – and you could have heard a pin drop. Austin's hand froze its ministrations on the back of her neck immediately as he pulled it away… and she turned to him, not looking at her parents.

"I don't want to wait any longer or have that stupid fence between us again," she breathed softly, looking into his warm eyes. "I want to grab at happiness, take our chances, and hammer out our dreams one step at a time. Do you want a church wedding with all the bells and whistles –

because I don't? I just want our story to have a happily ever after."

"Every time you smile at me, it does," he assured her, leaning forward and kissing her tenderly in front of her parents. "Tomorrow then, my love – or the day after?"

"Did you bring your dress uniform?"

"I did – did you?"

"Yes. You never know when you need something proper or nice to wear."

"This is true," he smiled softly. "Tomorrow?"

"Yes," she said hoarsely, touching his cheek. "Meet you at the fence?"

"Dinner and drinks, babe."

They both laughed softly, pressing their foreheads together in this sweetly stolen moment of wonder surrounding them. He had proposed only hours ago, and they were jumping in with both feet, together.

"You are...? Max? Is our baby getting married... *tomorrow?*"

"Sounds like I should steam my suit tonight."

"I need to call your brothers and sisters," her mother spurted nervously, her hands trembling as she touched her hair. "I need to roll my hair, and you should have some champagne on your wedding day."

"I can ask Greg to bring some over..."

"Get Georgia or Gemma to pick up a little cake..."

"We need balloons and maybe we should..." her mother fluttered happily, her eyes glistening as Giselle looked at her happily when Austin kissed her on the temple sweetly.

"Mom – we just want you there. I don't need anything big or fancy. We just want the memories and maybe some photographs to start our own hallway collection someday," she said, looking at Austin – who smiled at her knowingly.

"You never know," he said softly. "It could start any day... or perhaps in July?"

"Maybe," she acknowledged, knowing they probably needed to talk away from her parents, so they had privacy.

So much had happened today, so many reveals, twists and turns, that she just wanted to have a few minutes to share with him alone – to savor these moments, she realized as it dawned on her that she really hadn't even looked at her ring much or studied it.

Glancing at her hand, she saw the classic engagement ring and smiled. A thin gold circle surrounded her finger, almost as if it was meant to be there, while a round diamond sat perched on top.

There was no brashness, no 'flair' or ornamentation, which suited her perfectly. She wanted a symbol, not a flashing neon light, that would garner unwanted attention. This was their moment, their relationship... and it was perfect.

"Do you like it?" he asked softly, tucking a lock of hair behind her ear. "We really didn't get time to talk, and I know it was a surprise..."

"I love it – and it's lovely. I just don't know when you had time to get it unless..." her mouth dropped open in shock as she stared at him. "Did you bring it from the base?"

"No," he said nervously, smiling shyly. "I bought it at the jewelers the other evening when I went out with the guys. I was standing there, talking with X-Ray while Firefly was holding Betsy in his lap for her earrings... and found something that made me think of you – just like your earrings. It was perfect."

Her father interrupted them, getting to his feet and smiling warmly.

"It sounds like we all have a very busy day tomorrow – and we are really glad to have you both here. Giselle, your

Austin is a fine young man, and we are both very happy for you."

"If you two need anything, just knock on our door. Get some rest and try to sleep. You've had quite a busy last few days and before you know it, you'll be heading home once more," Her mother said, unknowing that was a sore spot with the two of them, as she got up and walked over, kissing them both on the forehead. "Sweet dreams."

"Goodnight, Mrs. Beck," Austin said dutifully and saw her frown at him, causing him to laugh. "I mean, Gigi…"

"That's better," she smiled happily at Giselle. "'Night honey."

"'Night, Mama… goodnight, Daddy."

She watched as her parents walked off and rose to her feet – only to have Austin move in time around her. He turned off the kitchen lights as she turned off the lamp in the living room, before meeting her at the hallway.

"Are you okay with tomorrow?"

"I'm thrilled with the idea of you becoming my wife so quickly," he admitted. "I'm not a very patient guy and never have been, so this absolutely works right into my nefarious plans to have my wicked way with you…"

He smiled playfully, wagging his eyebrows at her, and chuckling softly as she 'shushed' him nervously, laughing with him. He took her hand in his, pulling her towards the room where he'd dropped both of their bags and sat down on the bed.

"Let's talk for a few," he offered – and that touched her.

Austin wanted to know how she was feeling, to talk about whatever was on her mind, and just reconnect the two of them without having anyone point out flaws, question them, or plant the seeds of doubt.

She could do that all on her own.

"Okay," she said gingerly, sitting down facing him. "What

did you want to talk about? I'm really delighted right now and…"

"I just wanted to make sure of that," he admitted. "We've barely had any time alone, and I wanted to touch base with my favorite person in the entire universe."

She smiled softly at him.

"I'm very happy… and Giselle Calder sounds rather nice, doesn't it?"

"It sounds like perfection," he whispered emotionally, looking at her. "I don't want you to be nervous, frightened, regret any of this, or decide this isn't for you… and well, I just wanted…"

She interrupted him immediately.

"Austin," she said tenderly, reaching up to touch his face as she looked at him. "I want this with everything in me – and I don't plan on going anywhere or leaving you alone ever again. Okay? Don't be scared to open up to me, because I'm here… and we are wonderful."

"It's just hard," he breathed, looking away. "I can handle all those moments from my past, hearing the phone calls saying that they didn't want me there and needed child services to pick me up, or the rejection in their faces just before my ride arrived…" he swallowed hard, sitting there so still it broke her heart.

"Seeing that would destroy me, if you ever got sick of me. I just need to be sure. Call it self-preservation, fear, desperation, or lack of confidence… I just want things to be right for you so you don't regret any of this – or choosing me."

Tears stung her eyes as she looked at him.

"Oh Austin," she began painfully, her heart shattering for the sweet man before her. "I would choose you a thousand times over… and I'm thrilled to become your wife tomorrow. If there is ever something wrong, or something feels off, if I'm scared? I assure you – you will be the person I look to for help, support, and everything I could ever need to keep me going."

"So we're good?" he whispered insecurely, looking at her sideways from where he'd turned away, reaching for her hand.

"We are amazing," she smiled tearfully.

"What are we going to do about July?" he asked softly. "Do you want to look at a different location? I don't want to risk us trying to find a home somewhere and with there being no base housing…"

"Let's see what orders come up – and maybe we make a change?"

"It's something we can decide together."

"As a family," she acknowledged, clasping his hand tightly. "I love you."

"I love you too – and I will always be there for you."

"Good, because I'll probably be a mess tomorrow during the ceremony," she admitted and saw him smile.

"Now, I might not be such good help… because I'll be a mess, too."

"Maybe we can cry on each other's shoulders?"

"Dress uniform, Sarge… Jackets come off first."

"True 'dat," she laughed, winking at him. "They are a bear to clean and put back on all the ribbons."

"I know, right?!"

They both laughed softly, sitting there, holding hands as she smiled at him. "I love having these moments with you – and I think that we should always take time to talk in the evenings when we can."

"That would mean a lot to me."

Austin stood up regretfully and gave her a small smile.

"And I'm going to do the right thing, letting you rest and respecting your father's requests… even though everything in me just wants to hold you close," he admitted. "I'll be in the next room in case you can't resist me."

"Oh, yeah?" she chuckled, smiling at him as he winked.

"I'll be helpless…"

"I don't think there is a 'helpless' bone in your body, flyboy…"

"I'll be all alone… scared… and vulnerable…"

"Austin…"

"Poor me…" he said dramatically, giving her a lopsided grin. "You don't have to be so strong-willed, you know. I'll still love you if you can't resist me. Trust me – I'll manage somehow."

Her cheeks were hurting from the smiles that just would not stop as she gazed at him, realizing that her life would never be boring and always full of moments like this.

"Nothing? No, *'Please Austin don't go'*… nothing?"

"I'll manage," she replied saucily, using his own words – only to see him roll his eyes.

"Fine. I get it. You don't need me, I suppose…"

"We should sleep because tomorrow is going to be a very big day."

"I'm going," he conceded after a moment. "Goodnight – and I'll leave my door unlocked … just in case."

He hefted up the bag and left the room, before looking back at her, and then leaving it again.

"I'm just over here…" he called out in a loud whisper.

"I know," she replied, fighting back a laugh. "Goodnight."

Giselle grabbed her things and disappeared into the bathroom to brush her teeth, wash her face, and get ready for bed. As she donned a pajama, she opened the door and darted back to her room, shutting the door and half expecting to see him sprawled all over her bed… and he wasn't.

She was alone.

Sitting down on the edge of her childhood twin bed, she held her hand and admired her ring once more, touched and beyond happy to be marrying such an incredible person. He was everything she could have hoped for in her very own Prince Charming — complete with ketchup and a wooden spoon.

… And that was when an idea struck her.

CHAPTER 24

AUSTIN

AUSTIN WAS up at the crack of dawn and already in his dress uniform, drinking a cup of coffee while putting his thoughts down on paper what he wanted to say during their vows. He'd started the coffee before the house ever started stirring – and managed to slip the paperwork into his pocket just before Max, her father, walked in.

"You're up early, son," Max began, pouring a cup of the strong coffee for himself. "Couldn't sleep?"

"No, sir."

"Max," he reminded Austin again, smiling in silent under-standing. "You are doing better than me when I was getting married to Gigi."

"Oh?" Austin asked immediately, hearing the man laugh softly to himself as he sat down to join him.

"I was a mess," Max admitted. "Scared, intimidated, a little alarmed, because I didn't want to let her down. I mean, I was a twenty-one-year-old idiot that was stationed in Fort Bliss

231

when I met her there. Gigi is originally from El Paso, and she just swept into my world like a tornado."

Austin listened, fascinated, remaining silent because he wasn't sure if he could speak at this moment. He didn't have anyone sharing their memories with him, only having his own to cling to and they weren't worth really reliving... but this man was savoring them, and it was clear to see.

"She told me that we were getting married and I went along with it, because I'd never seen a prettier woman in my life... and I was a twenty-one-year-old man," Max admitted, winking at Austin, who laughed nervously.

"... But there was a light in her that just drew me in and we never looked back," Max smiled, looking at his coffee mug. "She's my best friend, keeps me in line, and has given me eight beautiful versions of us. I see her smile on my son's face. Gemma has her laugh, Georgia has her gusto for life... and my precious Giselle has her soulful eyes."

Max cleared his throat and looked at Austin, his eyes shiny.

"And I know you understand what I'm saying, because I see it in your face when you think no one is watching you. You look at Giselle like that impulsive young man looked at his wild bride nearly thirty-five years ago... and I'm glad," Max admitted.

"She's my best friend and I love her."

Both men stopped when they heard a noise in the distance. Austin hesitated as he realized it was Giselle moving around in the background.

"Excuse me just a second..." he apologized, smiling shyly as her father winked at him knowingly.

"Go ahead, son. I'm going to put the biscuits in the oven."

Hurrying, he poured her a cup of coffee and knocked on the bathroom door gently – only to see her jerk it open in a rush. He couldn't resist the smile that touched his lips as he saw her look of surprise, confusion, and then utter horror as she stood there... and immediately tried to slam the door shut.

She was so dang cute in the mornings, he mused, holding up the cup of coffee. Her hair was mussed, and she had a pink crease on her cheek from where she slept on the pillow. A toothbrush was hanging out of her mouth from where she was brushing her teeth already... and her pajama top was askew and halfway tucked into her pajama buttons.

... This was going to be his wife.

His heart nearly burst with the joy and understanding that he was going to get to experience this side of her, this raw reality and perfect imperfections, so many times over the years... and she had never looked more beautiful to him than she did right now at her most vulnerable.

"Good morning, Gorgeous – I'm looking for my blushing bride and thought she might want to start the day with a cup of coffee?" he asked tenderly.

"So you're farsighted, huh?" she said flatly, right after spitting in the sink and trying to calm her hair down, frowning. "I look a mess and seriously need to shower. This," she continued, pointing at her face and hair, "is gonna take some serious work to be presentable."

"Take your time, my love," he smiled and leaned forward to kiss her cheek, before setting down the cup of coffee. "I just couldn't wait to tell you good morning and wanted to surprise you."

"I'm surprised, alright..." she grumbled and looked at him, "and not much of a morning person."

Giselle looked at him then and he felt his chest swell up with pride as her expressive face told him that she liked him in uniform... and he couldn't wait to see her in hers.

"I clean up alright."

"You look... incredible," she admitted. "Wow."

"Get ready," he smiled, happily, needing to step back before he pushed his way into the bathroom and offered to wash her back in the shower.

He was a guest in their house and would need to be on his best behavior, but knowing that the woman he loved thought he looked handsome and was standing there in just her pajamas… well, it was certainly tempting to break a few rules.

No, he could wait… because he would wait forever for his paladin, princess, and partner.

"Enjoy your coffee, take your time getting ready, and I'll see you soon," he offered, stepping back and giving her a salute that caused her to smile as she shut the bathroom door… but not before he heard her breathy sigh of happiness.

Gosh, he loved that woman!

THE MORNING FLEW by for Austin and every time he felt a momentary twinge of nervousness or anxiety, he would see Giselle's smile or feel her touch his hand. It was like she just understood how nerve-wracking this was for him.

That scared boy that had once been rejected and abandoned so many times over the years was shaking in his boots, afraid that this might be the time that truly broke him.

If Giselle ever got sick of him, was done with their relationship, or decided to move on… there would be no recovering from that heartache. He was all in, no matter how hard he tried to hold back at times, and understood Max's words this morning in a way he never imagined.

That light drew him in uncontrollably… and he wanted to bask in her smile. Whether they were standing at the fence, sweaty from their runs? Or dancing awkwardly on the airstrip in the darkness, just because he wanted to hold her close. Breathing in that essence that was Giselle, was everything to him.

… And now, Giselle was standing at his side at the courthouse, looking so beautiful before him.

Her dress uniform felt so strange yet almost surreal compared to his own blue one. She was dressed in drab greens and tans of the Army, in a fitted jacket that nearly matched his – except it was belted. Her arms proudly displayed chevrons, patches, and other insignia that gave her rank.

Giselle's hair was pulled back in a bun low on her head, as was regulation, with a woman's garrison cap angled on her head. Everything about her looked perfect. The only stray from her military ensemble was the bouquet of red roses that she held in her hands from her sister, Gemma, that saw them married this morning.

"Beck and Calder wedding party?" a voice called out, and they shot to their feet almost in unison, causing him to look at her, seeing that precious smile as she looked at him.

They took their places in front of the magistrate and Austin reached for her hands immediately, only for them to hesitate as Giselle looked for a place to set down her bouquet… opting for a nearby table.

"Sorry," she whispered anxiously – and he smiled.

She was just as nervous as he was.

Listening absently, he couldn't help but admire this woman before him and hoped he could make it through the ceremony without completely breaking down or making a fool of himself. Glancing around, he saw a box of Kleenex on the table where Giselle's flowers lay and felt eyes on him.

Giselle was looking at him curiously – and angled her head at the magistrate.

"I'm sorry, what?" he asked sheepishly, feeling like a heel.

"I asked if you took this woman for your bride, Mr. Calder," the magistrate asked, smirking knowingly.

"Oh I absolutely do, sir – but I wanted to say something too," Austin began and dug in his jacket pocket immediately.

He hadn't even realized that they were saying their vows now and pretty much missed it, but that was just a formality... these words were from his heart, he thought emotionally, looking at Giselle and saw her brilliant smile.

"Giselle," he began nervously, clearing his throat and felt it getting thick with emotion already, his hands trembling as he began to read.

"Once upon a time, long, long ago...," he started and chanced at glance at her, only to see her beautiful eyes widen with recognition as her hand fluttered up to her face, covering her mouth emotionally as a tear streaked down her cheek, knowing that she recognized their story.

"There was a handsome knight, and a frustrated but breathtakingly beautiful paladin with infinite patience, who put up with the devilish rascal - because it made them both incredibly happy to take five minutes a day to see each other, share brief messages, and snack on unexpected delights in the moonlight," Austin paused, smiling at her knowingly as she moved her hand from her face, revealing that joyous smile that captivated him.

"But what that knight didn't know was the paladin yearned for what she could not have, searching the world over for a treasure few would discover... What a journey it would be, especially if they traveled together, pairing their skills and attributes that made each of them special."

He sniffed and felt tears burning in his eyes as the paper before him blurred wildly as he tried to hold back.

"Though she was scared, the paladin was intrigued – wanting to know more... and the valiant knight vowed to sweep her away to a foreign land – far, far away," he glanced at Max and Gigi sitting in the front row, holding each other close and saw Giselle's father nod at him proudly.

"She took his hand, feeling more alive and happier than ever before. That knight wasn't stupid - he grabbed her hand, smiled at her, and whispered, *'Baby, let's run away together and never look back...'* "

Austin paused, smiling at her.

"I had to add a bit more," he explained, seeing her chuckle tearfully and nod at him. "That beautiful paladin, laced their fingers together, holding fast to this miracle before her, and whispered, 'I'm ready when you are...'" his voice cracked as he looked at her tearfully, folding the paper he had kept close to his heart for the entire day, hiding it.

"Our story of how we met is a beautiful mix of where we were both at when falling in love, but nothing prepared me for this moment. I'm staring at my paladin and partner, standing at the brink of forever, and beyond blessed to have met you, Giselle," he breathed shakily and wiped his eyes, clearing his throat again and trying not to cry as he looked at her.

"I cannot think of a more beautiful soul to share my life with and experience the rest of that prose that is just waiting to be written... knowing that someday, we can pass down our beautiful beginnings to our children someday. I love you more than you will ever know," he whispered tenderly and kissed her hand where he'd just placed a thin gold band on her finger, resting it against the engagement ring.

"I absolutely, one thousand times over, emphatically say 'I do'... repeatedly," he uttered proudly.

Giselle squeezed his hands, laughing tearfully, and nodded happily as she spoke to him directly – not even waiting for the magistrate to speak. She was amazing in so many ways and he loved her spark, her flare for life... and would never look back from this moment.

"Austin, the day I sent that first email? I was hooked. There was such a playfulness, such a delightful persona that came out with every word that was written... and you drew me out of my frightened shell, bit by bit, step by step," she smiled at him.

"Dinner and drinks?"

"Yeah," she chuckled, nodding. "Every time I thought you couldn't get more perfect? You would surprise me. I would see you standing on the horizon, my eyes searching for you so many times, hoping and wondering if you would notice me... and you did."

She drew in a shaky breath as he remembered those moments that they first met. The fascination had been over-whelming, the anticipation thrilling, and the love... encompassing.

"You amaze me in so many ways and just when I think I couldn't be surprised more, there is another facet in the diamond that is you. You are more incredible, more rare, more beautiful than all the treasures in the world... and you are mine," she said strongly, making him feel so humbled to be there, taking her as his wife.

"I want to live our story, hold your hand during the trials and celebrate the victories in our lives together. I want to turn to you knowing that my soulmate is waiting to hold me, comfort me, or love me... and I, Giselle Amanda Beck, do most heartily take you, Austin Elijah Calder, as my husband."

Austin gazed at Giselle, as she took the matching gold band that he'd given her earlier that morning and slid it onto his trembling hand, where it came to rest on his finger, silently vowing to never remove it.

He let out a shaky sigh of relief as he listened to the magistrate finally pronounce them husband and wife. They stood there for a brief moment, just waiting, before he stepped forward and pulled her into his arms.

"I love you so much," he whispered, just before kissing her.

THAT AFTERNOON AND EVENING, Austin could not take his eyes from Giselle. Her parents had thrown together an impromptu party for them all that seemed so strangely perfect. Instead of having some fancy meal or majestic wedding cake? They decided to go with his bride's favorites, which suited him perfectly fine.

They had Whataburgers, onion rings, and spicy ketchup... and for dessert? Warm pecan pie with a scoop of vanilla ice cream.

He didn't have the heart to tell her that the wedding cake tradition was already being handled. They would be celebrating once again in Yonder when they landed.

It was meant to be a surprise.

Austin wanted Giselle to celebrate and love every moment with her family... before they could do it all again with his makeshift one.

They took photographs together – and he felt like he truly belonged, the sensation nearly bringing him to his knees. There were photos of him kissing Giselle, others of just the men of the family... including him. There were photographs of the women together, candid shots taken of people laughing, and others where he tried to sneak a kiss only to hear a faint giggle from his bride's sister, Gemma.

Greg had brought several bottles of bubbly for them to make toasts and the man had several quips that were lost on Austin, because he hadn't been there among the siblings... but didn't care.

It made Giselle laugh, and that was all that mattered.

Her happiness was first in his heart, his reason for living.

CHAPTER 25

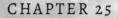

GISELLE

SHE WAS TIPSY... and nervous.

Today was such a beautiful day, married to the man she loved more than life itself with a joy just seemed to go on and on. She had never laughed or smiled so much, felt so wonderful, or so aware of that silently ticking clock in the back of her mind.

The days were passing much too fast.

Even now, as she glanced at the clock on the wall, she was shocked to see it was almost midnight when the last of her siblings had left the house... and her parents disappeared to go to bed, leaving her there with Austin.

Her new husband.

If life had been normal, if this had been an elaborate wedding – they would have gotten into a limo or a car, driven off into the sunset, to go to some honeymoon or exotic destination in order to be alone.

Except she was here... at home.

There was no veil, no groom's cake, no dancing… and the music was fun, upbeat music that they were all singing or playing around to while in the midst of talking, hanging out, and simply spending time together. It was lovely, fun, and she wouldn't change it… but it certainly didn't set the mood for a romantic honeymoon.

No, she was feeling a little out of place, knowing that her parents were on the opposite side of the house – and her new husband was standing before her.

… And if by magic?

Austin smiled, picked up two empty champagne flutes, and the bottle they'd just opened about twenty minutes ago.

"C'mon," he invited, walking down the hallway towards her room – and the temperature in the house just surged to a thousand as her face flushed in awareness. She had removed her jacket and tie earlier in the afternoon to keep from getting anything on it… and was grateful she had because it was probably the only thing keeping her from fainting.

"Are you hot in here? I'm burning up," she asked nervously. "Maybe I should open a window or something. It's only thirty-eight degrees outside, right? That should help things and…"

"Giselle?"

"Yeah?"

"Sit down, honey. You are nervous and making me feel anxious. Let's just talk for a bit."

"Talk? Okay. I can definitely talk. We can talk about anything. What do you want to talk about? Maybe we should talk about… talking – you know? Like pronunciations, dialects, and different languages? I used to know Spanish when I was in high school and… I think I will stop now," she finished lamely as she sat down, perching on the edge of the bed, and grimaced. "I'm really nervous."

"I can tell," he smiled tenderly, handing her one of the

champagne flutes and got up from his seat. She took a sip of it, only to see him shutting the door to the bedroom and moving her childhood desk chair under the handle – to block it.

She sprayed bubbly all over her Army dress jacket that was hanging on a hanger from the hat rack on the wall and began coughing as the fluid went down the wrong way. She hoped it dried clear because she wasn't sure if she had enough time to get it dry-cleaned before leaving… and there certainly wasn't one in Ghazni.

He immediately began patting her on the back as she waved him off, struggling to catch her breath.

"I'm… fine…" she croaked out, and he took a seat opposite of her. He was sitting sideways on the bed, one leg on and one leg off, watching her.

"You know," he began and stood up, holding out his hand to her. "One of my favorite moments that we shared was when we were splitting that cream soda and the gummy worms," he smiled… and then leaned forward to take her hand, pulling her to her feet.

He stood there, holding her hand, looking at it and turning it over in his, before looking up at her.

"I cannot tell you how much it made me smile to see you trying to hang onto the gummy worms while trying to squeeze this little delicate hand back through the chain-link fence," he chuckled. "Hands are such amazing things… don't you think?"

"Hands? No, why?"

"Just look at them," he began, holding out her hand and putting his next to it. "So similar, yet so different. They are tools that we use to function, made up of so many tiny bones, tendons, and joints… but there is so much more to them, too."

"I guess I didn't think about that," she whispered as he slowly slid his palm against hers, making her shiver.

"They hold glasses, needles, apply bandages, and feed us – but the list goes on and on," he breathed, trailing his fingers against hers. "Hands can bring joy, comfort, and hurt – but can also soothe that same hurt, too."

Her breath held as he turned over her palm and traced a line on her hand.

"Years ago, people used to tell fortunes, make blood oaths, wave hello in greeting or shake each other's hands," he began, and hesitated. "They are also incredibly tactile and sensory. Close your eyes."

She did so, fascinated by the way his mind worked.

"You can feel cold and wet," he whispered, pressing her fingertips to the side of the bottle. "Warmth, softness," he continued, her hand rubbing against the VELUX blanket on her bed, "And roughness."

Her hand touched his cheek where she felt stubble.

"Keep your eyes closed," he invited softly, and she nodded silently.

"Hands are miracles and extensions of the mind, soul, and body," he continued. "They can trace outlines," he breathed, drawing a finger from her palm up her arm, making her shiver as he chuckled. "They can give you goosebumps, too."

"You're tickling me," she smiled, keeping her eyes closed as she stood there waiting for him to keep going, fascinated.

"See?" he chuckled softly. "They can tickle, scratch, or…"

"Or?"

"Or stir the beginnings of something more," he whispered, kissing her fingertips slowly, before kissing her palm, and then her wrist as she caught her breath in awareness.

"They can show love," he promised tenderly, "transfer emotions from one person to the next, and…"

"And?" she asked hoarsely, her mind, heart, and soul thrumming with anticipation of what he would say next.

"They can create desire between a paladin and a lowly knight who is completely under her spell," he confessed lovingly as she opened her eyes slowly to see him before her.

Neither said a word as he slowly pulled her to him, and moved to kiss her before pausing. He nuzzled her cheek tenderly, his lips so close that it made her heart stagger.

"You are the queen of my heart... and there will never be another so long as I draw breath, Giselle. You are everything to me. My happiness, my comfort, my joy, and my very life," he promised, placing her hand on his shoulder. "Let me show you what you mean to me... my precious bride."

His lips finally met hers.

CHAPTER 26

GISELLE
Two days later...
Yonder, Texas

As the Cessna touched down, she shared an intimate and knowing smile with Austin, knowing what the next day and a half would be like. There would be no peace of mind, no solitude, surrounded by their friends... and stealing moments together where they could before they were on a plane back to Ghazni.

Just being here, sharing this part of his life with him, was more than she could have asked for – and she didn't want him to ever think she was ungrateful...

She just wanted to make sure they could spend some time alone too – especially before they couldn't.

"I have a surprise for you," he admitted shyly, his eyes searching hers.

"Does this involve another dissertation of the miracle of

hands?" she teased playfully, unbuckling and leaning over to kiss him.

Austin immediately grabbed hold of her, making her yelp in surprise for a moment as the plane was still taxiing to a stop on the short airstrip as he pulled her across his lap bodily. He cut the engine, pulled her against him, swooping forward and kissing her passionately as she clung to him.

They were both lost in that stolen kiss.

"Sparky," the headphones crackled, causing them to slowly open their eyes and look at each other, sharing another smile of awareness, before he kissed her again.

"I know you hear me, cause the Cessna is right in front of Harley's office and I saw you come up for air, bro," Houdini announced in the mic. "Taxi down to the hanger and tie her down – the plane, not your wife – and let's get going. Everyone is waiting for us."

Giselle pulled back and looked at Austin.

"What does he mean *'everyone is waiting for us'*?"

"That's the comment you got stuck on?" he laughed softly. "My brain stumbled, tripped, and belly-flopped *hard* on the 'tie her down' comment…"

She laughed and swatted at him, blushing wildly, as she moved back to the bench seat… seeing him laughing happily next to her.

"I seriously love you," he grinned.

"I love you too – but I also noticed you didn't answer my question," she replied knowingly as the plane coasted forward, looking at the window to see Houdini waving silently. She waved back and turned back to Austin.

"It's part of the surprise," he smiled, cutting the engines once more as he opened the door. "Wait here, Beautiful…" He climbed out and tied down the plane before opening her door, offering his hand.

She awkwardly made her way down and laughed merrily

as Austin pretended to catch her simply so he could pull her against him and manhandle her playfully for a moment. He grinned impishly as she swatted his hand away, only to see Houdini walking up towards them – also laughing because he'd seen her husband's not-so-slick moves.

"Stop that," she hissed, laughing.

"Later?" he said pertly, perking up happily, and she didn't answer him – only to hear his husky, supremely masculine voice behind her answer his own question. "Ohhhh yeah, later it's definitely on…"

She turned to look at him, smirking, and winked… causing him to fist pump the air in happiness.

"I don't want to know – do I?" Houdini said openly, extending his hand to her. "Congratulations, Mrs. Sarge…"

Giselle laughed aloud at the affectionate term as he greeted Austin not a second later. "Sup, Spark-N-Roll… you ready?"

"I was born ready!"

"What are you two up to?" Giselle asked, shaking her head and smiling. "Should we get our bags out of the plane?"

"I'll get it," Austin called out, jogging back, as Giselle turned to Houdini immediately.

"What's going on?"

"I'm not telling you because it will ruin your husband's surprise," he said openly. "But I can tell you it's sweet, and he's a good man."

"I know that…"

"Then relax and just go with it."

FIFTEEN MINUTES LATER, she was staring in shock at the two men sitting in the front seat of the car, who had their heads turned to see her reaction. She couldn't believe any of this as people literally swarmed the vehicle, and she was being pulled from the car quickly by a flurry of hands.

"Hands up," Harley ordered... and a mass of tulle and satin encapsulated Giselle, just before sticking her limbs out of the arms of a very loose dress.

... A wedding dress.

"What is going on? Whose is this?"

"Someone get Sparky inside..."

"Who has the veil?"

"Who has the sash?"

"Bouquet?! I saw it a second ago..."

"Garter?"

"Lucky penny?! I need the lucky penny, people!"

"Sophie, do you have a little hanky-panky for our newbie?"

"You know I do..."

"What is..."

"SHHHH!" Glory pressed and looked at Delilah. "Didn't you have the makeup?"

"My makeup – and considering I woke up with a zit on my forehead at thirty-three years old? I didn't figure she would want to wear my stuff."

"Whoa... whoa... WHOAAA..." Giselle said loudly, putting out her hands and staring at the seven women surrounding her. "Hi?! What is going on?"

"We missed your wedding," Melody smiled at Marisol, before turning back to Giselle. "Soooo? We decided to throw together a mock-one, Flyboys style."

"*Redneck...* redneck style," Meredith coughed under her breath, causing Harley to laugh easily and nod at her friend.

"A... wedding?" Giselle repeated, stunned, as she looked at the satin dress on her where her combat boots stuck out from underneath. The satin skirt was too short and stopped at her ankles. No one could zip the back because while the dress was short in stature, it was also exceedingly tiny in the waist and didn't fit.

"Whose dress is this?"

"I picked it up at a yard sale and Meredith had the brilliant idea to donate it for Angel Gowns."

"I always pick them up if I see them," Meredith admitted quietly. "Yard sales, Goodwill, wherever I spot one – I buy it. They gave me an Angel Gown for my first son, Aaron, and never looked back. This will make number thirty-five that I've donated over the years… so try not to get it stained for me – please?"

"Her first child was stillborn. People donate wedding gowns and burial gowns are made for infants with them, giving them to the grieving mothers," Glory whispered – and Giselle's eyes widened as she looked at Meredith to the wedding gown on her and back, nodding immediately.

"I had no idea," she admitted softly.

"We all look for them now and just give them to Meredith. She likes to give back, so if you spot one? Grab it. Now, are we going inside or what?"

"Let's go!"

Two sets of hands grabbed her arms while another set pushed her from behind, causing her to laugh in amusement… this was not a problem in the slightest and she was touched by how sweet this all was.

As they entered the small shop that said '*Dixie's Café*' – she realized it was actually a bakery, smelling the sugary sweetness almost immediately just before she spotted Austin.

… Standing next to a three-tiered wedding cake with tan, blue, and yellow roses, with Army green leaves on it. It was strangely perfect. No, she never imagined her cake to have pink roses, but to see the Army and Air Force colors combined was a little… chaotic.

"Hit me!" Austin called out – and Firefly threw him a

wooden spoon as someone turned on the music. Her husband began singing to the tune of Journey's *'Don't Stop Believin'*... but with very, *very* modified lyrics.

> *Just an Army girl,*
> *Livin' in a lonely world,*
> *She took the plane going anywhere...*
> *Just a poor Flyboy...*
> *Born and raised in Arkansas...*
> *He took the plane going anywhere.*
> *A singer in a bakery room,*
> *The smell of sweets, margaritas, and cheap*
>   *perfume...*

"Oh gosh, this is utterly terrible," Firefly muttered openly causing Alpo, Thumper, and Romeo to laugh easily... as they grabbed wooden spoons too.

Her heart was beating wildly in disbelief that this was an actual party, a reception, to celebrate their marriage. Her 'cup' was overflowing with happiness, as the guys all started belting out the actual lyrics, which sounded so much better.

She clapped her hands together, holding them over her heart, as she stood there in a too tight wedding dress, watching the 'wedding party' serenade her badly among their friends.

Austin walked over, grabbed her around the waist and spun her around for a moment, singing to her...

"Never stop believing in our fairytale," he smiled, just before he dipped her slightly. "Even when I fly back, believe in this magic, because I am never giving this up... and we'll figure it out."

"I believe you," she smiled lovingly.

"Good," he said simply. "Wanna cut the cake, Sexy?"

"Heck yeah, I do!" she smiled.

While she loved the moments she shared on her wedding day with her family, this was just as wonderful and yet supremely different. The guys were dancing, acting up, and having a great time. The children were enjoying their snacks and occasionally you would see a finger covered in frosting where one of them had mauled the first layer of wedding cake.

She had anticipated it would bother someone that the children were sticking their fingers in the frosting, but when she saw Austin kneel down near Betsy and Luke who were looking very unsure of themselves - and a little guilty – she found herself marveling at the man, she'd married once more.

He had a beautiful heart... and it showed. She wondered if someone had taken him aside when he was a boy, treating him tenderly at some point before he'd been in and out of foster homes.

She hoped so.

"Watch me," Austin said, conspiring with the two small children. "Take your finger and make it look like a candy cane, like this." He held up his index finger and curled it. "Now, it makes God's perfect little scooper for sneaking a treat... see?"

Austin stuck his finger along the base of the cake and scooped up a flower made of frosting, grinned at the children's amazed faces, and proceeded to teach them how to curl their fingers the 'right way' helping them pick at the wedding cake.

She glanced over to see Delilah and Armadillo smiling lovingly – and saw Firefly put his arm around Melody's shoulders, watching the scene, and smiling proudly at his best friend.

Thumper was standing beside Harley, holding their daughter. Alpo and Glory were seated beside each other, each holding a child in their laps, feeding them bottles as they sprawled casually across mommy and daddy with such adoration on their innocent faces.

They were a family just as much as her own – and it showed. They left no one out, caring for everyone, from the smallest babe… to the biggest Flyboy.

Austin looked up at her and whispered loudly to the children.

"Isn't she the prettiest bit of sweetness you've ever seen?" he said tenderly. "She is so special, just like these frosting flowers… Don't you agree?"

Betsy and Luke nodded with wide eyes, still looking disbelieving that they weren't getting in trouble for sneaking the cake.

"Austin? Do you think maybe we can have a few magical pixies help us cut the cake – all together?"

He smiled brilliantly at her – before looking at the children where he was kneeling.

"Did you hear that? My queen wants some help cutting the cake… Do you think you could help us?" he asked, sounding almost childlike.

Austin had so much love to give and just wanted to be a part of a home, a family, a world where he felt secure… that it was breathtakingly beautiful to behold.

She bit her lip realizing suddenly that he would be an incredible father someday to their children - and she couldn't wait. She could see this clearly in their future… and it was priceless.

Austin stood up, scooping Betsy up in his arms and holding out his hand to Luke as he met Giselle's eyes. A look passed between them, and she knew in that moment that this was the place that they were meant to be.

She wanted to be a part of this world, this family, with her own family close enough to reach. They could hop in a plane every weekend if he worked at Flyboys, and they built their lives together... which surprised her because she had always thought she would serve her time in the Army.

No more.

She was now imagining a much greater victory than one she ever anticipated... and even more thrilling.

Pulling up two folded chairs, Austin set Betsy down carefully and Luke scrambled up in the chair beside her. Both of them carefully 'spotted' the children to make sure they didn't fall.

"Okay team," Austin said quietly, his eyes scanning the room and grinning as he met their eyes watching them. Melody was filming on her phone while Delilah was taking photos.

I'm going to hang one in our hallway someday, she vowed silently.

"... Now, we have to take it slow and be careful because knives are dangerous – and it will take all four of us to cut the cake," Austin began, smiling at her. "Luke and Betsy, you put your hands there... and my love?" he said simply, taking her hand in his and placing it above the children's sticky fingers, smiling at her.

His own finger was stained with food coloring where he'd scooped up the blue rose. She began to chuckle, seeing it, and looking at his warm eyes that were crinkled at the corner as he smiled at her.

This was happiness... sharing this joy with others and Austin gave as much as he could, holding back nothing. Delilah came over quickly with the camera, zooming in on the four hands and taking a photograph quickly.

A moment later, Austin kissed her cheek, whispering 'I love you' as he pressed gently with her, and the knife began to cut into the cake. He slipped into his roll once again...

"Oh goodness, the cake is fighting us! We have to press harder team…"

"I pwessing!" Luke screeched emphatically and Betsy said something unintelligible to Giselle, seeing Austin shrug out of the corner of her eye, and began laughing again.

"Keep going… arrrghhh… it's fighting us, Luke," Austin egged on the children – only to have the children begin getting irate. Luke slapped at the cake with his other hand and Betsy did the same, not a second later.

"Oh no…" Firefly jumped forward as Armadillo did the same.

Things were escalating fast – and everyone was laughing now as the frosting was being knocked off. Thinking quickly, Giselle shoved the knife down with the children and Austin immediately chimed in.

"You did it! You won!"

She grabbed two red Solo cups, turned them over, and shoveled some mauled cake inside each, popping a spoon in each cup.

"For our mighty victors… thank you for helping us defeat the cake," Giselle smiled, giving each child a plastic cupful of cake.

They stared at her and smiled, just as both men scooped up their children, quickly getting them out of the way and letting them feast on the sugary gift from Dixie and Romeo.

Turning back to Austin, she uttered 'Whew' under her breath… as he hugged her easily and laughed, drawing her back into his arms as he leaned over her shoulder.

"Let's try this again… just us."

She angled her head, against his, touching their foreheads together and nuzzling his cheek.

"This is the best wedding and reception that a woman could ever have… and I am so lucky to have you at my side," she said tenderly.

"I hope you always think that," he murmured openly, kissing her.

"Alright… alright!" Alpo said, getting to his feet with his son propped in his arms. "Are ya' gonna cut the cake or not? Dixie makes a darn good wedding cake and we're ready for our slices, right Glory?"

"I'm on a diet, Hunter," Glory replied in a loud whisper.

"Why on Earth would you want to do *that*?" he said, looking aghast at his wife. "What am I supposed to hang onto? Besides, I love how soft you get and those…"

"Hunter – enough!" Harley said, slapping her forehead as Glory winked at her husband happily. "Nobody needs details from either of you. We get quite enough of that already."

"Two pieces of cake please," Glory said pertly and sighed. "I love him."

"That's right, babe," Hunter winked obnoxiously, causing several to laugh with him.

Austin smiled, kissing Giselle's cheek tenderly.

"I think I'm beyond ready to feed my bride some cake…"

"No shoving," Giselle cautioned only to see him wink as he smiled proudly, leaning close and whispering softly in her ear.

She burst out laughing and buried her face against his shoulder, shocked at the words that were coming out of his mouth, hoping no one else heard him.

"What?" he said innocently, laughing.

"Cake, then dancing…"

"You got it, my love," he smiled.

THAT NIGHT, when they were finally alone, lying in the bed cuddling at the bed and breakfast that belonged to Sophie and Reaper… Giselle broached the subject that had slammed into her mind, heart, and soul this afternoon.

"Austin?"

"Yeah, babe?"

"Can we talk for a few minutes about something?"

"Always…" he began, stroking her hair and kissing her forehead. "What's on your mind, sweetheart?"

"July," she hedged and felt him tense. "I think I want to come home and build a life here… in Yonder."

He sat up, his dog tags rattling noisily as he looked at her in surprise – and relief.

"I thought you'd want to go to Wichita Falls or…"

"I think I want to be here," she admitted. "I really feel like I am starting to fit in, and your family is here. We can see mine whenever we want and if we needed anything? Everyone is close and it feels… good," she finished lamely.

"Are you sure?"

"Very," she nodded looking at him. "Tonight, when I saw you talking to the children, I realized that I want our own to have friends around them and not just their cousins who are kinda obliged to love them, in my personal mind - but true friends to hang out with, play with, go to school with? I would like those bonds to continue to grow," she hesitated.

"Does any of that make sense or am I being silly? Family means a lot to me, and I don't want to choose one over the other, but take advantage of having both available to us, while building our own."

"You're sure," he asked hoarsely, his eyes sparkling as he looked at her.

"I've never been more certain of anything," she admitted. "The more I think about it, the more I love the idea. We could find a little place for us close by and maybe I can look at getting my nursing license… oooh," she perked up. "Maybe a paramedic or EMT? That would be exciting!"

He laughed, pulling her into his arms and kissing her tenderly.

"If I hadn't already fallen in love with you – this would certainly seal the deal, Mrs. Calder," he teased, holding her close. "I would love to build a life with you here, watch our children grow up with our friends, and visit Grandma Gigi and Grandpa Max on the weekends."

"So… July?"

"We're done," he said firmly and smiled. "Honestly, this is a relief because I wanted to come back the moment the guys talked to me about a job. I was just too scared to say anything because I didn't want to let you down."

"You are never going to let me down," she smiled up at him, touching his temple. It was amazing to think how such a big life-altering decision was made so easily, simply, because she felt supported by him. "Just love me and have my back when I need you."

"I'm there… always, Giselle," he promised.

CHAPTER 27

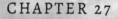

GISELLE
Ghazni, Afghanistan

THIS WAS PROBABLY the hardest thing Giselle had ever done.

Climbing into the back of the covered truck, donning her helmet and vest, while trying to act brave in front of the driver was hard. Austin was trying to help her fasten her vest, his eyes full of pain, as they took their seats... immediately clinging to each other's hands as they sat silently.

"All aboarrrd," Selkirk announced playfully over his shoulder. "Woo-wooooo..." as the truck lunged forward, the transmission going into gear on the massive vehicle.

Her heart was breaking because she knew they were about to be separated once again and the only thing keeping her from breaking down completely was the idea that it was for a limited time. They had to get through a few months and then they would be starting a home, a life, and reuniting once more.

"It's gonna be okay," Austin said softly, bringing her

wedding ring where it rested on her finger to his lips. "I promise."

"I know, but it doesn't mean that I have to like this."

"How about dinner and drinks tomorrow night, wife?" he teased gruffly, and she looked at him in the shadows of the truck, seeing his devastated expression, and knew he was hurting too.

"That sounds wonderful... husband."

"I would say tonight, but I'm pretty sure that I'm not going to get a second of privacy or peace once I walk in the barracks. Word travels fast and the guys are a bunch of gossips."

"... Not just the Zoomies," Selkirk announced – and Austin frowned heavily. "And congrats, you two."

They had an audience that was actively eavesdropping.

Giselle smiled ruefully and caressed Austin's cheek where he sat glaring over his shoulder at the man driving.

"Selkirk, can you pretend you aren't listening, buddy? The next time I have to dig shrapnel out of you or give you an IV, it might be a very dull needle..." she taunted, knowing that wouldn't be the case but enjoyed threatening the lively guy that she had helped a few times in the past.

"I see and hear nothing... but the road, Beck, ah... what's your new last name, Doc?" Selkirk said playfully.

"Calder," she smiled proudly at Austin, smoothing her thumb over his frowning lips, drawing his attention once more almost immediately. "I'm going to need to re-stencil everything or get new name badges embroidered."

"Leave it," Austin leaned forward, whispering in her ear with a hushed voice. "We aren't staying long enough for it to be an issue. We'll just file the paperwork but as for every- thing else? As slow as stuff takes to get here or get processed... I wouldn't worry."

"I'm proud of us... and I want people to know."

"I do too – and if we were staying, I'd say to change it. Five months is nothing in the grand scheme of things."

"True…"

"Now, if he's done listening," Austin said bluntly, glancing over his shoulder again, "We don't have long before we end up back on base."

Giselle immediately reached for him as he pulled her close, their helmets banged noisily together causing them to chuckle softly as the truck hit a pothole in the road. It was hard to kiss her husband because they kept getting jostled and bumped…

That kiss turned out to be them laughing softly, their lips touching occasionally, and their teeth bumping once.

She touched his face, cradling his cheek in her palm.

"I love you so much," she smiled tearfully as the truck slowed down, alerting them that they were arriving at the checkpoint gates. "Don't forget that and keep your chin up, okay?"

Austin nodded silently, his throat working as he looked at her.

"Dinner and drinks tomorrow night?"

"I might try to run tonight if I can get away…"

"Why don't you rest, relax, take a minute for yourself," she encouraged. "You barely slept on the plane and we both know it."

"I've barely slept the last three days cause my wife is insatiable," he teased tenderly and heard a gagging sound over his shoulder. "… And you aren't listening, remember?!"

"You're welcome for the ride… zoomie," Selkirk grunted under his breath, causing Austin and Giselle to share a look as they rolled their eyes. "This is our stop."

"I love you… and I'll see you tomorrow, okay?" she said quickly, trying not to cry or tear up in this moment as she met his turbulent eyes. "It's gonna be fine and will be just like we are dating again."

"I love you, too – and always will," he whispered, kissing her softly before getting to his feet on the truck and yanking off his protective gear that he'd borrowed. "Moonlight and magic tomorrow night, babe… or at least until the speakers interrupt us talking along the fence line."

"I can't wait," she smiled tearfully, trying to hide how hard it was to watch him store his helmet and vest, before climbing out of the truck. "I love you," she called out in a rush.

"I love you too," Austin replied, just before the drape hid him from her sights as the truck lurched forward again, driving her onto the Army installation after letting him off at the gates. It always amused her that the two bases were shaped in almost opposing images of each other – like two inverted L's.

The entrances were exceedingly close for deliveries or making it easily defensible if necessary. There was a long runway on the Air Force side – and on the Army's mirror image? It was actually a series of parking lots, munitions depots, and storage lockers covered with scrim to hide it from anything flying overhead. The barracks were in the same locations and the running paths were almost identical.

The truck rolled forward, before coming to a stop.

"Last stop… King's Beach," Selkirk called out, laughing.

They both knew Ghazni was no beach. The corner of the base off in the distance was dubbed 'King's Beach' because of a former soldier who orchestrated an impromptu 'beach' date with a civilian, before marrying her and going back home to take a job in Washington D.C.

Getting up from her seat, she yanked off the helmet and bulletproof vest in the warmth that seemed to permeate everything… even during the winter. The nights were cold, but during the day? It was awfully dry, warm, and arid – no matter the month. The summers were sweltering, but in January, it could still be a very tepid fifty degrees with the occasional spike… and the sand?

That accursed sand got everywhere.

"Home sweet home," she whispered to herself, stowing the gear before picking up her bag and throwing it over her shoulder.

Climbing down carefully, she turned to Selkirk.

"Thank you for the ride – and for giving us a few moments."

"Why a *zoomie*?" he asked, surprising her as she looked at him for the first time. He looked almost… disappointed? None of the guys on base had ever interested her because they felt like '*buddies*' or '*brothers*' – and honestly, she couldn't even fathom talking to someone that she worked with.

"He's my best friend," she answered, not holding back. "I signed up with Logan to get a pen pal and…"

Selkirk rolled his eyes and cursed.

"Never mind," he muttered. "Say no more."

"Why?" she chuckled, surprised at his response.

"I was wondering why the guys were suddenly pushing so hard for everyone to get a pen pal… and the first email I got was a doozie. I didn't reply."

"You should," she smiled. "There might be something to Logan's Romeo Squad…"

"Talbot's single," Selkirk winked at her, grinning. "You didn't have to go slumming you know. You could have had your choice of guys on base."

"No thank you," she said nervously, feeling very weird about this whole conversation. "I'm married, not looking, and you guys should work your whole angle with your pen pals – not me."

"Morrison? What about Peña?" he teased, following her as she turned to walk away.

"Selkirk, that needle is getting duller by the second, buster."

"Keyes? Although the stick-in-the-mud might be a little boring…"

"NO!" she snapped, whirling around and glaring at him. "Not interested and happily married. Do you not understand what '*no*' means?"

"Awww relax, Doc…" he grinned, playfully pushing her gently on the arm. "You are like a sister to all of us and it would be just creepy-weird anyhow. I'm happy for you – even if you were slumming."

"It's not slumming," she muttered, smiling at the man. "I feel like I won the lottery, actually."

"I'm happy for you."

"Thank you," she acknowledged, "…And you should go write your friend."

"Well, maybe I will…?" he mocked, making a face before walking off shaking his head, before saluting her loosely.

Giselle looked over her shoulder towards the Air Force base, seeing the planes in the distance… and one lone figure standing beside a building holding his duffle bag, watching and waiting.

Austin.

Unabashedly, she waved her hand '*hello*' high above her head, touched that he was looking for her as much as she searched for him. If she knew him, he was probably making sure she got '*home*' safely and was touched by the little things he did to show he cared.

Walking into the building, she passed the clinic and went straight back to the wing that was being used for the female barracks. Crossing the room, she dropped her bag down on the bunk as exhaustion hit her.

It had been a very busy week… and a long fourteen-hour flight with two layovers. While she wasn't ready to be away from Austin, she was glad to finally 'stop' for a moment to catch her breath from the whirlwind that enveloped them both.

Unzipping the bag, she began taking out her uniforms and smiled at the small box inside that had been taped carefully with bubble wrap to the point it was almost a puffy ball. She'd laughed so hard at seeing him packing her spicy ketchup he'd smuggled out of the Whataburger in a baggie.

As she picked up the box, she hesitated.

Underneath the hastily packaged bundle of bubble wrap and masking tape, was a tiny white box tied with a red ribbon.

"… What did you do?" she whispered aloud in disbelief, her heart thumping wildly at the realization that Austin had snuck something special in her bag without her being aware of it… which was funny because she had done the same thing to him.

She had taken the wooden spoon that he used at her parent's house and wrote 'Sarge's Man' on the back of it and hiding it in his bag for him to find.

Slowly, she pulled on the ribbon and lifted the lid, before folding back the tissue paper and hesitated. Inside, there on a cotton bedding, was a resin heart. It looked almost like a paperweight with flecks of silver encased in the tinted creation… along with a note.

> You have my heart… always.
> ~ Austin

Teary-eyed, she marveled at the heart that was about the size of a deck of cards, turning it over in wonder and admiration for the man that constantly knocked her socks off.

Closing her eyes, she pressed the heart against her chest as if it could remotely make her feel closer to him… and let out a heavy sigh.

It was going to be a long five months.

CHAPTER 28

SPARKY

Three months later...

PARADOX, Ricochet, and Riptide were gone for the next week on vacation, heading to Texas, and it made the barracks feel kinda empty. Copperhead was put in charge while their squadron leader was out and personally – not that Austin would ever say it aloud – he was pretty sure Reaper was testing the man to see how he would hold up under the pressure.

Austin got along well with his new wingman, but he hadn't breathed a word to anyone about getting out in July. He was sort of afraid to jinx something or create an issue due to seeing it several times in the past with Reilly.

Reaper wasn't anywhere close to Reilly... but he also didn't want to test the quiet man, especially after hearing through the grapevine that his wife had miscarried at ten weeks. Just hearing that, had him wondering if Giselle just hadn't told him or if she was pregnant and trying to surprise him.

They hadn't discussed any of it, but then again... they also hadn't been trying. He kinda hoped that she wasn't, but only because they still had a lot to take care of before returning to Texas.

He had contacted a realtor in Yonder that came highly recommended to him from Harley and was silently checking the listings online, ready to make a jump if needed. The idea of surprising Giselle with a place just for them made his knees weak with unbridled joy.

Harley was ordering his business cards for Flyboys, his coveralls, and had set up his email with them already. Once he had his return date, she promised to put him on the schedule, so he had no interruption in his pay.

Giselle had mentioned that she was trying to get some of her credits to transfer to the state for accreditation to get her license to work in the medical field, but it was a slow-going process.

Everything seemed to be trudging along, moving at a snail's pace, that it felt like July would never get here. Even Giselle made a comment that surprised him yesterday, because of the alarming truth and simplicity of her words.

"It's too quiet," she'd said, smiling at him. "We did inventory again this week because we ran out of things to do. No dehydration, no wounds, no scrapes or injuries. It's like either the dust is finally settling or the poop's about to hit the fan."

"Duck and cover?"

"That's not funny," she chuckled. "I kinda like this because it gives me a chance to get my head sorted out regarding all the accreditation stuff... oh! I meant to tell you the news... you are never going to believe this," she gushed happily.

"What's up?" he asked, holding his breath, and praying that she didn't announce she was pregnant. He wanted a little version of her so badly, but in a about a year from now. First, he wanted to get her home, settle into their jobs and lives together, and then have some fun creating their little family...

"Talk about 'Six-degrees-of-Kevin-Bacon'..." she chuckled. "Ready to follow this mess? So apparently, Captain Logan's best friend is a police officer in Tyler near Yonder, and a bunch of soldiers live in the area that used to be stationed here."

"Okaaaay?" he drawled, unsure where this was going and a little surprised that she'd told Captain Logan about their marriage so easily. Maybe things were different on that base than they were here.

"So, Logan and Griffin are friends – and one soldier that used to be stationed here still works for Griffin. I'm not sure what he does at the station, but that guy's sister... is married to a firefighter in Ember Creek, which is next to Yonder."

"I'm still lost," he laughed nervously as the speakers went off in the distance announcing, 'lights out'. "Keep going... but hurry, babe."

"Okay. The firefighter knows the chief, who is apparently 'talking' to one paramedic in Ember Creek, and they need an EMT. He told her about me! Which means, if I can figure out my licensing quickly? I might have a lead on a job when we get out in July," she said excitedly, jumping up and down excitedly.

"Sweetheart, that's incredible," he smiled proudly. "I'm absolutely thrilled for you – and even if we had to figure it out when we got to Yonder? There's hope we are going to hit the ground running."

"Exactly!" she beamed. "You've got your gig already at Flyboys and I might have something lined up, just one town over."

"I'm so proud of you," he said tenderly, leaning forward and kissing her. "I love good news."

"And I love you," she said tenderly, their fingers touching each other where they rested on the chain-link fence. "Have I mentioned that if I never see chain-link again? It won't be too soon. I'm growing to hate the stuff."

She made a face and scrunched up her nose.

"A necessary evil," he said evasively, wondering if she guessed that he was looking at homes. "Maybe we could get a puppy someday – or perhaps have a pool?"

"Maybe," she shrugged, just as the speakers went off again. "We need to go, or we'll be walking in complete darkness."

"I was just thinking that," he admitted, quickly kissing her. "Go, babe."

"Be safe and I'll see you tomorrow night."

"You got it."

THE NEXT MORNING, as Austin was walking out to his plane for their planned, normal recon mission... he stared in horror at the unexpected moment unfolding before him.

Trigger Warning

CHAPTER 30

GISELLE

"*WHAT?*" Giselle whispered, painfully aware of the eyes on her as the question slipped unconsciously from her before she could stop it.

"Sir! Yes, sir!" she quickly recovered, seeing the look that Captain Logan and Gretchen were giving her.

"I get it," Captain Logan began. "Usually Minors always goes, but he's off-base. I need a 68W to go with the squad. Gear up, Beck."

"Will there be an AXP?" she asked Gretchen, trying to get a gauge of what exactly she was being sent into. If there was an ambulance exchange point, then she was going deep into a mess today. The AXP were used to get someone from the front line away for help, before they could be moved to the medical treatment facility – or the base.

"No," Gretchen said in understanding.

Swallowing hard, she nodded, trying not to let her innate relief show.

A sixty-eight-whiskey was a designation for a combat medic. Here in Ghazni, they hadn't been sending them on the patrols and things had been calming down – or at least until Corporal Reed had almost died.

She had been sent before on a mission and this wasn't her first rodeo, but it made her very uneasy after working in the plush clinic for almost the last three years without having to go out with the team.

Putting down her things, she immediately disappeared for her locker to get her gear… hating how much her hands trembled. She wasn't going to the front line of a battle, but riding along with the boys and would be present if something happened.

Sliding her firearm into her holster, she strapped on her bulletproof vest before hefting up her IFAK bag. Each combat medic carries an individual first-aid kit with them because you never know what will be needed – or when.

Her bag was stocked with bandages, gauze, chest seals, and gloves. She always brought two or three pairs of gloves because if things got bad, or she had to change them out… she needed them available in a pinch.

There was also duct tape, scissors, and a combat casualty card for herself – filled out and ready to go should she fall in the line of duty and need aide herself. It gave another medic your vitals, name and rank, along with any allergies. She had an allergy to penicillin that could be lethal. That was a tough moment the first time she ever filled out one, but if she couldn't speak or was unconscious… it was vitally necessary.

She also brought a tourniquet, EPI pen, a space blanket, and a nasal airway and tactical cric kit. Having used one before, it always made her uneasy. A cric was so much easier to use than to perform a trach in the field to establish an airway. It took less time, there was so much less bleeding, and could save a life if there was a blockage that couldn't be removed.

Grabbing her helmet, she took a second to take several deep breaths before putting a confident look on her face. It wouldn't do well to show the guys that 'the little girl Doc' was scared.

No, you had to earn your place with the team – and she had. She had been in the trenches with them and had been the first medic on the scene when Corporal Minter lost his leg and had been hauled in unexpectedly several years ago.

That chaotic moment had scared that 'kid' who'd just arrived, and it took shoving his squad commander with both hands on his chest, yelling at him to get out of her way, and saving that soldier's life to earn their respect. She would never tell them how much she cried that night, nor how much she had thrown up.

That was the first time her boss, Houghton, had pulled them all together in a huddle, talking to the staff like they were a family unit... and this team needed her today - if something happened.

She was the 'Doc' for this mission... and there was no going back now.

Exiting the building, she saluted Captain Logan and made her way to the truck where the guys were standing. Several knowing looks, men she'd given IV's to, guys she'd dug shrapnel out of their legs, backs, and other parts of their bodies, were standing there together... with the prettiest and meanest looking dog.

"Guys..." she said simply in greeting.

"'Sup Doc!" Selkirk grinned. "You riding shotgun with us today?"

"Suns out, guns out – right, fellas?" she smiled and heard their laughter, their easy acceptance, as one of the guys offered a hand to help her in the back of the truck.

She cast one glance towards the other base – and saw Austin standing there in the distance... as he dropped his helmet on the ground.

She wished she could talk to him, comfort him. He was probably in shock at seeing her getting in the truck with the rest of the team that was heavily armed and heading into town.

Tonight, she thought sagely. *She would talk to him tonight and reassure him that everything was fine.* This was a normal thing, and it was her 'turn' on the roster that they kept.

Honestly, this was going to be a breeze for her because she was going out with two trucks... which meant two teams of ten men – and a medic could be assigned to handle up to forty men.

She raised her hand in a silent wave before disappearing inside.

THANKFULLY, the afternoon passed easily, and it was truly a sunny day. Giselle was glad there was a breeze because the temps were already reaching an almost unbearable warmth as they fried slightly under all their protective gear.

Keyes insisted she stay in the middle so they could protect her as they marched. She had Talbot and Peña flanking her, with Morrison in the lead with his dog, Trigger. Selkirk was bringing up the back and running his mouth the entire time, making comments here and there to cause the guys to crack up laughing at random moments.

Yeah, it could have been so much worse.

As they all filed back into the truck, she smiled as they handed out water bottles to everyone and treated her like 'one of the guys'.

"So, are you coming on the next one too, Doc?"

"She's not as mouthy as Minors and a sure lot prettier."

"Minors *is* mean."

"Because you told him that having your back meant being your 'golf caddy' for the afternoon when you put a 'hole in one', Selkirk."

"Hey! I put a hole in one… just before he put a hole in me!"

Giselle couldn't help the laughter that escaped her as everyone chuckled at the man's pun… just as they began to slow down, arriving at the base, and she heard Trigger yelp.

… Right before the world exploded around her.

The truck was launched upwards into the air and she barely had time to think, grabbing onto the framework that was covered with sheeting to keep them hidden inside. Her body swung wildly in that split second as she was hit by another man, who was being thrown clear of the truck.

Her mind could barely grasp what was happening as it was so sudden, filled with rapid fire movements, that sent the vehicle careening and tumbling wildly.

She couldn't tell which way was up and heard Trigger yelp loudly as Morrison's shouts became hastily barked orders not to be countered or argued with.

"DOC OUTTA THE TRUCK – KEYES, COVER HER AND REPORT BACK! PEÑA, COVER KEYES AND MAKE SURE HE DOESN'T GET SHOT."

Giselle was moving, grateful she hadn't removed her pack from her back, because she was going to need it…

"WHERE'S TALBOT?"

Keyes was exiting the truck, rifle drawn and swiftly surveying the area, as Giselle ducked behind him, looking for hostiles, pulling her own weapon for protection.

"Just don't shoot me…" Keyes said bluntly. "Adrenaline is high right now."

"I know that!" she snapped hotly and heard the klaxons

wailing in alarm, the sirens filling the air... nearly dulling out the voices.

"Oh my gosh..." she whispered, staring in disbelief at the men in the distance making a run at them. They were carrying guns and other weapons, bottles with rags sticking out of the top, shovels, pitchforks, and other items to attack them with.

Did they seriously think they were going to take the base like... *this*?

The base would never fall... however the soldiers surrounding her could.

"MORRISON! WE'VE GOT HOSTILES COMING IN HOT..." Keyes screamed out as Selkirk appeared with blood running down his temple, quickly drawing his gun – and waving?!

"You don't have to all surrender at once, you know..." Selkirk hollered in a sing-song voice, causing Morrison and the others to laugh in disbelief.

Laughter was probably the only thing that kept them from crossing the line of *'protective'* and *'duty-bound'* to *'primal rage and panicked self-preservation'*.

"One at a time," Selkirk continued, wiping the blood off his face. "You can surrender *one at a time*... it's probably better that way, too!"

"Let me see you," she ordered – only to have him push her hand away as he gave her a hard look, all joking aside and forgotten. His duty was to protect her, so she could help them... and he took it seriously.

"It's just a scratch. I'm fine... and get down!"

Selkirk grabbed her by the pack, yanking her bodily down behind the truck that she only just realized was on its side. She saw him looking around, his expression dark.

"Where's Turner and Collins?"

"Peña? You okay, buddy?"

"I don't know…"

Keyes, Selkirk, and Peña swung their rifles up in unison… as she heard screaming behind them.

"**GISELLLLLLE!**"

She glanced over her shoulder to see Austin there, being held back by three men as a fourth was running towards him. He was struggling, trying to free himself, kicking and trying to leave the base – all to get to her side, as bullets began to ring out.

Trigger ran to her side as Morrison stood over her, blocking her view. The tall man swung up his rifle, protecting her, and began firing.

The sounds were jarring and alarming, like jackhammers going off in her skull as she began waving at Austin to get back. If he got shot in front of her eyes…

Just the thought was sending sheer panic up her spine – and she slapped at Morrison who was standing over her, almost obscenely close, trying to get him to move to the side.

"Get off me and let me look for the others!" she screamed out – and gratefully he did so.

Austin had no idea just how safe she was with these men, because they would do anything to keep '*Doc*' safe… because nobody messed with '*Doc*'.

Soldiers were already flooding forward to help them… and she screamed quickly at Austin at the slight break in gunfire as Selkirk and Peña were reloading.

"GET UP THERE AND PROTECT US!" her voice warbled and strained with the effort, screaming out the words at him, and pointing at the sky.

Austin wasn't going to do any good down here, but get in trouble – but up there? He was their eyes and ears from the sky and could fire, if needed.

Her words must have struck a chord, because he turned and ran off with the other men towards the planes… and they roared overhead within minutes, one right after the other.

Giselle moved along the protective shell of the truck, her eyes scanning the horizon looking for anyone that might be trying to get the surprise on them.

What exactly had happened?!

Could someone have detonated a bomb? The truck was monitored the entire time they were in town on patrol. Wasn't it?

Grabbing a knife from her belt, she sawed off the ties holding down the covering to gain access to the back of the truck and spotted Muldoon, Pendergast, and Ortega shaking their heads as they struggled to stand. One man was bleeding heavily from his head, while another had blood coming out of his mouth, and the other was holding his ribs. They probably hadn't been fast enough to grab onto something and bounced around inside the truck several times until landing.

She grabbed her penlight and shone it in their eyes, checking for pupil dilation, before inspecting their wounds.

"Muldoon, can you fire?"

"Yeah…"

"Go! They need you…" she ordered bluntly. The man had split his head and would have a throbbing headache, but he would live and wasn't urgent in her opinion as she ran through her mental stats, registering them in order of priority.

"Pendergast," she barked, getting his attention and checking him. This one, not so much… his pupils were slow and he was groggy. "Can you fire your gun, soldier?"

"Huh?"

"Stay here," she said, pushing him back down into a seated position and shoving a rifle in his hands – just in case. "Don't fire unless you hear me scream."

"Doc? I don't feel so good…"

"I know Pendergast, just stay awake for me and we are getting some help soon, okay buddy?"

She moved to Ortega just as he coughed up blood.

… This *was* an emergency!

He was holding his side and bubbles were coming out of his mouth – the man had a punctured lung. She quickly moved about, trying not to create any more problems for the man that had to be suffering… or dying.

"Stay put!" she ordered and peered out of the truck. "Morrison! Do you have a radio? I need the medical team now!"

"You *are* medical!"

She gave him a flat look.

"I need him in the clinic! Ortega is dying…" she said bluntly and winced, hearing Pendergast crying out in alarm as she looked back inside to see the other man slumping over.

"Oh Jesus save us…" Pendergast was whimpering, holding the other man's slack hand in his. "Ortega?! Ortega! Hey buddy… man… you gotta hang on…"

Giselle looked back at Morrison.

"I NEED THE CLINIC NOW!" she roared hotly, turning back inside and grabbing the unconscious man under the arms, pulling him from the truck limply… and proceeded to start dragging him towards the gates in the distance.

Morrison was swiftly cursing her up one side and down the other – before barking orders at Trigger to stay put. The German shepherd was growling angrily but remaining still as the other soldiers ran forward to the gates and moved to help Giselle.

"There's two more men missing – I think they were thrown from the truck," she snapped, seeing Gretchen running towards her… and she was grateful.

Overheated, scared, alarmed, muscles aching, and throat hoarse... it was still a sight better than poor Ortega.

The two women dropped to the ground, falling on Ortega and began working to stabilize him as some others finally arrived moments later with a back board to carry him to where the lifesaving tools were located.

"Go..." Gretchen ordered. "There are more injured, right?"

"Yes!" Giselle barked, snapping like Houghton would have done – demanding obedience because there was no room for discussion or error. They needed to get Ortega inside and could carry the backboard. "We've got this..."

A plane roared overhead, swooping low and giving recovery fire to them.

Everything was happening so fast, in such a blur. There was such an organized chaos as men moved forward, armed, and taking steps to defend the base's entry... as the attackers started to dissipate, hiding from those that were now fighting back with everything they had, protecting their own.

Out of the corner of her eye she saw Logan carrying a limping soldier, Turner, maybe? They were moving towards the base as someone else had Collins, helping him forward by physically dragging him.

Collins obviously had two broken legs – one of them severe.

Lifting the back board with Gretchen, they began to move quickly towards the clinic in the distance... and she took a second to view the nightmare around them.

Looking around, she could hear the radios, the engine roaring of the Falcons above, the deafening sound of bullets... and the cries of pain. The smell of diesel mixed with gunpowder, combined with the salty smell of sweat and blood... no that would be a scent she would never forget.

Giselle's arms ached and she desperately wanted to check

on Austin, but she couldn't stop. She couldn't let herself break yet, and set back to work once more trying to stabilize the man before her.

IT FELT like hours had passed, and Giselle was moving from cot to cot checking on the men – feeling a tap on her shoulder. Glancing up, she saw Captain Logan's grimy face… and Austin's beloved one.

That was when she broke.

A sob welled up from deep inside of her as she crumbled. Austin and Captain Logan, both grabbed her by the arms, pulling her away from the wounded – before pushing her into a small doorway.

A bathroom.

"Pull it together, Beck…*ah*… Calder," Logan hissed firmly. "Congrats, but those men out there cannot see you break down yet - and we both know that! Our duty isn't done, and you can't give in to this. Swallow it down, and put that confident face on. Take ten minutes for yourself with your husband… and then I need to see my medic back in her place - at one hundred percent. Am I clear?"

Giselle nodded tearfully, sniffing and wiping her face as she looked at Logan's harsh stare and heard his voice crack as he continued, revealing what was truly in his mind, just before his eyes softened.

"Crying comes later when you are alone, and it hits you hard at what just happened today. I'll be the guy in the chapel bawling like a baby, if you need company."

Giselle laughed tearfully as Austin hugged her close – and Logan shut the door in their faces, giving them privacy.

"Oh my gosh," Austin breathed, his arms seizing her as he held her close, whispering rapidly, his emotions racing. "I was so scared I was going to lose you... are you okay? I just kept seeing them shooting at all of you, and the truck on it's side..."

She clutched at him and sobbed painfully, smelling the sweat and grime on him, combined with something else she didn't recognize. Was that jet fuel or...

It didn't matter, she realized, because he was here, holding her.

He was... here?!

"How did you get on base?" she asked, pulling back and looking at him tearfully in alarm.

"I caught the captain and Selkirk trying to drag another two bodies towards the gates. I ran off base to help them, immediately asking to see you for a few minutes. I was kinda shocked that the captain gave in and Selkirk told him we had gotten married a few months ago... and... well, I'm here for just a few moments before I'm going to be escorted off again."

Austin paused as he swallowed, completely overcome with what had just happened... and nodded silently.

It was a lot – for both of them.

She immediately moved forward, needing to draw comfort *from* him and provide it *to* him. He was her rock, her reason for every smile and every laugh... and the singular person that would always have her back in so many ways.

"Kiss me," she whispered, putting her hands on either side of his face and drawing him towards her... only to feel him take the reins as two tight bands of sinewy corded arms closed around her waist, holding her against the wall of his chest as his lips crashed against hers.

He needed this as much as she desperately did – this reassurance that there was nothing separating them, they were there for each other... and *alive.*

... So blessedly alive!

Austin was still kissing her when she moved to unzip his flight suit at the same time that he was reaching for her pants, his hands shaking and desperate. She needed to feel him close, to revel in the ragged emotions still surging in her... and it had to be the same for him.

No words were said.

They looked at each other as their kiss ended... both brokenly chuckling in sheer disbelief at this stolen moment neither expected, yet trying to hold back tears of joy, love, overwhelming relief needing this connection in a way neither could explain.

"Clocks ticking, flyboy... time for the Petersen Maneuver?" she said huskily, as he locked the door to the bathroom, pinning her hands above her head.

"As you wish, Sarge," he smiled, kissing her again.

CHAPTER 31

SPARKY

AUSTIN STARED at his beloved bride, nearly brought to tears as he realized just how truly precious that she was to him. If the world ended right now, he would die a happy man just staring into those eyes. Those feelings combined with the abject relief coursing through him, grateful they were both alive, and reveling in this stolen moment together...

He was humbled.

Weak.

"Dinner and drinks tomorrow night, my love?" he breathed, seeing the gentle expression of hers that seemed even softer somehow to his eyes.

"You got it, handsome," she whispered, caressing his cheek as they shared a smile – just before they jumped nervously at the knock on the door.

"Calder... *both Calders* – wrap it up," Captain Logan said bluntly, and she could hear the laughter in his voice as she realized he was quite aware of what was going on in here.

"Oh my gosh..."

Giselle was chuckling nervously, and her cheeks were pink with embarrassment as her eyes danced with horrified amusement.

Austin had no such issues. He grinned baldly, ready to strut happily back to his station, if required. They quickly righted their clothing, just before he stole another quick kiss.

"You look perfect to me."

"I look like some alley wench..." she hissed, smoothing her hair, and let out a small giggle as Austin winked at her.

"'Alley wench' is the sexiest look – and my favorite."

"You need to behave..."

"But you like it when I *mis*-behave..."

"I do," she admitted tenderly, smiling at him. "I love you."

"I love you too – and you take care of yourself for me. We've got a month left before we are out of here. I'm going to go ahead and turn in my resignation to Reaper tomorrow."

"I will too. We are going home to start our life, our fairy-tale, together."

"Our happily-ever-after..."

... And then Captain Logan knocked again.

"Time's up," the man said bluntly. "Don't try my patience because I will take this door down, airman."

Austin yanked the door open and saw the other man's knowing smirk.

"Walk of shame?" Captain Logan asked, holding back a laugh.

"Ain't no shame in my game... sir," Austin grinned happily and stuck out his hand to shake the other man's in sheer gratitude for this unexpected moment of happiness.

Logan glanced at his hand – then back at him pointedly, raising an eyebrow.

"You know why I'm hesitating..."

"This hand never made contact," Austin volunteered with

the other man as they both started laughing – especially at Giselle's mortified voice.

"Austin! You both need to stop... I swear, I could die of embarrassment right now between the two of you having a good time at my expense."

"You had a '*good time*' too..."

"Oh my gosh," Giselle muttered, covering her face as Logan laughed a little harder.

"Stop it, you two. You are just making me miss my wife..." Logan admitted, patting Austin on the shoulder. "I'm going to have someone provide an armed escort for you back – and your wife is going back to the clinic, right?"

"Yes, sir!" she said immediately, snapping to attention perfectly, which gave him a sense of pride at seeing her there.

"Bye, babe," Austin said swiftly, leaning forward to kiss her as she darted off back towards the clinic, watching her go before turning back to the captain that had given him this unexpected blessing.

"Thank you, sir... from the bottom of my heart. I cannot tell you how much I appreciate you understanding that I just needed to see her and make sure she was okay."

"I understand – and we need to keep this quiet," Logan said quietly. "Nobody is to know about this, because I don't need people migrating back and forth between the bases... especially after today."

"I understand."

"I'm glad you and your pen pal hit it off," Logan began as a soldier walked forward.

"You called, captain?"

"Keyes – can you escort Lieutenant Calder back to his hidey-hole? I believe he got 'lost'..." Logan said, smirking. "Make sure he gets home safely and then report to my office."

"Yes, sir."

... And it hit Austin.

"How did you know she was my pen pal?" Austin asked, stunned and staring at the man in surprise – only to see his knowing smile widen with a smugness that was irritating.

"Who do you think gave Beck your information?"

"... What?"

"Perhaps you should just count your blessings, airman, and quit asking so many questions. You don't have to know every detail, just know that it was handled... and handled well by those of us that care about our team. Now, go."

Keyes grabbed him on the shoulder, pulling Austin away from the captain before he could question him further... and he shrugged off the other man's hand.

As they walked out into the evening air, Keyes brought up his rifle, surveying the darkening landscape in the distance before walking Austin past the security gate. Walking towards the other gate, he was shocked to see Reaper standing there, arms crossed over his chest with a security guard.

Keyes elbowed him lightly, indicating Austin should go ahead and take the lead, before Keyes paused in his steps – waiting.

"Thank you, soldier," Reaper said loudly. "I'll take it from here."

Was he in trouble?

"Welcome back, Sparky," Reaper said quietly, before signaling the security guards and they walked off. "Did you have a good time playing in the Army's sandbox next door, *airman?*"

Ouch.

"I should have asked or..."

"Yes, you should have," Reaper said coolly in an icy voice, staring at him, his black eyes piercing as Austin realized that the man was livid. He'd never seen him this angry and it was slightly terrifying.

"I'm so sorry, sir," Austin began, feeling a touch of fear in his chest as Reaper closed his eyes and took a deep breath to calm himself. "I just was so scared that…"

"You think I wasn't?" Reaper bit out angrily. "You think I like being told by security that you ran out of the gates… *and hadn't come back?"*

… Just as Austin was about to open his mouth to apologize again or defend himself – the unexpected happened…

Reaper shoved his shoulders hard, unseating him and knocking him to the ground, screaming at him. His commanding officer was standing over him, leaning over, putting his finger in Austin's face.

"DON'T YOU EVER DO THAT AGAIN – AM I CLEAR?"

Austin stared up at him silently and saw the fear in his eyes, realizing that he had truly scared the man that had befriended him, watched out for him, and had taken him under his wing since he first arrived.

"I'm so sorry, brother," he breathed openly, putting his hands up in surrender… only to see something fracture in the other man's face.

Reaper didn't say a word, he only extended a hand to Austin, pulling him to his feet - and hugging him.

Shocked, Austin heard him speak.

"I was scared that you were gone," Reaper said quietly. "I've got a year left and I can't lose…"

"If Sophie had been out there, would you have checked on her?"

"I wouldn't have her here – period."

"And I'm not," Austin agreed. "Giselle is going home in July."

"Well, crap…" Reaper uttered under his breath before chuckling in awareness of what his announcement meant, releasing him and rubbing his face. "I know what that means. Ghost, X-Ray, Firefly… and you too now, huh?"

"I can't take seeing her and not being able to hold or touch her. It's terrible and I don't know how you do it."

"I understand," Reaper admitted in a sigh. "I can only do it because she's not in my face daily. If I had to look at Sophie on a daily basis and knew I couldn't hug her, touch her, or hold her hand for months on end? It would kill me. The separation is hard enough… but those homecomings?"

The man got a distant smile on his face that Austin understood in a way he never did before, thinking of what had happened between him and Giselle not twenty minutes ago.

"… Sophie's welcome makes the sacrifice worth it all in the end," Reaper said hoarsely, before clearing his throat. "No more escapades next door – am I clear?"

"Yes, sir."

"Good," Reaper replied – and smirked. "Now, report to Hawkins because you unequivocally just volunteered for an additional duty assignment."

"What?!"

"Hawkins – now! And just be glad that I am not turning this in for abandoning your post. You never leave when things are this hot – and you should know better. Stop thinking with your pants and use your head, Sparky."

"B-But…"

"Was she worth it?"

Austin didn't even hesitate as he saw the glimmer of understanding in Reaper's eyes – and the faint smirk on his face. The man was 'punishing' him without actually doing so.

"Very much so."

"Then quit arguing with me and get moving."

THAT EVENING, exhausted and emotionally drained from the day's events that unexpectedly dragged into the evening hours thanks to his new duty shift... Austin emailed Giselle to apologize that he was going to miss their rendezvous tomorrow evening – only to see that she had emailed him first.

> *Hey sweetheart,*
>
> *I am so sorry, but I am not going to make our date tomorrow night. Because of everything that happened, the supplies we used, with the people we are still treating for wounds and injuries... we are doing another check of our supplies and prepping.*
>
> *I've got my screen open right now on the other tab and typing up my resignation letter. I always thought I would be scared to do this, nervous, or much older... but I cannot tell you how happy this makes me feel right now.*
>
> *I also got an email about my EMT license online... and nailed the test! I feel like things are working out for us – and I'm truly excited. I emailed someone named Eileen Ballantine to verify if they still had the opening, explaining that I've passed my EMT licensure online, where I am stationed, and our move to the area... so I'm hoping I get good news back. If nothing else, I've got the first step done.*
>
> *Austin, I can't stop thinking about you and if we have to sleep on the floor of some crummy apartment, eat ramen noodles for a month, or worse – I'm finding that I don't even mind. I just want to be close, make a home with you, and enjoy that glimpse of what life can be like together that seems so long ago.*
>
> *My contract end date is July 11th – and hopefully we will be close on the time frame. Should I start looking at apartments?*
>
> *I love you,*

Giselle

AUSTIN SMILED SOFTLY TO HIMSELF, as he realized just how wonderful their future was going to be together. They thought very similarly, and he had already been working with a realtor looking for a place for them already - on the sly.

It was time to show his cards... because he was considering putting down the earnest money on a place and already had his VA loan approved.

Now, he wanted Giselle's approval on the place he finally had settled on.

Beloved,

So, I guess maybe I should admit just how infatuated I am with you and what you do to me... because I already got pre-approved for my VA loan and have been looking at homes for about three months now. I've got quite a nice deposit to put down on a place – and think this would be perfect for us.

There is a craftsman style house about three miles away from Flyboys – closer in town. There is an elementary school at the very end of the street (for in the future) and while it needs a little updating? I think it's something we can handle together and make it our own.

The yellow paint and white trim just make me think of 'home' – and I could see myself carrying you over the threshold or passing out Halloween candy to the neighborhood children. The railings on the front porch would be so cute with Christmas lights – or maybe some silly flower baskets.

(Look at me getting all 'domestic' now...)

Look around at the photos, tell me what you think... or if I'm crazy. I love you darling – and don't worry about tomorrow. I'm on duty for the next three nights because of my little stunt... I might have left without telling anyone. Ha ha ha!

Get some rest and be ready to be 'wined and dined' on Friday. I've got a bag of Twizzlers with your name on it, my lovely Paladin.

Always your knight,

Austin

CHAPTER 32

GISELLE

STARING in disbelief at the computer, this email was just the thing she needed after her conversation with Captain Logan and Gretchen Perry. Boy, it was not pretty in the slightest.

Giselle had laid down her resignation paper on Captain Logan's desk the moment that Gretchen was there, in the office, talking to someone... only to get yanked in to have a 'discussion'.

As Gretchen walked in, took one look at Giselle, and then glanced at the captain, who was putting his head down in his hands... and the sparks flew.

Gretchen slammed the door behind her.

"I TOLD YOU THIS WOULD HAPPEN!" Gretchen snarled angrily, putting her finger in Captain Logan's face, shocking Giselle like she'd put her tongue on a nine-volt battery.

"You told me this wouldn't happen! You promised me that

this was just a friendly communication, and nobody was leaving my team. This isn't fair, Logan, and you know it."

"I'm good," he smirked… but that smile didn't reach his eyes. "What can I say?"

"You can say 'NO'," Gretchen stormed hotly. "I do not want the 'Romeo squad' infecting my department. It's like… *lice*! Spreads like wildfire and takes forever to get rid of it. Most of the time, it's disgusting to boot. I mean, just look at some of the team you have now? … Bunch of goofballs and airheads, I swear!"

"Ewww…" both Giselle and Logan said in unison – making faces.

"That's disgusting, Perry. Falling in love is not like catching lice. That's just plain nasty – and your husband is rubbing off on you," Logan uttered. "Not in a good way either, I might add."

"Ha!" Gretchen snapped, crossing her arms angrily and glaring at Giselle before continuing. "So what? You are wanting to go home and live a boring life? You know medical credits don't hardly transfer to the civilian world and you have to get your license or…" and then hesitated as a look of shock crossed her expressive face.

"Is *this* why you asked to use the printer? You've already been working on it, haven't you?"

"Yes, ma'am," Giselle acknowledged quietly. "After hours – but yes."

"Can you blame her after what happened?" Logan said heavily, sitting back in his chair and looking utterly defeated. "I've had three already today requesting transfers and two resignations – not including this one. People get scared or want safety – and I can't really blame them."

"I don't care about anyone else," Gretchen said weakly plopping down in a chair looking almost as defeated. "Sit down, Calder. I need to think."

Giselle sat silently, not sure what to say.

"I wanted her there, in my clinic, because she's the best we have," Gretchen began, looking at Logan, and Giselle was shocked by her words as she listened to the woman speak.

"She's smart, quick on her feet, and can put me to shame inserting an I.V. in someone quickly. I'm more of a 'get it done' mentality... but she's got a gift and the soldiers respond to it. I mean, just look at the men when she walks around? They treat her like a respected family member – she's like a sister to them and we don't let 'family' go, remember?"

"Gretchen, we can't hold her back," Logan said quietly. "As much as I hate to say it, but we just can't. I won't do it when you and Perry are ready to return to the States either."

He paused and met Gretchen's eyes without faltering.

"I will freak out, have a small panic attack, and then scramble to get someone with a half-a-brain to take your place... because let me tell you? Angels just don't drop into your lap like you did for me when you and Randy got married – and I will be forever grateful for you both."

"Ughhhh," Gretchen said in frustration, rolling her eyes. "And there you go with the flattery..."

"It works," Logan smiled, giving Giselle a quick wink as she sat there quietly, not sure what to make of this easy camaraderie between her two bosses. Nobody talked to the captain like this – yet there was something there between Gretchen and Captain Logan.

A friendship that went deeper than just work-related, making Giselle wonder at what happened behind the scenes to create this between them.

"Where are you going?" Gretchen asked Giselle quietly, not looking at her but still watching Logan's face. "Back to Wichita Falls?"

"Actually, there's this place outside of Tyler..."

"OH, FOR PETE'S SAKE..." Logan snapped hotly, doing a complete 180 degree turn and glaring at Giselle. "Did Griffin put you up to this? I'm gonna have that man's front teeth made into earrings if he doesn't stop..."

"Isn't he your fr-friend? W-What? N-Nooo?!" Giselle stammered interrupting as the man leaned over the desk angrily looking at her – just as Gretchen started laughing uproariously next to her. "I'm getting a job as an EMT in Ember Creek and Austin has a job already lined up in Yonder, just southwest of Tyler."

"So, neither Lily or John had anything to do with this?"

"You did this..." Gretchen reiterated bluntly.

"Fine! Is that what you wanted to hear me say? I did this, Gretch... this is my fault, and I will get you someone else here as quickly as I can," Logan snapped hotly, signing off on Giselle's resignation paperwork.

"Heads up – your former life doesn't end the moment you walk off this base. You'll end up seeing both of us again, so don't be a stranger, and be prepared to have company over for coffee one of these days. Got it?" he said in a matter-of-fact voice. "I can't believe any of this..."

"Did something else happen?" Gretchen began as Logan gave the other woman a knowing look.

"Juliet is looking at homes in Tyler," Logan muttered, but there was a rueful smile on his face. "She wants our kids to grow up in the area – and I'm not sure I'm going to win that fight with her. My father is in D.C. and well, it's really hard to pick your wife and child over your parent. I told her to find a place with an In-Law suite that is separate from the house... and do you know she found one? Now, I'm stuck. I've got nine-kinds-of-hell going on in my personal life... and now three weeks to find you another medic, Gretch."

He slid the paper towards Gretchen and she signed it –

before sliding it back towards Logan, and turning towards Giselle.

"Coffee, BBQ, whatever… but you need to stay in touch, okay? Family is family – and I feel like you are part of mine. While I'm happy for you both? I'm jealous at the same time because all our friends are there… and I'm speaking for both of us," Gretchen said openly, glancing at Logan.

"If your EMT gig doesn't work out? Go to the Tyler Police station and ask for Officer Griffin," Logan began… and smirked. "Tell him I sent you and they'll help you find something, I promise. I might be mad at him stealing my people… but it's only because he has a heart of gold and can't say 'No' to family."

"Thank you both," Giselle whispered, tearing up. "I'm gonna miss you both."

"Enough to stay for another year or two?" Gretchen perked up.

"Noooo…"

They all three laughed and got to their feet, just as Gretchen hugged her… and then Captain Logan.

"Congratulations again, kiddo… and I mean it when I say 'barbecue' or coffee," he smiled. "None of that cheap stuff either – good strong coffee and smoked Texas brisket."

"Yes, sir," she smiled, saluting him.

"Get outta here," Gretchen laughed, nudging her on the shoulder. "He's got work to do and needs to find me another medic."

LOOKING AT THE EMAIL AGAIN, Giselle clicked on the link and held her breath. The house Austin was looking at was breathtakingly beautiful and full of character. She grabbed a tissue as she stared in disbelief and comprehension that he was planning on buying them a home to start their 'forever' together.

The flowerbeds were overgrown badly – and there was an untouched area in the backyard that looked like a garden. She had never planted a thing in her life, but now? Just looking at that photograph of the home, she was wanting to put down roots permanently... and plant vegetables.

The bedrooms were tiny and so was the living room – but the kitchen was immense... and she loved it.

Massive golden cabinets soared to the high ceilings and the backsplash was covered with an old, circular tile that needed a good cleaning. The countertops were a god-awful swirled, peanut butter-ish color that was horrifying... and she almost laughed. Those countertops probably kept the house from selling out of sheer disgust.

The light fixtures were dated, and massive drapes covered the windows, making her wonder what it would look like if she yanked them down and let in the sunshine.

Her heart was fully 'in' on this house, and she was beyond touched that he had found them a home.

Hitting reply, she began to type... hoping he understood just what she meant.

> *Beloved,*
>
> *I cherish the house so much. I have some money set aside as well (since we've never discussed this before) and it's simply magnificent. I guess we should get settled first before we start browsing for planes – and I need you to teach me what to look for so I can be your partner on our next adventure.*
>
> *I'm sitting here, staring at the screen and keep scrolling through the photos, picturing moments and events in that home... but those countertops?*
>
> *Can that be our first project together? Ha ha ha!*
>
> *Oh Austin, I'm so overwhelmed right now – and so in love*

*with you! I can see 'spoon karaoke' together, lazy Saturday
mornings sharing coffee on the porch, and... I want to fill those
rooms someday with babies.*

*I never thought I would say that, but I want to hold our
baby someday and just thinking about it has made me all
emotional. I love you so much – and you are the best thing that
has ever happened to me.*

*Put in the offer, my fearless knight, and let's take hold of
our 'castle', making it our own.*

XOXO,
Giselle

THE NEXT MORNING, she couldn't help the tearful laugh that
escaped her as she opened his email – overcome with sheer
happiness at his obvious exuberance.

My beloved Paladin,
To quote the greatest 'poet' in the world...?
On a boat...
Or in a plane!
On those ugly counters,
Or in the rain...
In a chair?
In a lair!
Every time we are alone... and everywhere!
We already did it in the bathroom,
I think you're incredible...
And you make my heart zooooom!
*(Still rhymes... but it's definitely losing something if I keep
going)*

*I'm gonna give you those babies – and enjoy making them
with every breath I take! That is no hardship, and I mean that*

sincerely. Say the word, or better yet? Just walk into any room where I am... you won't have to mention a thing because I am CRAZY about you, Giselle!

We'll know in twenty-four hours if the house is ours.

I miss seeing your smile, so how about that hot date tonight night? Are you up for a little 'fence-rendezvous' with you-know-who?

I love you,
Austin

THAT EVENING, she immediately spotted him as she rounded the corner along the line of the fence, trying to ignore the soldiers that were now posted every so many feet watching for insurgents.

As she jogged up to the fence, she saw Austin's proud smile.

"Hey homeowner..." he said simply, unable to hold back his excitement.

"You're kidding?" she gushed wildly, reaching for him through the fence and trying to hug him as he tried to kiss her. His lips barely pressed against hers. They were awkwardly smashing their noses and foreheads against the metal chain links.

"I hate this freakin' fence..." he whispered. "I'm so ready to go home... now that it has a meaning to me."

"Oh Austin," she breathed, knowing just how much this must mean to him. "I can't believe we are getting that house... it's so beautiful."

He chuckled softly, his fingers holding onto the links as she reached for him... and he whispered, unexpectedly singing to her softly.

"... On those ugly counters - Or in the rain... In a chair? In

my lair... I will love my wife just everywhere," he sang softly, his voice playful, kissing her forehead, her nose, and her mouth, as she laughed gently trying not to draw attention to them.

"Your last day is July 11th? Mine is July 7th ... I reached out to Harley and Thumper to tell them what was going on and the closing date is set for the 13th, so I will pick you up at the airport and take you home," he said proudly and she beamed at him happily.

"Take me home and be mine?"

"Always, sweetheart…"

"You've got to promise me something though."

"Anything."

"You've got to be careful when you are leaving – and feign sickness if they try to send you out again. I'm terrified something will happen to you and wish that I could…"

Austin froze and angled his head for a moment, thinking.

"I'm going to talk to Reaper and see if I can stay for a few more days so I can fly out with you," he said suddenly. "I'll let you know in the next few days for sure. I'll just tell him I can't get a flight."

"You think that will work?"

"They aren't going to want to send anyone out for a little while due to lockdown… so we might be stuck. I need to let the realtor know or see what I need to do about a power of attorney."

"I think they would understand that we are active duty and things are hectic. I mean, if you can do most of it online and I'm sure…"

"Giselle," he said softly, smiling at her. "It's going to be fine. We'll figure it out and go home together – I promise."

"I'm so happy," she admitted. "I can't wait."

"Neither can I," he hesitated. "Wanna celebrate?"

"I thought we were celebrating?" she laughed easily –

only to see him reach down and grab two things. "Ohhhh mercy, the Twizzlers?"

"Heck yeah – I love me some sugar," he drawled playfully, "And I have an Afghani chocolate bar."

"Really?"

"Yup. Don't ask questions," he chuckled. "I don't know what's in it except chocolate, and that it's supposed to be good. You aren't allergic to anything, are you?"

"Penicillin… so if I'm ever sick, don't give me that."

His eyes widened in surprise.

"Good to know," he said openly nodding. "Penicillin. Nope. Never getting that stuff ever…"

He broke the chocolate bar in half, looked at it tentatively and raised an eyebrow at her. She truly loved his personality, these moments, and treasured the fact that something so simple or silly as a chocolate bar turned into an event between them.

"Life's an adventure, remember?" she whispered.

"Always searching for treasure in faraway lands, my love…" he agreed immediately, tapping his part of the chocolate bar gently against the half she held. "Here's to the sweetest happily ever after a lonely boy could ever imagine."

She nodded tearfully, smiling at him.

"Here's to finding home in your heart – and in your arms."

"Oh gosh yes…" he breathed reverently. "I couldn't have said it better, Giselle. *You* are my *home*."

CHAPTER 33

GISELLE

IT WAS TIME.

The last few weeks had dragged by but her time in the Army was over. She was so excited, so thankful for these opportunities, but also incredibly ready to start her life with Austin.

She cried bitterly leaving her friends, hugging them, making them promise to write her, and just when she didn't think she could cry anymore?

Gretchen and Captain Logan were waiting at the truck where Selkirk was standing to drive her - with five other armed men.

She recognized their faces, knew their names, they had been like cousins to her on base, watching out for her... and now they would protect her one last time as she made her way to the airport.

"Let me just say," Captain Logan began, smiling at her. "While I am not a huge fan of this? I understand."

Giselle was struggling, eyes burning as her nose ran, swallowing several times before she spoke. She desperately hoped wherever she ended up working that had people like this around her – because it was obvious the captain and Gretchen cared.

"Brisket… I promise," she choked out, wiping her eyes and smiling.

"And don't forget the coffee," Gretchen reminded her, letting out a whimper as she moved to hug her. "I really am so happy for you – and will miss you terribly, but I know we'll see each other again soon."

"But not too soon," Logan interjected, frowning, as Gretchen and Giselle laughed tearfully, hugging once more.

"Alright, alright," Selkirk said pointedly in a very macho voice. "There's only room for one set of ovaries on this truck and if me or the guys start boo-hooing? It's over. You are gonna miss your flight if we don't get moving soon, *Beck-Calder-Whatever-Your-Name-Is-Now…*"

Giselle laughed softly, seeing their smiling faces, meeting each one of their eyes before she patted them each on the shoulder, saying her goodbyes.

"… Thank you, my friends," she whispered to all of them, knowing the danger she was putting them in to make this final flight.

"We like barbecue too, you know," Talbot volunteered.

"And mac & cheese…" Peña added, smiling. "Just sayin'…"

"Pie," Keyes announced, surprising all of them. "What? Just because I obey the rules doesn't mean I can't like pie, you dorks. I love pie. It's like God's perfect gift to humans… crust, sugar, fruit – what's not to love?"

Morrison smiled, kneeling to pet Trigger, before looking up.

"I think everyone would be happy with anything if they got a break from here – and I speak for all of us when I say,

'Just be happy' and we hope to see you again sometime, Doc. Now, you know the drill. Get in there, yank your *'bone dome'* on, and let's get moving."

"We've got three more…" a voice called out, interrupting them and Giselle fought the urge to throw herself into Austin's arms as he was brought to the truck that was waiting at the gate – along with another two men.

"Up and at 'em, everyone… Zoomies, too. We need to get moving and there's no reason to let our 'buddies' get in position."

Everyone climbed into the truck – including Giselle, Austin, and the other two men, one who immediately stuck out his hand towards her once they were seated.

"Reaper, miss," he said simply. "Congratulations – even though I'm late."

"Riptide," the other volunteered simply, sitting back in the truck as the other soldiers settled around them.

"Reaper's going to visit his wife in Yonder," Austin volunteered, smiling easily at her. "Sophie. We met her at dinner and again at the reception."

"Oh my gosh… *that's* Reaper?!"

"I guess my wife talks about me?" the man chuckled quietly with a slight smile on his face. "I miss my bride and want to see my son… and thought this was a perfect chance to disconnect for a few moments, because I might not be able to again if things liven up. Besides, Ricochet's got this under control for a week."

"Hang on," Selkirk yelled from the driver's seat. "Formula One Racing - eat your heart out, babiessss…!"

The truck surged forward at a breakneck pace, causing all of them to look at each other in a little bit of surprise, alarm… and a silent joy as she took Austin's hand in hers.

"We're going home," she whispered, smiling at him.

*

Fourteen hours later, they were landing in Texas... and beyond exhausted. Shockingly enough, the man that Austin said was quiet all the time, talked the entire second half of the trip.

She was surprised that Riptide had gotten their seats all rearranged so the four of them were sitting together and listened fascinated as they talked about all sorts of things... including Austin's call sign.

"... Did he ever tell you how Sparky ended up in Ghazni?"

"No?"

"Oh geez..." Austin muttered, laughing. "One stupid mistake and it haunts you for life."

"They could have called you 'Pyro' or something with that stunt."

Giselle looked at Austin, shocked and a little nervous that maybe she didn't know him as well as she thought.

"They are making a mountain out of a molehill," Austin said quickly. "It wasn't like that – at all. I was just a stupid kid trying to fit in... and did stupid things."

"Very," Reaper quipped, laughing.

"Why did they call you Sparky?"

"Well, so, ah..." he hesitated, rubbing the back of his neck nervously and smiled at her. "I was getting quite well-known for being this dumb, playful kid around the Academy and I was put to a dare."

"Okay?"

"One of the guys said, *'Hey Beavis, bet you won't hit this with a hammer?'* – and I was motivated to do whatever he was saying because I did not want to get stuck with *Beavis* or *Butthead* as a call sign," Austin laughed nervously. "A lot of times when you are dubbed something? It sticks and suddenly everyone just calls you that name – eh Riptide?"

"It's true."

"I just assumed you surfed a lot…"

"Nope."

"Ohhh, weird. Okaaaay," she drawled and looked at Austin again just as the 'Fasten Seatbelt' sign illuminated overhead and the announcements came on that they were landing in Tyler within the next twenty minutes.

"Soooo," Austin drawled in embarrassment, "It turns out I *was* actually young and incredibly stupid."

"Why?"

"Well, the guy had a hammer… and a bullet."

"Oh nooo," Giselle whispered in horrified understanding of what he was about to explain. "You didn't?"

"I did," he admitted and winced. "Left a nasty little scar on my shin – and everyone started calling me 'Sparky' because of the sparks that went flying the moment I nearly killed myself because of a stupid dare. I had no idea how badly it would go – or how much trouble I would get into."

Giselle laughed softly, meeting his warm eyes as he laced his fingers with hers.

"One of the officers at the Academy saw the whole thing, said that sparks went flying as the cap of the bullet exploded like a small firecracker."

"Geezzzz, Austin," she chuckled and heard the other guys laughing.

"I know. I never claimed to be a genius," he admitted, grinning at her. "And you are stuck with me."

"Happily so," she smiled, leaning to put her head on his shoulder.

"Who's picking us up at the airport?" Riptide asked.

"My wife," Reaper answered, grinning.

Not twenty minutes later, Giselle was gawking at the man that obviously had zero shame when it came to his wife. As they all walked down to the baggage claim together, the dark-haired man began to sprint... grabbing Sophie in the distance, who threw herself bodily into his arms.

Giselle sighed openly, seeing the sweet reunion as the man kissed her happily, lifting her off the ground, and spinning her around for a second, before scooping up the child in the stroller, nuzzling and kissing his son, openly affectionate.

Just seeing the small family before them, she turned to look at Austin and already saw his eyes on her.

"I love you," he breathed, holding her hand.

"I can't wait until we are alone," she whispered.

"And I feel like a third...," Riptide muttered from nearby – and froze, stopping mid-sentence before completing it – weakly.

"... Wheel?"

Giselle and Austin both stopped walking, looking at the man's shocked expression as he stood there, staring off into the distance near where Sophie and Reaper were holding each other and talking... only to see a woman waiting there – with a rose.

"*Budddyyyyy*...," Austin drawled pointedly, chuckling. She laughed softly at the tone of his voice and the lack of response from Riptide as it didn't even get a rise out of the other man. "You stud?! Keepin' secrets, eh, Riptide?"

Instead, Riptide walked forward towards the woman... and drew her into his arms, hugging her.

"Awww," Giselle smiled, touched at the unexpected greeting that obviously meant a lot to him.

Riptide moved to hold the woman's hand and they walked out of the airport into the parking lot, without a word to anyone else. It was obvious they wanted to be alone, and she was there only for him.

"That's so sweet. I'm happy for them."

Giselle met Sophie's tearful smile and saw Reaper watching the other man leave curiously, as they finally caught up with them.

"Ryan, are we ready to head out?" Sophie asked.

"Yes," Reaper acknowledged. "Let's go home."

"We're gonna drop these two off first – and then go home."

Giselle smiled happily, knowing that it was going to be a brief madhouse of paperwork, picking up the keys at the title office, and then finally heading to their new home... before setting off to try to figure out how the rest of this was going to play out eventually.

She would need to get in touch with the station in Ember Creek. Austin would need to get on the schedule with Flyboys. They were going to need to start their search for a plane, figure out the car-situation, and get so many other things ironed out that the list seemed almost overwhelming sometimes.

As they piled into the vehicle, Austin and Giselle sat in the back with Ben in the car seat, she tried to keep her mind off of things by playing and talking to the toddler that was watching her with such innocent, enormous brown eyes full of happiness.

Ben was a sweet child and was making talking noises at her, trying to get her attention even if she couldn't understand him. Even Austin was touching the child's hand, trying to hand him a toy, and playing with him... only to feel the vehicle come to a stop.

Giselle looked up... and hesitated.

"What's going on?" she whispered in disbelief, staring at the crowd of people that was milling about... in front of their house that she'd only seen in pictures.

"I thought we were... *wait...* I don't understand. What

is…?"

Her voice trailed off as she saw several of their friends turn to them and smile where they sat in the car, stunned. Austin opened the car door and got out, as Sophie turned to look over her shoulder, smiling happily.

"Welcome home… and to Flyboys, Giselle," Sophie began. "You are part of our family now and we take care of each other. When someone is starting out, we each help out a little bit, so the burden isn't quite so overwhelming. I hope you like our gift."

"Whaaat?" Giselle whispered tearfully, staring at the woman before looking at the crowd again who was waiting as Austin opened her car door.

"The dining room table," Sophie smiled. "I'll be over next week for coffee and we'll talk more, but right now? I just want to go home."

"Baby-makin' time, my love?" Reaper said quietly, causing Giselle's mouth to drop open in shock as Sophie laughed, touching the man's face.

"You know it, handsome. I'm so glad you are home, Ryan."

"Mrs. Calder," Reaper said bluntly, not looking away from Sophie. "Time to get out of the car, ma'am… I've got a hot date with my wife."

Sophie's intimate laugh combined with Reaper's words were enough to cause Giselle to flee. She hopped out of the car quickly, shutting the door behind her, as Austin took her hand.

His face looked almost as stunned as hers – and she realized he had no idea any of this was going on either.

"Hey Spark-dog," Firefly grinned. "Surprise!"

"What in the world is going on?"

"It's moving day… Can't you see that?"

"But…"

"It sucks to sleep on the floor," Glory interjected.

"Or not have any hot water," Alpo volunteered.

"No plates or utensils," Thumper added.

"Or a shower curtain..." Harley smiled.

"Towels, a trash can, or a broom," Romeo chimed in, smiling at his wife who also commented. "Or sheets, a chair to sit on, and a microwave."

"T.P.," Delilah said sheepishly, as Armadillo burst out laughing, hugging her.

"Ceiling fans," Valkyrie said bluntly. "This is Texas and ceiling fans are a must in every room because it can get quite sweltering here with no ocean breeze and the humidity isn't like Ghazni, my friends."

"I don't understand," Giselle said numbly as they were brought forward, tugged towards the house – only for Austin to scoop her up into his arms as he carried her over the threshold at the last minute, causing several knowing laughs around them, just before he set her down.

"What is all of this?" Austin asked pointedly, looking around as Giselle's eyes took in everything in disbelief.

She and Austin had talked in hushed voices at length about what they were going to do to furnish the house. She suggested hitting up Goodwill or Big Lots in order to grab a few necessities. They would need to get groceries, paper plates, and figure out the rest... but neither of them expected *any* of this!

There was a small dining room table, a recliner, and boxes everywhere. Someone was installing a ceiling fan in the middle of the living room and wires were dangling from the ceiling with the box just underneath a ladder.

It was chaos... but a blessing, too.

"We are helping you move in," Delilah volunteered, smiling tenderly. "Now this is only to help you get started, but you won't be sitting on the floor nor sleeping there... and I'm sure you will want to get a few things as you get situated.

I put a notepad and pen on the counter so you can start making a list of items you need as you discover something missing – and then we can come up with YOUR box from that list, for the next Flyboy that comes to live in Yonder."

"Our box?"

"We pay it forward," Dixie explained, smiling. "As one of us gets settled, the others get the call, and we bring our individual boxes to help establish the home. We brought the bathroom items."

"Kitchen," Firefly volunteered, holding up a hand.

"Ceiling fan," Mary smiled at Ghost – who waved at Austin near the ladder where he was standing beside.

"Enough yammering," Alpo said pointedly. "We've got classes this afternoon and the newlyweds are gonna want to be alone. Let's get back at it. Who's on childcare duty because *Thing One* and *Thing Two* are pulling each other's hair – again."

"On it," Glory yelped, running for the children angrily sobbing in the hallway, with fistfuls of hair.

"Oh geez," Alpo muttered, rubbing his forehead. "My wife is on child duty… and those are *my* kids. Good thing I can't live without any of them, because they make me want to pull out my hair sometimes."

"Cueball," Thumper taunted – causing Alpo to immediately touch the back of his head and glare at his best friend.

"Shut up. I am *not* losing my hair, Thumper…"

Everyone burst out laughing at the exchange between friends – and a box was pressed in each of their hands.

"The sooner we unpack, the sooner you are alone," Armadillo drawled pointedly, winking at them and grinning. "And let me tell ya', the bed's already set up and made."

"On it!" Austin blurted out, dropping his duffle bag and digging into the box immediately. "I've got spices and utensils… kitchen. Which way is my dang kitchen?"

"That way!" several people hollered, laughing and pointing.

"Thanks," he grinned, sheepishly. "I can't remember from the photographs, and it's been almost a month since I've seen the place."

Giselle looked in her box and grimaced.

"Switch with me, Austin."

"Sure, babe... what have you got?"

"Hammers, screwdrivers, measuring tape, duct tape, and other junk... and you are *not* setting up my spice rack," she smiled, swapping boxes with him right away.

"... And hurry," she whispered pointedly, looking him up and down, before he gave her a lazy smile in awareness.

"Yes ma'am," he acknowledged huskily, before clearing his throat. "Uh, guys? Which way is my garage?"

"That way..."

Austin winked at her playfully as she stared after him, knowing that this was just the beginning of their chapter unfolding, especially as she heard him.

"... Tumble out of bed and stumble to the kitchen," he began dancing and singing, *'9 to 5'* by Dolly Parton, strutting his way towards the doorway where everyone had pointed a moment ago, only to hear other voices chime in.

Moments later, everyone was singing, laughing, and dancing about as they unpacked boxes – including Giselle, who was grinning and smiling at her beloved husband.

If life was a series of events, chapters, lyrics, moments, and realities crossing? Then by golly, hers was an unimaginable fable with lessons learned, trials endured, treasures discovered, with a happiness she could have only fathomed in her wildest dreams... and shining brightly behind Austin's beautiful eyes.

Hours later, when they were finally alone, the two lovers exchanged a warm and tender smile as they held each other close, in their new home they would share for years to come.

"... The handsome knight and his beautiful paladin lived happily ever after," Austin whispered in the darkness of their room before kissing her softly once more. "The end."

"No, my love," she smiled tenderly at him, admiring his face in the shadows and marveling at the truth of it all. "Never an end, I promise you that."

"... This is only our beginning."

EPILOGUE

Nine months later...

"'NIGHT, EILEEN..." she smiled, waving at her friend and coworker from Ember Creek. She loved her job, feeling so thrilled right now and couldn't wait to get home to talk to Austin. He was flying tonight, taking students up, and mentioned he might be home a little late.

That was actually perfect, because it gave her time to put together her gift for him, she thought happily, glancing at the bag of things she'd picked up during a brief lunch break as a surprise.

... Except her phone rang.

"Hello?"

"Hey there," a strained voice said, and it took her a minute to realize it was Sophie.

"Are you okay?"

"Nope. My water broke and Marisol is at the doctor's office with Nicolette getting tubes put in her ears... of all the days, too. Dixie just got home from the dentist where Luke fell and busted his tooth royally, Harley is at Flyboys, Glory is babysitting – *and I'm panicking..."* Sophie sobbed wretchedly. "I need help and I'm alone – and if you breathe any of this to my Ryan, so help me God I'll…"

"Whoaaaa, calm down Mama-bear…" Giselle chuckled in understanding.

One of the things the women talked about in hushed voices on their Saturdays alone was that they didn't want any of their spouses to know how hard watching them leave was, how scary the idea of being alone during emergencies was, or how frightening it was to think that they couldn't rely on them if there was a problem overseas or with the business.

That was their only income and maintaining Flyboys was exceedingly important – and Reaper was stuck in Afghanistan for another week before he could come home for good.

"I'm on my way now."

"Oh gosh, thank you, Giselle. I just need someone to drive me and to watch Ben. If you don't mind keeping me company for a little bit while I 'do my Mom-thing'… ugh, hang on… contraction…"

"You're fine, hon… and I'd be happy to watch Ben for a bit."

"Glory and Alpo are going to keep him overnight – so they'll come get him shortly so he can play with the twins."

"Sophie," Giselle smiled, trying to calm the panicked mom who was under a lot of physical, mental, and emotional turmoil right now with the baby, Ryan coming home, and trying to raise the rambunctious little boy… oh she understood very well. "Please don't worry and no one will tell Reaper – I swear it."

"I'm sorry… I'm just freaking out a bit."

"You have good reason to, my friend. How far apart are your contractions?"

"Nine minutes."

Whoaaaa boy, Giselle thought to herself. Second babies come fast usually, and it was no wonder Sophie was panicking. She probably would be too.

"Alrighty. I'll be there in just a few and we'll head straight to the emergency room together. I'm going to hang up and let Austin know that we're heading in, okay?"

"Don't tell him I'm nervous."

"I promise – it's our secret."

"Thank you," Sophie uttered. "I'll be waiting by the door and…"

"Why don't we take your car, so I don't have to fool with moving the car seat for Ben?" Giselle suggested, afraid that the woman might have the child in the car or the parking lot. "Let's cut corners where we can and make it easy on ourselves?"

… And sped up.

"Okay. I'll meet you at the car."

"Perfect. See you in four minutes."

Giselle hung up the phone and immediately called Flyboys because she knew Austin was in the air with a student pilot.

"Flyboys, this is Harley…"

"Harley! Oh my gosh, hey, can you radio Austin and tell him I'm going to the E.R. with Sophie? The baby is coming…"

"WHAT?"

"Yep. Contractions are less than ten minutes apart and…"

"Reaper will never make it back to the States in time."

"I know."

"Ohhh man – and he wanted to be here, too."

"Not gonna happen," Giselle said bluntly. "Tell Austin to pick me up because I'm taking Sophie's Toyota – and will you let Glory know to pick Ben up from the waiting room? She's keeping him overnight so he can play with the twins."

"Of course. Do you want me to bring you something for dinner?"

"No. I might need a ride back to my car, but we're good. Just let Austin know and…"

"I'll send him with the Jetta since your car will be at Sophie's and you aren't picking him up."

"Perfect – and thank you!"

"Is she nervous?"

"She's upset Ryan won't make it… and doesn't want him to know."

"Nope. I gotcha. I never told Jackson that I was beyond overwhelmed giving birth to Samantha because he would only feel guilty and be a basket case. I merely told him I was happy with one perfect child – and didn't need another," Harley said sheepishly. "I'm certainly not Delilah, who is pregnant again, by the way."

"Oh my gosh, someone get those two an aspirin to put between her knees!" Giselle uttered wildly in disbelief. This was going to be the fourth child together – and with Luke – the couple had five children total.

"I know right?!" Harley laughed boisterously. "Text or call me if you need anything…"

"Will do," Giselle grinned as she pulled up to see Sophie standing there, holding her stomach, while making a face that had an obvious fake smile on it, trying to comfort Ben… who looked very disconcerted right now.

"Oh, thank goodness," Giselle said happily, winking at Sophie. "Ben! You are just the pilot I'm looking for… are you ready to be my co-pilot?"

"Me?"

"Yes, sir! We are going for a ride, and I need a co-pilot. Can you do it?"

"Yeahhhh!" the boy said happily, racing to the car and trying to reach the door handle.

"Thank you," Sophie whispered softly, giving Giselle a grateful smile.

"I gotcha, hon… can you walk to the car okay?"

"Yeah, just slow going."

"That will give me time to get my… COPILOT BUCKLED UP AND GO THROUGH PREFLIGHT CHECKS," she said loudly, knowing the boy liked to play make-believe. She opened the door for Ben, who scrambled eagerly into his car seat. "Oh hey! You must be ready to take off, huh?"

"I ready, Auntie Gilly…"

"Alright! Let's gooooo," she said dramatically, trying to keep the toddler who was engaged so he didn't get upset as Sophie was breathing fast in the passenger seat and gripping the door panel as Giselle slid into the driver's seat.

Twenty minutes later, Giselle was playing 'patty-cake' with Ben in the waiting room and sipping on apple juice as Austin came around the corner.

"Hey Babe… how's Sophie?"

"Pushing, I'm sure," she smiled. "We got her into a room and they came to check her, ushered me out, and said the baby was coming quickly now…" her voice trailed off as she saw Valkyrie carrying Toby come around the corner as Marisol pushed a stroller, extremely pregnant, and looking exhausted, followed by Glory and Alpo, carrying the twins.

"Has she had the baby yet?" Glory asked easily. "Ben! Are you ready to be a big brother?"

Ben shrugged, looking suddenly unsure of himself.

Austin knelt down and smiled at the boy.

"You know, that being the big brother is the most special thing in the world, right? You have to be brave and strong,

319

just like your Daddy, because your Mommy will need your help... and trusts you."

Giselle felt tears sting her eyes, wondering if Austin had gotten the same speech when he was younger, being bounced around, and fed some lines by the people taking him in.

"It's true, you know," Giselle knelt down beside them. "A boy is the man of the house until his Daddy comes home and your sister is someone who will always be your best friend no matter what."

"Really?"

"She'll always be there to play with you... and sneak cookies at Aunt Dixie's house," Giselle smiled, seeing Ben's shy smile. "Don't think I didn't see you, buster... but it's our secret, okay?"

"Okay."

"Now, can you stay here with Uncle Valkyrie and Auntie Marisol. Maybe you can practice being a big brother and check on Nicolette in the stroller for me?"

"Oh, I could use the help," Marisol said immediately, catching on and nodding. "Aunt Giselle is going to go check on your mama – and we are going to keep Uncle Aeron here, so he doesn't pass out... *again*."

Austin chuckled.

Valkyrie glared at him... before smirking good-naturedly.

Everyone knew that the tall man could not handle seeing a baby emerge from a woman's body. Something about it made him pass out cold, whether it was nerves, anxiety, stress, or just the sight of blood... no one knew.

Nodding, Giselle started off towards the delivery rooms... only to have Austin pull her aside, as he looked at her inquisitively in front of the nursery.

"Do we need to... talk?" he said softly, his eyes searching hers.

"About what?"

"Giselle," he said hoarsely, staring at her with a shy smile on his face. "Valkyrie took me to get our car from Sophie's house and… I saw the baby stuff in the passenger seat. Are we… *are we gonna have a baby?*"

His voice was infinitely tender, disbelieving, and emotional with the understanding that they were going to be in this exact same position in approximately seven months. This was a man who had everything taken from him repeatedly over the years, with no home, no one to care for him, and drew himself up to stand tall.

She couldn't imagine how this news made him feel because it wasn't a kind world out there – and they both knew it.

"Yeah," she smiled tearfully and heard him drag in his breath as he pulled her into his arms, holding her close. "Are you happy?"

"Oh man, I'm so overwhelmed right now. I can't imagine what our baby will look like and… I already feel so lucky to have you, but now a baby too?"

"We're gonna have it all… Daddy," she whispered, laying her hands on either side of his face, touching his cheeks, and looking him in the eyes. "You are loved, treasured, and we have a beautiful life together, building a home… and now we are going to have a little baby to love together."

She saw his eyes, the fear buried so deeply, and kept speaking to him, needing to see so much more there.

Not fear or insecurity.

… *Never* fear.

"You are my life – and we are going to do this, Flyboy," she whispered firmly. "Don't be scared. Be my partner, my friend, and let's learn how to be parents together."

"Are you sure?"

"You are never leaving our home – and neither is our

child," she said tenderly, seeing his eyes glisten as he stared at her with so much hope and trust, seeing that what she suspected he was struggling with – and had guessed right.

"I love you – and no matter what happened in your past? I'm not giving up on our quest, my beloved knight. Are you ready to tackle another adventure… with me?"

That single question hung in the air between them as they looked at each other, before he slowly nodded, swallowing hard.

"I believe you – and I want this quest of ours so much," he said tearfully, smiling at her… and hesitated.

Both turned slightly to see a basinet being rolled into the nursery. Austin's arms came around her as he perched his chin on her shoulder, watching in disbelief as the name '*Baby Girl Merrick*' was emblazoned on the card at the end of the cart.

"She's tiny…"

"Look at all that dark hair…"

"She looks like a little pixie…"

"A scrunched-up pixie…"

"Austin," she laughed softly in disbelief.

"What? Do all babies look… pinched?"

"They've both just been through a traumatic event… and she looks beautiful," she smiled up at him as he looked at her tenderly.

"Our baby would be so much more beautiful," he whispered, before brushing a soft kiss on her lips.

"Let's keep that between us and let them have their moment," she mumbled, kissing him again briefly. "Okay?"

"Can we go home and hold each other for a little while? I've got a real need to refresh my memory of how we got onto this new quest," he teased softly, chuckling intimately telling her exactly what he was meaning without saying the words.

"I think maybe we should have a fence-rendezvous just for old times' sake…" she flirted softly, not taking her eyes off the baby as she tried to picture what their child would look like.

"Then we can," he agreed, surprising her.

"Really?"

"Oh yeah, want to know why?" he invited, his breath tickling her ear – but before she could answer he was speaking once more. "Because I plan on climbing that fence and ravishing my paladin, like I've wanted to since I first laid eyes on that soldier who captured my heart."

She met his eyes, saw the love in his eyes, and smiled.

"Sounds like a plan, my knight. Let's go home."

"As you wish, my love."

WANT EVEN MORE?

Click HERE for an additional scene from Forever Fabled.

This small 'slice-of-life' glimpse is a little something that I wanted to include for those of you that couldn't get enough of Sparky & Giselle's story, too.

Enjoy,

~ Ginny

AFTERWORD

Wow! What an adventure!

I just loved the idea of two worlds that 'shouldn't mix' suddenly colliding - and this brought together the group of Army from my Healing Hearts series and our Flyboys. Can you just imagine what it would be like to have a crush on someone, not being able to hold their hands or touch them?

I'm like that with ice cream. Yeah, I know that's not the same thing - but if it's in the house? I snack on it. If we don't keep it at home? Then I don't miss it.

Reaper & Sophie... are like my love of ice cream.

To quote Giselle - *LAME*.

... And the Angel Gowns? #emotionaldamage

I was watching the news and they were taking donations for used wedding dresses to make 'Angel Gowns' here for children that were stillborn like Meredith & Handsy's son - Aaron.

I can imagine that it would help Meredith heal some from the loss to search for a way to provide comfort to others that might have been in her shoes at one time or another. I would like to imagine she would motivate the others to also start

327

collecting used wedding dresses in support - which makes me want to do the same.

The Petersen Maneuver... I LOL'd writing that moment and had to explain it to my husband. I think it lost something in translation because he didn't think it was as funny as I did – but if you know Alpo and Glory?

Yep – I laughed.

… And we got a glimpse of Riptide and Megan's meeting. Someone cue the fireworks because our jaded, curvy girl is gonna get the handsome Cali-guy and I've got plans for them.

What did you think of Copperhead's book cover? Are you ready for Paradox and Mallory? I loved Selkirk's comments and cannot wait to dive into his character. He's going to be so stinkin' funny!

I'm so excited to share what is coming soon in the future in Yonder!

XOXO,
Ginny

FOREVER FEELINGS

Paradox's Story

Trust your gauges and bet on the unexpected!

Joshua *'Paradox'* Parr had no intention of taking his wingman's cast-aside friend out on some date as a favor. He wasn't *'stepdad material'* nor was he like the other love-struck members of the squadron.

There was something about Mallory that confused the stealthy pilot, making him curious.

… And curiosity could be a dangerous thing!

Healing Hearts Series - Including Gretchen & Captain Logan's stories

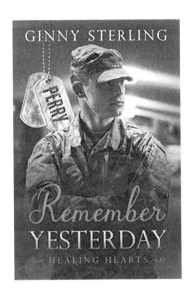

Remember Us is Captain Logan's story

Remember Yesterday is Gretchen Perry's story

If you love heartwarming, tough guys who fall in love unexpectedly – this is the series for you!

These standalone sweet, clean romances follow a team of soldiers that were once stationed in Afghanistan, bound by friendship.

Opposites attract, soulmates find each other at their lowest points, and friends become lovers across the miles.

A Wish for the Single Dad Flyboy

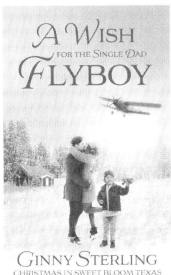

Deacon '*Cajun*' Josephs was stunned at the abrupt '*right turn*' his life had suddenly taken... and running from his demons wasn't feasible anymore. When he's unexpectedly grounded and favors are being called in by friends? Everything feels overwhelming – including the intense feelings for the mysterious doctor.

Dr. Shelby Bow wanted to throttle her sister! Secrets never helped anyone, especially when it's one that you cannot hide for long. When a scared plea tears at her heart, Shelby knows she would do anything to get to Sweet Bloom – including a blind date.

What if the wish you never imagined could happen... was now coming true?

***A Wish for the Single Dad Flyboy is book four in the Love in Sweet Bloom romance series

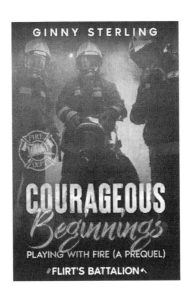

Flirt's Battalion Sweet Romance Series

EMBER CREEK, TEXAS

"I volunteered the entire team, so make sure that your Friday is clear of any activities or events. This is non-negotiable, team, and I really need your help with this charity event. The other shift will be covering for us, and they go up on the auction block this Saturday…" Chief Carpenter said openly, putting his hands on his hips, looking over the table at them.

They'd just gotten back from a roaring blaze that had engulfed a mobile home on the outside of town, and all Kyle could smell was smoke so heavy he could taste it.

It was everywhere, seeping from the pores of his skin and in his clothes, and each of the men at the table reeked of sweat. In fact, several of them had matted down hair that was strange looking because of their thermal gear and helmets.

Hat-hair, he mused, shoveling another bite in his mouth.

"This isn't bordering on harassment or some other rule? I

mean, I've never heard of any job condoning this, and while I know it's for charity… still," Justin began nervously. "I mean, are there guidelines to this… mess?"

"Huh?" Kyle said distractedly, reaching for a slice of corn-bread. "What'd the chief say?"

"Weren't you paying attention?" Austin hissed behind his hand. "Dude, this is exciting – and scary!"

"Honestly? Noooo… I'm hungry and we just got back from a run. I can actually smell the chili and the woodsmoke together. It's not half bad," Kyle said chewing noisily, before blowing his nose and wincing at the smoke-filled residue he left in the napkin.

"You're disgusting."

"Hey, at least I didn't do like Austin did last week…"

"Ugh, don't remind me!" Chase muttered.

"You didn't catch any of what the chief just said?" Justin muttered, frowning and kicking Kyle under the table that they were all sitting at.

"I heard him say *'You guys can eat while you listen'*… so I'm eating," Kyle whined, shoveling in a massive bite. "And listen-ing. I'm listening, too. Can you pass the butter?"

"What about the listening part?" Chase uttered. "With them big ol' ears you should have…"

"I just said…" Kyle choked out openly, chewing with his mouth full and talking at the same time, trying to keep anything from falling out.

Man, whoever made the chili this morning – it was fantastic! he thought wildly, stirring his bowl and reaching for the package of cheese once again.

"Did you have something you wanted to add, Rimes?" Fire chief Reese Carpenter said quietly, in a voice that brooked no argument.

It was said that the chief never yelled, never raised his voice, and commanded respect from his team easily by being in the thick of things with them – and treating them like equals. He liked Chief Carpenter – even if he set him on edge sometimes. The man just had a way of looking right through you...

"No sir!" Kyle said immediately, swallowing his food noisily before smiling and nodding. "I think it's a great idea."

"Good – you're going to be first," Chief Carpenter said openly, pointing at each man. "Marks, you're second..."

"Awww man... seriously?" Chase whined immediately, rolling his eyes. "Charity... it's for charity. You are not a piece of meat to be ogled... it's not a date. Charity auction, donating time, not anything else... relax and don't make this weirder than it already is."

Chase hesitated – and then spoke up.

"Do we really have to do this?"

"Yes," the chief said quietly, walking around the table as the men looked at each other in alarm, some in confusion, and Chase looked decidedly uncomfortable as Justin turned a weird shade of greenish-white under his tan.

Kyle's eyes grew wide as Chase slid down even further into his seat, looking almost despondent at the announcement.

What exactly did he get volunteered for – and why would Chase Marks be worried about being ogled like a piece of meat? he wondered silently.

"Olivera, you are third."

"Does this count as a blind date? I can check that off my bucket list of strange new things to experience..." Austin grinned and rubbed his hands together. "I do love me some fine Texas women, and I will happily go up on the auction block. Do I have to wear a shirt? Can I show off my muscles? I can oil my abs up and..."

"Blind date? What? *Wait* – I think I *really* missed something..." Kyle choked on the bite he'd just taken, spewing little pieces of cornbread – which everyone picked up off the table and threw at him at once.

"Dailey... you're fourth..."

"Sir, respectfully, can I just volunteer my time? I'm still reeling and going through recovery from my divorce... and I'd rather not be auctioned off for a dinner date."

"When the person bids on you, you are welcome to discuss your evening plans with the person. They will be made aware ahead of time of the rules and what lines not to cross. No kissing, touching, harassing, no sexual misconduct..."

"WHAT?" Kyle choked again, his eyes bugging out of his skull at the strange conversation that he was suddenly a part of.

This time, Austin slapped him hard on the back several times while Chase threw a paper towel at him, landing in his bowl of chili.

"Pennington... you're fifth. I will even participate and volunteer as the sixth person on the auction block, so that gives them plenty of chance to reach their financial goals for the charity event."

"Whoaaaa boy..." Andy grinned, looking at Chase and saluting him. "I might get my sister to come bid, just so Carpenter can come be my housemaid for the day."

"I'm not wearing the costume unless there is a reserve on the auction – and it will cost you, kiddo," the chief grinned... causing several of the men to laugh openly while Kyle looked around in disbelief.

The men started talking around him in a flurry, passing the bag of shredded cheese, the plastic container of chopped onion, and the tote of sour cream around the table, while Kyle was trying to comprehend what had just happened...

The chief leaned down and clapped a hand on Kyle's

shoulder, speaking softly beside his head in a hushed whisper.

"Thanks for your support, Rimes. I wasn't sure you had it in you, but really appreciate you stepping up to the plate and backing me. According to the Battalion chief, this barely squeaked by for approval, and I think it's going to do really well."

"Sir?" Kyle said, without moving. "Begging your pardon… but what exactly are we doing?"

"We are doing a charity auction for a *'Date with the Firemen of the First Battalion'* – and our entire team is going to be auctioned off to the highest bidder for a date…"

"We are?"

"Yep…" Chief Carpenter laughed. "Just be glad you aren't on the other team."

"Why is that?"

"Let's just say, it involves a photoshoot…"

This time, it was the rest of the team that nearly did a spit-take all at once as they looked up in horror. It was one thing to have to spend time with someone you barely knew, calling it a date for the sake of charity… but photography meant evidence – and they had all seen the firefighter calendars that people ogled all the time.

Kyle couldn't imagine any of them posing nearly naked with suspenders and a helmet for charity... well, maybe Austin?

He'd gouge his eyes out with a Bic pen first…

"That's right – the other truck is making calendars and auctioning them off for some lucky lady to be in the photo _with_ them."

"We got the better end of the deal," Chase said openly, his eyes wide. "My ex would absolutely nail me to the wall and show the judge that for evidence…"

"No kidding," Justin agreed quickly, frowning. "I don't

need any help with that foaming-at-the-mouth attorney that Lauren sicced on me..."

"Ah – so Honey and Lauren have the same lawyer?" Chase joked.

"She rides a broom in the night sky and cackles when she wins a case?"

"That's her!"

Austin, Kyle, and Andy just looked at each other with wide eyes as Chief Carpenter shook his head, walking off with his hands clasped behind his back.

"Are your ex-wives really that bad?"

"YES," both men said emphatically.

"I'm never getting married," Kyle muttered openly, scooping up the last of his chili with his spoon.

"No kidding..." Austin agreed. "I don't need the headache, the heartache, or pants-ache in my trousers. Women are bitter teases and extreme man-haters. There isn't a girl out there that is worth the trouble or drama she causes."

"That's why you date around and live life for yourself," Andy grinned. "It's cheaper. You are generally happier. There's no one to nag you, whine about you having one too many beers, or complaining that you spend too much time at the station..."

"Hear, hear," Chase muttered.

Attention: MVA – motor vehicle accident...

The announcement carried on, along with a bell ringing in the distance calling them all into motion.

Sure enough, the men were flying into their positions, throwing on their protective clothing. It was almost comical to watch, because shoes were being kicked off onto the floor and flying around them, as they started dressing.

"Grab your bunker gear and packs..."

Kyle ran, grabbed his bunker gear, and threw it down on the ground, kicking off his shoes quickly and leaving them where they lay as he stepped into his boots. He grabbed his pants, hiking them up over his trousers he was wearing, and donned his weighted jacket before making sure everything was fastened appropriately.

Checking his tank and the lights on his mask, he heard Chase start yelling for the 'round up'...

"Let's go! Let's go! Let's go!" Chase hollered, waving his hand quickly in the air in a circle.

Justin was already climbing into the driver's seat and the massive rig flared to life as the lights started spinning wildly.

Kyle knew he had seconds to hop on, because Justin would not wait for anyone to dawdle... and you did NOT want Chief Carpenter to find that you were left behind.

"Round it up fellas and let's get moving..."

Kyle leaped onto the truck and into his seat only seconds before the vehicle started lumbering forward and the siren began wailing in the air around him.

"Rock and Rooooooll..." Austin and Andy crowed happily, angling their chins to the air, and howling like a couple of playful mutts as the rest of them laughed.

It was showtime!

Friday afternoon...

Kyle was sweating buckets – and it had nothing to do with the temperature of this strangely warm, yet beautiful November afternoon. No, he was nervous, and with good reason. They had all loaded up on one of the smaller fire trucks to make sure to make a 'good show' for the sake of charity...

Before they left, the captain literally inspected each of them, instantly making him wary. He didn't, *shouldn't*, have anyone to impress – and the fact that he was told to tuck in his t-shirt once again… before they were all told to get their hefty, insulated jackets – to make a good show for the people attending the auction.

Listening in disbelief, he realized that this 'auction' was literally going to be an actual meat-market of men for all sorts of women to ogle and bid on. Chase was right! They were going to be ogled like pieces of meat!

He was going to be going on a date with some strange woman, all for the sake of charity.

"I need an adult…" Kyle whispered openly, swallowing nervously.

"You *are* the adult, dipstick…" Chase whispered loudly, grinning nervously, and sweating almost as much as Kyle was.

The temperature was perfect, and the sun was beating down on them, keeping the chill from the air despite the fact it was late in the year.

"God help us all…" Justin muttered, shaking his head and rubbing the back of his neck nervously.

"Seriously, I don't think I want to do this," Kyle whispered, looking down the line of firemen standing there in the sun wearing their heavy yellow jackets and helmets… and Austin, his partner, wasn't helping things in the slightest.

The outrageous man was posing for the crowd, grinning and smiling, right before slipping off his jacket, causing a group of ogling women to gather near them where they were lined up.

"Awww yeah, this is gonna be great!" Austin crowed happily. "Check this out!"

He flexed his biceps and kissed each one playfully, causing Justin to put his head down in his hands again in annoyance as the chief laughed from where he stood at the end of the line. Every man hesitated and looked down the line to gawk at the stoic man that led them, who was always so quiet.

"See?" Austin jeered happily, elbowing the two men closest to him – Justin and Chase, the two divorcees. "If Carpenter can loosen up and have some fun? Then you two spaz's should be able to as well. I mean, seriously?! It's a beautiful day, there's a breeze, we are off work…" and Austin's voice got louder, working the crowd as he stepped forward and jerked off his uniform shirt, much to Kyle's horror. "… And all these fine women are here to support a good cause – am I right, Ladies?"

A rowdy, boisterous thunder of appreciation swelled around them as Austin flexed again and showed off his tanned six pack, his tattoo, and then openly smiled, shaking hands with the women and kissing knuckles repeatedly.

Yep. The playboy could certainly work a crowd.

"Someone's gotta stop him," Kyle whispered in a hushed panic. "They're gonna expect us *all* to act like *that*…"

"Then *someone's* gonna be really disappointed, aren't they?" Chase muttered.

"No kidding…" Justin agreed.

Austin ripped… literally RIPPED… his t-shirt off of himself, causing several women to scream in excitement – and Kyle nearly died as he realized he screamed aloud as well, but in horror.

Like a girl.

What was his partner even doing?

"I can't do this!" Kyle balked, feeling faint and definitely disturbed at the fiasco that was about to happen. "Chief! Chief! H-Hey – s-someone g-get Carpenter for me… I c-can't do this!"

His voice was breaking and croaking like a boy going

through puberty – and he was thinking of his own pasty skin, if they put him standing next to Andy or Austin. Someone was going to laugh or chase him off the pergola where the auctioneer was…

"Alright… Alright… Alright! My lovely, esteemed ladies of Ember Creek – are you ready to play with fire? Are we having some fun yet? Just look at these fine specimens we have here today…"

"Not yet… but getting there, Mayor Winstead!"

"Right? You've got some flamboyant young men that are eager to get this auction started… and let's hear it for the Flirt's Battalion!"

"First…" Kyle hissed, mortified. "*First* Street battalion… not Flirt's!"

The mayor actually ignored him… and picked up a gavel to bang it on the small podium that she was standing at.

"We're here today to raise funds for the children's home, and every dollar spent is being donated one hundred percent to Sister Agatha's loving care. It will help pay for school clothes, supplies, bicycles, and computers for the children, bringing so much joy and support to our beloved community – that is supported so wonderfully by our wonderful fire chief Reese Carpenter and the Flirt's Battalion…"

"FIRST!" Kyle hissed, correcting her again. "You've got a typo, lady…"

Then Andy and Austin took their places, returning to the line, and Kyle listened in disbelief as he realized that the auction was beginning. He felt several sets of hands shove him up the steps, stumbling, as he walked forward, looking distinctly uncomfortable.

"Now ladies… remember this is for charity, and we have some pesky rules for this proceeding. Now, he might be a very handsome man, but remember this is for one evening with this young firefighter," the mayor smiled – and immediately Kyle felt a shiver of dread run down his spine.

"This fine, *fine* gentleman of the *Flirt's* Battalion…"

"FIRST…" he hissed again, pointedly. "She meant to say *First* Street Battalion Firehouse…"

"I think 'Flirt' fits so much better…" a woman called out happily, waving her wallet… causing Kyle's eyes to pop out of his head as he saw that it was Mrs. Kendall, who called them weekly needing 'assistance'.

It was the same call every single time.

Mrs. Kendall claimed that she'd fallen and couldn't get up – and specifically asked if Kyle was working that day. They would drive out and Kyle would have to endure the teasing of his coworkers, as he walked in to find her sprawled in various stages of undress, picking her up off the floor, and then suddenly?

She would have a miraculous recovery… asking him if he wanted coffee.

The guys always teased him about Mrs. Kendall – who was the same age as his grandmother Mae… and played bingo with the woman on Sundays at the Catholic church on Main Street.

"Hi Kyle…" she waved happily, wobbling her fingers at him, and making him feel cheap, sordid, and uncomfortable in that moment. He'd seen more of this woman than he would ever care to, and had requested that the team tell Mrs. Kendall that he was scheduled 'off' when she called.

"Hello, Mrs. K-Kendall," Kyle said nervously, hating the way his voice stuttered, and he could feel his cheeks heating up.

"Ruthie, you behave now, young lady…" the mayor laughed, causing several in the crowd to chuckle with delight – as Kyle wished the floor would open beneath him.

Maybe lightning would strike the pergola and they would have to evacuate?

In that moment, he was sincerely grateful that he wasn't having to pose for photos like Team Two… because he knew exactly who would mortgage their house or sell a kidney to be in some scantily clad firemen's calendar photograph with him.

Mrs. Kendall.

Kyle swallowed nervously and scanned the crowd as he listened vaguely to the mayor speak.

"This strapping young man is good with his hands…"

"What?" Kyle whispered, realizing how she was twisting the small paragraph they had to write about themselves. "I do carpentry, work on my truck, and am able do small tasks around the house, like painting and electrical work."

"He's *sooo* good with his big, strong hands and can really work a tool…"

"Oh my gosh," Kyle gaped, staring at her in shock and dismay as several people started to whoop excitedly, making his face turn even redder than it already was.

"He's the one that holds the hose, ladies…" the mayor teased playfully. "Charity, remember ladies?"

"I'm on the nozzle team," Kyle squawked, protesting. "I'm a nozzle firefighter, Mrs. Mayor. You're painting a terrible picture of me…"

"TWENTY-FIVE DOLLARS!" a voice called out.

"What?" Kyle said, whipping his head around to see who had bid.

"Make him take off that jacket so we can see his muscles…" a woman cried from the back of the crowd.

"Noooo," he grimaced, clenching it around him protectively.

"Take off your jacket, young man," the mayor urged pointedly under her breath. "It's for charity."

346

"Charity begins at home," he hissed back, glaring at her. "Why don't you make a donation and get me off this auction block!"

The mayor glared at him and slammed down the gavel to get their attention, causing everyone to look at her – including Kyle.

"Ladies, he said he's not taking off his jacket or anything else unless you get serious about the bidding…"

"I never said that!" Kyle balked.

"FIFTY!"

"SEVENTY-FIVE!"

"Do I hear a hundred?" the mayor asked openly, smiling happily.

"NOOOO?!" he yelped in shock, realizing this was getting completely out of control quickly every time he opened his mouth.

"ONE HUNDRED!" a woman said from the front row, not looking at Kyle, and her face was almost as ruddy with embarrassment as his was.

Her short cropped brown hair ended at her chin, and she was standing there looking like she'd just come from a funeral, wearing all black and dressed modestly despite the warmth of the day.

"There we go…" the mayor encouraged. "Did I mention that this young man, Kyle Rimes, is right at home getting on his hands and knees easily…"

"I scuttle up the fire engine's ladder, sheesh woman! Where did you get all of that?" Kyle hissed, looking at the crowd. "I know this is for charity – and I'm happy to participate, but I'm… *this*… this isn't what you are thinking, ladies…"

"Is he married?" someone yelled out – and the mayor looked at him.

"No," Kyle muttered, knowing that despite what he said, he had lost this fight long before it ever started. "I'm single."

"Do you do woodwork or paint things?" the woman with the short hair asked nervously, catching his attention again as a ripple went through the crowd at his words. He was getting a mental picture of himself having to work around a house, shirtless, wearing a blond wig and tossing his hair like some cover of an old romance book cover model.

"Yeah, I'm pretty good with a circular saw and a jig..." Kyle admitted, swallowing hard as he tried to avoid looking at Mrs. Kendall who was literally fanning herself, made eye contact with him, and then pointed openly at Kyle... mouthing at him.

'You're mine, sweet Kyle'.

Kyle cringed, crossing himself openly.

"TWO HUNDRED!" a voice cried out – and he saw the woman with the short hair had bid again, still refusing to look at him.

"What?!"

"Take off your jacket, mister..." the mayor hissed angrily.

"Look – I'll throw in two hundred to end the stupid auction right now," Kyle said angrily, feeling nausea roll in his stomach at the thought of Mrs. Kendall possibly winning him. The old woman was a terror, and he was afraid she would really cross the line this time! "Get me off this auction block and stop this insanity. I'm not exactly what you are wanting up here..."

"SOLD!" the mayor hollered, banging her gavel noisily. "Mr. Kyle Rimes of the Flirt's Battalion...

"First Street!" Kyle interrupted pointedly.

"... Is yours for one entire twenty-four-hour period, Miss Reyna Mattingly," the mayor continued speaking, smiling at the crowd – and grabbing Kyle by the arm before he walked away.

"Mr. Rimes – you owe the charity two hundred dollars, remember?"

He glared at her, feeling practically man-handled and discomforted as he realized that his time had just been auctioned off like a haunch of meat to a butcher.

Nodding, he dug out his wallet and quickly handed over everything he'd withdrawn from the ATM the day before, intending to get a few things for an apartment he was hoping to lease very soon, that now would just have to wait until next payday…

"Can I have a list of the stupid rules for this farce?" he muttered – and was handed a sheet of paper with the details lined out for him. "Thanks."

"Thank *you*, Mr. Rimes…" the mayor said in a saccharine voice. "Ms. Mattingly? If you'll pay the cashier – there is a small picnic bench where you can discuss your upcoming 'date'…

"Meeting," Kyle corrected as the woman walked up.

"Meeting," the winner of the auction agreed coolly, still not looking at him as she dug out her wallet and paid the cashier. "I'll need a receipt for taxes – please, and thank you."

"Of course, Miss Mattingly."

"Thanks, Dolly…"

The woman turned and looked at him, spinning carefully as to not dig her heels into the grass – and he felt something move within him as he realized she had the most beautiful turquoise eyes he'd ever seen.

"You can paint?" she asked candidly.

"Yeah?"

"Wonderful," she began, and held out her hand in a businesslike manner. "I need your help – and quite a bit of painting done."

"You don't want to go on a date?"

"No," she said nervously, her hand remaining out as she

waited for him to take it. "I need help with my café – and I can't do it alone."

"But we are _not_ dating…?" he reiterated, arching an eyebrow, feeling slightly disappointed and a little relieved that he was off the hook. He could definitely do manual labor, but a part of him kind of wished that maybe she wasn't so disinterested… because she was really pretty.

"One date doesn't make people _'dating'_, you know… besides, it really makes things quite sordid, if I've paid for your company. Don't you think?"

"So, this _is_ a date?"

"No, Mr. Rimes… this is me, hiring you, to help me with some manual labor."

"Is that code for something?" he asked warily, thinking of his partner Austin immediately. Austin was always throwing out things that had a different meaning – and frankly? So did Andy. Those two men spoke an entirely different language sometimes.

"The mayor twisted stuff, so are you doing the same thing? Is _manual labor_ code for some weird, kinky thing that I'm too dumb or naïve to understand?"

The woman, Miss Mattingly, smiled nervously, and her cheeks reddened even more than he thought possible as she held his gaze.

"No. Manual labor is just that: manual labor," she replied. "You are going to work with your hands - painting."

Kyle nodded and listened distractedly as the crowd suddenly roared in delight as the auction continued in the distance, and he gave the elusive Miss Mattingly his phone number and accepted her business card.

"Text me when you have a day off this next week, and we'll get this out of the way, okay?" the woman said bluntly. "Now, if you'll excuse me? I'm late for a meeting…"

Kyle stared as she walked off. She was crossing the street,

heading into the bank at the corner of Main and State Street, leaving him more curious and mystified than before at seeing her – and her reaction to his questions.

She looked almost like she was as bothered as he was regarding the auction, and the fact that she'd just purchased his time and company.

… And he was fascinated.

ABOUT THE AUTHOR

Ginny Sterling is a Texas transplant living in Kentucky. She spends her free time (Ha!) writing, quilting, and spending time with her husband and two children. Ginny can be reached on Facebook, Instagram, Twitter or via email at GinnySterlingBooks@gmail.com

Subscribe now to my Newsletter for updates

Made in the USA
Middletown, DE
30 June 2023